SUMMON

Content/Trigger Warnings:

PTSD

Torture

Flashbacks

Panic attacks

Detailed fire scene/escape

Discussion of past suicide attempts

Fade-to-black sex (consenting adults)

SUMMON

Darci Cole

Ember Rose Entertainment

This is a work of fiction. All of the characters, organizations, and events portrayed in this novel are either products of the author's imagination or are used fictitiously.

SUMMON

Book Two of The Unbroken Tales

Cover design by Kirk DouPonce at DogEared Design
Sword icon by Freepik, modified by Tiana Smith
Maps by Dewi Hargreaves
Formatting by S.D. Simper
Merlin's sketchbook pages by Danielle Prosperie

An Ember Rose Entertainment Book
Published by Ember Rose Entertainment LLC
Mesa, Arizona

www.darcicole.com

ISBN 978-1-955145-06-0 (paperback)
ISBN 978-1-955145-05-3 (hardcover)

First Edition: October 2022
Printed in the United States

0 9 8 7 6 5 4 3 2 1

To Annalee.

For instilling and encouraging my love
of books, magic, and happily ever afters;
and for always being there when I need you.

Thanks, Mom <3

TABLE OF CONTENTS

Map of the Unbroken Lands

Map of Medelios

Map of Reinos

1. Carina....1
2. Carina.... 11
3. Ahnri.... 19
4. Carina.... 29
5. Carina.... 35
6. Carina.... 44
7. Carina.... 54
8. Carina.... 72
9. Carina.... 93
10. Carina.... 100
11. Ahnri.... 114
12. Carina.... 121
13. Ahnri.... 139
14. Ahnri.... 148
15. Carina.... 155
16. Ahnri.... 161
17. Carina.... 165
18. Carina.... 171
19. Ahnri.... 186
20. Carina.... 191
21. Carina.... 198
22. Ahnri.... 210
23. Carina.... 213
24. Carina.... 229

25. Carina.. 239
26. Carina.. 242
27. Ahnri.. 248
28. Carina.. 254
29. Ahnri.. 262
30. Carina.. 272
31. Ahnri.. 288
32. Carina.. 295
33. Ahnri.. 304
34. Carina.. 306
35. Carina.. 315
36. Carina.. 327
37. Ahnri.. 333
38. Carina.. 336
39. Carina.. 340
40. Ahnri.. 344
41. Carina.. 348
42. Ahnri.. 354
43. Carina.. 357
44. Ahnri.. 363
45. Carina.. 367
46. Ahnri.. 370
47. Carina.. 374
48. Ahnri.. 387
49. Carina.. 393
Acknowledgements
Follow Darci for Updates
About the Author

THE
UNBROKEN
LANDS
N
Ignatia
KIWAN
Kiwa
Peak
Teao Mountains
GALANIS
River Tardus
Regania
Arontas
Mountains
Fugera
Cliffs of Antos
Vei Lake
River Veiro
ISILLE
REINOS
Nosar
River
Tiero Mountains
Medelios
The Hollow Desert
Avir
River
Avir
Lake
Somnuria
Shano
River
TAEJA
Calidar
ENSET
Avirmi River
Rico
Peak
Perdonio
CASIR
Property of the Royal Reganian Library

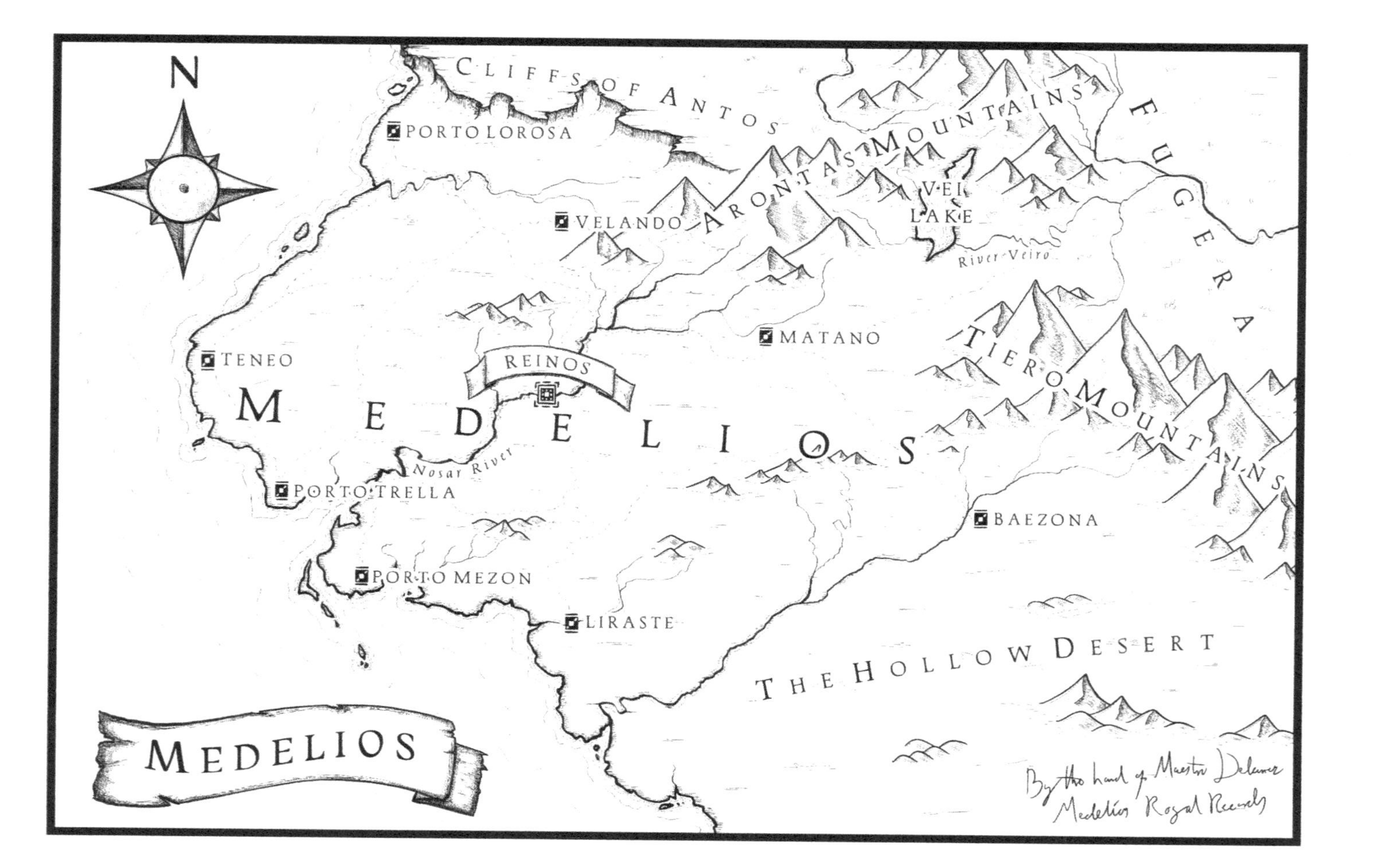
N
CLIFFS OF ANTOS
PORTOLOROSA
ARONTAS MOUNTAINS
FUGERA
VEI LAKE
VELANDO
River Veiro
MATANO
TENEO
REINOS
MEDELIOS
TIERO MOUNTAINS
Nosar River
PORTO TRELLA
BAEZONA
PORTO MEZON
LIRASTE
THE HOLLOW DESERT
MEDELIOS
By the hand of Maestro Delamer
Medelios Royal Records

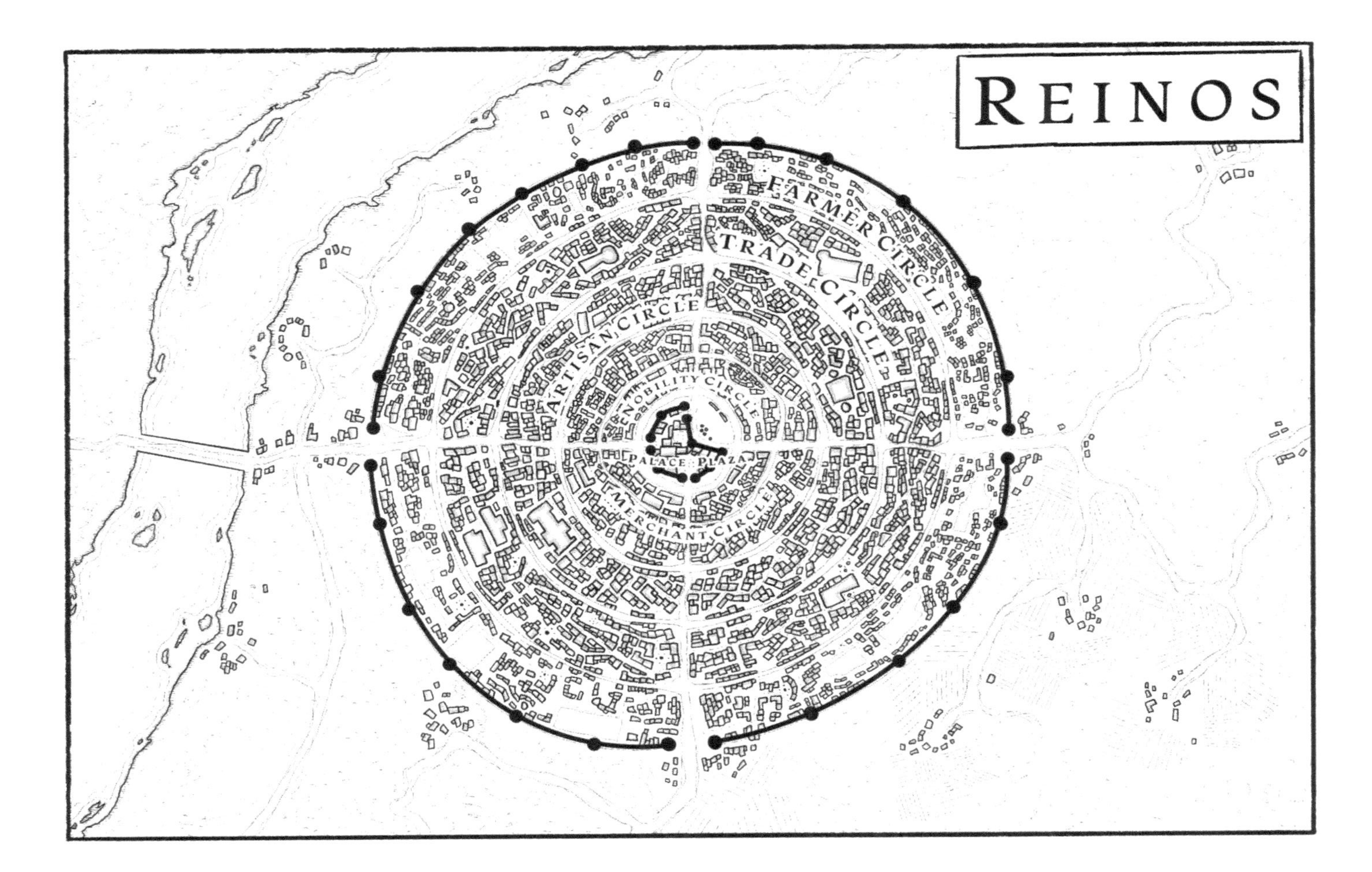
REINOS
FARMER CIRCLE
TRADE CIRCLE
ARTISAN CIRCLE
NOBILITY CIRCLE
PALACE PLAZA
MERCHANT CIRCLE

Part One

Destiny

I
CARINA

Carina Valio slowed her horse to a walk and closed her eyes, taking in the winter sunshine. The clouds parted above and a sharp smoke-like scent that she could only describe as *desert* came to her on the wind. She didn't bother patting away the film of gold-colored dust that caked her legs. Two years ago, she would've been sore from riding a horse for six hours—she remembered those days—but now, her muscles had hardened.

The desert road she followed had a towering cliff rising to her left and a flimsy fence on the right. The fence bordered farmland. The ground, covered in cut-off grain, looked as though the field had recently been cleared. A few minutes later, she discovered just how recently.

Not ten yards from the road, a woman worked cutting down the old stalks, gathering them in bunches, stacking them one on top of the other. Her skin was cracked and burned. Her mouth and eyes were turned down in such intense focus, she seemed sad. A small home stood a bit farther off, red shutters standing out against worn wood on the home, barn, and stables. The field was nearly cleared, only a small section was left here by the road, though it should've been done weeks ago.

Carina pulled her horse to a stop. The woman was worn, though she couldn't have been older than thirty or so. Sweat trickled down her face and arms. Dismounting, Carina tied her horse to the fence and went to the woman.

"Can I help?"

The woman blinked in the sunlight, but didn't fight as Carina took the scythe from her. The woman backed away, muttering a thank you.

"Go get a drink," Carina said. "Rest."

She went, her eyes glazed. Carina's heart ached at the sight, but turned to the work. Daylight would be gone in an hour or so, but work could still be done until then. Soon, despite the crisp autumn wind, Carina was sweating as much as the woman had been.

As she worked, Carina let her mind wander. Two years ago, she'd run from her home. She'd been fragile, afraid, uncertain. One year ago, she had entered Medelios, searching for a place to call home. She'd never found it, but serving the people in small ways like this helped her feel like she wasn't wandering. Helped her forget the pain. Or at least, distract herself from it.

"Water, milady?"

Carina turned to see a young boy, perhaps five or six, approaching with a large bucket. He barely held the thing above the ground. As he drew closer, the circles under his eyes and his slightly sunken cheeks made her heart sink.

"Thank you," she said, taking the cup he offered and dipping it in the water. She drank two fills then thanked the boy, going back to her task.

The boy's stare felt like needles on her back. She glanced at him without breaking her momentum.

"You have a question, might as well ask it," she said.

"You sound weird," he said immediately.

"I could say the same of you."

"And you look funny. You're not Medelian, are you?"

"I am, partly," she said, adjusting her grip slightly. "My mother was Medelian, but I grew up in Regania."

The boy's eyes widened.

"Is that your barn?" she asked, nodding behind him.

"Yes."

"Do you think your parents would mind if I slept there tonight?"

"No." He continued to watch her, twisting his hands. "Are you the one they call the Jewel?"

Carina paused, raising a brow at the boy for a moment, then turned back to the stalks, cutting down a handful. "That is not my name."

"But—"

"Enough," Carina said.

The boy's mouth clapped shut.

Carina continued working as distant hoof beats sounded. She blinked. A cloud of dust grew farther down the road, drawing nearer.

People had been calling her "The Jewel" since she'd saved a father and child from the threat of an overzealous tax collector with bad information. She still wasn't sure whether she liked the name. "Jewel." It made her sound like a saint, when her actions—everything she did—was only to keep her from feeling useless. To keep the voice in her head—and the anger—at bay.

At those thoughts, a flicker of resentment bubbled up inside her. All she'd ever wanted was to be *enough*. She'd never found it at home, and she hadn't found it out here on the road. At this point, she'd begun to doubt if she ever would.

She paused, closing her eyes and taking a deep breath. Her hands had tightened on the scythe and she forced them to relax. Set the emotions aside. Do the work.

"Lady?" the boy said.

Carina looked to him.

"Are you going to save us?"

A sharp pang hit her heart. His deep brown eyes and brown skin reminded her of her own. Her Medelian heritage. These were her people, and they were suffering. But like everything in her life, no matter how much she did, it was never enough.

The approaching horses finally reached them. To Carina's surprise, they stopped. Two large men loomed over her for a moment before they both dismounted and came closer. They glanced at her only a moment before their gazes fell on the boy.

One of them, a man with a thick dark beard, spoke. "Good day to you. I'm Pax, this is Mico."

Mico scratched at his hooked nose, and Pax pointed to the

boy.

"He yours?"

Carina squared her shoulders. "Why do you ask?"

Mico leered. "We're in need of a small person. He's the right size for the job we've got."

Carina was already shaking her head. "No, he's not for sale."

"So, he is yours, then?"

Carina gripped the scythe tighter, the anger inside returning. "You should be on your way."

Pax whistled. "She's got a mouth on her."

"She might work, come to think of it," Mico said.

"Nah, she's tiny, but not small enough."

Mico nodded. "Right. We need him."

Then Pax was stepping toward the boy, who had frozen in terror. In a flash, Carina raised the scythe to Pax's throat. He paused, beard twitching.

"I said," she hissed, "be on your way."

He turned slowly to examine her, his eyes glinting with anger. "As soon as I collect this."

As he'd spoken, hook-nosed Mico had quietly approached behind Carina. Not quietly enough, though. She waited until he was in range, and swung the scythe around, slamming the dull side into his temple. He fell with a grunt.

The boy screamed, and Carina turned back to see Pax carrying the boy over his shoulder, toward the horses. Her anger flared. Gripping the scythe in both hands, she followed him, spun to build momentum, then slammed the handle into the backs of his knees, bringing him down. The boy fell, tumbling away with a cry of pain.

"Run!" Carina shouted at him.

He ran. Pax roared, turning on Carina. "You think you can—" He cut off.

Carina immediately had her dagger to his throat. "I gave you a warning," she said, her voice low.

Excellent, the voice in her head crooned.

Pax sneered. "Who are you to—"

She pressed the blade harder against his skin, bringing forth a thin line of blood. He cringed.

"Me?" she asked. "I'm no one." She stepped back, out of his reach, still holding her knife before her. "Collect your friend, please."

Pax went to Mico and hauled him up onto one of the horses, tying him down before mounting the other. He glared back at Carina. "You'd better hope we don't cross paths again, little girl."

"Oh, I don't need to worry. I expect you'll be avoiding me in the future." She smiled sweetly—a trick she'd learned from her father—and the man's anger turned to uncertain fear.

Well done, the voice in her head whispered.

A knot twisted in her stomach.

She held the man's gaze until he kicked the horses into motion. In moments, they were gone.

"Wow," the small boy said.

Carina spun to see him peek out from behind a pile of dead grain. She sighed. "I told you to run."

"I did!" he squeaked. "Just not very far."

Carina shook her head. That had been a close call, and she didn't like close calls. She sheathed her dagger and went to him, checking for injuries. "Are you all right?"

He winced. "I…I think I twisted something."

A quick examination of his wrist told her it was worse: a bone in his hand had snapped when he'd fallen. Carina sighed. Even a young child's work would be essential in a family like this, and if he was this injured, he wouldn't be able to help.

"Wait here," she said, going to her horse. There, she reached under her saddlebags and extracted a small hidden pouch. From this, she pulled a cloth which she used to remove a simple ring made of silver. It was nothing special, not an heirloom or gift. She'd found it on the side of the road on her travels, and stopped at a temple to pay to have it filled with Life magic—healing magic. She went back to the boy. "Hold out your hand."

He did, and Carina gently touched the coin to his palm. The coin glowed with a white light, and the boy closed his eyes against it. A moment later Carina pulled it away and the light faded.

She watched him until he opened his eyes again. "Better?"

He blinked, twisting his wrist in a test. Then he beamed. "Yeah! What was that?"

Carina frowned. "Have you never seen magic before?"

The boy's eyes went wide and his face paled. "That was *magic*? But magic isn't allowed!"

Carina cursed inwardly. She'd heard of this, but in the

outer parts of the kingdom the rule hadn't been as stringent. Now she was approaching the capital, she should have known it was bound to be worse.

"Was it?" she said, frowning. "I didn't see any magic."

His fear vanished, replaced by a wide grin. "Suuure." Then he gasped. "I forgot! Mama wanted me to bring you in for dinner!" Then without another word, he took her hand and started toward the house.

"Wait," Carina said, laughing. "Let me get my horse!"

The woman she'd taken the scythe from turned out to be Dani, and the boy was Jes, her son. Jes's father, Bann, had arrived later, and they all sat together to enjoy a meal of thin soup and warm bread.

"I honestly thought I'd imagined you," Dani said, smiling wide. "I was so tired I told myself it was Bann coming home early. I should've recognized you. Everyone talks about your hair. Regania keeps to itself mostly, you know, so it's not a combination of colors we see often."

Carina knew, she'd heard it all before. In Regania, her two-toned hair had been a source of strangeness, something the nobility there thought odd. But in Medelios mixed blood—and therefore two-colored hair—was a sign of nobility more often than not. It seemed every commoner from here to the border had recognized her, not as Carina Valio, but as a noblewoman out of place.

"I'm glad I could help."

"Well, you certainly did that," Bann said, his voice soft. He'd been shocked to hear of Jes's near capture, and insisted Carina sleep inside by the fire instead of in the barn.

"Mama," Jes said. "Can she stay tomorrow too?"

Dani mussed his hair. "If she wants to, love. But I would assume she has places to be."

Carina took a bite of bread to avoid speaking. She had nowhere to be. She would leave anyway.

Bann cleared his throat. "Lady Jewel," he said. "I don't know whether you've heard, while I was in town today it was announced that the king is holding a tournament."

Carina swallowed. "What kind of tournament?"

He eyed her, seeming hesitant. "The winner of this tournament will be named heir to the throne."

Something fluttered in her chest, an odd feeling she didn't recognize. She ignored it. "I thought he'd already chosen one. The queen died a year and a half ago."

"Well," Bann said, "begging your pardon, but from what I've been told, that didn't happen. And so, the king is using this tournament to choose, and…" his voice trailed off.

Carina waited. "And?"

"Well, there's been talk. I've heard more than one person suggest *you* should enter, my lady."

Enter the tournament…to be heir to the throne?

Interesting, her father's voice whispered in her head.

"I don't know," Carina started.

"I'm not saying you should or shouldn't, my lady," Bann

said. "I only thought you ought to know what people are saying about you."

That she should enter? Become what, a princess? She was still covered in dust and grime from travel, her hair braided down her back and wisps of it falling around her face. They must have sensed her discomfort, because the subject changed and none of them spoke of the tournament for the remainder of the evening. Carina could feel it lingering in the air between them though, like steam off of boiling water, barely seen but acutely felt. Later, as Dani laid blankets out by the fire and spoke of their fields and livestock, the kind-faced woman paused and met Carina's eyes, a sad expression on her face.

"What is it?" Carina asked.

"I just realized; I never even asked you your true name."

Carina gave a wry smile. "Not many do, these days."

Dani folded her hands. "Would you tell me?"

"Carina," she said. "Carina Valio."

Dani bowed her head in respect. "It's an honor to meet you and to serve you in our home, Lady Carina."

Carina thanked her. Then, after the best night of sleep she'd had in some time, she woke before sunrise and left without a sound.

2
CARINA

Heir to the throne....

The thought had been gnawing at her for two days as she travelled the Medelian countryside. She'd trained herself to listen to her instincts, and something told her to make her way toward the capital whether she joined the tournament or not. At home, Carina's only instincts had been "stay still," "don't argue," and "show nothing." Aside from her oils, she'd never done anything for herself that wasn't protective. Mostly because anything she tried to do was subject to the judgement of her father. At least these days he wasn't able to harm her.

Physically, anyway.

As the sun touched the horizon and the sky melded into reds and pinks, Carina began to search for a spot to settle down for the night. The desert didn't have tall trees, but it did offer some cover. An outcropping of large boulders caught her eye, so she made her way toward it.

She'd run away at just over sixteen years of age, now she was eighteen and a half. Throughout her travels, she'd done her best to distinguish between her own thoughts and the voice of her father. Anything he said, she tried to do the opposite, unless her own thoughts agreed with him—those were unnerving moments. Even she had to admit her father had been intelligent. He'd very nearly usurped the throne in Regania. She herself had played a part in stopping him.

She'd never wanted power. She knew what it had done to her father and did not want the same to happen to her. Yet, something about this tournament tugged at her heart the way Jes's eyes had when he'd asked that question:

Are you going to save us?

An arrow flew past her, close enough to cause the loose hair around her face to whip like waves in a storm. Carina kicked her horse into a gallop, hurrying toward the boulders.

A glance behind told her that the two men she'd bested to save Jes had somehow found her.

She rounded the largest boulder and leaped from her mount, sending the animal farther and drawing her sword at once. A moment later, her pursuers appeared.

"There you are," Mico sneered. The knot on his temple where she'd hit him had turned purple. "We've been meaning to have a word with you."

"Well, here I am. What would you like to discuss?"

"How about," Pax said, putting his bow away and drawing a sword, "how you nearly killed us all for the sake of a kid."

"First of all, I did not *nearly kill* you. I injured you. There's a difference."

Both of the men dismounted, keeping their eyes on her.

"Second," she said, taking a defensive stance, "the life of that boy is equally as valuable as yours."

"Valuable my arse," Mico spat. "We're all just fodder for the nobility these days."

Despite the gravity of the situation, Carina's heart ached at his words. Something inside her seemed to click into place.

"You don't have to be," she said.

Pax leaped forward to attack. Carina barely managed to block him. A moment later Mico had joined to her left and she was at the mercy of them both. The fight was not a fair one, and in a matter of a few heartbeats, Carina had been disarmed and backed against the stone, Pax's sword at her throat.

"You think you have any idea what our lives are like?" he muttered.

Behind him, Mico picked up Carina's sword. "Nice blade, this. We could get some good coin for it."

Carina rose onto her toes to keep away from Pax's blade—as far back as she could, given she had a boulder at her back. She didn't *think* he would slit her throat, but her chin trembled anyway, and she couldn't stop it.

"I could enter that tournament," she said. "Make changes."

Her horse gave a low whinny nearby.

"We don't need you or any other mucking nobility to try to fix us," Pax growled. "We have accepted our lot."

A snap sounded from somewhere to her right. Frowning, she glanced over Pax's shoulder and her blood ran cold.

Two yellow eyes huddled low to the ground, hidden beneath a scrubby desert bush on the edge of the remaining daylight. The animal's gaze was trained on Mico, who stood a few paces away from her and Pax.

"Listen to me," Carina said, keeping her voice low and calm. "There's a wildcat behind you."

Pax's eyes widened and he turned—too late.

Carina watched in shock as the huge cat toppled Mico onto the hard dirt. Pax pulled a knife from his belt and dove onto the cat, trying to draw its attention. But the animal threw him off. He landed with a grunt, his head slamming against the ground just as Carina managed to get free.

Weapon. She needed a weapon. Where had her sword gone? Eyes darting around, she caught the flash of metal from between two of the huge stones she hadn't noticed before.

Somehow, irrationally, a sword was embedded *into* one of the smaller boulders, framed by the larger ones with the sunset as a striking backdrop.

Carina didn't think. Didn't wonder why a sword was here in the middle of the desert or why it was encased in stone. She leaped forward, gripped it, and *pulled.*

The blade came free far easier than she'd expected, dirt and pebbles flinging as she swung it around toward the animal. A heartbeat, three steps, and she plunged the sword into the cat's chest.

The animal whined for a moment before it slumped to the side, dead. Sweat dripped from Carina's brow, though the entire incident had only taken a moment. Mico lay barely breathing, and Pax stared at her from nearby.

She had never killed anything before, animal nor human. The cat seemed smaller in death. The sight brought tears to her eyes, though they didn't fall. She knew, given the chance, she would've done it again to save the lives of these men. Without her consent, her hands began to shake.

Close your eyes, she told herself. *Deep breaths. What next.*

She opened her eyes and laid down the sword, kneeling beside Mico's damaged form. It was obvious he couldn't move. He would need magic if he wanted to survive. Luckily, that was something she had a little of.

She took a steadying breath, then went to her horse.

"What are you doing?" Pax asked.

"Wash his wounds," she told him.

He stared at her.

"You have water?" she snapped.

"Y-yeah, I—"

"Do it now," she said, more firmly.

She waited until he'd begun, then went to her horse. She pulled out the swatch of fabric, and used that to pull out the tiny silver ring. She knew there wasn't much magic left.

Wasteful, said her father's voice.

Shut up, she replied to him.

She could refill it soon. Life magic was meant to be used. Carefully, she brought the ring to Mico, and set it in his palm.

When the metal met his skin, it began to glow white. Carina held it there. A minute passed. When the light faded, Mico's injuries, while not fully healed, they appeared a few days old at least. He would have scars, but at least the scratches were closed and safe from infection.

"Was that magic?" Pax said.

Carina met his gaze. His face had gone slack, his eyes wide. "Yes," she said. "Unfortunately, that was all I had left. You'll have to take good care of him while he heals. He should be well enough to move him. Get him to an inn or something."

Pax stared at his friend with an expression more tender than she could've imagined on such a gruff man's face.

"You love him," she said.

Pax scowled at her.

"Get him somewhere comfortable and make sure he doesn't move much for a few days."

"I know what to do," Pax snapped.

Carina stepped back, letting out a breath. The sword she'd pulled from the rocks caught her eye, then. She took it up and used a spare shirt to clean off the animal's blood before sliding it into a metal loop on her saddle. She looked around for her old sword, finally locating it on the ground a few feet away from Mico.

She stared at it for a moment. Her father's sword. Or rather, the sword her father had given her. It had never really belonged to him; it had been a gift from him to Carina. But she'd begun to think of it as his. He'd had it forged for her specifically when the swordmaster had deemed her training complete at the age of thirteen. The blade had never felt truly *right* in her hand, though she could never articulate why.

She slid it into its sheath, thinking of her father. He'd

trained her up, given her the best he could. He'd been using her, of course, but did that mean *she* couldn't use those skills?

She'd been traveling for two years now, helping in small ways, hardly using the education or training she'd gained as a lady of court. Maybe it was time she did....

"You really going to enter that tournament?"

She paused, glancing back at Pax. "I'm considering it."

His eyes lowered, then raised, as though inspecting her. "You really are that one, aren't you? That Jewel people talk about."

"I don't really like that name."

"Well," Pax said. "Whoever you are, there are some of us who could use the help. Someone up in the ranks who knows what it's like in the dirt."

A thought occurred to her then. "If you could make one change to Medelios, what would it be?"

Pax's eyes went wide. "Oh, I don't presume to understand the workings of politics and nobility, my lady."

She faced him, met his eyes. "I'm not asking you to understand all that. I'm asking what change *you* would make."

"Ah," he paused, considering for a moment. "I suppose, making it easier to find work? Seems as though if you're not a farmer or a tradesman, you're muck out of luck when it comes to earning coin."

Carina cocked her head to one side. Surely there had to be a way to make that possible, even in more remote areas. "Thank you."

In a few motions she tightened her saddle bags, making

sure she had everything. Except, she left a few coins for them. She couldn't promise anything at this point, she had no idea what she'd be getting into with this tournament, and winning it seemed so unreachable as to be impossible…still, something told her to try.

She mounted her horse.

"You're leaving?" Pax said.

"Are you going to stop me?"

He hesitated. "It's dangerous in the dark."

She tugged on the reins, giving a final nod. "I'll risk it."

3
AHNRI

Ahnri enjoyed being invisible most of the time. Hired as a spy, he'd managed to make it a whole month in the Matano's service without actually doing much. Based on the Medelian king's reply, that could be about to change.

The Matano manor house stood in the northern reaches of Medelios, within view of the Arontas mountains and only a day's walk from the springs where the River Nosar began. Ahnri liked it here, though he had to admit he missed the heat and views of Isille, his home city in Fugera.

He took a moment to rearrange things on the tray he carried, then slipped a slice of chicken into a napkin and stuffed it in his pocket. The king's letter to Barón Matano and another missive lay between a bowl of oranges and cup of berry wine. Ahnri strode through the corridors of Matano Manor. The shuttered windows were covered in carpets, thick fabric lining the walls to keep in warmth.

A set of double doors brought him into the practice room. A long, narrow space with velvet curtains framing tall windows, left uncovered to allow the cold in while they practiced, and intricate tile designs on the floor. Empty chairs were set up along the walls, leaving a space clear in the center.

There, Lady Rosaline Matano moved through a practice routine, her sword reflecting light in flashes while her private swordmaster watched nearby. Ahnri watched her work too as he passed. She was very good, but he admired little else about her. Her copper skin was like his. Her hair, black with streaks of pale white blonde, was evidence of her dual heritage: native Medelian, and Fugeran. The only thing they shared were the color of their skin and those pale strands of hair.

Ahnri found it fascinating that the Medelian blood mixed the way it did with other races. Medelian features nearly always shone through, the secondary features coming through in the hair specifically. All throughout Medelios were people—nobility mostly—with streaks of color in their dark hair. Gold blonde of Regania to the northwest, red or auburn of Somnuria in the east, Fugeran-white-blond from the central desert kingdom, blue from Calidar to the southeast.

Cool sunlight reflected off Rosaline's sword, drawing Ahnri's thoughts back to the present. He could almost feel the pull and release of his own muscles as he watched her move. She was a true talent.

Beyond her was Barón Matano. He also moved in a practice dance, but stumbled through the motions until he accidentally hit his leg with the blunt blade. Ahnri winced internally, keeping his face expressionless. The man's knees bothered him. Matano paused, holding up the broad sword as though sparring with an invisible opponent.

Ahnri waited. He usually did. Though he was getting more bored every day. He hadn't planned to stay this long.

Barón Matano lunged and cut, turned and brought the sword down in an arc. He nearly lost his balance. Ahnri raised an eyebrow at the old man. If he were fighting a real opponent of even minimal skill, he would already be dead. His hold was weak, his aim off, and his stance too narrow.

The swordmaster didn't comment on it. From Ahnri's view, the man only had eyes for Rosaline. Neither Matano nor his daughter would ever take instruction from someone who was not a Medelian weapons master. Even if Ahnri *had* learned from masters in three different styles and crossed blades with dozens of others before he'd turned ten. Even if Ahnri *had* been wielding a sword since he was four. Even if Ahnri knew more about combative arts than anyone in this whole mucking kingdom. True or not, Matano would never know. That was the point.

A moment later he noticed Ahnri standing there and stumbled in another imaginary attack. "Food. Right," he said, wiping his forehead and neck with a handkerchief. "Set it on here, boy."

Ahnri did as he was told, setting the tray on a chair and watched as the large man eased himself into the one beside. For a few minutes he ate in silence. Ahnri kept his face impassive.

Barón Matano handed the letter to Ahnri. "Read it."

Ahnri took the paper and popped the wax seal, unfolding it to read through the short reply. "The same, sir," he said. "His Majesty is intent on holding the tournament. He states that he is determined to do it the way he feels is best."

"*Hmph.*"

Ahnri's eyebrow twitched.

"That prideful old—" Matano stopped himself. Even in the company of a servant, he wouldn't dare speak ill of the king. "Well, I'm running out of time then. When is it, one week?"

"Registration opens in three days, sir," Ahnri corrected, tucking the letter away.

"Right. Read the other, then."

Ahnri opened the second letter and scanned it. "It's from one of your contacts in the Liraste lands. There are hints of a foreign noble rumored to be entering the tournament, a favorite of some of the lower class."

"What's this?" Rosaline said, approaching.

Barón Matano waved a hand. "A foreigner won't be able to enter. The king said they have to be of Medelian descent."

Ahnri cleared his throat. "Pardon me, Barón, but this person, a girl, is said to be half Medelian and half Reganian."

Matano grunted. "She's of no concern to us. Fetch my armor, boy. It's time I crossed blades with my daughter." He stood with some difficulty, and went back to his practice.

Ahnri took his leave and made his way to the armory. As he reached the manor entry he passed Stara, another servant, coming in from a hunt. She wore riding leathers, a bow and quiver slung across her back, carrying a package in her arms.

"What is it?" he asked, nodding to the bundle.

She shrugged. "Like I know. It's for the Barón."

Ahnri nodded and moved on, continuing toward the armory.

Gathering Matano's armor, Ahnri asked two other servants to help him carry it. Back in the practice room, Ahnri was surprised to see Barón Matano moving with more ease and skill than he had earlier. It unnerved Ahnri, but he supposed some people took longer to warm up.

He and the other servants assisted the barón into his armor, then were quickly dismissed. The barón apparently wanted complete privacy while they practiced. Ahnri didn't linger. He'd fulfilled the tasks assigned to him and they hadn't given him new ones, so maybe he could get a nap.

His footsteps were silent on the carpets while his mind worked out possible scenarios for the Matanos' conversation. Most likely they were discussing how to win the tournament, along with every other member of every noble house in Medelios. It would be difficult though. King Jaltér, selfish though he seemed—Ahnri hadn't gotten close enough to tell whether those rumors were true—wanted the best, and only the best. Sword fighting, an obstacle course, tests on Medelian history, strategy, and economics. Ahnri could probably outlast most if he'd wanted to enter. If he'd been allowed to, that is, not being of noble blood.

Lady Rosaline would probably win—she was by far the most capable of the young nobility Ahnri had met in his short time here—though she didn't strike him as a very benevolent ruler. Regal, certainly. Intelligent, yes. But also, incredibly arrogant.

In the stone-walled basement room he shared with the other male servants, he opened the single window high in the wall, then lay on his cot and closed his eyes. A moment later, a soft weight settled on him, and he opened one eye to see his hawk standing on his chest, head cocked to one side. The message carrier on his leg was empty, but that was nothing new. Ahnri laughed as the bird began pecking at his shirt, tickling as he went.

"Not there, Kahn," Ahnri said, reaching into his trouser pocket for the slice of chicken. The bird snatched it up and pulled it to the floor to eat.

With Kahn's pecking in his ears, Ahnri closed his eyes again. Visions filled his dreams of anklet coins flashing in bright sunlight, warm Fugeran sand beneath his feet, and the weight of a sword in his hand.

"Ahnri?"

He shifted in his sleep, blinking to see Stara leaning through the door.

"Barón Matano wants you."

Ahnri groaned, covering his head with a pillow.

"I believe the official summons is, 'Barón Matano wants you to accompany him and Lady Rosaline to the capital.' Ahnri, they're leaving in an hour. You'd better get your things together."

"What things? I've got nothing of importance."

"A change of clothes, perhaps? You will be there for a week or more."

Stara left, and Ahnri rubbed at his eyes. When he was certain she'd gone, he knelt beside his bed. From beneath, he took a satchel, and shoved some clothes inside. Then, checking again that he was alone, he reached into a tear in his thin mattress. For a moment, his heart caught, wondering if it was gone. Then his fingers brushed the soft leather bag.

He untied the drawstring then poured out five flat wooden sticks. On one side of each stick was burned a symbol. Ahnri could never remember what it meant. A lucky number in some foreign language.

It was a game he'd played many times with Damond, his second father. Ahnri's birth parents had been servants in the palace at Isille, the Fugeran capital. They died of fevers when he was only three, and Damond—one of the queen's personal guards—took him in. Trained him, taught him, paid for his education, let him explore the city and spend time with his friends, all while being a father to Ahnri.

He shook the sticks a moment, the sound bringing back memories. Damond said the real name of the game was Bones, but Ahnri liked to call it Sticks, since that's what they were. The two names had become interchangeable in his mind by the time he was twelve. How many times had he and Damond had out-cheated the cheaters in dusty alleyways of the Fugeran capital? He'd lost count. Never for the money, just for the fun of it.

A pang of grief struck his chest for a moment. He quickly slid the game back into its bag and put it in his pocket—at the same time, locking away the pain in a box in one corner of his mind. It would stay there. He didn't have time to feel it right now, nor did he want to.

He packed the few things he owned and went up to the ground-level floor. The huge entryway was crowded with people carrying trunks and loading carriages, dust filling the air as they worked. Their plain canvas clothing was marked with sweat despite the cool air.

Outside, Ahnri first made sure Kahn was flying above, then found Barón Matano's carriage. With it he found Matano as well and approached, avoiding anything on the ground that might spear through his boots. This desert wasn't the same as the dunes of Fugera. The dunes were soft and deadly; Medelios was all cactus and brambles. Still dangerous, but in a different way.

"—doesn't matter, you hear me? Just get it, and bring it now," Matano said. The servant, a boy of perhaps twelve, ran off.

"Barón," Ahnri said, bowing. "You summoned me?"

"Yes. You'll be my daughter's sparring partner on this trip. Understand?" He raised an eyebrow at Ahnri.

"You have a more specific job for me, sir?" Ahnri asked quietly.

Barón Matano checked around as though to make sure they wouldn't be overheard. "I want information. Anything that feels off, I need to know about it."

"Yes, sir."

Ahnri bowed as Matano got into his carriage. A sudden shout came from in front of the carriage. Ahnri hurried forward to see the horses stamping the ground while the driver held their bridles, trying to calm them. Slowly, as Damond had taught him, Ahnri approached and ran a hand over one horse's back as he passed. The animal nickered and flinched at his touch. He stopped next to a servant holding the bridles, a young man he didn't recognize. Probably new.

"Mind if I help?"

"Go ahead," the man said. "The driver made me hook them up, I'm not sure what I did wrong."

As the man backed away Ahnri took hold of the bridles. He held them firm, whispering *sshhh*, and waiting for the mares to calm. When their heads stopped bobbing, he rubbed their noses. They nuzzled his chest and let him move between them to check the harnesses. He winced. The traces were far too tight, it was no wonder they were upset. Ahnri loosened the straps and rubbed the coat beneath on each horse to let the mares settle. After a few moments, he re-tightened the straps just enough and sidled to the horses' heads again.

Switching to his native Fugeran tongue, Ahnri whispered to the mares, "You'll take us there safe, yes?" They nickered at him, rubbing their noses against his chest and arms. "Of course, you're welcome."

Satisfied the horses were ready for the journey, Ahnri took his place beside the driver's seat, while the driver was still tightening luggage down at the back of the carriage. Kahn drifted down to perch on the carriage beside him. The hawk crowed and Ahnri ran a finger over his wing.

"No messages today, my friend," Ahnri said in Fugeran.

Kahn clicked his beak, rolling his head slightly.

"We can't leave," Ahnri said. "Not yet. I'm sure Matano is in contact with him as well. If we leave now, they'll come searching for us."

The hawk seemed annoyed at this, but calmed as Ahnri continued to smooth his feathers. He was always nearby, always waiting to carry another message, another update, that Ahnri refused to send.

4
CARINA

Hungry and exhausted, Carina kept her head down and hood up as she entered the first town she'd seen since the wildcat incident. Young men in official-looking uniforms stood on street corners shouting about the King's Tournament to begin in three days.

"Come see Medelios's finest make their bid for the throne! Races! Duels! Celebrations! Support your nobility and show your love for our beautiful kingdom!"

Bumps rose on Carina's arms. The tournament had floated through her mind as she traveled; the possibilities, what might be required....

You could do so much.

She sighed. And every time she considered entering, her father's voice tempted her. If he were here, he would tell her to enter for all the wrong reasons, she knew that much. This was, she had to admit, the kind of thing he'd trained her for, wasn't it? Every lesson she'd had since her mother died was in preparation of marrying her off to Alexander—the Reganian prince, now king, who hadn't wanted her in the slightest. So, that plan hadn't worked. But Carina had the knowledge. She had the training. She knew what was required of royalty. Maybe—

Her reverie was broken by a vendor shouting about fresh rice and pork. She was surrounded by brightly-colored buildings of one or two stories, walkways formed from rooftop to rooftop, and a wide market she now approached. The awnings of the stalls were wide, their colors clashing against those of the buildings.

Tying her horse to a post, she caught the sharp scent of spices mixed with too many bodies. In the center of the square was a well, wide and low. She filled her water skin and took a long drink before filling it again. Sitting on the edge of the well, she checked the food prices and winced. She had saved a good amount of coin over her travels, but at this rate she'd be lucky to last a week. She was of noble blood, she could enter the tournament, but she would be laughed at if she was begging for food on the streets between events.

She wasn't sure why she'd been traveling toward the capital, even before she'd learned of the tournament. Something had pulled her that direction. Two years of solitude had taught her to trust those instincts.

The sword she'd found drew her attention, hanging from her saddle. It wasn't extravagant, but it was very well-made. If she sold it, she could probably afford food for a month or more, possibly even lodging. By then, the tournament would be over. If she won, she would be cared for in the palace, she was sure. If she lost, well, she already knew what this life was like. She could go back to it.

But the thought of parting with that sword, even after only a couple of days, felt…wrong.

A cry sounded from behind and Carina flinched. She knew that sound. She'd once made it herself.

Pushing her way through a now-silent crowd, she took in the scene. A girl, no more than thirteen, was on the ground. A bag of dried angfruit had spilled, its bright reds and greens spreading over the brown stones of the street.

"Your carelessness will cost you," a woman said. She was tall and exquisite. Her perfectly-styled hair was inky black streaked with deep red, and her features were sharp.

An older man leaned over the girl. "Please, Baronesa. I can replace the goods. I only need a week or so."

Baronesa. A noblewoman.

"I need them today," the baronesa said, slow and precise. She brushed the skirt of her fine Somnurian silk dress, though the intricate embroidery was spotless. "If you cannot provide because of your daughter's mistakes, then I will hold her until you do." She waved a hand, and one of the guards reached out to grab the girl.

Anger flared in Carina's chest. "Leave her alone!"

The guards paused, and the noblewoman raised an imperious brow. She seemed not to even *see* Carina among the surrounding crowd.

The woman said nothing, and casually gestured to another guard. He stepped forward, beginning to shuffle the crowd away as the rest again went toward the girl.

Carina's heart raced. She had to stop this.

Then, as if drawn there, her eyes found a young man standing against the building, watching her. He was too pale, with dark hair, and his eyes were intensely focused on her. When she met his gaze, he winked at her. Then, with a snap, he flicked something from his hand. It shot out to hit the rump of a horse, causing the horse to buck and kick. The kick snapped one of the poles holding up the fruit stand's awning, bringing the frame down to crash right into the noblewoman's head.

The crowd scattered, the guards went to their mistress, and the fruit vendor snatched up his daughter and fled. No one would be near when the baronesa awoke.

"Pretty good, huh?"

Carina's mind was reeling. She shook her head and turned to see the boy beside her, grinning. His eyes were a striking grey, and seemed to be about the same age as her, perhaps a bit older.

Carina's eyes narrowed. "How did you—"

"I mean I wasn't sure it would work, but it did! We should probably get out of the area though. You hungry?"

Without waiting for an answer, he wound her hand through his arm and began to walk. Carina didn't fight the escort, but her entire body tensed. "Who are you?"

"We'll get to that," he said.

"What do you want?"

"I was thinking some of that meat in the flatbread over

there. I can't pronounce the name but I've had it twice already today and—"

"I meant," Carina said, stopping their progress and drawing her knife, "what do you want with me?"

The boy's eyes went wide, more in surprise than fear. "Threatening? Really? Come on, there are better ways to get people to do what you want. You of all people should know that."

"Why are you speaking as if you know me?"

"Fair question," the boy said, gently pushing her dagger aside with one finger. "I don't know you. But I do know that sword on your saddle over there, and I know the kind of people it likes."

Carina's gaze flitted from him to her horse—which was still tied at a post behind him. He spoke fast and his accent was unfamiliar. Not Medelian, not Reganian, not from any place she recognized.

"You're the one they call 'The Jewel,' right?"

Carina frowned in thought. He wasn't being offensive, or threatening, or dangerous in any way. He seemed genuine. Which only made her *more* suspicious.

He matched her frown. "Are you all right?"

She took a breath, letting it out slowly. "I'm fine. You still haven't answered my questions."

"I would like to offer my services," the stranger said. "And my sponsorship as well. I know people are talking about you entering the king's tournament. I assume you'll want someone to help with your supplies, armor, weapons, etcetera?"

Her heart said this young man was not a danger. The part of her mind occupied by her father however, didn't like him. That was important. Her father had never wanted what was best for her and her own heart had never led her wrong.

She eyed him, suspicious. "I can't pay you."

"That's all right, I'll do it for the exposure."

"That's stupid. Why?"

He shrugged.

She raised a brow.

"Okay, okay, okay," he said, waving a hand. "Let's start over. My name is Merlin, and you are?"

"Carina."

"Would you believe me if I told you I have a lot riding on you winning the tournament?"

"You've bet on me? Before I've even entered?

"It's complicated." Merlin paused, bouncing on the balls of his feet. "Can we get out of here, and I'll explain?"

Ironically, his nervousness put her at ease; at least, a little. She *was* curious what reason he would have to help her. As much as the people had encouraged her thus far, no one else had offered their assistance. It intrigued her, and, she had to admit, she would need the help.

"Well, go on," she said. "Lead the way."

5
CARINA

On the edge of town, Carina pulled her horse to a stop and dismounted. She didn't want to go any farther with this boy until she got some answers, and though she was curious, she kept a tight hold on her horse in case she decided she needed to leave quickly. Beyond the town were fields of grain and citrus; the sharp scent of the latter made her straighten, feeling more awake and energized. That was good. She needed to focus.

Merlin dismounted nearby. "Is it always this hot here this late into winter?"

"I'm not from here. But last year it was about the same."

"Well," he said, "first, can you tell me where and how you found that sword?"

She eyed at the sword she'd pulled from the boulders two days earlier. She hadn't found a suitable sheath for it yet, so it hung on her saddle wrapped in leather. She also hadn't polished it or cared for it much at all, yet it appeared brand new.

"It was stuck in a stone," she said. "Embedded in it."

"Right, that's a favorite." Merlin said. "And what was happening when you pulled it out?"

"There was a wildcat. It attacked someone."

"And did you save the person?"

"Yes."

"With the sword?"

"Yes. Well, and some magic."

"Excellent."

Carina stared at him. "What's that supposed to mean?"

Merlin walked to her horse, examining the blade, but not touching it. "This sword's name is Excalibur. Its sole purpose, its only reason for existing, is to name the person who will become the next ruler—and generally savior—of a kingdom. You obviously don't have that legend here, but I promise you: the sword is never wrong."

Carina looked from him to the sword and back. "You're saying the sword is magic?"

"Technically, yes, though a different kind than you're used to. It's not going to grant you healing or a clear mind or change your appearance the way your 'gods' grant to your priests. It shows up and draws to it the person most worthy and able to do the job. In our case, that would be you."

"So, you're saying a sword wants me to win the King's Tournament?" she said cynically.

Merlin sighed. "You were drawn to the sword. When you joined the sword, I was drawn to you. The sword's only job here is to identify you, and I come along with the sword."

Carina frowned. He was speaking as though he'd memorized this speech, given it a hundred times.

"My job," he went on, "is to take on the magical abilities of the place we're in—that's your world—to help me keep you in peak mental and physical condition, and to coach, teach, and encourage you, until your position is acquired."

Position…"As heir to the throne?"

"Yes! See? You're catching on!"

Carina paced away and had to laugh. She hadn't even decided whether to try her luck in the tournament. This boy though was talking of prophecy and fate and things she did not believe in. She knew of the high priests—men and women who taught of the Gods, their Powers, and their Will for the people of the Unbroken Lands—she'd learned of their teachings of love of all kinds, and the command to worship and seek the Gods' guidance; but never had she heard things like Merlin was saying. Was he simply mad? Or was there a better explanation?

She crossed her arms. "What do you know about the tournament?"

Merlin cleared his throat. "All those of noble blood, age eighteen to twenty-five, are invited to enter if they wish. The first thirty-two people who show up at registration and are able to verify their lineage and pass an entrance interview on the day of registration will compete."

"Interview?"

"That's what I'm told."

Carina let her gaze follow the road all the way to where it disappeared over the horizon. Then something else Merlin said crossed her mind. "You mentioned magic?" she said.

He glanced to her out of the corner of his eye. "Yes."

"What kind of magic?"

"Back up slightly. Can I assume you're familiar with the four branches of magic in this world?"

"Of course." She began to recite the poem she learned as a child.

"*Life to heal the body ill,*
Growth to turn young at your will.
Stability, the mind ascends,
then Death at last a life to end.
With these, the Gods have blessed our lands,
To use in service, be their hands."

"Well, that was adorable," Merlin said, his mouth curling up on one side. "Have you seen them all used?"

"Yes. Though there was never much call for Death where I lived. We focused more on the other three."

"Good," Merlin said. "Now, understand that I have the ability to access all four powers at this time. And while I do require fuel, as any Vessel would, I do not hold any trinkets to channel the powers."

"That's impossible," Carina said, disbelief coloring her voice. "You can't possess more than one, no one ever has."

"True," Merlin said, "until me. I took on these abilities when the sword drew me here. I am the Companion of Excalibur—capitalized—and like I said, I take on the power of a place in order to do my job."

She understood the words he spoke but not what he meant. Her head was beginning to ache. "Remind me what you get out of this arrangement?"

"I told you, I'm only here to help you. Whatever you need. Within reason, of course. I'm not a servant, though I can pretend to be one. Call me a councilor. No, mentor. I like that better. Has a certain, *je ne sais quoi*."

"A certain what?"

He grinned. "I don't know."

Carina forced herself to take another deep breath, loosen her hands and the tension in her shoulders. "You don't make sense."

"Yes."

"Where are you from?"

"Where do I look like I'm from?"

She paused, noting his pale skin and dark hair. "Ignatia," she said. "The snow kingdom up north. I had a servant from there. You could be her brother."

"Good. Then that's where I'm from."

"But that's not *really* where you're from."

"No, it's not."

"And you're not going to tell me the truth?"

He chuckled. "Maybe once we know each other a little better."

Carina closed her eyes, pressing fingers to her temple. "You want me to simply trust you?"

"Not necessarily," he said, his voice softer now. "I wish to *earn* your trust, my lady."

She frowned, scrutinizing him. He was thin, not too tall. He seemed like an average able-bodied young man. If she *was* going to enter the tournament, she would need help. So far, he'd been the only person to offer.

You could use him…

She froze. That voice plagued her. It came and went, but was never fully gone.

"Then again," Merlin said, "maybe simple is what you want to go for."

They don't deserve the crowns they wear…

Her heart beat faster. She forced herself to take deep breaths. Shove the voice away. Listen to Merlin. She thought of the noblewoman back at the town. If someone like that gained the throne, the commoners would suffer more than they already were. It was possible the nobility would have a revolt on their hands. But if *Carina* was in power….

She flinched at that word—*power*. Her father had sought power and that had not ended well. She didn't want power for power's sake, but she *did* want to help people. All her life, she'd only wanted to feel like she'd done enough—*been* enough—was this how she could do that?

From the corner of her eye, she noticed her father's sword, the one that had been made for her. The one she'd been carrying for the past two years.

Stupid girl, her father's voice said.

Her hands curled into fists, and she closed her eyes. A memory flashed before her; her father gripping her arm, slamming her to the floor, the scent of burning wood.

After everything I've planned...

Curled up beside the fire pit, a foot striking her stomach. Her father's words flashed through her mind.

Not good enough!—get control—Stupid imbeciles.

The scent of citrus filled her nose, and she opened her eyes. She was not at home. She was not being beaten. She was in Medelios. Safe. On her own.

She shook her head.

"Lady Carina? Are you all right?"

She shook her head, turning back to face him. "I'm fine." She wasn't.

You're pathetic.

Then she was back there again. In her rooms, in her old home.

"My lady," Merlin said. "Should I—"

"Shut up!" she snapped. "Just—just stop talking, all right! Gods, you have the patience of a child!"

She turned toward her horse to hide her face against the saddle, a lump rising in her throat. The red of the curtains in her old room clouded her vision, shards slashing through it—the shimmers of light that used to reflect off her oil distiller. The wave grew and crashed over her, the panic, the rage. It flooded her mind as it had so many times and she couldn't stop it.

You never think! He'd shouted. *I always have to clean up your mucking mess!*

The impact of her father's hand stung against her face, then the stab of his foot to her side.

"Lady—"

"Stop!"

Tears welled up in her eyes. She held them shut. Her nails pierced her palms. She would *not* let it out. Not in front of this stranger she barely knew. He should know better than to speak to her when she'd already told him not to.

The simplest of instructions, and you can't even do that, he'd said. *Pathetic.*

The worthlessness, the loathing, it tore at her from the inside out. She turned her thoughts inward, focusing on her breathing. In, and out. In, and out.

Carina gripped at the saddle and straps as she struggled to survive, to let the attack pass through her. It had been some time since *this* had happened—this visceral response to her father's voice. Weeks at least, perhaps a month. She'd always known it would come back. It was always there. Always waiting.

She wished she could be rid of it.

There was part of her mind that recognized she'd been running from it all this time. Or trying to, and never succeeding. The more she tried to get away, the more the anger took hold—and the more like her father she became.

She didn't know how long she stood there with Merlin waiting silently behind her. She tried to visualize the waves of anxiety and anger—over the years on her own, she'd begun to imagine them as lines of darkness surrounding her—slowly draining from her body, into the soil beneath her feet. Never fully leaving; there would always be puddles and drips left behind. She allowed the pain to take its course.

Finally, she opened her eyes, and turned. Merlin was watching her, concern written in his furrowed brow.

Use him…what was the opposite of using him?

The answer came to her as soon as she'd thought the question: Trust him.

She needed help; she knew that. And she'd been traveling alone for so long, it might be nice to have company. And then there was the tournament.

She swallowed, trying to sort through her jumble of emotions. On her saddle, that sword—Excalibur—was there, hanging by a strap of leather, and beside it her old sword. It seemed like a sign, somehow. She couldn't keep doing what she'd been doing these past two years, that was clear. She'd thought helping others would help her move on, but it hadn't.

But the tournament. If she could win—though it seemed impossible—she could help in a way she hadn't been able to yet. And then, maybe she could do what her father had failed to. She could do it *better* than him. And maybe then…perhaps she could get him out of her head.

"You can travel with me to the capital," she said. "I will enter the tournament, and I accept your offer of help and sponsorship."

Merlin nodded, wary, but seeming pleased. "Deal."

6
CARINA

The first community Carina and Merlin came across was out in the open; a small castle guarding the northern edge, a patchwork of homes and buildings, surrounded by barren fields. The buildings of the small town were low and old, formerly-bright paint faded and peeled from walls that had fallen in on themselves in places. Red shutters on one building reminded her of Dani, Jes, and Bann. For a moment she wondered how they were doing.

As they approached the center of the circular town, children began to surround them, jumping and calling that the Jewel had arrived. As they shouted, more and more people came to their doors to wave and catch a glimpse of Carina.

They reached the far end of town where a pile of wood was already being erected, big enough for a bonfire. An elderly man with shaking hands approached Carina and bowed.

"Lady Jewel. I am Loran, the elder of this town. Word that

you were heading this way had reached us this morning. Would you stay tonight for a meager meal and celebration?"

Carina bowed her head. "I would be honored."

The man grinned, delighted. "I believe the children have something of a performance to show you. It's one the rest of us have all seen, but they wish you to be their audience tonight. Food will be ready once that is over."

"Thank you."

The man turned, shouting to other townspeople and shooing the children to their places. Carina was led to a patch of grass to sit, while Merlin took their horses to a stable. He joined her as the children began a dramatic show. At only a minute in, Carina realized it was a reenactment of her own acts.

The time she saved that father and child from a misguided collector.

Once when she helped a family gather support to build a home.

A day when she drove off a pack of wolves, intent on a town's meat supply.

There were more. So many that Carina hardly remembered, but when presented with them, it refreshed her memory.

"You've certainly been busy," Merlin said after the seventh scene.

"I…" She didn't know what to say.

Merlin eyes her. "Are you all right?"

"Fine," she said. And she was, but she was also flattered, and confused. "I had no idea these kinds of stories were being told about me."

"Are they exaggerated?"

"Not really," she said. "I mean the words aren't exact but the events are true so far."

"You seem bothered by it."

"It's just…why me?"

"Why not you?"

"I'm no one. I'm nothing. All I've ever been—" She stopped herself. Those were her father's words. "I know I've helped here and there, but I never did it to build some kind of reputation or legend around myself."

"My dear lady," Merlin said gently, "that is precisely the point."

A young man approached then, kneeling in the grass and offering a cup of water to each of them.

"Here you are," he said. "I'm afraid we have no wine. The water's clean at least. I'll be over there, let me know if you need more."

"Thank you," Carina said.

The boy lingered, however, and a moment later said, "Lady Jewel, may I ask you something?"

"Of course," Carina said.

He adjusted his knees a little, side-eyeing the crowds. "Our town elders would never admit it, but things are bad for us right now. And they only seem to be getting worse."

Carina frowned, glancing at Merlin, then back to the boy.

"Some of the younger ones, they've placed their hopes in you. You seem to be the only noble who cares at all about people like us, so…" His words trailed off. "Well, we all hope you'll consider entering the king's tournament."

The run-down buildings, the tattered clothes, the peeling paint…Carina took it all in, along with this young man's words. It didn't sit right with her.

"I am entering the tournament," she said, "you can confirm that rumor. Also, could you tell me: I'm familiar with some of the rural farming areas and how their production is divided between the nobility and themselves, does it differ between areas?"

"I don't know about others," he said. "We're forced to give three-fourths as tax to the Barón of our land, Barón Liraste, then he gives half of that to the king." His face fell a little and he lowered his voice. "Don't know why they need so much, though. There's an awful lot more of us than there are of them."

Similar to other towns she'd visited, if her memory served. Though the percentages seemed to vary depending on the noble house. "Thank you."

"My uncle is the town elder. He could probably tell you more."

"The man who greeted us?"

"Yes, my lady."

"I'd like to speak to him."

"I'll let him know." The boy gave a hasty bow, then ran off.

Merlin bumped her shoulder with his. "Well?"

"I never wondered why the nobility take what they do, I only thought it was too much. Ever since I entered Medelios, it was obvious that the commonfolk were being drained of resources. It's possible that the practice has a purpose, or did at one time," she said. "Whether it's to store up for emergencies or to redistribute to other towns in the area…"

He watched her. "But?"

"But," she said, watching the children waving swords before them, "if the resources were being used, it should be in places like this. Not taken away from here."

Merlin gave a small nod. "Well-reasoned."

"What kind of ruler allows this?"

"Probably one who either doesn't know, or doesn't care." He had emptied his cup, and was swinging it on a finger by its handle

Carina's mind was spinning. Something here did not add up. "The queen died a year and a half ago."

"Yes."

"All this damage couldn't have happened in only a year and a half. This has to have been going on for much longer."

"So it would seem." He paused and leaned forward on his knees. "In your home kingdom of Regania, King Stephan and Queen Larissa didn't *know* his people were suffering because the lines of communication were corrupted. Things were rough for the common people until Prince—well, King—Alexander and that outlaw Robyn girl began to fix things two years ago."

Carina glanced at him as he spoke. How did he know so many details about those events?

"Here in Medelios," Merlin continued, "I'm not sure what the trouble is. We'll have to wait and find out. Maybe do some reconnaissance." He raised his cup to eye level, staring at it.

Then he lowered it, still staring, placing his other hand on the ground. A moment later, the cup began to glow a deep red.

Carina checked to see if they were being watched. "What are you doing?"

"Nothing," he said. The light was gone, and the rocks where his other hand had been were a dark black. He held up the cup, which appeared exactly as it had before. "Giving a little Stability to whoever figures out it's there."

"Did you just put magic…into that cup?"

"Yep," he said.

"Do you do that often?"

"Sure. I can only affect things I can touch, and I can only draw from the sources of nature like any Priest, or Vessel. So, when I get the chance, I give. I figure I have access to the powers, why not share it?"

"You never run out?"

"Haven't yet."

"Do you ever get…I don't know, tired?"

"Hasn't happened. That's not to say it wouldn't."

She snatched the cup from him. Immediately, her mind cleared. It was like she'd had a fog in her way before, and the magic blew it away. "It goes to whoever touches it, right?"

"Yup."

She handed it back to him, feeling the power of Stability leave her mind. "Can you make me one to wear?"

"What for?"

"For the tournament."

He grimaced at her. "You'd cheat?"

"Is it cheating?"

"Magic is outlawed in Medelios."

She raised a brow, glancing from him to the cup and back.

"Right," he said. "But I don't get *caught*."

"That's not a very good reason, if you actually want me to win."

"I mean," Merlin said, leaning back in the grass. "I could, if you really wanted me to. Keep in mind you've got me here if you need help, and when necessary, I won't hold back. Magic isn't *completely* illegal here anyway, rather it's strictly controlled by the monarchy. Only the king or queen can order its use, and usually then only in extreme cases of healing and such. It's probably going to be against the tournament rules except for taking care of serious injuries."

A half-circle of people had gathered behind them to watch the children's performance. Boys and girls were now grouped before them, dressed as knights, pledging to keep their families safe in the name of the Lady Jewel. When they bowed, the audience surrounding them cheered and whooped, and Carina's heart grew a little lighter.

A moment later, the town elder approached, followed by a few youths carrying plates of food which were set before Carina and Merlin. The food was simple: a small cut of pork, a scoop each of rice and beans, and stewed yellow tomatoes with onions.

"Thank you," Carina said, taking the plate they offered. "Sir, would you sit with me for a moment?"

The town elder turned back, and slowly sat beside her. "How can I help you, my lady?"

Carina took a breath, then met his eyes. "Do you remember a time when your town was more prosperous than this?"

He took a breath and his gaze grew distant. "Yes. It's been a long time since we could be called prosperous. It has gotten much worse in recent years."

"Since the queen died?"

"Since she grew ill," he clarified. "Which was nearly five years ago now." His gaze locked onto her. "My nephew says you're entering the tournament. Is that true?"

"It is," she said. "But I don't know if I can win, or make any difference if I do."

"I can understand your nerves," the man said, scratching at his beard. "A kingdom is complex. I know I wouldn't have the abilities necessary, but if I had the king's power, there are some things I would change."

"Do you mind telling me what those changes would be?"

He straightened his back. "I would create a system that punished wrong-doers whether they are of noble blood or not," he said softly. "I would use the army of this kingdom to train local troops to protect our small towns from thieves and wild animals, and put in place a system to check *them*, and keep them accountable for their actions. I would make absolutely sure that everyone had enough to eat, and whoever was able could work to do their part to keep this land functioning." He paused. "You think you could do all that, young lady?"

Impossible.

She tried to ignore the voice. All around her, the people, the bonfire, the run-down town behind them, told her that something needed to change. What could she say?

She sighed. "Change takes time, friend."

The old man's face softened. "Then I wish you as many years and more as I have had."

He stood and left them to their food. A weight settled in Carina's chest. She wanted to help, and she had some ideas. Would that be enough?

You're never good enough.

"Well done," Merlin said. "That could've gone much worse."

Carina shook her head, trying to clear it. "The more I think about this, the more frightened I become. To do everything he said," she muttered, "it would take years. Decades."

"Or," Merlin said, "it could never happen. Sometimes all it takes to make change is one person with power standing up for those without."

the outer walls are
so short they dont
even look good
in the
sketch...

7
CARINA

During the journey to Reinos, the Medelian capital, Carina ate and slept better than she had in months, thanks to Merlin and the people of the Medelian countryside. Merlin even helped her acquire some comfortable riding dresses in one of the towns they passed through. As time passed, she shared small bits of information with Merlin, and he with her. It was refreshing, to have someone to speak to.

They were only a day or so out from the capital when, in one town, the local barkeep—a woman who couldn't have been more than a few years older than Carina and Merlin—insisted they stay at her inn for the night. As they entered her establishment, she eyed them both.

"Will you be needing…two beds, then?" she asked. "Or just one?"

"Two," Carina and Merlin said together.

"All right, all right," the woman said, smirking. "You never know."

They followed her up to a room where two beds sat on opposite sides. She took to one and began spreading blankets, so Merlin went for the other to do the same.

"I heard," the woman said, laying out blankets on a bed, "that the two of you have quite the history together."

"Oh," Carina started. "No, we only met recently."

Merlin fluffed a pillow. "I'm her sponsor, and servant. Sort of a dual-role I'm playing."

"Really?" the woman said. "Hmm. Not sure where that came from then. You, Lady Jewel, you're from Regania, right?"

Carina tensed. It wasn't that she was afraid of her past, but she didn't really want to talk about it. "I am."

"Beautiful country up there," the barkeep said, tossing her braid over her shoulder. "Trees for days."

Carina nodded politely, wishing she could avoid the conversation.

"Regania is lovely, yes," Merlin chimed in. "Except the bugs are *maddening*. I couldn't go two days without something biting me."

"Better than the snakes down here," the woman said. "I'd take a bug bite over venom any day."

"Ah," Merlin said, "but would you like venom *in* a bug bite?"

"No," she said. "That's not real."

"It absolutely is."

Carina kept near the doorway, letting Merlin take the conversation. This, she'd noticed, was something he often did.

Whenever something made Carina nervous, tense, afraid, he would steer things in a different direction. For not the first time since she'd met him, her shoulders loosened, and a small, sincere smile lifted the corners of her mouth.

Maybe it was part of his mentoring, or whatever he'd called it. This ability was something no one had ever done for her before. It was subtle. Most people wouldn't even notice him doing it. Carina did.

Merlin played his part well as they went on, posing as Carina's servant wherever they went. The closer they came to the capital, the worse the circumstances became. She'd worked on farms and in villages, and she'd never seen people so poor as these. As a child, when her mother described Medelios, Carina always imagined bright buildings, open fields, and prosperity. If that had ever been the reality, things had changed.

Carina spotted Reinos as a smudge on the horizon a full day before they arrived. That afternoon they rounded a bend in a small group of hills and saw the circular city laid out before her.

A wide river ran around the bulk of the city, running north to south. The outer walls were of baked clay bricks, and painted a light grey that reflected the red of the afternoon sun. The streets were laid out in circles surrounding the palace in the center, which stood a few levels higher than the rest of the city. Most of the buildings seemed to be made of wood, though some closer to the palace were of the same brick as the outer wall. But the thing that surprised her most, was the colors.

The buildings in the center were mostly painted white, or

grey. From there, the entire city was painted in the order of a rainbow. A circle of red, then orange, yellow, green, with blue and purple on the outskirts. There was an occasional dot of brown or black here and there throughout the city, but otherwise the pattern was unbroken.

"Merlin, have you been to Reinos before?"

He shook his head. "First time for me."

The next morning when they finally reached the city, Carina eyed the outer walls. They were short, no more than fifteen feet high, with guards patrolling every hundred yards or so. It made her wonder about the city's defenses. She wasn't aware of any battles that had been fought here, but one could never be too careful. Even the Reganian capital's walls were thirty feet, and Regania had mountains guarding its borders.

Being arranged in circles surrounding the palace at the center, Reinos had four main avenues in each major direction and tiny side streets winding throughout, as well as alleys and some empty fields here and there. Carina and Merlin rode down a road called East Arm, passing through a labeled gate with each circle. Carina realized the colors were meant to distinguish between each. Farmer Circle in blue and purple, Trade Circle in yellows and greens, Artisan Circle in orange, Merchant Circle in red, and Nobility Circle in whites and greys. The brown buildings were apparently chapels, and the blacks were inns and taverns.

She was mesmerized at the organization, the brightness and variety of shades within each circle. It took her by surprise to notice a few commoners and workers seemed to recognize her as she passed. It wasn't long before one approached.

"Pardon, miss," the woman said, a baby on her hip. "Are you the Lady Jewel?"

Carina swallowed, nerves rising in her chest. "I am."

The woman beamed, her eyes lighting up. "Welcome to the city, my lady. We hope you'll do well in the tournament."

"Thank you."

The woman bowed and moved away, returning to her friends. Carina's stomach twisted into uncomfortable knots.

A commotion broke out behind her, and Carina turned to see royal guards pulling a man toward the city's center. His feet dragging, the man appeared terrified, shouting for them to let him go. Carina pulled her horse to a stop.

"Carina," Merlin said. "Don't—"

She ignored him, dismounted, and stepped up behind a group watching the commotion.

"Wasn't he licensed?" one woman said.

"I thought he was," a man said. "Maybe his papers were forged."

"Idiot," another woman said. "Those poor kids of his just lost their mother, didn't they? Now this?"

"Well, he is a Cure," the man said. "He's got a chance, especially with the tournament starting up."

A Cure. A worker of Life magic. The group continued on their way, leaving Carina to piece together the situation. She turned back to mount her horse. Merlin had remained in his saddle, a deep frown on his face.

"I told you magic is strictly controlled," he said.

"I knew already," she snapped.

"You could change that, you know."

Carina nodded, thinking of how magic was handled where she grew up. Every baby born with the ability to channel magic became a priest or priestess in training, learning to use and control their abilities. As adults they could do as they wished with their talents, but they were taught to use it for the good of the kingdom. She had—naively, she realized—assumed Medelios would be the same.

Nobility Circle, the road between palace walls and nobility homes, was wide and pristine. The cobblestones looked as though they'd been swept that morning; the noble halls, while only two stories tall, were wide both side-to-side and front-to-back. Carina noted that each one, though mostly white and grey, had a different colored banner flying before the entrance. Between these were taverns, inns, restaurants, and a few merchants who, Carina guessed, were granted the privilege of putting their shops within easy reach of the wealthy.

Here, the people walking about stopped and blatantly stared at Carina. Where the expressions had been mostly curious and excited in the rest of the city, the nobility raised subtle brows and pursed their lips.

They hate you.

Shut up, she spat back in her mind.

She forced herself to straighten her spine, square her shoulders, and meet their gazes. Let them stare, she would stare right back. She didn't have to wait long for them to look away.

A few minutes later Merlin turned them toward an inn

called *Cait's Corner* and passed the animals off to a stable boy along with a handful of coins.

On their way around, Carina received more stares and whispers from a well-dressed group nearby.

She met their eyes. "Something to say?" she asked.

They exchanged glances, but no one spoke. A moment later, they moved on.

Good.

Merlin chuckled. "You have a reputation among the nobility, it seems."

"And what is that?"

"Well, some obviously see you as a threat, and some seem to think you're worth less than the dust on their boots."

He laughed. His final statement hit a nerve, sending a chill down her back.

You're worthless, her father's voice crooned. *A pitiful excuse for a daughter.*

She shut her eyes tight, trying to ignore the emotions that flooded her. Despair and indignation mixing like paint on a canvas, forming something new. Hearing Merlin—this person she'd decided to trust—speak words her father had; it was too much. The nerves that had plagued her since arriving in the city burned into her temper, her hands gripped her skirts.

"How dare you," she said.

"Sorry?"

She glared at him, the anger inside rising to overflow. "Worth less than the dust on their boots?" she snapped. "You're such an idiot. Maybe I should never have agreed to this if that's how you're going to speak to me."

"I—what?"

"I must be weak, or unfit, right?" she said, letting herself say everything that came to her. "Because I'm not from here? Because I'm an outsider?"

"Carina, I didn't—"

"They're all laughing at me, right? I'm a stupid foreign girl, too simple to win the crown. That's what they're all thinking. And you know what? They're mucking right."

People were staring now, and she knew that would only make things worse. She stomped into the inn, leaving Merlin behind. She tried taking slow breaths to let the anger subside, but it lingered like a fire burned low into the night. She clenched her teeth together, trying to keep herself in control.

Don't react. Wasn't that always what she'd told herself when her father beat her? It was always worse when she cried, or begged, or asked him to stop. It would only make it go on longer.

Control. Keep it inside. Locked away.

Merlin entered the inn behind her, but she did not look to him. Instead, she took in the entryway. A long tall desk stood empty in front of a curtain, with stairs to the right over a hallway of doors, and to the left was a common room with a bar where people in fine clothing were grouped together eating or talking. Everything was made of dark, smooth wood, with plush cushions on the chairs and barstools—much of it appeared imported.

Now out of the sunshine, Carina took a moment to

breathe. Merlin paused beside her, not speaking. A moment later a woman with short-cropped dark hair and wary eyes swept through the curtain and greeted them.

"How can I help you?" she asked.

"Are you Cait?" Merlin asked, "of Cait's Corner?"

Carina glanced at him. If he was bothered by her outburst, he didn't show it. A tightness grew in her chest—something like guilt—but she couldn't bring herself to apologize. His words had hurt, and at the moment, all she wanted was to disappear.

"I am she," Cait said, nodding. "Who's asking?"

"My name is Merlin, and this is Lady Carina. We need rooms," Merlin said. "Two, side-by-side, if possible."

"That'll cost you," Cait said. "How long?"

"The length of the tournament."

"Observing?"

"No, actually," he motioned to Carina. "Lady Carina will be competing."

Cait paused glancing at Carina again. Then, eyes narrowed, she turned back to the curtain and called, "Mar? Got a question for you."

A moment later, Mar stepped through the curtain. With pale skin and blue hair, they appeared part Calidian, part Ignatian.

"Yes?"

"Lady Carina," Cait said. "Isn't that the foreign girl you heard about?"

Mar glanced at Carina. "Oh! It is, yes! Will you be staying with us?"

"We'd like to," Merlin said. "If you have two rooms beside each other."

Cait's grin sharpened. Without another word she opened a book on her counter and turned a few pages. "Favored contestant, staying at my inn. You wait 'til this gets around."

Mar leaned forward. "I keep the bar; Cait keeps the inn. I'm the one you come to if you need feeding."

"And I'm the one who brings you baths," Cait said, "which I imagine you'll be needing. Follow me."

Cait led them through the ground level hallway to the very end where two doors stood across from each other. There, she turned and handed them each a key. "There's a door connecting the two rooms, it must be unlocked from both sides to be opened. There's a small field out the back—most inns have one, but ours is far nicer, I tell you. Use it for practice or exercise or whatever you need."

Carina and Merlin thanked her, and Cait left to return to the front desk.

"I like them," Merlin said. He opened the door to their right. "Nice enough space. We can get cleaned up and then go get you registered. How's that sound?"

"Fine," she said, unlocking her door across from his, and closing the door tightly behind her.

The space was small, but comfortable. No windows, a single bed of sturdy dark wood, and a thick down blanket over smooth sheets. There was a dresser and nightstand as well, and a small fireplace. Carina quickly took her vial of rose oil and stood it open on the bedside table. The scent calmed her.

Her hands shook as she set down her things and got used to the space. She'd now been traveling with Merlin for four days, and that was long enough that she no longer suspected he would hurt her, but not long enough that she'd told him her whole story.

He knew she was a runaway Reganian noble, and that she was defensive about her past. That was really all she'd revealed.

A knock came as the door, and Carina answered it to find a few young girls carrying a small tub and buckets of warm water for a bath. She let them set it up, watched them leave, then locked the door behind them.

After cleaning up, Carina felt truly refreshed for the first time in months. Her nails were free of dirt, her hair smooth, her skin clear. She donned one of the dresses Merlin had bought her, a soft deep red fabric with white accents on the cuffs and collar. It seemed a ridiculous amount of fabric compared to the robes she'd grown up with in Regania, but it was comfortable, and easy to move in. She'd not worn this style much and was surprised to find she liked the way she looked in it. She took time to brush out her hair and braid back the sides so they wouldn't fall in her face. She'd barely finished when Merlin knocked.

"Ready?" he asked through the door.

Opening the door, she blinked at the sight of him, clean-shaven and wearing a deep blue tunic with black trousers and belt. Nothing extravagant, but it was clean and well-cared for. His brows raised as he bowed to her. "You look lovely, my lady."

"Thank you, as do you."

"You're too kind," he said, leading her out of the inn.

As they made their way, Carina kept picking at the skirt of her new dress. "Merlin," she asked, "Where did you get all your money?"

"All over," he said. "I had a job in northern Regania for a while, did some things in the capital and the surrounding forest lands, worked some mines in the mountains on my way down here—"

"And you're fine spending it on me?"

"You're the entire reason I'm here, my lady," he said, holding the door open for her. "So no, I don't mind at all."

She frowned at that. Surely she wasn't the *entire* reason. And if that was true, the thought made her uneasy.

The north east quarter of the Palace Plaza—the central circle of the city—was nothing but open space, cleared for the King's Tournament. It seemed as though it was usually all manicured lawns and trimmed hedges. Now, however, it was a frenzy of movement and dust. A huge arena was set up to the east, and small sparring rings were sectioned off with poles and rope. Carina watched young nobility spar each other as men and women in fine tunics and dresses watched.

"Merlin," Carina said. "Will I be cheating if I use Excalibur?"

He raised a brow. "Have you decided whether you're comfortable cheating or not?"

"Well, you made such a fuss about it, I figured I'd ask."

He half-shrugged. "Fair. No, you won't be cheating if you use Excalibur."

"Didn't you say it's a magic sword?"

He shook his head. "It's not any kind of magic that'll make a difference to you while you're dueling. The sword is basically unbreakable, so that might help a little, otherwise it's like any other sword."

"I'd need to practice with it if I'm going to use it."

"All right, we'll find you someone to spar with."

"Can't I spar with you?"

He shook his head. "I can't do it, I'm no good with a sword."

Carina let out a small laugh. "You're the Companion of Excalibur—capitalized—and you're no good with a sword?"

"I am not that bloody blade's keeper," he snapped.

The sharpness in his voice made her flinch. She watched him for a moment, until he let out a breath, almost a sigh.

"Sorry," he said. "It's a long story, I'll have to tell you later."

She dropped the subject, and part of her was confused by how quickly he'd apologized. He was obviously angry about it, but…

"Carina," he said. "There is something I'd like to ask you about."

"Yes?"

"You shouted at me outside the inn."

She clenched her teeth. "Yes."

"I am sorry for what I said that upset you. However, I want to make it clear that while I understand it made you angry, I don't think I deserved to be yelled at the way you did."

Carina pressed her lips together. Kept her emotions inside.

Locked away.

"Can we agree to speak respectfully to each other, even if we're angry?"

"Of course."

"Thank you," he said.

Well. At least now she knew where she stood with him.

A minute later they reached a canopy set up in the center of the madness. More finely-dressed men and women were gathered here, shuffling through papers and discussing things Carina couldn't hear. As they approached a table, one of the women stepped forward, adjusting a set of spectacles on her nose.

"Registering?"

"Yes," Carina said.

"Name and lineage, please?"

Carina squared her shoulders and lowered her hood, taking a breath. "Carina Valio, daughter of Reganian High Lord Maximus Valio and Condessa Ariana Soran, of the Soran shipping company."

The woman wrote it down, then shuffled through a few papers, muttering Carina's surname. Carina gripped the fabric of her skirts. Was this the right thing to do? She seriously doubted she'd actually win, no matter what Merlin said. But if she did…

"According to my records," the woman said, staring hard at Carina over her round spectacles, "High Lord Maximus Valio was killed and stripped of his title two years ago, after attempted usurpation of the Reganian throne. Do you have anything to say on this?"

Carina swallowed. Despite her father's crimes weighing on her, she squared her shoulders. "He was dealt with justly. His crimes were real and he deserved to be stripped of his land and title. However, King Alexander kept my title intact. I am nobility without land or inheritance, but nobility nonetheless."

The woman nodded, satisfied, and began to fill out a pedigree chart. Carina let out a slow breath of relief. So, her father's actions had spread this far. It shouldn't have surprised her, it had been two years, though she hadn't thought much about it. Had actively tried *not* to think about it. Merlin leaned toward her.

"I wondered if you were *that* Carina."

"What do you mean?"

"Nothing particularly, but I have heard of you."

She glared at him. "What have you heard?"

"Later," he said, nodding to the woman, who was waiting for Carina.

"You will be interviewed by one of the king's advisers. You are to answer as accurately and honestly as possible," she said. "Please follow me." She led them to a nearby tent, lifting the flap and entering. Carina followed, her eyes adjusting to the dark. The woman handed over her papers to someone before turning to leave—and stopped Merlin as he tried to enter. "Only the combatant, please."

Carina caught a look of protest on Merlin's face before the flap dropped and her view cut off.

"Hello, my lady."

Carina turned to face the interior of the tent. A tall man with thick arms and wide shoulders stood behind a small desk. He gestured to a seat across from him.

"Please, sit."

She went to the small wooden chair, taking the moment to glance over the adviser. His dark hair and beard stood out against light brown skin, and she could see dark freckles sprinkled across his nose.

"Lady Carina," he said, reading her name from the paper he'd received. "I am Sir Ilian Teneo, an adviser to his Majesty, King Jaltér Salina; may the Gods bless him."

Teneo. She'd have to remember the name. There were five noble houses in Medelios, all charged with caring for the people of their lands. While she hadn't paid much attention to the names of nobility during her travels, she hoped she would recognize some of the names from her studies.

"First question," Sir Ilian said, "can you define my role as an adviser to the king?"

She took a deep breath, her hands gripping the folds of her skirts to help her focus. "You are one of twenty-five advisers, five from each noble house, managing the day-to-day responsibilities of the palace and seeing to small issues that arise."

"Very good." He scanned through her information once more. "I see you've arrived in Medelios recently, correct?"

"If one year ago is recent, then yes."

He nodded, making a note. "May I ask why you wish to compete for the crown when you grew up in Regania?"

She wasn't certain how to answer that yet herself. "My mother was Medelian, my father Reganian," she said, falling back to the reason she'd traveled here in the first place. "I lived there until his crimes became too much to tolerate, then I left. I'm simply seeking a new home, and...I very much wish to make a difference in the lives of people who need it."

Oh, how benevolent of you...

Carina shook her head.

"Very good," Sir Ilian said. She got the sense that he hadn't listened very carefully. "We'll be glad to have you join us regardless of the tournament outcome. Now, can you tell me what specific responsibilities the king and queen have?"

The facts came to her as though she had studied them that morning. "The queen is usually in charge of seeing to foreign relations, as well as trade agreements and the import and export of goods. The king sees to the kingdom's finances, budgeting, and citizen care such as food, water, and waste. Of course, each one has advisers like yourself assisting them, and they also make public appearances when circumstances deem it necessary."

"I'm impressed," he said. "Even some of our own people don't know that much detail. Where did you learn all this?"

Her face flushed slightly. "My father made certain I had the best education. He had high hopes for me."

"I see," he wrote something down. "Your final question is two-part: first do you have any magical abilities or inclinations?"

Carina swallowed, remembering the man being taken from his family. "No, I don't."

"Related," Sir Ilian said, "the king will have his Cures on

standby during the tournament. Are you willing to consent to them healing you if necessary?"

This was easier. She'd been healed by Cures many times in her life. "Yes, I am."

Ilian stood. "Thank you, Lady Carina. It's been a pleasure to meet you."

"Am I entered, then?" she asked, standing too.

He stood and extended his hand. "Yes, you are entered. I wish you the best of luck."

8
CARINA

Carina shivered at the cold as she left the adviser's tent. Immediately, Merlin was at her side, matching her pace out of the cacophony of tents and people.

"Well?" he asked.

"I'm entered."

"Excellent." He clapped his hands, rubbing them together. "So. Opening ceremonies tomorrow. Would you like to go back to the inn to rest?"

"No," Carina said, something tugging at her. "I should see more of the city."

"We can absolutely do that." His smile, if possible, widened even more.

Despite the afternoon sun shining brightly above, the air around them was chill. She rubbed her arms through the long sleeves that covered them, and pulled her cloak tighter.

Merlin bounced, skimming the crowds with a glance. "We

should ask around to find the most interesting things to see."

"Do I have to talk to people?"

Merlin eyed her. "You went all over Medelios meeting new people and helping villages for how long?"

"That was different. Those people were kind. Nobles are always judging and trying to put others down to make themselves look better."

"Carina," he said. "I hate to tell you this, but *you're* nobility."

She gave him a flat stare, but said nothing.

They walked side by side down the cobbled street of Nobility Circle, people passing by in every direction. A group nearby seemed to be close to Carina's age, finely-dressed and on their way into one of the large homes she guessed was for the nobility, with a few servants following behind. As Merlin approached, one of them mentioned the tournament.

"Pardon me, sirs, ladies," Merlin said, bowing. "My mistress is new to Reinos. Do you have any recommendations of sights to see in the city?"

They stared as though he were speaking a different language. Then, a boy with dark brown skin, and blue streaks in his dark hair stepped forward.

"That depends on what her preferences are, of course. Is there a reason *you* are addressing us? Can she not speak for herself?"

Merlin, playing the part of Carina's humble servant, bowed low and backed away, carefully eyeing Carina and motioning for her to approach them.

Straightening her shoulders, she approached.

As the blue-haired boy drew near to meet her, his entire demeanor shifted to one of casual kindness with a smile that made his eyes crinkle at the edges. "My name is Sir Eron Baezona. And you are?"

"Lady Carina Valio." The rest of the group had relaxed now that they were addressing Carina and not Merlin.

A girl came forward beside Eron. Tall and beautiful with shoulders as wide as the young men around her, her mouth a demure bow, and her brows perfectly arched. "Lady Rosaline Matano. It's a pleasure to meet you, Lady Carina. How long have you been in Reinos?"

"I only arrived a few hours ago."

Sir Eron chuckled. "I know just the thing. Take South Arm down to Artisan Circle, and turn right. There's a blacksmith there who built a fountain, taller than two men."

"Or," Lady Rosaline said, "You could visit the chapel on Nobility Circle. Its architecture is beautiful, I've sent many a visitor to see it."

"There's also the river," another young man chimed in. "To the north, the Nosar flows across the desert. It's a little low right now, but still lovely."

"Oh," Eron added, "and if you do go see the metal fountain, there's a lovely little glassblowers shop near it. Not really a sight, but Zanne makes the best glasswork in the whole city."

"You're constantly telling people about her, Eron," Rosaline said. "I hope she's paying you for your advertisements."

They all laughed, and Carina gave a small "Thank you," and curtsied. "These all sound like beautiful sights, I very much appreciate the recommendations."

"Lady Carina," Lady Rosaline said, brushing hair of black and pale white away from her shoulder. "What brings you to Reinos?"

Absurd ambition...

Carina shook her head, then said, "I'll be competing in the King's Tournament."

Eyes widened all around. Eron grinned. "Wonderful!"

"Sir Eron and I are both competing as well," Rosaline said.

Eron looked Carina up and down. "If you're nobility...I mean to say I don't recognize you or your name. Are you a distant cousin of one of the noble houses?"

"Actually, I grew up as Reganian nobility," Carina said, clasping her hands tightly before her. "My mother was a Medelian condessa and my father a high lord of Regania."

Lady Rosaline put a hand to her heart. "Well, I for one am glad to see an unfamiliar face joining in. It should certainly make things interesting."

"Thank you," Carina said, then added, "I haven't heard much about the king himself since arriving. Is he in good health?"

Rosaline waved a hand. "Oh, I'm sure he's fine. Things have been better since the queen died, in my opinion, may the gods bless her soul."

"Right," Eron said. "He's had his advisors taking care of things since then, and everything's been much more relaxed.

Quite nice, to be honest."

"That's…good," Carina said, trying not to betray her discomfort.

"Indeed," Sir Eron agreed.

"Lady Carina," Rosaline said, "Is there anything you need, since you're so new to the city? Anything I could do personally to help you prepare for the tournament, perhaps?"

Carina thought for a moment, glanced at Merlin, then something came to her mind. "Actually, I am trying to find a regular sparring partner. Preferably someone not competing. Can you recommend anyone?"

Rosaline turned around, waving a hand. One of the servants behind the group came forward.

"It's your lucky day," Rosaline said. "My father assigned this one to be my fighting dummy, but I would really rather work with the combatants myself. You're welcome to use him. He's decent with a blade."

The servant she motioned toward was tall and lean. With brown skin and white-blonde hair, he looked pure Fugeran. His expression was serious, focused. He bowed to her, the perfect picture of an obedient servant.

"Thank you, Lady Rosaline," Carina said. She turned to the servant and nearly spoke to him before remembering how Merlin had been treated by these nobles. So instead, she addressed Rosaline again. "Could he meet me tomorrow around midday? I'm staying at an inn called Cait's Corner; they're letting me use the back field for practice."

"Of course," Rosaline said. "I'll be with family for most of the day, anyway so I'm certain he won't be missed."

"Perfect, thank you."

Rosaline curtseyed. "Have a wonderful day, Lady Carina. And welcome to Reinos."

Carina moved on, feeling Merlin's presence follow behind her. She didn't glance at him until they'd passed into the next section of the city, and there she stopped. "Why were they so rude to you?"

"I've been in Medelios a month or so," Merlin said, "and only interacted with the lower classes. I'd guess that servants aren't allowed to speak unless spoken to."

"Well, that's ridiculous," she said continuing on. "It's not unusual for a servant to speak on behalf of their master, that happened in Regania a number of times."

"Cultural differences." He shrugged. "I've seen worse. Which of those things did you want to see?"

"Let's go to that fountain. I am interested in the chapel, but that's closer to our inn, so I can go another time."

They turned down South Arm, Carina's mind still processing what she'd heard. The king was, apparently, not doing much by way of ruling, and instead letting his advisors run the show. So was the tournament the council's idea, or the king's? And if it was the council's, would they even relinquish their power to a new heir?

The buildings they passed were painted bright, each circle of the city in shades of a different color. The citizens were as varied in appearance as their buildings, and Carina found herself feeling more at home than she had in Regania. There, her darker coloring and two-toned hair made her stand out in a way she hadn't wanted. But here, she was simply another face.

Carina watched Merlin as they made their way through the city. He wore a content expression, his hands clasped behind his back, nodding in greeting to everyone they passed. She'd only known him a short time, but she had to admit, she enjoyed his company more than anyone she'd met in the last two years. More than anyone she'd known previously as well.

They made their way down South Arm toward Artisan Circle, as Sir Eron had recommended. The sun was past its peak by this time, and Carina was beginning to grow hungry. She tugged Merlin to a food cart and purchased a grilled meat wrapped in soft bread, with spices she didn't recognize but that tickled her lips when she licked them.

As they made their way, she noticed Merlin's posture shift. He walked with his eyes on the road at his feet, his brow wrinkled.

"Merlin, you seem quiet. Is something bothering you?"

The corner of his mouth twitched. "Yes, actually."

"What is it?"

"I'm starting to worry about your interaction with those nobles. Your question about the king could've revealed too much. If it spreads that you're poking about for weaknesses..." he trailed off.

He didn't say more, for which Carina was grateful. No corrections to her behavior, nothing to say she'd done anything wrong. He was simply speaking as an adviser.

"It's a valid point," she finally said. "I'll try to be more mindful of my words."

"I'm only concerned for your safety," he said. "You must be careful whom you trust."

He was right. Ever since she'd escaped from her father, she'd been telling herself that, relying on her gut instincts to tell her whether someone was being honest. But the fact was she wanted to believe people were good. With what she'd seen of the nobility though, particularly that Liraste family, she would need to be careful.

"What did you think of Lady Rosaline?" Merlin asked.

"I like her," Carina said. "She seemed kind, and intelligent, and her offer to let me spar with her servant was generous."

"She seems quite likeable, yes," Merlin agreed. "And you are correct in all those conclusions."

Something in his tone made her pause. "You're concerned?"

He raised a brow. "You're getting very good at reading me."

"I would hope so."

He breathed a laugh, then grew serious. "She just handed over her own servant, Carina. It's extremely likely she'll instruct him to spy on you."

"Right. But I do need a sparring partner."

"You do."

"I think it's worth the risk."

"Very well."

She blew out a breath, trying to relax a little. His agreement brought a lightness to her, a validation, like she'd actually done something right. Followed by a twinge of guilt in her chest for her outburst earlier.

"Merlin, I—"

"Oh!" Merlin said, drawing her attention. "Wow, when he said fountain, he really meant fountain."

Carina looked up from her food to see a huge structure that took up the front of one building and jutted into the street. It was made entirely of metal, the pieces melted and bolted together in a way that seemed precarious, about to fall. And yet, water spouted from three levels to fall into a ten-foot circular pool at the base. The fountain was surrounded by people, some reading or chatting while sitting on the edge of the pool, some simply admiring the sight, and some children trying to touch the water as it fell.

Carina had seen fountains like this, more impressive ones in size at least, made of stone in Regania. But she'd never imagined it was possible to build with metal.

"Did they weld this?" Merlin muttered, stepping close to peer at one point where a spout arm was joined to the central pillar. "This kind of technology is very advanced for this time period."

"It's beautiful," Carina said.

"Yes, of course, and nearly impossible."

"What do you mean?"

Merlin shook his head. "Sorry, just doing some math. Whoever figured this out is *way* ahead of everyone else here."

"I'm sorry?"

He waved a hand. "Not important. You'll want to keep an eye on this blacksmith though, once you move into the palace.

You want them on your side."

Carina rolled her eyes. His assumption that she *would* move into the palace seemed entirely too premature. Then she paused, her eye catching on the glassblower's shop Sir Eron had mentioned.

"Merlin, could we go in there?"

"Hmm? Oh, of course. I do want to come talk to that blacksmith later though."

As they entered the glassblower's shop, a blast of warm air hit them, and both removed their cloaks, Merlin taking hers.

The walls were lined with shelves covered in trinkets as well as more practical items. Flames flickered from behind a counter where multiple ovens and fires stood, two people working at them in heavy leather smocks. One of them, a short woman with long red hair and freckle-stripes native to Somnurians, put down her work. "How can I help you?"

"Are you Zanne?" Carina asked.

"I am."

"It's lovely to meet you," Carina said. "Sir Eron recommended we see your work."

"Ah, he's a favorite customer," Zanne said. "If you see anything you like, let me know. I'll give you a good price."

Carina thanked her and began to browse the shelves. She passed spectacles, goblets, bells, candelabras, each one unique and lovely.

"Carina?"

She turned to Merlin who stood on the other side of the shop.

"You like roses, yes?" He pointed toward a shelf. "You'll like this."

She went to him and he held out a small rose charm, no bigger than her thumbnail. Red petals just beginning to bloom, with a green stem wrapping around it providing a place to be strung onto a necklace or bracelet.

"It's beautiful," she said, breathless.

"It suits you."

"Out! Fire! OUT!"

Carina turned to the back of the shop where Zanne was shouting, shoving a young man around the counter. And a line of black smoke filling the space beyond.

"Get out!" she screamed.

Merlin took Carina's arm and pulled her from the shop. Behind them, Zanne and her apprentice exited, followed by a blast of fire and heat.

Carina dropped to the street, covering her head with her arms. Merlin leaned over her, blocking her from the brunt of the danger. When she finally opened her eyes, she met his gaze.

"Are you—?"

"Fine," he said. "Give me a moment to heal and I'll be all right."

"Heal?"

He grimaced, exhausted and pained. "I told you. Magic. It still stings."

Moving to check his back, she winced. The skin was badly burned and charred. As she watched, it began to turn back to pale healthy pink, knitting together one burn at a time.

"You—" she stammered. "Life magic?"

He shook his head, grimacing. "Later."

Carina's hands shook as she stood. The shop behind them was in flames, bright against the darkening sky. Already, people were lining up from the nearest well, and the fountain, and passing buckets to attempt to control it before it reached the other buildings. She spun around and found Zanne lying on the ground nearby, swatting fire from her clothing.

"Let me help," Carina said, going to her. She used the skirts of her dress to snuff the last of the embers on Zanne's trousers.

"Thank you," Zanne said. "I'll be all right. I got Sam out, and I got far enough I only got caught on my clothes. We'll be fine, but…my shop."

The building was in blazes. Carina doubted anything would be salvageable.

A group of soldiers approached at a run. "What happened here?"

"Sir?" Zanne said, waving him over. "We were working glass, these two in my shop. Then something came in from the back window with a spark on it. I got us all out as fast as I could before it exploded."

The soldier grunted. "Did you see anyone?"

Zanne shook her head. "I was focused on my work. Sam might've seen something though, here." She led the guards to where Sam was standing.

"Carina."

Merlin came up beside her, throwing her cloak back over

her shoulders. He already had his on, hiding the ragged back of his tunic.

"Let's get back to the inn. Now. Keep your cloak tight, try to hide the burns on your dress."

She let Merlin lead her away. Minutes of silence passed before she spoke the single thought floating through her mind.

"Who would blow up the shop of a glassblower?"

"Not anyone we want to be friends with, that's for sure." Merlin shook his head. "Here I was hoping we could avoid assassination attempts."

Her gaze snapped to his. "You think that was meant for me?"

Merlin raised a brow at her. "Though to be completely candid, the attempt was messy and stupid. What kind of assassin relies on an explosion that causes so much collateral damage? And obviously isn't even guaranteed to work?"

Carina put a hand to her head, feeling dizzy. Why had Merlin saved her from injury and let himself be burned so badly? Why would someone attempt to blow up a glassblower's shop to get to *her*?

Because you should *be dead, child.*

Carina stumbled on nothing, nearly falling to the cobbled street but Merlin caught her by the arm.

"Easy," he said. "Are you all right?"

"I'm fine," she said. She couldn't let him see. Keep it locked up.

He doesn't care.

She hurried along the road, not speaking, the anger inside

burning hotter every moment. She wasn't worth a spot in the tournament, why was she bothering to be here? She couldn't do any good, why try?

The sun was low in the sky, so maybe she'd have an excuse to get away once they got back to the inn.

"Carina?"

"What?" she said, harsher than she'd intended.

"Do you want to tell me what's bothering you?"

She clenched her teeth together. "No."

Merlin sighed, which only made her hands curl into fists.

"Carina," he said, "I can't help you if you don't tell me what's wrong."

"Right, because you care *so much*," she said, rolling her eyes.

"I *do*," he said, stepping in front of her.

She balked, backing away. "What do you think you're doing?"

"Getting your attention," he said, his voice low. "You yelled at me earlier, called me an idiot, and you haven't apologized. Now, you're angry and you're not—" He sighed. "I know it's only been a few days; do you remember when I said I know the kind of people that sword likes? I know something is wrong here, but I can't fix what you won't communicate."

"I'm not supposed to!" she said, louder than she'd intended. People around her stopped to stare, and her nerves got the better of her. She squared her shoulders. "We can have this conversation back at the inn."

"Good," he agreed, turning to fall into step beside her.

It seemed every eye in the city was on her now, and it made

her stomach turn. From the corner of her eye, she turned toward a building on Nobility circle she hadn't noticed in their afternoon of walking—a chapel. It had to be the one Rosaline had mentioned. Made of sunbaked stone, painted deep brown, with intricate engravings of the four Gods lining the doors and windows. Her curiosity piqued, but she didn't have time or energy to visit it now.

By the time they got back to the inn, Carina's anger had faded a little, though she was still annoyed at Merlin. She stormed into her room, letting him follow behind her, then closed and locked the door.

"Well?" he said, gesturing with his arms out. "Let me have it."

"Let you have what?"

"Whatever it is you're pissed about," he said. "I don't know what I did, but we've got to work through it."

"It's not *you*, I'm angry about," she lied. "The explosion has me shaken, that's all."

"Well, why didn't you tell me that?"

"Because," she said, fighting to keep calm, "you said I shouldn't get angry."

"What? I didn't—"

She spun to face him. "'I didn't deserve that'? 'Let's speak respectfully'? What do you call that, if not 'don't get angry'?"

Merlin's shoulders fell slightly, and his eyes lowered. "I see. And now you're feeling angry about the explosion?"

"Yes!" she said. "You think someone tried to kill me!"

He took two steps toward her, an arm's reach away.

"Carina," he said. "You absolutely *should* be angry about that."

Her retort caught in her throat. For a moment she could only stare. "What?"

"Let's start with this," he said. "There is a very significant difference between healthily expressing your anger, and lashing out at someone who is trying to help you."

As he spoke, a tightness grew in her chest she didn't understand. "Explain?"

He extended his hands, offering them to her. For a moment, she just stared at him. She had decided to trust him, hadn't she? And he'd shown today that he was willing to sacrifice his own well-being to protect her.

She put her hands in his, and told herself to listen.

"I care about you," Merlin said. "I want you to succeed, and I'm here for you. Now, no one likes to be yelled at for making simple mistakes—which is what you did to me earlier. I had no way of knowing what I said would trigger—I'm sorry—would provoke you the way it did. And I apologized for that."

She nodded. He had apologized, she could acknowledge that.

"However. Me causing that anger—that hurt—in you," he went on, "doesn't make it acceptable to demean me. Do you understand?"

She wasn't sure she did. The last seven years of her life—since her mother died—had been one long lesson in the opposite of what Merlin was saying. She would make her father angry, and he would hurt her. Over, and over, and over. But, then…she knew her father. He was not a kind person. So, wouldn't he be wrong to do that?

"Carina?"

She gasped, looking up at Merlin.

"Would you like to talk about it?"

She let go of his hands and turned away. "I'm still thinking through all of this. What does it have to do with the explosion?"

"That's the other part," Merlin said. "Someone tried to murder you, Carina. You have every right to be angry about that, and to express that anger—so long as you're not harming others in doing so."

"But," she turned back. "Anger means hurting. That's what you do when you're angry, you—"

"Carina," he said, holding up a hand. "I'm sorry, but, no."

Dizziness overcame her, so she went to the chair and sat, head in her hands.

Merlin approached, and she could feel his presence as he knelt beside her. "You don't have to tell me everything. I don't need to know why you feel this way. If you're willing, I can promise to help."

She rubbed at her eyes. She had just spent hours in a crowded city with a young man she'd only known for four days. They'd been in great danger, and he had protected her. The memory of heat and the sound of the explosion came back to her.

"You really think that explosion was meant to kill me?"

"I do," he said. "Why else would a glassblower's shop be a target? Unless Zanne is smuggling illegal goods or something, you were the most valuable thing in that shop."

Carina took a slow breath. She'd faced death before, but not knowing her attacker was more unnerving than she cared to admit. Merlin believed she was worth more than an entire shop of intricate artwork, and if it were anyone else, Carina would agree. She just couldn't think of herself that way.

And now, this realization that she had apparently taken on far more of her father's habits than she cared to admit….

Finally, she spoke. "I could use the help. Learning the differences, like you said."

"Learning to channel anger in healthy ways is not something most people think about, but it's a valuable skill. One that will serve you well as a leader."

"Right. I'm sorry," she added. "For shouting at you. I'll try not to let it happen again."

"All is forgiven, my lady."

Part Two

Choice

9
CARINA

The morning of the tournament's opening ceremonies, Carina woke to the scent of her rose oil and sounds of a parade from outside the inn. Blinking, she rubbed her eyes and sat up, then made out something else…singing?

She couldn't make out the words, but Merlin was definitely singing in the room next door. His voice was practiced and clear; smooth, as though he'd been at it for many years. She shook her head. She hadn't known him long at all. The song was slow moving and held an energy to it, a momentum that made her want to move despite not understanding the language. She pulled her knees to her chest and waited for him to finish. When he stopped, she went to the door they shared, unlocked her latch, and knocked.

"One moment," he said. He shuffled around a bit, then the door opened.

"Good morning, my lady," he said. "Or rather, afternoon."

"I did sleep late," she said, yawning. "What were you singing?"

"Oh, that." He turned back to his room, making his bed. "A little song from one of my favorite musicals."

"Favorite what?"

He stared at her for a moment. "No, no you wouldn't know what I'm talking about. Sorry, I'm a little stuck in the past this morning. Well, my past. Different place. How are you feeling?"

Carina frowned in confusion. Choosing to ignore his nonsense she said, "Much better, actually."

"Good. I was about to try to wake you anyway. That servant is supposed to be here soon to spar with you."

Energy sparked in Carina's muscles at the thought. She hadn't properly sparred in months.

"I got you some armor this morning," Merlin said. "It might not be exact but I did my best to have it adjusted to your size."

Once they got everything on, Carina was grateful to find that the hardened leather and brass guards fit relatively well. Merlin left first to check the field and make sure they would be alone, and Carina turned to the corner of her room where she'd set Excalibur, and her father's sword.

Despite having practiced with her old blade for so many years, the sight of it simply made her anxious. It was the thing her father had given her, and she didn't want to be reminded of him just now. She took it, and propped it against a chair on the side of the room in case she needed an extra weapon, then took up Excalibur—a sense of calm coming over her as she hefted it in her hands.

Out in Cait's empty field, she began her practice dance with Excalibur. Merlin brought out a pad of blank paper and sat against the building, watching her and sketching with a charcoal pencil.

Carina had been warming up for ten minutes when Rosaline's servant came through the inn's back door. His eyes were narrowed, his jaw tense. No false smile, no smile at all. He wore armor like hers except steel where she had brass, and carried a sword and scabbard. He gave a single nod of greeting to Carina before turning to warm up himself.

She watched him warily, wondering how talented he was, whether he'd give her a challenge. As soon as he raised his blade, the anger in his body vanished and a new kind of tension took its place. Her worry evaporated. In this, he was like her.

He moved with ease, comfortable in the armor and swinging the sword as though he had been his whole life. Carina knew how to dissect a fighter's abilities, and this young man was certainly gifted.

When he finally turned to face her, she stared for a moment. His smile was now wide, bright and genuine, as though he'd finally come home after a very long journey. He swung his sword, stepping into fighting stance as excitement flowed off of him.

His energy was contagious. Carina grinned back and mirrored his position. She watched his eyes, which never wavered from hers. Impressive. A less-confident fighter would be scanning her for some sign of attack or weakness.

He struck first.

She blocked, gripping Excalibur tighter as she did. He was definitely stronger, but she would have the advantage of speed. She shoved him away and slashed at his leg and was met by his blade. He spun her sword out. Carina used the momentum to propel herself backward a few feet. He advanced again.

She moved with the grace she'd practiced at home for so long. Her muscles remembered their training, and she let her body move on its own. Luckily, this servant was very good, as she'd guessed. He blocked every one of her attacks. This made her nervous as well. If this boy—the servant of her opponent—was so talented, how practiced were Carina's competitors?

Time passed easily as water over smooth stones, though they couldn't have been at it for more than a few minutes. First Carina gained the advantage, then his style would shift slightly and she would lose the ground she'd gained. She let him push her while she watched, learning his strategy by his movements, then she used his own forms against him and pushed back.

Carina's clothes began to stick to her skin from sweat despite the chill air. Her muscles burned but she would not be the one to call the spar. He seemed as tired as she, his movements beginning to lag as much as hers. She only had to keep at it a little longer....

The opening came. He blocked her strike, and instead of making his own, he staggered, losing his footing. Carina took the chance. With a burst of strength, she spun his sword with her own, forcing it free and out of his hand. He fell to his knees, leaning forward and breathing deeply.

Carina focused for a moment on breathing. When her heart slowed enough, she spoke. "What's your name?"

He gave a wry grin, and Carina wondered if any nobility had ever asked him that before. "Ahnri."

"It's a pleasure to meet you, Ahnri."

He laughed then stood, shaking his head.

"Are you all right?" she asked.

He nodded, still breathing deep. "You're very good."

"As are you."

He bowed his head in thanks as Merlin approached holding two mugs.

"Thank you."

"You're welcome, sir," Merlin said.

Ahnri snorted. "Don't 'sir' me. I'm as much a servant as you are."

Carina exchanged a glance with Merlin and caught his sly smirk. "Ahnri, would you like to keep working?" she asked.

"I think so." He stood, handing his water back to Merlin. "Thank you again."

"My pleasure," Merlin said, also taking Carina's.

They continued on. The more they sparred, the more equal parts relief and amazement came to her. She remembered so much more than she'd expected to. She was glad to see that as she worked, her motions became smoother and her thoughts clearer. Maybe she would have a chance at this tournament after all.

She was also surprised at how much Ahnri taught her as they worked. Unlike someone she might be working against, he had no qualms sharing with her the actual forms and strategies of the styles he knew. The entire time, Merlin leaned back against the inn, sketching, watching.

When her arms began to ache, Carina realized they'd been going far longer than she'd planned. She backed away, raising her hand in surrender, before leaning forward on her knees. "I think that's enough for today," she said.

"When would you like me to come again?"

She straightened. "Well, my race is tomorrow morning but I'd love to meet in the afternoon."

"I'll be here." He cleared his throat, sheathing his sword. "How are you feeling about the tournament, my lady?"

"As prepared as I can be," she said, rolling her shoulders. "Not knowing what to expect can make anyone nervous, I suppose."

He frowned, beginning to unbuckle and remove his armor. "Yes, I believe most of the combatants feel the same. How do you find Reinos? Is it to your liking?"

Then Merlin was there. "If you'll excuse us, Master Ahnri—"

Ahnri laughed. "Just Ahnri, friend."

"Ahnri, then. Forgive my interruption but Lady Carina does need to prepare for the festivities this evening."

Ahnri raised a brow. "Of course, don't let me stop you."

Carina thanked Ahnri, then followed Merlin into the inn. She turned back once, and Ahnri gave a small smile, a real one, she thought, before the door closed behind her.

In the hallways, Carina spoke softly. "What was that for?"

"He finally remembered he was supposed to get information," Merlin said. "Lousy spy he is if that's how he works. He was preoccupied enough during your training that he hadn't asked a single question about you. Though I daresay he got a lot from your fighting style. His asking how you feel about the tournament? That was a warm up. And even your vague answer will give the Matanos something to speculate on."

Carina sighed, putting her face in her hands. "If he wasn't working for my competition, he could be a friend. An ally."

"I know," he said. "All the more reason to be careful around him. Ahnri is talented enough to give you a good fight, and you're lucky he knows and has shown you more than he seems to let on to others. As long as we can keep him from getting any real information, we should be fine. Now, you have three hours until the presentation of the combatants. Go clean up a bit and eat, then I have something to teach you."

"Something besides my destiny?"

"Carina, please." He placed a hand over his heart. "That is not something to be taught, it simply is."

She rolled her eyes. "Then what are you teaching me?"

"A strength and relaxation exercise," he said. "It helps with mental focus and muscle control, somewhat similar to your practice dance. If we can strengthen you in those areas, you'll be prepared for anything you have to face, and it will help you to calm and focus your thoughts before the presentation."

She tilted her head. "Thank you. I hope it does."

"Good." He grinned. "Now, go get cleaned up and meet me outside in half an hour."

10
CARINA

After she bathed and ate, Merlin gave her a loose linen shirt and pants to wear. Once again in Cait's back field, he had her mimic his motions. She moved her arms in slow, funny circles, occasionally lifting a foot from the ground to hold it there before setting it down as gently as possible. He called it *t'ai chi ch'uan*. Carina enjoyed the slow but specific movements of each form. After a few minutes, however, her entire body became tense and tired, and she wanted to put her arms down. Merlin kept her at it for half an hour before letting her rest, and she ended up more exhausted than she had after sparring with Ahnri.

She sat on a bench, her back against the inn's wall, head tipped to gaze up at the fading afternoon sky. Despite the early winter air, she was sweating for the second time that day.

Merlin sat next to her. "Had enough?"

"How is it possible that I can wave a sword around for over

an hour and not do your silly exercise for more than thirty minutes?"

"It's just a different kind of exercise," he said, offering her water. "You're more used to one than the other. Doing both will help you, I promise."

She took a deep breath and a few sips of the water. They sat in silence for a few moments. "Thank you, Merlin."

"For what, my lady?"

"Your help, your faith in me, for being honest...you've been a good friend."

His cheeks actually tinted slightly pink as he regarded her. "Well, you make it very easy."

She closed her eyes, letting the cool air raise the hairs on her neck. After a few minutes, she opened her eyes again to see Merlin doing the exercise on his own in the small, enclosed field. She hadn't even heard him stand.

His eyes were closed, his face serene. She watched as he moved with grace, ease, strength. As though he'd been doing it for years. She was certain her movements weren't as controlled. He was so precise, and yet his body held tension. His very skin rippled with pent-up energy. Carina tilted her head to one side in curiosity.

"Merlin?"

"Yes?" he said, not pausing his motions.

"How old are you?"

His lips quirked in a half-smile. "What makes you ask?"

"You're very good at a lot of things, insightful, knowledgeable, it's as though you've been around for a long time. Aside from your magic and the sword I don't know much about you. I thought your age would be a good place to start."

"And yet, that's probably the most confusing place to start," he said.

"Confusing how?"

He opened his eyes and gave her a curious look. "All right, we're doing this now." He released the tension in his body and glanced around, his gaze settling on a tree at one corner of the small field. He gestured to it. "Join me?"

More curious by the moment, she followed him to stand beneath the branches of the tree. It was wide and low enough that the boughs blocked their view of the nearby buildings and gave them a bit of privacy.

Merlin reached out, placing a hand on a low hanging branch. "You know I channeled Stability, yes? With the cup the other day?"

"Yes."

"Here is Growth." He closed his eyes, and Carina watched as the branch he touched began to glow with a soft green light. Like the ground that had fueled his Stability magic, the branch gradually turned dark, withering while Merlin drew magic from its very essence.

What made bumps rise on her skin was not that Merlin was now proving he could access multiple magics, but that instead of getting younger—as a Growth Vessel could only change form within ages they'd already reached—he grew *older*.

He was still himself, but his face became more mature, his jawline more defined, shoulders filled out. And then, his dark hair began to turn grey, then white. His youthful skin gained lines and experience, and his shoulders stooped as though weighed down.

And then, as quickly as it had come, the age began to melt away. Then, as the branch he held disintegrated into dust, Merlin opened his eyes. He appeared again how he had before, perhaps nineteen or twenty. When he opened his eyes, Carina's breath caught in her chest.

"So, you see," he said, "I'm much older than I appear to be."

She blinked. "How?"

He shrugged, ducking back out from under the tree's shade. "I've been doing this for a very long time. I go where the sword goes, and my job is to help the person the sword chooses. I've tried to find patterns in the process, but those are the only constants. I've had to assume that my life is connected to Excalibur. I'll probably live until it's destroyed, and seeing as how it can't be destroyed…" He left the sentence unfinished, and Carina's heart twisted at the expression of inevitability on his face.

"Do you even know how old you actually are, then?"

"Not exactly." His voice was low when he spoke. "I've lost track, to be honest. It's been centuries."

"Centuries?" she squeaked. "More than one?"

"Definitely more than one," he said, closing his eyes and beginning his exercise once more. "Last I remember I was seven or eight hundred. But that was a while ago."

Carina's mouth hung open. "How…Merlin, people don't live that long."

"I'm not people," he said.

She stood there in the late afternoon sun, watching him. The immensity of who he was and why he was here seemed to finally sink in. She found herself rapt with curiosity about him.

She joined him, mimicking his movements. "Tell me about your life."

He watched her closely for a moment, then shook his head. "My life is not a very happy story."

The smile he gave her was forced and full of pain.

Carina shuddered. "My story isn't either."

He met her eyes. "I would like to hear it. If you're willing to share."

If people knew about her past, what she'd been put through they would call her weak. Yet, part of her longed to voice it. To tell *someone.* Even someone she'd only known for five days. She'd never spoken the whole story to anyone.

Carina closed her eyes, letting her body move in the patterns he had taught her while her mind wandered through her life, choosing where to start, and what to say.

"My mother got sick when I was nine," she began. "One night she started coughing and couldn't stop. It went on for hours. Then she began coughing blood. She was confined to her bed so that Cures could work their magic over her for a few hours every day, but she seemed to only get worse. At some point, Father changed. Before, he'd been loving and kind, if perhaps a little prideful. When Mother's brightness began to fade, it was like he slipped deeper and deeper into darkness. Away from Mother, and away from me.

"She died when I was eleven. Father had been keeping mistresses for a while so he barely noticed her death. He attended the funeral; personally, I think that was more so people wouldn't ask questions. After that I rarely saw him. I turned to my oil distilling to keep my mind occupied and threw myself into my training and studies, to help me forget. It was a few months after Mother died the first time he hit me."

The crunch of dirt sounded; Merlin spoke. "He hit you?"

"Yes, he hit me." She continued the motions, but opened her eyes to see him staring, mid-motion, his arms tense before him. She met his grey eyes, like an anchor to the present, keeping her from being sucked too far into the past. He nodded. An acknowledgement. Her heart beat an unsteady pace in her chest as she went on.

"That first time, I think he did it on accident," she said. "He seemed as surprised as I did, and the bruise on my face was difficult to explain away. He never made that mistake again. He was always careful. Always precise.

"Then there were the mistresses. As I got older, they were closer and closer to my own age. Always commoners, usually some poor girl off the street or from an isolated town who thought she was getting a chance at a better life. Then three months later, a body would be carried out of the basement."

"Carina," Merlin said, his voice pained.

She knew it wasn't easy to hear. It wasn't easy to say. Merlin's back was to her, anger apparent in the stiffness of his shoulders. She understood. She'd been angry too. Still was, sometimes.

"He hit me often," she said. "All the while telling me I wasn't good enough, wasn't doing enough. No matter what I did, he was never satisfied. I was never worth his love."

"Don't say that," Merlin growled.

"Why not?" she snapped, her arms falling from the forms she'd been so careful to maintain, and her words spilled out. "It's the truth. I'd like to think he loved me before my mother died, that he at least cared about me. I don't think he did. He only ever viewed me as a tool. A means to an end. It wasn't until some very kind people—King Alexander being one of them—risked their lives for me that I was able to get away. Five years he beat me, Merlin. I always thought it was my fault. It took me months of travel and work and praying to gods, who I'm still not sure bother to listen, to realize—it never would've been enough. *Never*."

The steadiness of her voice surprised her, though her chest ached at the memory of longing. The determination to do anything, *anything*, to gain her father's approval. She hadn't spoken these things in two years. She'd thought them many times, wondered what she would say to her father if he could see the person she was now. Wondered if she'd be able to draw her dagger on him to defend herself as easily as she defended others.

"I pushed myself so hard in my schooling and training, thinking maybe if I did better, he would be pleased." Now that she'd started telling the story, she wanted to finish it. She turned away from Merlin. Her hands clasped before her, she stared up at the sky. "One day he brought in stylists to make my hair beautiful, do my makeup, make me perfect. I thought I'd done something right, that things would get better. But he only put me on display. Praised me in public and beat me in private. He wanted me to marry Alexander, so he could control the throne and kingdom through me." She took a slow breath. "He was killed as a result of his scheming. Lex kept my title intact, gave my lands to another noble, and I left."

Carina watched the blue sky beginning to fade to pinks and purples, the sun slowly making its way to the horizon.

"Were you running away," Merlin asked, "or searching for better?"

She wrapped her arms around herself, her eye catching sight of a bird circling above. "It started as running away. It changed."

"Because *you* changed," he said.

She sighed. "I've heard his voice in my head ever since I left. I've never been sure if it's magic-related, or just my imagination."

"As far as I've seen, magic doesn't do that here," Merlin said. "But trauma can cause a person to hear or see things, like re-living bad memories. Is that what's happening to you?"

"Maybe," she said, a shudder passing over her. "I don't like to think about it too much."

"Understandably," he said. "Shall we talk about something else?"

"Yes, please."

"Have you given any thought to how you'll implement changes in this kingdom?"

Carina took a breath to clear her head. "I haven't had the

time," she said. "Medelios is unbalanced. The nobility are starving and swindling their people while the king turns a blind eye. A king I know nothing about, who—even if I am named his heir—might be too ill or too selfish to teach me anything worthwhile. Not to mention the lower class who now have me on some kind of pedestal, and—"

"Woah, slow down," he said. Moving to step in front of her, he placed his hands gently on her shoulders. "You don't need all the answers right this second. I only wondered if you'd thought about it. You have time. Once you get into the palace and have some authority, you'll have more information and you'll be able to figure things out."

Liar...

Her hands formed fists on instinct. She shook her head, blinking away that voice. Her father's voice. Heat flared inside her.

What did you do?!

Her chest began to constrict, her breathing became shallow. Her eyes shut tight, and suddenly she was in her father's office, curled on the floor from a slap to her face.

That voice had started to fade since meeting Merlin, since entering the tournament. She thought if she could only win her events, it might even go away altogether. But it was here, now, and she couldn't take it.

In the memory, her father's foot slammed into her stomach, her body curling around the pain, trying to protect herself.

Before Merlin, her knees weakened, she fell to the ground,

dead grass sharp against her hands as phantom pains wracked her body.

"Carina?"

Merlin's voice sounded muted, as though coming through water.

"Stop this!" she shouted. "You're a horrible person!"

She knelt, one hand on the ground, the other on her chest where the pain was growing, a fist gripping her heart.

You did it wrong!

"I hate you!"

"Carina, look at me."

Merlin held her shoulders, kneeling in the dirt before her. He lifted her chin and met her eyes.

Foolish child.

"I'm not—"

"Breathe. Stay with me, Carina."

She did. In, and out. Her breaths were shaking, and she had to consciously tell her lungs to open each time, to let the air in. She didn't know how long it had been before the sensations passed. It could've been minutes, or hours…until, finally, her breathing became smooth, slow, and steady.

And Merlin's eyes were there, unwavering; a stone giving shelter from the waves that threatened to drown her. Her own eyes were blurred with tears that refused to fall.

The tightness in her chest eased, and the voice in her head was gone.

Carina's voice was small when she finally spoke. "Thank you."

"Of course." He stayed close. "Better?"

She could only nod.

"Would you like to sit?"

He helped her to the bench near the back door of the inn, and he sat beside her. She was grateful that Merlin didn't ask what happened or what caused her to crack. It was minutes before she finally spoke.

"You must think I'm mad."

Merlin snorted. "No, no. You're not mad. Everyone has scars, everyone has demons. It seems to me that yours like to fight you back sometimes. Trauma will do that to a person."

She rubbed her head. "Demon is a good description for the memory of my father."

"Was it him you were shouting at?"

Her voice was small when she spoke. "Yes."

"Carina," Merlin said. "You know, in your heart, that you are stronger than him, right?"

She paused. "Sometimes."

"Sometimes you're stronger?"

"Sometimes I believe it," she corrected. "Other times, it's difficult."

"You deserve so much better than him."

Despite herself, Carina smiled. She had loved her father, but he had never loved her. She knew Merlin was right. That didn't make it easy to let go.

Beside her, Merlin shifted, staring at her intently. "How can I help you see yourself the way I do?" he asked.

Something in his eyes made her pause. "What do you

mean?"

He held up a finger. "Wait here."

She frowned as he went into the inn, and was gone for a few minutes before appearing again, his sketchpad in hand.

"I like to get at least one portrait of each of my friends, as I call them. The people I help. Your practice time earlier seemed like a good opportunity." He flipped through a few pages, then held the pad out toward her.

She took it, an image of a girl staring back at her. Features smooth, a determined jaw, round cheeks, and brow set in concentration. Dark hair streaked with pale flowed around her face, and her mouth was held slightly open as though taking in a breath. The shadow of a sword blade rose behind her, ready to swing at an attacker. Her brows were drawn, her dark eyes focused and intense.

"She's lovely."

"She's you."

She blinked up at him, confusion making her head spin a little. He gave a slight nod toward the sketch, as though saying, *look again*.

She did so, and didn't know what to say. She could only stare at the girl in the drawing. Vibrant, determined, capable. The sight of it overwhelmed her. Was this real, or was Merlin exaggerating in his art?

He leaned forward, elbows on his knees. "I've met a lot of people in my lifetime, and I rather pride myself on my ability to see potential in others even if they cannot see it in themselves. You, Lady Carina, have great potential. We all have our trials and struggles, and I dare say you've had more than most. What matters is how we handle them."

She couldn't look at him. At his words, her throat tightened with emotion.

"You beat those demons down every time they rise up, and you get stronger and stronger each time. Maybe they'll never go away, but you will learn better and better ways to hold them back. You are a good person, Carina. You are doing good things and making a difference in people's lives. And you *can* change things for the better. You will."

That sharp prick of tears had begun behind her eyes as he spoke, as she stared at his sketch...of herself.

"How?"

"Be the best *you* you can be." He watched her, then, after a moment of consideration knelt in front of her. "May I take your hand?"

She set down the sketch pad, and held her hand out to him. He took it, then pressed his forehead to the back of her hand, followed by his lips. She shivered at the contact.

"I swear myself to you, Lady Carina. I will do all I can to lift you up, to never make you feel less than the queen you are meant to be. I will stay at your side as long as I can, until my work is done, to give you strength and support in whatever form you ask of me."

11
AHNRI

Ahnri's eyes narrowed. He watched through leaves and branches as Merlin knelt before Carina and pressed his forehead and lips to her hand—some sort of gesture of loyalty? He was already her servant, wasn't he? Why would he only now swear himself to her? Ahnri couldn't hear them from where he hid on a nearby roof, and made only a half-hearted attempt at reading their lips. Stories, some kind of bonding moment. It wasn't important. Matano would only care that Carina was truly alone in the city, save for a single servant who looked like he'd never lifted a sword in his life.

They'd talked until the sun was low on the horizon and Ahnri knew he needed to leave soon to make it to the presentation. He couldn't be late, that was where the best gossip usually happened. His back was tired of hiding, crouching on the edge of a nearby roof. As Merlin and Carina stood, Ahnri yawned. At the door of the inn, Merlin paused and glanced around. Ahnri held very still as Merlin's eyes roved over his hiding place, then moved on. Once the door closed, Ahnri relaxed.

Re-tying his long white hair back, his mind returned to the sparring session. He suspected he'd learned as much from Carina as she had from him, which was impressive. He'd never seen anyone so skilled at adaptation. Most duelers were so set in their training it was difficult to pick up on tricks from other methods. Carina did not have that problem. Might be a Reganian thing, or maybe just a Carina thing.

Ahnri stood and bent back and forth, stretching his stiff muscles. He sniffed the fresh air and stepped to the edge of the building, scanning the alley there, with Cait's Inn on the other side. Kahn took that moment to drift down onto Ahnri's shoulder. Ahnri arched a brow at the bird.

"What? You want something to do?"

The bird clicked his beak indignantly.

Ahnri sighed. "I know you're tired of staying put, but I have nothing to say to anyone."

Kahn cocked his head to one side, staring.

Ahnri sighed, running the back of his fingers over smooth feathers. "We'll find you an errand soon, I'll think of something. Just promise you'll come back."

Kahn jumped and took off, seeming satisfied for the time being. Ahnri watched him go for a moment, then refocused on his task.

He chose a section of wall where there were no windows on either building, then lowered himself over the edge. Holding on with his fingertips, he anchored his feet against the wall, took a deep breath, then jumped. He pushed off the wall, turning mid-air while throwing himself toward the opposite building. His legs and arms absorbed the impact, keeping him silent, before pushing off again back to the first building. He continued, moving a few feet down each time, until he reached the cobbled alleyway.

It felt good to move again after sitting for so long. Music and laughter from Cait's taproom tempted Ahnri. He still needed to clean up before the event that night, but he had a few minutes. Perhaps he could gather a bit more to tell Matano. He had been threatened with losing his position. He wouldn't mind getting dismissed, in fact, he thought as he entered the inn, it might be better for him if he was.

Maybe then the Fugeran queen wouldn't be able to find him.

The taproom of Cait's Corner was full, but not crowded. A small band played against the far wall, and were surrounded by giggling dancers. He went to the bar and ordered wine, sipping at it while watching the dancers and listening to the conversation around him.

"Not a chance."

"She's as good-for-nothing as the king himself."

Ahnri nearly choked on his wine.

"Quiet! We're in Nobility Circle, you idiot."

He stood from his seat and went to a new spot at the edge of the dance floor. Couples spun and held each other close, while a few single men and women danced alone across the polished wood floor. One woman met Ahnri's eye, and winked.

He sighed, slightly annoyed. He hated flirting. So much work. And the woman wasn't his type anyway. She had dark eyes framed by thick lashes, and wore a dress of purple Somnurian silk that flowed over her curves as she danced. Aesthetically pleasing, certainly. Ahnri, however, took a drink and turned away.

"Nice view," a voice said. He turned to see ChaNia, a Somnurian servant of the Baezona house, sit beside him, eyeing the dancer.

"I'm sure I'm not enjoying it nearly as much as you are," Ahnri said. "How are you?"

She braided her red hair back as she sat. "Everyone's talking about the tournament. The Lirastes are planning murder, the Teneos are seeking out ways to profit, and the Velandos are ambitious but not nearly as cunning as they think they are."

"Not the way I heard it."

She raised a brow. "Oh?"

"Earlier today, Barón Matano had a brief but pointed conversation with the good Sir Leon of house Velando, and if I'm not mistaken—"

"Which you never are."

"—coins were exchanged."

"Hm," she said. "A royal adviser being bought. I might have to check on that."

"Mmhmm."

"And the Matanos?"

"Confident as ever," Ahnri said. "There is no doubt in their minds that Rosaline will win."

"And do you think she should?"

"Eh," Ahnri said. "She has all the right qualities, I'm sure she'd be fine."

"Right," ChaNia said. "Because *fine* is exactly what Medelios needs."

Ahnri grinned. "And the Baezonas?"

"Baronesa Baezona wants young Sir Eron to make a good show, but doesn't honestly expect him to make it past the first round of duels. He's fast enough he might do well in the races, and he can study to pass the exam. Put him in a ring with a sword, though, and he'll only embarrass himself."

"Mm. Poor man," Ahnri said.

"Indeed. I'll see you at the presentation?"

"Most likely."

She smiled and left the inn. Ahnri closed his eyes and let his head fall forward, stretching his neck. Opening his ears.

"No way it'll work."

"I'm not so sure. They are neighbors."

"They've been rivals for generations!"

"Who's to say it needs to continue?"

No idea what that was about, but might be important.

"I'll wager ten silver that Lady Genai wins her race tomorrow. I've seen the Velando girl, she's too fragile for the tournament."

"I'll take that bet. Sophia Velando has a stubborn streak. She can run that course as fast as anyone."

Ahnri's head began to ache. Then something poked his

shoulder.

"May I speak to you?"

The voice was firm, and close. Ahnri opened his eyes to see Merlin staring down at him, his arms crossed. Somehow, he appeared significantly more imposing than he had a few hours ago.

"What about?"

Merlin's jaw clenched. "Outside."

Ahnri stood and followed the servant through the inn's main entrance and around the side of the building where he'd come down from the roof. Then he turned to Merlin. "How can I help—"

Merlin's fist slammed into Ahnri's jaw. He staggered, his hand instinctually forming a fist to strike back, but he held himself, shaking his head. It wasn't a very hard hit; more surprising than anything. "What was that for?!"

Merlin shook his hand out. "You were on the roof."

Ahnri's eyes narrowed.

"You can spar with her," Merlin said, breathing heavily, "but do not spy outside of those hours. Matano probably wants information from the entire city. You can go anywhere else and get any other information you want but you stay away from Carina. Do I make myself clear?"

Ahnri stared at him. The defensiveness, the loyalty, this…protectiveness. There was more to Merlin than Ahnri had assumed. How had he not seen it before? "You're not a servant. But you swore yourself to her, so what are you? Who do you work for?"

Merlin raised a brow. "Come on, you really think I'm gonna answer that?"

Ahnri actually laughed. "All right, fine. I'll keep away outside of sparring."

"Too easy," Merlin said. "You'll just hide better next time."

"Probably. Why don't we see if you can spot me?"

At that moment, Kahn flew down and perched on a nearby stack of empty crates, and clicked his beak at Merlin.

Merlin pointed to the bird. "Is he yours?"

"Yes."

Merlin watched Kahn for a moment. Then, in a surprised voice, said, "He trusts you."

"How would you know?"

Merlin met Ahnri's gaze and said with a completely straight face, "I speak hawk. With his vote of confidence, I'll give you another chance. Do *not* spy on Carina again."

With that, Merlin bowed to Kahn, then turned to go. He'd gone two steps before he stopped and faced Ahnri once more.

"You need to know I'm serious. I may not hit very hard, but I have other weapons at my disposal and I will use them if I have to. She's too important to risk." He turned and went back inside.

Ahnri stood for a moment, reviewing the exchange multiple times. He was left *still* confused. Merlin was short, skinny, and too pale to be healthy. What weapons could he possibly wield? As Ahnri made his way toward Matano Hall, he decided he would not tell Barón Matano about that exchange. He had enough information to satisfy the Barón, and this particular bit was one Ahnri wanted to look into on his own.

12
CARINA

Carina tried to decline Mar's offer of a carriage, saying the distance was short enough to walk, but Cait was adamant.

"All the other combatants will be in carriages," Mar chided. "I like you, and I'm not going to give them an easy reason to slander you. You'll arrive in style."

Half an hour before they were due to leave, Merlin had brought her a dress—deep scarlet, with a bodice made of gold-colored lace in rose patterns. Even at home she'd never had a dress that fit so perfectly. Not only fit her body, but fit *her*. Despite his peculiarities she had to admit: Merlin paid attention.

"Are you sure?" she said when he'd given it to her. "It seems too fancy for a presentation ceremony. I was thinking I'd wear my armor."

Merlin shook his head. "There's a small gathering of the combatants and their families after the presentation. You'll need to dress to impress for that."

When their carriage pulled up in front of the palace entrance, Carina let out a slow breath. She'd been trained in court interactions. She'd never been particularly good at them, but she knew what to do and how to behave. She would be fine.

Merlin opened her door and offered a hand to help her out. He wore a suit of matching color to her own, with gold accents that clashed with his grey eyes. An errant thought came to her that she much preferred him in blue.

Crowds of people lined the small drive, and a platform was set up to one side of the palace entrance. Merlin led her toward the stage where Sir Eron and a few others were lined up near a set of stairs.

"Lady Carina!" Sir Eron came to her, his expression eager as he bowed low before her. "I hope you're enjoying Reinos?"

"I am, thank y—"

"Men and women of Reinos!" A voice broke over them, coming from the stage above where an adviser held an amplifying funnel to his mouth as he spoke. "It is time to meet your champions! May I present to you, daughter of Baron Leon Matano and the late Baronesa Helena Garino, Lady Rosaline Matano!"

Carina covered her ears, watching as Rosaline made her way up the stairs to greet the roaring crowd. She was perfect. Strong and confident. Carina straightened her shoulders. She could match that.

The announcer was already introducing the next person, and Carina turned to ask Merlin what she was supposed to do, but he was gone. Where, when did he—then she spotted him behind the stage, his eyes on her. His gaze was calm. He nodded once, and her nerves eased. Then they called her name.

"Your turn," Eron said, placing a hand on her back.

Carina pulled away from him, making her way to the stairs as her name echoed over the madness. The people were cheering, shouting her name. As she looked out over the crowd, a strange peace came over her. She smiled, waved once, and was led to the other side of the stage and down another set of stairs, toward the main entrance of the palace itself.

That was all. The presentation was over.

"Well done," Merlin said, appearing beside her.

She laughed. That had been easier than she'd expected. Then Merlin led her through the main palace entrance, and her breath caught.

The corridor was tall and wide, with artwork lining the walls, and crystal chandeliers casting light over glittering treasures. The beauty of it all made her feel small and plain. She closed her eyes for a moment as they walked, letting Merlin lead her while she focused on her breathing.

Her shoulder slammed into someone. A plate crashed to the floor and Carina opened her eyes in time to dodge a spill.

With a short exclamation, the woman snapped her sharp eyes up from the mess, and Carina stepped back again. This was Baronesa Liraste, whom she'd stood up to in the market on the day she met Merlin.

"Apologies, Baronesa," Carina said, bowing. Her heart pounded fast in her chest.

Baronesa Liraste straightened, smoothing her expression. Servants were already cleaning before them.

"No harm done." The Baronesa said, waving a hand. Then her eyes narrowed. "You must be Lady Carina, am I correct?"

Carina's cheeks went warm. "Yes, Baronesa."

"You have a familiar face. Have we met before?"

Carina swallowed a lump in her throat, her eyes flickering to the spot on the baronesa's forehead where she'd been hit by the post that day. It was little more than a smudge now. "No, Baronesa. I'm certain I would remember making your acquaintance."

"Hm." Baronesa Liraste smiled politely, but there was a venom to the sweetness there. "Then welcome. And of course, good luck."

The Baronesa moved away and Carina curtseyed. A knot twisted in her chest.

"There, see?" Merlin said. "That was by far the worst thing that could possibly happen tonight, and you survived. You'll be fine."

"Right," she said, rolling her eyes. "Because things can never get worse."

"Honestly, fair." She met his gaze and saw a twinkle in his eye. "I'll be against the wall there," he said. "Not far, and I'll keep an eye on you. If you need me, raise a hand and I'll come."

"Thank you," she said.

"You can do this."

She watched as he strode away, back straight and head high. She mimicked his posture. She was not known here, could not expect the young nobility to leave her to sit alone in corners the way they had in Regania. She'd been trained for social situations all her life. She could handle this.

The room he'd led her to was small by royal standards, intimate. Heavy curtains hung at wide windows, and carpets muffled the many footsteps of people crowding into it.

"Lady Carina?" a voice said. She turned to see Sir Eron approaching. "That was fun, wasn't it?"

"Indeed," she said, keeping distance between them. "What was your surname, again, Sir Eron?"

"House Baezona," he said.

Baezona, she thought to herself. *Calidian heritage, hair blue or black-blue.* "And, do you have family in Calidar?"

"Cousins and such, yes," he said. "I spent some time there as a child but haven't been back in years."

They spoke of the tournament, when each of them would be competing, and she learned his mother was full Calidian and his father one-quarter, but mostly Medelian. Their family was one of the richest noble houses because of trade with the east, but the way Eron described it made Carina wary. It sounded as though they might be treating merchants the same way the Lirastes treated their farmers.

"It's a bit warm in here," he said finally. "Would you like a drink?"

She glanced toward Merlin. He still stood against the wall, watching, not interfering.

"Yes, please," she said.

Eron brought her a glass of starflower wine and raised his cup. "To new friendships?"

She forced a smile. "To new friendships."

They drank, and soon were joined by a few of Sir Eron's friends and cousins.

"Eron," one young man said, "What are your plans if you win the tournament?"

Eron grinned. "It'd be nice to move in here, don't you think?"

The others laughed.

A girl with wide eyes said, "Personally I want you to do something about the beggars. Put them to work. The slums practically stink up the whole city because those people never *do* anything."

Eron waved a hand. "We'll figure something out. I'm sure there's already plans in place from the king."

Carina doubted it.

"And the outskirts?" she asked him. "The rural areas? Have you considered them?"

Eron laughed, then seemed to realize she was serious. "I don't know anything about them. I assume they're fine. Would you like another drink?"

"Oh, no thank you." She paused. She'd lost track of Merlin. "Actually, I need to find someone. It's been a pleasure, Sir Eron. If you'll excuse me."

Carina slipped through the mingling nobility. She greeted those who met her eyes as she went. No sign of Merlin. She did however catch Lady Rosaline among a crowd. She wore a deep black gown with silver accents, and seemed the obvious leader of whatever this group was. Carina was about to pass by them until Lady Rosaline caught sight of her.

"Ah, Lady Carina, so good to see you."

"And you, Lady Rosaline."

"Is my servant a sufficient sparring partner for you?"

"He is, thank you. You're too kind."

Rosaline waved a hand. "Oh, it's no trouble at all. I'm glad to help. Have you met my cousins Marius and Constance? And this is our friend, Sir Kemin Velando. They're all competing as well."

Rosaline's cousins were as tall and strong as she was. Though the other boy, Kemin, was closer to Carina's size.

"It's lovely to meet you," Carina said. "There are so many competitors, I think it'll be difficult to keep track of them all."

They laughed. Rosaline said, "It's true. And interesting to wonder how different the kingdom could be depending on who wins."

"That seems to be the topic of conversation tonight," Marius said, chuckling. "I heard Lady Betania saying she'd burn the outer circles of the city and send all the commoners to work the fields."

"She would," someone added.

They all laughed again, as though murder and driving people from their homes were everyday activities.

Carina couldn't laugh.

What was happening here? Did these people really not

know how cities worked? How a kingdom functioned?

"Well, when I win," Rosaline said, a sly smile on her lips, "I won't need to burn anything down. The people will do as I say because they love me."

"What about you, Lady Carina?" Kemin said, his eyes skimming over her.

"Oh," she said, surprised that anyone would care to hear her opinion. She didn't really have much of a plan yet, though she did have some ideas. So, she spoke them. "I would love to evaluate the resources we have, where everything is going, and possibly alter the justice system to be fairer for all."

Her words were met with silence. Rosaline's expression was unreadable; the two young men looked as though she'd slapped them across the face.

She quickly added, "And, of course, take advantage of the comforts of the palace," and raised her wine goblet.

The boys laughed it off as Rosaline took a sip of wine. Carina met the other girl's gaze, and for a moment wondered what Rosaline's keen eyes could see when they looked at Carina.

The conversation continued, and Carina scanned the room again. Where *was* Merlin? Not that she needed him, but he *said* he'd be there.

"I've heard a lot about you, Lady Carina," Sir Kemin said. He placed a hand on her arm, and Carina forced herself to not pull away, wanting to appear comfortable, like a normal person. "There are some lovely gardens outside, would you care for a walk?"

She wanted to say no, but he wound her hand through his

arm and led her away without waiting for an answer. She kept an eye out for Merlin as Kemin led her to an archway she hadn't noticed at one end of the room. They stepped outside onto a cobbled sandstone path, and cool air sharpened her senses.

"You've gained quite a reputation, my lady," Kemin said, his voice low.

Carina cleared her throat, forcing herself to speak. "Thank you."

"I'd love to hear about your travels sometime. There've been some interesting rumors."

"I'm sure my reputation has been exaggerated." Carina glanced at him, half expecting him to be staring at her, but his eyes were on the gardens around them.

"Still," he said, "you've done much to be lauded for."

Carina frowned. "What was your surname, Sir Kemin?"

"Velando." He chuckled. "Are you having a difficult time keeping track of us all?"

"Yes, actually," she said. "You'd think after knowing Regania's ten houses that five would be simple."

He squeezed her hand as they rounded a corner, and paused.

"Ah," Kemin said. He released her arm, stepping away. "Pardon me, there's someone I need to meet."

Not ten paces away, a servant girl peeked out from behind one of the nearby trees, a blush on her cheeks.

"Sir Kemin," Carina said, putting a hand to her heart. "Did you use me only to accommodate a secret meeting?"

"I'd be lying if I said no." He adjusted his coat. "Thank you for your company, Lady Carina, and—I hope—for your discretion."

Carina curtseyed as Sir Kemin approached the girl, who smiled brightly as he drew near.

She made her way back to the main room, weaving through the crowd, and out into a corridor of the palace. The space was extravagant, to the point of distraction. Leaning against the wall to rest herself, she glanced back into the room behind her for Merlin. Again, he was nowhere in sight. She was beginning to get truly worried. He said he'd be there. Where *was* he?

She made her way through the corridor, reviewing the noble houses in her mind as she tried to keep calm. *Baezona, part-Calidian, kind. Liraste, part-Somnurian, cruel. Matano, part-Fugeran, richest house but generous. Velando.* She realized then she didn't know where the Velandos lived based only on Kemin's appearance, and she hadn't learned anything about his house or himself, except that he had a secret relationship with a palace servant.

There was one other house she needed to identify: the Teneo house. She'd met someone by that name already, hadn't she? Yes, the adviser she'd spoken to at registration. By the gods and goddesses, there were so many to keep track of.

A few small groups were speaking quietly in the hallway. As she moved farther the talk faded, and she found herself staring at a tapestry on the wall. It was a weaving of the four great Powers as represented by their worldly counterparts: Mountains for Stability, Trees for Growth, Water for Life, and Shadows for Death.

A group passed behind her, laughing about something one of them said. A mention of the gardens again, and something about a secret passage. She ignored them, then wondered: they must spend a lot of time in the palace if they knew its secrets.

She continued down the hall, eyeing the finery. A huge painted vase, a rug she didn't dare step on for its beauty, gold-inlaid doors.

Excessive. That was the only way she could describe this place. The treasures here could feed hundreds, and instead it was locked away and ignored by the king and his nobility. The Reganian palace, Carina remembered, had been old, strong, and well-kept. The royal family always had fine clothes, weapons, and enough to eat, but they'd never had so much to spare as this.

She stood before one wall panel, staring at the intricacy of the carving, when the echo of a scream sounded from a small side corridor.

It was abruptly cut off.

She spun around, expecting guards to come running. Someone who had more authority than she. No one came. No footsteps approached. Without another thought, Carina turned in the direction the scream had come and followed it.

The passage she entered was narrow and low, turning left, then right. The walls were of plain stone, and bare save for torches sconced every ten feet. And then suddenly, there were none.

She stared into the blackness where torchlight faded. If anyone was there, they would see her silhouette. She pressed her body to the wall and crept slowly forward into the darkness. The wall ended, the corner against her back. She turned with it, and caught sight of a dim light farther down. A candle? No, a lantern, being carried.

She followed it and the bodies surrounding it. She counted three girls in ball gowns, but they were carrying something between them, and the something was moving. A person, tied up, and with a sack over their head. One of the girls grunted in frustration and the burden they carried fell to the floor, writhing. The three girls knelt, and the lantern was set down. Carina hurried to get closer.

"We should go farther. Aren't there secret passageways in the palace? I've always heard—"

"Shut-up, Sim! Betania, do it!" a voice hissed. "We're not that far from the party. If he screams again, they'll hear."

"I'm going to, but it'll take a lot of pressure. Hold him still, and tighten that sack."

Bile rose in Carina's throat. She had to do something. Her skin prickled, her hands forming fists. She didn't have Excalibur, didn't even have her dagger, but she didn't care. She approached, no longer trying to be stealthy.

"Pardon me," she said, brightly.

The three girls turned, eyes wide.

"I heard there were some gardens this way. Am I mistaken?"

They exchanged looks. Carina could only make out minor features in the dim light, but she could tell they were ready for a fight. One of them, a girl in a light blue dress, stood and brandished a dagger, her eyes sharp and cunning. "You'll regret following us."

For the first time since arriving at the palace, Carina's mind was clear. "I'd regret the chance to stop you from hurting that boy."

"You should mind your own business."

"And yet," Carina said, "I'm here now. Leave him alone."

The blue-dress girl came at her, and she was fast. But Carina was expecting it. She leaned away from the blade and swung a hand at the girl's arm, twisting it behind her back. Carina snatched the dagger and shoved the girl away in time for a second girl, this one in red, to grip her hair. Carina was yanked backward and shoved against the wall; her face pressed against the cold stone.

"Keep him tied," the girl in blue said. "We'll do this one first."

Carina's arms were held behind her back, the dagger pulled from her hand, and the girl in red shoved Carina along the wall, scratching her face. Carina shifted a foot, sliding it across the floor, searching. Then her toes came in contact with a foot behind her, and she slammed her heel down on the foot of the girl at her back.

The girl in red shrieked in pain, jumping away and freeing Carina. She kept the wall at her back as blood trickled from her nose, and she spat.

"Ugh," the girl in blue shrieked. "You got blood on my best dress!"

Carina took a deep breath. "You shouldn't have worn your best dress to a kidnapping."

The blue girl advanced again and swung at Carina's already bleeding nose. Her neck twisted; her heart raced. The girl sidestepped and attacked again, grabbing onto Carina's dress to pull her close. The knife she held was to Carina's throat now, the blade biting into the side of her neck, warm blood trailed down her chest. She closed her eyes, grinding her teeth to distract her from the pain. Separate herself from it as she had so many times.

"You're that foreign scum, aren't you," the girl in blue said. Her laughter was light and airy in the darkness. "Do you really think the gods would allow someone so pathetic to win the crown?"

Her words were drowned by the rush in Carina's body. With a fluid motion, she slammed an elbow into the girl's side, took the knife from her hand, and spun to shove her against the stone wall.

Spinning, Carina met the girl in red, gripping her arm and twisting it, then slamming a hand sideways into her neck to send her falling to the tiled floor. The last girl, one wearing a pale-yellow dress who had been watching the boy on the floor, charged Carina with a growl. When she drew near enough in the dim light, Carina spun out of the way and shoved her against the wall. She crumpled to the ground, holding her head.

The girl in blue shook her head and stared for a moment at her two friends, then at Carina. A heartbeat passed, and then she turned and ran.

Carina followed, leaped on the girl's back, and knocked her to the ground.

"Who are you?" Carina asked.

"Why do you care?"

Carina slammed the knife's pommel into her head, knocking her out.

Carina straightened, heart pounding and breath scratching her throat. The small corridor now smelled of sweat and blood, and these girls would be coherent in a moment. If she was caught here….

As she thought it, there was a sound of footsteps running away in the darkness. Someone *had* seen them. Whether they knew it was Carina or not, she might never know. She shoved the thought away. She'd done the right thing, hadn't she? And that was what mattered.

The three girls incapacitated, Carina went to the boy. His hands were tied, and a sack covered his head. She reached for the sack, then stopped.

"I'm going to leave you tied."

"What?" the boy shouted, fear making his voice crack. "No, no please. If they wake up and I'm still here—"

"No." She didn't even know who these girls were. They could be servants, or nobility, or workers.

"Please," the boy said. "I know them. They're Lirastes. Betania, Cora, and Simata.

Liraste, part-Somnurian, cruel...

"They grabbed me," the boy said. "I-I was going back to the party, I didn't even see them coming, please—"

"All right," Carina said. She pulled the sack off.

Kemin Velando, the boy who had snuck off with his

servant girlfriend, stared up at her. His eyes widened. "Y-you? But you're half their size!"

"Yes," she said. "And I'm holding the knife, so don't try anything."

He tensed, and for a moment Carina thought he might attack her, even tied up. Then slowly, he looked away, cowed.

She cut the ropes around his wrists and ankles, then gestured with the knife. "Go on," she said.

"Go where?"

"Wherever you want that isn't here."

He swallowed, then started down the corridor, back toward the party.

"And Sir Kemin?"

He turned back.

"I'll appreciate your discretion in this matter."

Shaken, he nodded, and continued on his way.

Carina sighed, letting her arm fall. He'd likely be back soon with guards. Nearby, one of the girls began to stir. Carina had to get away. She laid the knife on the ground next to one of the girls, and slipped down the corridor after Kemin.

Back in the hall with tapestries and artwork, Kemin was nowhere to be found. She quietly made her way toward the party, watching for guards, but instead, she found Merlin. Leaning against a pillar, eating an angfruit. She stormed up to him and knocked the fruit from his hand, sending it flying.

"Hey!" His eyes went wide at the sight of her. "What happened to you?"

"'I won't be far,'" she said, throwing his own words at him.

"'If you need me, I'll come.' Where *were* you?"

His face fell. "I went to catch sight of the king, but he was gone before I could. I—"

"Merlin," she said, her voice breaking.

His hands hovered over her, glancing at each injury but not touching. "I'm so sorry, you were doing so well on your own, I never—I should have—who did this?"

"Not important." She pressed a hand to her head, the anger fading to exhaustion. "Someone screamed, and no guards came, so I followed—"

"You followed them?" he asked. "Do you really think that was wise?"

"They were going to hurt someone! Besides, we are talking about *your* disappearance, not my decision making. I don't regret what I did. I'm angry with you for not being here when I needed you."

His expression softened. "You're right. I'm sorry."

The sincerity in his eyes struck her, and she put her face in her hands, remembering his lesson about anger. "I'm sorry for yelling, but I am *extremely* frustrated with you right now."

"You have a right to be." He placed a hand on her shoulder. "Here. Come this way."

He made his way farther away from the party, and she followed. Once they'd turned a corner, he stopped.

"Now, let me see these," he said, indicating her wounds. "May I touch?"

She braced herself, then raised her chin and let him gently prod the skin at her neck where she'd been cut. His fingers were chill from holding the fruit, his gaze focused, analyzing. He moved to the scratches on her face, then to her head where she'd knocked against the wall.

"Well, the cut on your neck is minor, and the bump on your head should fade quickly, especially if we get some water and let me heal you. There's a side exit this way, let's get you back to the inn."

13
AHNRI

Disgusting.

Ahnri frowned at the bits of half-finished food on trays leaving the party with each servant. These nobles took a single bite of an orange and if it was too bitter or dry, they let it go to waste. In Fugera, one never let any scrap of edible food go by without eating it. Medelios was a rich kingdom, yes, but it never failed to twist Ahnri's stomach with how short-sighted they were about it. The amazing thing was, they didn't even realize it. He kept his face impassive. If he was seen sneering at a plate of food, he might be asked to dispose of it, and that would put him out of hearing range.

"There's no way he'll make it past the fourth round," someone said to Ahnri's right. "You know he'll be up against Rosaline; he's got no chance—"

"They've been sparring since they were six," a woman's voice said. "And he has the upper hand in strength. I'm certain

Marius will be the victor."

Well, that wasn't new information. Ahnri quietly stepped toward a table that held drinks and took up a tray of wine goblets. He swept through the crowd offering fresh wine to those he wanted to listen in on.

"Have you heard about this foreign girl?" Barón Liraste asked a group as he took wine from Ahnri's tray. "Some bumpkin from Regania who *claims* to have Medelian blood. I don't care how accurate her information is, she should not be allowed to compete."

"I met her myself," Baronesa Liraste added. "She's smaller than my dogs, I give you my word."

"I beg your pardon, Barón, Baronesa," said Sir Ilian, one of the king's personal advisers. "I interviewed the girl myself, and I must say she has quite the mind. She might surprise us all."

Barón Liraste gave a forced smile. "I highly doubt it, sir."

Sir Ilian placed an empty goblet on Ahnri's tray and gave a nod.

Ahnri bowed himself away and went to re-stock his wine goblets. One more tray would be the limit though. After that people might begin to notice that he wasn't in palace servant attire. He carried the tray of full goblets to the other end of the room. Lady Rosaline sat on a sofa in a corner, surrounded by a group of friends.

Out one of the tall windows, Kahn swooped by on an air current, his dark form a shadow against the star-lit sky. Ahnri made his way to where Baronesa Teneo sat speaking with her daughter and one of the Baezona cousins. Ahnri bowed to them, offering wine. They ignored him entirely, making it simple to eavesdrop in plain sight.

"You can't expect me to take your word, I hope," Baronesa Teneo said.

The young Baezona boy ran a hand through his blue-black hair, looking suave. "You'll have to, I'm afraid. That's all you're getting."

"Now, sir," the young Teneo girl said. "We have all been disappointed with how things have fallen but there's no reason you can't provide verification in writing."

"Syla is right," Baronesa Teneo said, standing. "Tell your uncle that unless I see a signed document, we have no deal."

The boy bowed as Baronesa Teneo swept away, then he turned back to Syla. "Is she serious?"

"I'm afraid so," she said. "She does business, Diman, not trust."

First names, casual, Ahnri thought. *Interesting.*

"Hm." He took a drink from his goblet then absently set it on Ahnri's tray.

"We need it in writing," Syla said again.

"Well," Diman said, meeting her eyes. "Perhaps I could be persuaded to provide it. Over dinner?"

She arched a brow, a smile tugging at her mouth. "That could be arranged."

Ahnri's fought to hold his surprise behind his usually impassive face. According to his sources, the Teneo and Baezona houses had been financial rivals for nearly a decade. A relationship between two who might one day be head of their houses would cause all sorts of rumors and drama.

Ahnri returned the empty goblets to the servant's station and moved to a relatively empty corner of the room. He scanned the crowd, taking a moment to mentally catch his breath. It seemed that Rosaline was a favorite to win the tournament—no surprise—and there was that foreign girl Barón Liraste spoke of. That had to be Carina. And he had to admit after sparring with her that she stood a decent chance.

He spotted a familiar face against the wall nearby and went to stand by her.

"Evening," Ahnri said.

ChaNia gave a nod of greeting. "Evening."

"Hear anything interesting tonight?"

"Lady Rosaline obviously the favorite, yes?"

"As expected," Ahnri said.

"Baronesa Velando continues to press Kemin despite his apathy toward the entire tournament."

Ahnri snorted.

"Do you know about the Baezona and Teneo situation?"

"Yes, I saw them speaking earlier. Diman, is it?"

"And Syla, yes," ChaNia said. "They've been spending quite a bit of time together. Much to their parents' dismay."

"That should be interesting to watch."

"Quite. See you at the races tomorrow?"

"I'll be there."

Ahnri made his way out of the room toward the servant's exit, stopping when he passed a side corridor. People were shouting. Ahnri might not be much help, but if something was happening, he needed to know.

He approached the voices and found a few young men surrounding three ladies, all seated and being fawned over. Ahnri recognized them as Liraste girls, all three with varying degrees of red streaked through their black hair. Cuts and bruises decorated their arms and faces. The blood had dried, which told Ahnri it had been a while since whatever incident had given them the injuries.

A moment later, one of the king's healers arrived and shoved everyone back, then began to examine them. He sent some servants to fetch water and towels and bandages, and in a matter of minutes he'd cleaned and dressed their wounds and sent a petition to the king to allow him to heal them with magic.

Sir Eron, one of the young men, drew the healer aside, worry clear in his eyes.

Ahnri made his way around the crowd, just close enough to listen.

"Did they say what happened?"

"Attacked, or so it seems," the healer said. "They won't talk to me."

Eron frowned. "Will they be all right?"

"Fine, fine. No permanent damage done. I'd prefer to heal them if the king sees fit, but they should be able to participate in the races regardless. None of the wounds are too deep." He turned back to the girls. "Ladies, please stay here. I'm going to see to your healing petition myself."

With that, the healer left, and young nobles surrounded the three Lirastes.

"Where were you?"

"What happened?"

"Did someone attack you?"

Lady Cora blinked, putting a hand to her head. "I—I don't remember anything."

Betania, beside her, nodded vigorously. "It's all black," she said. "We were headed to the…the gardens, and then we woke covered in all these injuries, in a servant's corridor."

"Magic?" Eron muttered.

Ahnri rolled his eyes. That wasn't how magic worked.

The crowd began to murmur, but Ahnri watched the eyes of the three young ladies. Cora in particular seemed to be glancing from person to person, testing the reaction of her words.

She was lying.

Someone had attacked them, though it seemed they didn't want to accuse anyone. Why would that be?

Curious, Ahnri passed through the party once more, taking particular account of who was present and who had left. Only two combatants were not present—Kemin Velando, and Carina Valio.

Kemin wasn't the smartest, but even he should know not to go against three Liraste knights at once. Carina, on the other hand….

If Ahnri's guess was right, Carina had not done the initial attacking. Which, most likely, meant Cora, Betania, and Simata had attacked, and Carina had taken them all down.

Ahnri's mouth quirked up at the corner. Three on one were

bad odds, especially considering these three were taller than Carina.

Ahnri would have to find her in the morning. He took a moment to review the injuries on the girls, and couldn't help feeling impressed. Perhaps the foreign girl *would* give these nobles a surprise.

The party ended soon after the attack was discovered, and Ahnri rode with the driver of Rosaline's carriage back to Matano Hall. Kahn flew above the entire way. Ahnri kept his face stoic as he helped Lady Rosaline step down and led her into the building. He took her cloak, then bowed as she left for her rooms. Ahnri stepped into the parlor nearby, where Barón Matano stood near a window.

"Report?"

"Lady Rosaline is a favorite to win, sir."

"Unsurprising. What else?"

"While she is a favorite, there is talk of whether she'll be able to beat Sir Marius. He is seen as her biggest threat, at the moment. Bets are being placed, of course. Those discussing the matter spoke of the two dueling since childhood, knowing each other's strengths, weaknesses, and patterns. Some sided with Lady Rosaline, but there were strong voices for Sir Marius as well. I would guess that he is training specifically to surprise her in the duels."

"Hm. Go on."

"The Teneo and Baezona families may have an alliance in the works, whether financial or otherwise I was unable to determine. One of the king's advisers expressed a vote of confidence in the foreign entrant, Lady Carina Valio from Regania, which was dismissed by others present. The Lady Carina accepted an offer from Lady Rosaline to use me as a sparring partner for the duration of the tournament, and, while sparring with her I gathered that she is more nervous than not at the prospect of the tournament."

"Good," Matano said. "We want to keep her that way. Anything else?"

"Before we left the party tonight, there was an attack."

He turned to face Ahnri, his brows knit together. "An attack? On whom? By whom?"

"Three of the Liraste cousins were covered in cuts and scrapes. They say they were heading for the gardens when they must have blacked out, and woke in a servant's corridor bruised and injured. They insist they didn't see their attacker."

"Hmm," Barón Matano muttered, staring out the window again. "Any suspicions who might've done it?"

"No, sir." He'd decided right away he would keep this from the Baron. It was his job to bring the information, not draw the conclusions.

"Very well, boy. You say you're sparring with this new girl?"

"Yes, sir."

"Gain whatever information you can from her. Get her to trust you if you can."

"Of course, sir."

"Dismissed."

Ahnri bowed and left the room. He took the stairs to the second floor and slipped left into a sitting room to check that his game—his set of Sticks—was safe, behind a loose brick at the back of the fireplace. They were. Pleased with himself for finding the spot, he returned the game and brick.

It wasn't even midnight, and Ahnri was not tired. Taking up his cloak, he left the hall through the back door and made his way to the nearest alley. With ease, he ran at one wall, jumped to another, pushed off, and reached the top of the closest building. He pulled himself up and took a deep breath of the cool night air. Kahn circled above, and the city lay before him, all bright lights and dark shapes, waiting to be explored.

This wasn't the kind of spying Matano would expect of him, but it was the kind Ahnri preferred. Pulling his hood low, he leaped from the building.

14
AHNRI

On the day of the races, Ahnri made his way to the tournament field early. There would be sixteen races today: each of the thirty-two entrants competing in pairs, and being scored on ability, fairness, speed, and probably other things the advisers hadn't seen fit to announce to the public. Those moving forward would be announced the following morning.

The stands formed a rectangle, open at the corners, and held perhaps a thousand people, with the obstacle course laid out in the field below. On his way in, Ahnri caught sight of high metal bars, ropes, wooden tunnels. As he ascended the stands, the course was blocked from view.

Sheets of canvas covered the course to keep future competitors from gaining an edge on the early racers by seeing their mistakes. A nice concept, Ahnri thought, but it did make for less of a show for those watching. And there were many who had come to watch. The sides of the course came up against the underside of the stands, and were open to allow the king's advisers a view of the racers' progress. They would mark off points for mistakes or cheating.

Ahnri took a seat near the top of the stands, right in front of a particular group he knew for their heavy gossip habit.

"Fifty?" a woman shouted. "Why on earth would he agree to that? The girl doesn't stand a chance!"

"I warned him," a man said. "Lady Rosaline has all the advantages in the races. There's no way she'll lose."

Ahnri stared out over the growing crowd. Lady Rosaline stood at one end of the course, next to her cousin Constance, preparing for their race. Rosaline's hair hung down her back in a long two-toned braid, exposing her face. He was quite far away, but Ahnri thought she seemed bored. Constance had some Somnurian blood, showing in the deep auburn hair held back in a tail. The girl was thin, and barely came to Rosaline's jaw. Unless she had great speed—which Ahnri doubted—Constance would most definitely lose to Rosaline. Ahnri let his sight un-focus, and let his hearing drift to the conversations around him.

"Who's up after this?"

"Simata Liraste against one of the Teneos."

"When's the foreign girl racing?"

"Not for another hour or two, I think."

"Check the program."

Ahnri scanned the stands opposite him.

"You know, I think that's right smart of the king to give them a test."

"It's not the king who's organizing this. It's the advisers."

"Surely, he's got some say, though?"

"I doubt it. Some say he hasn't left his bed in weeks."

Ahnri frowned.

Across from him he spotted Lady Carina, her faithful servant at her side. Though he was far from them, Ahnri reevaluated the young man now, remembering the punch he'd given the day before. Not too tall, with skin so pale he stood out among the surrounding crowd. He eyed those nearby with suspicion, but he was always polite, and never more than a few paces from Carina.

"There she is, the foreign girl!"

"Where?"

"Right across and down a bit. See?"

"Is that her servant?"

"He's quite nice to look at, isn't he?"

"I heard she uses his *services* quite a bit."

The group laughed.

Interesting rumor. Ahnri turned his head, keeping his eyes on Carina. There was something in the way she held herself. She was no bigger than Constance Matano, yet her presence held much greater strength. A calm firmness only gained by weathering constant storms. Ahnri thought of the walls surrounding port cities, built high and strong to take the force of breaking waves. Carina was that wall.

"She stayed at our house!"

Ahnri blinked, focusing on the child's voice.

"Surely it was someone else," a man said.

"Oh, it was her," the child's mother said. "She saved our little Jes from being kidnapped, then stayed for dinner and left the next morning."

The man grunted. "Someone said she did things like that. Thought it was rumors."

Ahnri frowned. Truth as rumors and rumors as truth….

A fanfare sounded below and two of the king's advisers stepped up from below the stands to address the crowds. The taller of them held his hands up for silence, then spoke. "Good people of Reinos! Today we witness the first competition of the King's Tournament, an obstacle course. This course is designed to test both physical and mental agility; ability to perform under pressure, as well as calmly managing the challenges faced. Points will be given for finishing first and completing each obstacle, and taken for cheating or mistakes. If the racers and advisers are in their places?"

He paused, then received a nod from another adviser.

"Very well. Let the races begin!"

The crowd began to cheer and all eyes went to Rosaline and Constance. A moment later a bell rang, and the two girls dashed into the canvas-covered course. Ahnri crossed his arms. Nothing to see now but who would come out the other side.

The canvas covering shook and shuddered in places, but it wasn't two minutes before Rosaline came out the other side. She finished a full half-minute before Constance and didn't even seem fatigued.

From the talking around him, Ahnri gathered more judgments about Carina, word of Fugeran nomads visiting the city during the tournament, two knights whispering which advisers would be the easiest to bribe, and a few comments about the Baezona and Teneo drama.

Ahnri frowned as he left the arena. It was all good information, but none of it seemed important. To him, anyway. Barón Matano might very well find it priceless. He stopped near one of the main exits and leaned against a support beam, closing his eyes. As citizens and nobility passed, all he heard was praise for Rosaline winning by a wide margin.

When the flow of people became a trickle, with about half the audience staying in their seats for the next race in less than an hour, Ahnri slipped away and headed back to Matano Hall. He found Barón Matano in a small dining room lit by sunlight streaming through wide windows. The scent of warm bread and hot soup made Ahnri's stomach clench. He bowed, then stood staring at the far wall.

"Report?"

"Lady Rosaline finished first, sir."

Barón Matano rolled his eyes. "As expected. Get on with it."

Ahnri relayed everything he'd gathered from every source, reliable and not—making sure to point out the difference as he spoke. His personal thoughts, he kept to himself. As always.

Matano ate carefully, every movement concise. Ahnri frowned at the precision with which the old man sliced his meat. Matano listened, nodding occasionally or grunting in acknowledgment.

"Good enough," Matano said when Ahnri finished. "Not

the standard I'd hoped for, though."

Ahnri wanted to roll his eyes, but he kept his face blank.

"I need more. I was promised a spy of quality when I hired you, boy. You were a fair servant at the Manor, here is where I need the skills I paid for. So far, you've given me nothing more than what I could hear on my own by going to the local tavern."

That wasn't necessarily true. People wouldn't say the things they meant if Barón Matano were nearby.

"I need dirt. I need secrets. I need something I can use against the other houses. Find it. If you can't do it, I'll replace you."

"Understood, sir."

"Go."

Ahnri bowed, then turned and left the room, shaking his head. He was wasting his time here.

He made his way through Matano Hall, passing rooms where family members lounged, drank, talked, but his steps led him through to the room he'd been given to stay in. Simple, unadorned, but with the basics of a chair, writing desk, and a bed that was much nicer than the cots at the manor.

He opened the window, expecting it when Kahn drifted in to settle on Ahnri's shoulder, his talons sharp, but not cutting through the tunic and vest. A moment later, a second carrier hawk followed, taking a perch on the back of a chair. There was a note tied to the new bird's leg.

Ahnri took a deep breath to steady his suddenly racing heart. It had been weeks since his last contact, and he'd begun to hope there wouldn't be any more. But the queen of Fugera was not a forgetful woman.

Ahnri loosened the leather strap and unrolled the paper.

A-

Progress report. Rumors of new heir? Confirm.

-E

Queen Elya, of Fugera. The woman was old, but she was cunning. Ahnri gritted his teeth, turning to toss the note into the fireplace and then to the writing desk. Pulling out blank paper and ink, he scribbled:

E-

New heir to be named. Will send word when confirmed.

-A

Perhaps the hurried scrawl would portray a sense of busyness. Ahnri rolled up the note, and slipped it into the new hawk's carrier. The bird flew off without delay.

Ahnri pulled his cloak tighter around him, and rather than stay inside, ducked out of the room and headed for the busy street. He needed to let off some steam.

15
CARINA

Her race hadn't even begun but Carina's heart pounded with excitement. She'd been wished good luck by an eager Sir Eron and a demure Lady Rosaline, stepped up onto the platform next to the royal advisers, waved at the people gathered to watch, and caught Merlin's glance amid the sea of faces. His eyes were like steel, holding her to the earth. Even from that distance he told her, *you can do this.*

While they'd watched—or rather, not watched—the other races, Carina had complained about the whole thing.

"The obstacle course is ridiculous," she had said, crossing her arms. "What does an obstacle course have to do with ruling a kingdom?"

"Improvisation," Merlin had replied. "How you act under pressure. A monarch deals with problems every day. They want to see whether you keep your head in a stressful situation."

"They should give us actual problems to fix," she argued,

her annoyance cutting through. "It's not like they don't have them."

"Have what?"

"Problems."

"You're not wrong." He'd smiled then. "I'm glad you're feeling better."

She had sighed then, feeling guilty for her frustration. She should be grateful to be alive—she *was* grateful to be alive—and here she was complaining?

Now, she faced a canvas curtain through which her own obstacle course laid wait, and she tried not to let her annoyance at the process get to her. To her left, Nando Liraste bounced on the balls of his feet, apparently full of extra energy and ready to race. Carina dusted off her pants and stretched her muscles, taking deep breaths to help her focus. Then, a face in the crowd caught her eye.

"Jes?" Carina ran toward the stands, recognizing the young boy, and then his mother behind him.

"Lady Jewel!" Dani waved frantically, a wide grin on her face.

"Why are you here?" Carina said, reaching her hands up to hold theirs.

Dani laughed. "To support you, of course! Once we knew you'd officially entered, Bann insisted we come and see you."

A burning sensation rose behind her eyes, tears she couldn't let fall at the moment. "Thank you. You don't know what this means to me."

"Oh," Dani said. "It's not much, dear."

"It's enough," Carina said, squeezing Dani's hand.

Jes was shaking her other hand. "Did you know they have *ice cream* in the capital? Mama says we can make some at home this winter if we freeze enough ice!"

Carina laughed. It was at that moment she noticed the crowd around them staring. Dani and Jes's plain but well-maintained clothes stood out stark against the finery of the nobility, and the latter were not happy that Carina was giving the peasants such attention.

Carina squeezed their hands once more. "Thank you for being here, it means a great deal to me. Come see me this afternoon and we can visit more? I'm staying at the inn, Cait's Corner, on Nobility circle."

"We'll come," Dani said. "Good luck!"

Carina made her way back to the start point, and jumped when another voice screeched through the air.

"Nando! You'd better beat her, or I'll disown you!" The voice came from the stands behind her. Betania Liraste leaned over the rail with a smug smile and keen eyes. She laughed, a tinkling bell-like sound at odds with her rudeness.

Of course, she would be here. To support her cousin—or whatever Nando was to her—and to taunt Carina. Betania's voice continued to carry down to them. Carina ignored it. She had to get through this race. She could worry about other things later.

"Sorry about her," Nando said. Then he reached a hand out to Carina.

Hesitantly, she took it and they shook.

"Good luck," he said.

Well, maybe he wasn't as bad as his relatives. "Good luck."

The signal was given for them to take their places. Carina took a slow breath and leaned into her back leg, ready to push off and dive through the canvas. Why a mucking obstacle course?

A bell rang, and she dashed forward.

Inside the canvas sheet was an eight-foot wall. Straight upward, polished wood, with a rope hanging down from the top. Carina swore, then grabbed the rope and began to pull herself up. Twenty feet to her left, Nando was already halfway up. She cursed again. Then she watched him and mimicked his movement, perfecting as she went, and managed to reach the top at the same time as him. He dropped to the ground. She followed but lost her footing and landed on her hip. She groaned as she rolled to her feet. That would be a bruise.

Next was a low tunnel also made of wood. She scurried through her tunnel, which turned left, then right, right, then right again, and left, before ending at a wide pit filled with mud. There were two ropes stretched across it, one at her feet, the other at eye-level. Without a thought, she took hold of the top rope and stepped onto the bottom. She wobbled and shook, her heart racing and her hands burning to hold on despite the sweat on her palms.

Relief flooded her when she made solid ground. It didn't last long. A forest of thin poles stuck up out of the ground before her. With no way around it, she had to go through. They weren't so close that she wouldn't fit, but it was painful. Bending and twisting to move from one awkward position to the next, her foot caught and she cried out in pain. She had to backtrack to get it out, which slowed her down, making her more frustrated. She emerged from the other side with a twisted ankle.

Mucking obstacle course, she thought, frustration brewing in her chest.

She was met by a steel bar situated over a deep pit. Nothing dangerous at the bottom, but the fall would hurt and she wouldn't be able to get out. Either side was blocked off by ropes, where the king's advisors watched with interest. The pit was only ten feet across, surely she could keep her balance that long, even with an injured ankle. She stepped onto the bar, and didn't think. She ran across, and when her balance began to slip, she dived the rest of the way, rolling as she met the ground, pain erupting from her already injured hip.

Covered in dirt, with small cuts tearing at her hands, forearms, and knees, she stood and took in her next obstacle: a high line of steel bars with about two feet between each one. She would have to swing from one to the next to get across. Funny, there was no pit or mud here. She could easily run to the other side, but she guessed that wasn't their intention. She jumped up to grab the first bar, and swung her body weight to catch the next one. There were ten, and by the end her hands were burning, her forearms on fire. Her entire body begged to stop. She ran forward, determined now to beat this stupid task.

Another wall to climb stood before her, rope ready. She wasn't even sure where Nando was anymore. She tried not to think about her blisters, or her bruised hip, or the way her ankle was bending, or the dust suddenly clouding her vision and filling her throat. She took hold of the rope and climbed, coughing through a brown cloud.

At the top, she heaved herself over and dropped—landing flat on her back—before staggering to her feet and running through a second canvas sheet.

Two bells sounded, and she was surrounded by healers. They took her to a shaded place as hands began to examine her, poking and prodding, Life magic flowing into her. She couldn't open her eyes for the dust.

"Let me through, *let me through*!"

"Merlin?" she called.

"Yes, I'm here." He pushed stray hairs from her eyes.

"He threw dirt into her face, we need water," someone said.

"He did *what*?" Merlin cried.

"A handful of dust to her eyes and mouth," the voice said.

Carina coughed. No wonder her throat was so dry.

"*Ese hijo de*.... Carina, you're going to be all right, you hear?"

"Yes." She coughed. "Did I win?"

He laughed. "They won't decide on that until after all the races are done, remember?"

"I know, but," she coughed again. "Did I beat him out?"

"From my perspective, you came out at the same time." He squeezed her hands. "You were incredible."

She let out a breath. "Stupid obstacle course."

Merlin laughed.

16
AHNRI

Ahnri prided himself on being able to read and understand people, but Lady Carina was different. Everyone tried to *appear* honest, few ever succeeded. Everyone had a giveaway: a twitch of the eyebrow, itching an ear, some body language inconsistent with their statements. Ahnri could always tell. So far, from what he'd seen of her, Lady Carina seemed to be completely genuine. Ahnri watched her get carried away on a stretcher and couldn't help wondering when he'd catch her. Everyone lied about something. It was only a matter of finding out what.

The dirt was hard beneath his feet as he ran away from the crowds at the races and toward the palace. Where the palace wall came to a corner before going south, he stopped and waited. His fingers tapped his thumb in a quick beat, the only part of his body he allowed to fidget.

Only seconds passed before ChaNia was approaching. "How's the morning?"

"Rosaline finished first—"

"As expected."

"—along with Marius and Beatrice."

"Matanos are making this quite the show."

"Exactly. The last Matano, Leo, is racing this afternoon."

"What about the foreign girl?"

"Carina? She came out even with Nando Liraste. He threw dirt in her face though, so he'll get marked down for that."

"You think she'll win?"

"I do."

"Hmmm."

"What else is happening in the city?"

ChaNia smirked. "Baronesa Velando continues to press Kemin despite his *accident* at the party last night."

"Accident?"

"Apparently, he was attacked by 'three huge men' whose faces he never saw, dragged into a dark corridor of the palace, then saved by a palace guard who made him promise to keep his identity a secret."

Ahnri's brows shot up. "And he has no idea who his attackers were?"

"None at all."

"Well, that's ridiculous."

"Quite."

"So, the Lirastes don't want the Velandos able to compete."

"Apparently."

"But why? If you're going to eliminate the competition, why start with Kemin Velando of all people?"

"My thoughts exactly," ChaNia said. "What of this so-called 'palace guard' who saved Sir Kemin? To willingly put oneself against three attackers—no matter one's talent, that is not a smart choice. Why save Kemin at great personal risk?"

"It seems to me," Ahnri said, leaning forward, "there may at last be a person in this kingdom who actually has…a conscience."

ChaNia gasped. "No. A conscience?" she looked side to side before meeting his eyes again. "Truly?"

Ahnri lifted his shoulder in a half-shrug.

ChaNia put her hand on Ahnri's arm, lowering her voice. "You are the best I know at spotting deceit, Ahnri. Is she actually as good as that?"

"I've been watching her closely for two days and I have yet to see her lie about anything," he said. "And if what you say is true, I'm confident it was she who saved Kemin. The Liraste girls' stories about their unknown attacker didn't match up, and Carina was gone before they were even found. The fact that someone else has already nearly killed her makes me even more convinced that she's worth supporting."

ChaNia leaned back against the palace wall. "The lower classes love her."

"Quite a lot."

"Should we perhaps put our support behind her?"

"What support? We're servants, ChaNia."

"We control more of the information in this city than the king himself."

"That's not difficult these days."

"Then the advisers. We can make people think what we want them to. If we got together and told the other servants she's the best option, we could have most of the nobility supporting her by the end of tomorrow."

"Except the Matanos."

She waved a hand. "I never count them."

Ahnri laughed. "You're right. Let me think about it. I'll see if I can get anything else on her."

"Good. I'll see you this afternoon, then? Under the south stands?"

"I'll be there."

17
CARINA

Back at the inn, even though her eyes had been thoroughly cleaned, Carina could still feel grit in them. Her hands were wrapped in bandages, and she had taken half an hour to bathe and change into a clean dress. At a knock at her door, she let in Merlin who carried a tray in his hands. Hearty meat stew, a few slices of fresh bread, and a goblet of dark wine.

Carina's stomach rumbled.

Merlin's brow raised. "I suppose you're ready to eat, then?"

"Wouldn't you be?" she asked.

"I most definitely would."

She sat on her bed, putting the tray on her lap as Merlin took the chair beside her bed.

"How are you feeling?" he asked.

"Fine, I suppose. My hands still hurt a little, but I'm not tired."

"I'm impressed," he said. "Your hands were torn up like

streamers, you got a twisted ankle and bruised hip, plus splinters and scrapes all over your arms and legs. Just out of the course you looked like you'd gotten attacked by a horde of angry bees."

She gave a soft laugh, taking a bite of stew.

"I'm much less concerned with you getting injured than I am with you winning the tournament," he said. "As long as we get you on the throne, I can fix just about anything else."

"I'm allowed to get cut up, as long as I win?"

"Sounds a lot more callous when you say it like that, doesn't it," he said, crossing his arms. "But you're not wrong."

Carina simply smiled.

"The races are still going," Merlin said. "There's been a lot of people cheating, according to Cait. You're one of the few who hasn't."

"How does anyone know who is or isn't cheating if they can't see the course?"

"The advisers talk," he said, "people listen in."

"You'd think they'd be more discreet."

"They are, as much as they can be. But there will always be spies."

"Did you tell Cait to let me know if Dani and Jes come to visit? I want to see them."

"I did, and gave her their descriptions. She seemed rather pleased."

Carina continued eating in silence until she was full and sat back, content.

Merlin moved the tray to her nightstand, then sat on her bed, facing her. "If I may, would you allow me to examine your hands? The Cures healed you some before bandaging you up but I'd like to double check their work."

She glanced from him to her hands, then held her left out to him.

"Thank you," he said. He untied the knot holding the bandage in place, and began to unwind the fabric.

"Meh," he said.

The skin was technically healed over, but still red and raw. She flexed it, feeling the tightness of new skin and a slight burn from beneath. She winced.

"Not fully healed."

"No. Does it need to be?"

"If you want to practice with that *boy* this afternoon, you'll need to be at full strength."

"Merlin," she chided. "That boy's name is Ahnri."

"I know his name," Merlin said. "Now let me finish healing this." He stood and went to the dresser, taking up a bowl of water. On the way, he bumped the chair, knocking over the sword propped against it. Her father's.

"Oh, sorry," he said, picking it up.

"Could you slide that under the bed, actually?" Carina asked. She'd hardly thought about her father's blade since she'd gotten Excalibur, and the sight of it made her uneasy.

"Of course," Merlin said, doing as she asked. Then he came to the bed and sat, facing her, placing the bowl on her nightstand within his reach. With one hand in the bowl and the other over her palm, he closed his eyes.

This time, Carina watched. A white light shone through

his fingertips, and a tickling sensation covered Carina's palm, then the pinpricks. The light grew so bright she turned away, then began to fade, along with the tingling. When the light faded, she noticed the water seemed less clear, and the level was lower.

His touch was sure, confident, even tender. Merlin's fingers ran across her palm, putting pressure on the fully healed skin. A shiver ran up her arm from where he touched, and she pulled away.

He frowned, holding his hands still. "Did I hurt you?"

"No, just…no." Her heart was only beating faster than it had that morning before the race. Feeling nervous—and somewhat curious—she held out her other hand.

"I'll be more careful," he said. And he was. His motions were gentle, and the magic even lighter than before. Again, he ran two fingers across her palm. Something about the gesture made her breath catch.

"Why do you do that?" she asked.

"Do what?"

"You touched the skin after healing it."

"To make sure it doesn't hurt you anymore." He released her hand, and she ran her thumbs over the healed palms in turn.

"Thank you."

"You're welcome," he said. "How does your ankle feel?"

She twisted it, and winced at the pain. Merlin breathed a laugh and went to the foot of her bed. He shifted her skirts carefully to reveal only her bare feet. One hand in the water, one on her ankle, his thick brows came together and the white light appeared again. Then his fingertips trailed over the healed areas, testing them for weak spots. She wasn't sure whether she imagined that his touch lingered, and a blush rose to her cheeks.

"All done," he said. "Unless you want your hip healed as well?"

The heat in her face deepened at the thought. "No, that's all right. I think they fixed that entirely."

"Good. Ahnri is coming to spar with you in a few hours, so you should probably rest while you can. I can bring you a book if you don't want to sleep."

A frantic knock sounded at the door. Merlin hurried to open it.

"Lady Carina!" One of Cait's girls said, breathless. "I'm so sorry to bother you, I know Master Merlin said you need to rest, but—"

"No bother. What is it?"

"There's a line of people who'd like to visit with you, my lady."

"A line?" Carina blinked. "But, why?"

"I assume it's regarding the tournament, my lady?"

Still confused and tired, she sighed. "Thank you. Let me clean up a bit first. Would you please ask Cait if there's somewhere private I can meet with these visitors?"

"Of course, my lady." She curtsied and hurried off.

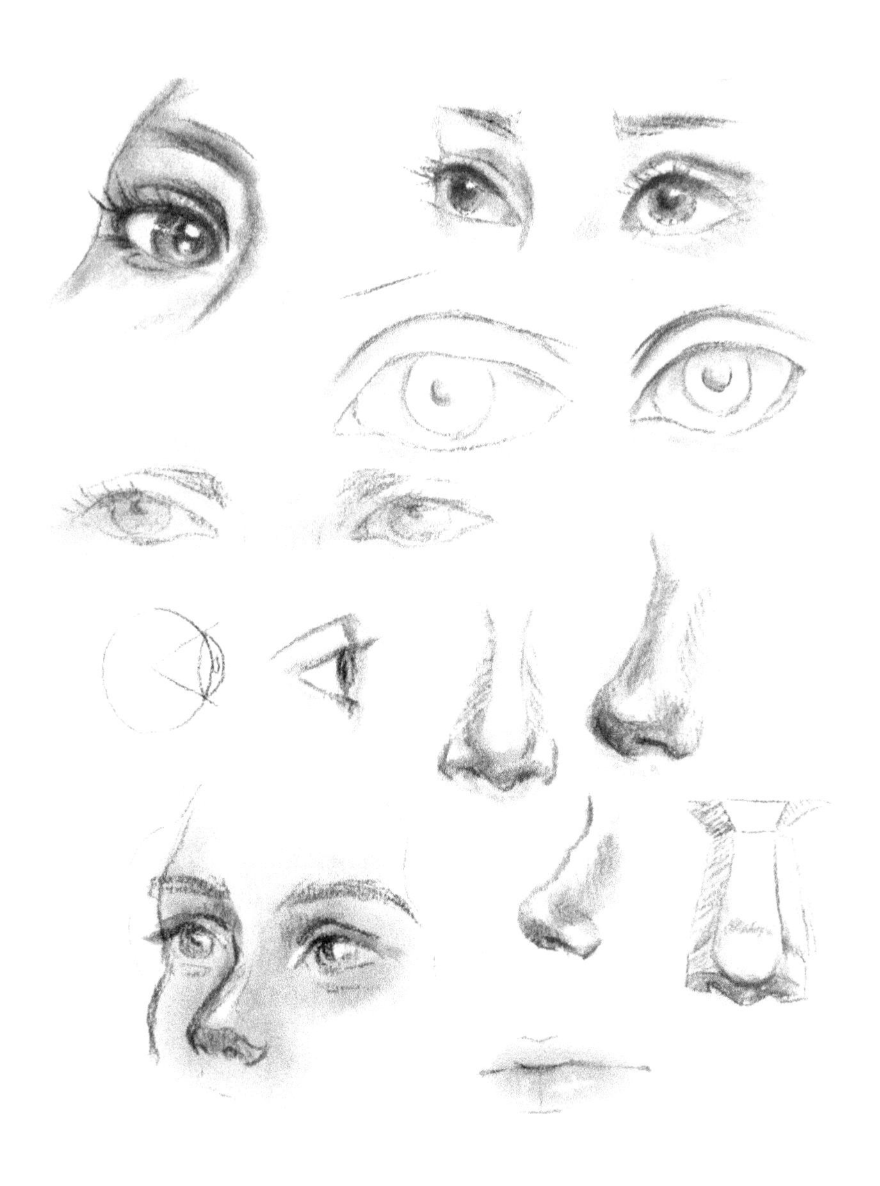

18
CARINA

"Who wants to see me?" she asked as she and Merlin made their way to the front of the inn. "This morning no one cared."

"You were cheated against," Merlin said. "And you still came out even with the cheater. That makes you interesting. Are you sure you're rested enough?"

"Do I have a choice?"

"You could send them all away."

"Oh, I don't want to do that," she said, frowning.

"Why?"

She paused at the threshold to the bar area. "Well, wouldn't it be bad? Make them say I was rude or inconsiderate?"

Merlin leaned a shoulder against the wall. "Do you care what they think?"

Did she?

She had to, in some sense. She was nobility, and that meant a certain level of expectation. Seeing that she was competing, she did want to make a good impression. As the events of the last few days shuffled through her mind, she realized there were only a few opinions that truly mattered to *her*.

"Not particularly," she finally said. "But I do think I might be able to gain some insight by visiting with others."

Merlin nodded, a sly smile on his lips.

Carina turned into the bar, searching for Cait, or the servant girl who had called her out. "So, I'm intriguing now?"

"You're an enigma to them," Merlin clarified, following her. "The nobility don't understand how someone they had no expectations for could have done so well, and the lower classes are ecstatic that you were successful."

"I suppose it's a good thing then."

"Indeed," he said, pointing out Cait near the bar. "Not to mention we've officially gone a whole half a day without anyone trying to murder you. Let's not break that streak."

"Parlor, there," Cait said. "I'll have Lyn send them in one at a time and give you a few minutes with each. There's quite a number lined up outside."

Carina entered the room, and Merlin followed. Two sofas faced each other over a low table, and a fire crackled in the hearth beyond. A moment later the serving girl, Lyn, entered with a tray of sunsetberry tea and orange pastries. Setting it on the table, she turned to them. "Shall I bring the first person in, my lady?"

"Yes, thank you."

Merlin went to the tea and poured a cup, placing an orange slice on the saucer before handing it to her. "You are capable, strong, powerful, and kind. You can handle a few visitors."

The surety in his eyes made her face grow warm. "Thank you, Merlin." She sipped her tea. The drink, combined with Merlin's praise, calmed her rising nerves.

"It occurred to me," Merlin added, and she could tell he was attempting to keep a casual tone, "that whoever was behind the explosion yesterday could be coming here to try and get close to you."

This was good to keep in mind. She could read people well enough, maybe she'd be able to guess who her attacker was. In any case, she would have to be careful what she said no matter who came to visit.

"Speaking of all that, look what Mar gave me," Merlin said. He pulled a small vial from his pocket and held it out to her. Clear water flowed inside.

"Mar gave you that?"

"When I brought you back last night and asked for a bucket of water, then another one this morning, she brought this in. I think they've guessed."

Carina frowned. "Do you think they'll report us?"

Merlin shook his head. "I think Mar's a cure. They'll keep our secret safe."

The door opened then, and Carina set her tea down as Dani and Jes entered. She stood and, without a word, went to hug the woman. The warmth and support in that embrace brought a calm to Carina's heart she hadn't felt in years. It was like being held by her mother.

She pulled away, smiling. "Thank you for coming."

"Of course, dear," Dani said. "We're so proud of you."

Dani and Carina sat on one of the sofas, while Jes went to Merlin and started asking him questions.

"You're doing so much good," Dani said. "How are you feeling? Everything all right?"

"There's a lot happening," she admitted. "I wonder sometimes if I'm doing enough."

"Well, you can't help anyone if you're not helping yourself," Dani said. "Are you eating? Drinking enough? You know, even though it's winter here, it's still a desert. You still need to be drinking plenty of water, not wine."

Carina laughed, nodding. "Yes. Thankfully, I have Merlin to help me remember things like that."

Dani glanced over at him, and Carina's eyes followed. He was doing some kind of slight-of-hand trick for Jes, who watched in amazement, trying to figure out how it worked.

"He seems like a good man," Dani said.

"He is." Carina blinked, then, hearing the implication in Dani's tone. "Oh, not like that. He's not—"

"It's none of my business what he is or isn't to you, my lady," Dani said. "All I know is that a woman needs good supportive friends, and if that's all he is, then it's enough. Everyone from our town is proud of you. I don't write, you know, but someone from our town volunteered to be a messenger for us, so he's sending news straight to them, faster than news usually travels. They'll all come in for your coronation though."

Coronation. Carina didn't think she could handle thinking

that far ahead yet. She shook her head. "Dani, thank you. I needed this."

"Of course, my lady. We're staying at the Playful Pony inn on Farmer's Circle until the tournament is over, if you want to visit again."

"How are you affording that?"

Dani waved a hand. "We'll make due."

Carina shook her head. "Merlin? Can we see that Dani and Jes's stay at the Playful Pony is paid for?"

"It shall be done."

"Lady Carina, you don't have to—"

"I know," Carina said. "We want to."

Dani stood and hugged her again. "Well, you have much more important people to see than us, so we'll let you get to it."

"Thank you, again," Carina said. "I'll try to come visit you soon."

"Jes, time to go."

Jes frowned. "But I didn't get to hug Lady Jewel!"

"Then get over here," Carina said.

Jes ran to her, hugging around her hips and burying his face in her stomach. She ruffled his hair, then Dani took his hand, and they were gone.

"That kid is hilarious," Merlin said. "And your tea is getting cold."

Carina sighed, taking her seat again. Her heart just a little lighter than before.

A moment later Lyn entered again, followed by a wide-eyed Eron Baezona. Without a word, he approached Carina and knelt at her side, taking her hands in his. Carina's entire body tensed.

"Carina, I'm so relieved to see you're well." He shook his head. "I feared something terrible had happened."

She swallowed, taking her hands from him. "Well, as you can see, I am fine. A little sore, but the magic has done its work. Please, will you sit?"

She motioned for the seat opposite. He sat beside her. "I'm so glad I could come visit with you."

She tried to shift away from him. "Would you like some tea?"

"No, no. I know I don't get much time, so I'll speak plainly." he said, locking his eyes on hers. "Carina, there are those in Reinos who would do you harm."

Carina raised a brow.

"Some may even be planning to meet with you this very afternoon. Please, allow me to stay with you while you take calls. I'm sure you are a formidable opponent, nevertheless, you are quite small and recently injured in your race. I wish no harm to come to you."

His dark eyes were so eager, desperate and deep beside the blue streaks of his hair. Still, she couldn't let him think it was his place to be overprotective for her.

"*Sir* Eron," she said, trying to inject formality into his casualness, "I appreciate your warning, and your offer of assistance. It's very kind of you. Rest assured I am perfectly safe here. As you said, I can hold my own in a fight. I'm a door away from help, and I have my servant here in case anything happens."

Eron's brows came together in confusion. He looked around until he spotted Merlin standing next to the fireplace. The two eyed each other, and the energy in the room seemed to shift.

After a moment Eron squared his shoulders and turned back to Carina. "Very well. Promise me though, if you need help you won't hesitate to send for me?"

"I promise. It won't be necessary, but thank you."

Eron's face fell a little, then was quickly replaced with a bright grin. "My parents asked me to invite you to dine with us tomorrow, after the oral tests are completed. Would you like to come?"

Carina glanced at Merlin, who gave a tiny shrug. She'd have to try to make allies at some point.

"That would be lovely," she said.

Eron's grin widened. "Wonderful! I can't wait for you to meet my parents."

His joy was contagious. As he bowed and left, Carina couldn't help a smile.

"Prat," Merlin said.

Carina blinked. "I'm sorry?"

"He's far too familiar with you," he said, crossing his arms. "Did you notice? He didn't address you properly the entire time he was here. First name basis he thinks he's got. You may not have feelings for him, but he certainly has intentions for you."

Carina pressed her lips together. She knew he was right about Eron, and the thought made her stomach twist. She stood and began to pace. "I'm not ready for that."

As she spoke, she ran her thumbs over the palms Merlin had so recently healed, and a memory flashed through her mind.

Damari, the boy she'd thought she cared for. He'd helped her, been so eager to be with her. That had been before she'd left Regania though, and he had betrayed her. Funnily enough, he'd been part-Calidian as well, though very different from Eron. Damari had always been erratic, unpredictable. Eron at least listened when Carina asked him to leave.

"Carina?"

"Yes?"

Merlin met her gaze, understanding in his eyes. "You don't have to think about it. Don't let him pull you into anything you don't feel ready for."

"Thank you." She took a deep breath and returned to her seat, smoothing her skirt.

The door opened again, and Lady Rosaline entered followed by Ahnri. Rosaline's hair was pinned up in an elegant knot, the pale streaks criss-crossing through midnight black. Her dress was deep blue with gold at the edges, and a welcoming smile lit her face. Carina couldn't help a small stab of jealousy at her beauty.

Rosaline came to Carina, taking her hands. "You did quite well today, Lady Carina."

"Thank you, Lady Rosaline," Carina said. "As did you."

Rosaline squeezed Carina's hand, then took a seat on one of the sofas and waved for Ahnri to pour her a cup of tea. Rosaline was confident, she was kind, and generous, and talented; everything Carina aspired to be.

Ahnri handed the cup and saucer to Rosaline, then took a place next to the door, as stiff and unemotional as he usually was. Carina watched him as she took a sip of her own now-lukewarm tea.

Rosaline hummed as she drank. "How are you feeling?"

"Well, I suppose. Excited for the next event."

"I feel the same," Rosaline said. "I have to say, with the injuries you sustained in that race it appeared you'd been beaten."

Carina's throat tightened at the choice of words. At least this beating she'd obtained of her own choice. "Yes, it was rough, I'll admit."

"The worst is probably over for you, though," Rosaline said. "You seem incredibly intelligent, and talented with the sword if you spar so often. I for one am confident you'll go far."

A blush rose on Carina's cheeks. "Thank you. It is comforting to hear you say so."

Rosaline's expression was warm, then her face fell slightly. "I know how it feels to go without positive affirmation. I try to give it where I can."

Carina watched her carefully. "Are you feeling all right?"

"Yes. It's only…my mother died a long time ago, and you look quite a bit like her. It's very surreal sitting with you."

Carina's throat tightened. She spoke without thought. "My mother died when I was young as well."

Carina let out a soft laugh. "It seems we have more in common than we thought."

"Indeed."

The door opened and Lyn stepped in. "Are you ready for the next visitor, my lady?"

Carina wanted to keep talking to Rosaline, but she had more people to meet with. So, she stood and the two young women held hands again.

"Thank you for coming to see me," Carina said.

"I'm glad I did." Then she wrapped her arms around Carina's shoulders and pulled her in for a hug.

Carina hugged her back. The tenderness of that gesture made her feel brave, that Rosaline viewed her as an equal.

Rosaline swept from the room, and Ahnri followed. Carina took a moment to glance at Merlin, whose face was a mask of concern.

Carina said it before he could. "You think Rosaline is trying to spy on me."

"Carina, I think everyone is trying to spy on you," he said. "It's kind of in the job description."

She sighed. "I know. But I feel different around her."

Merlin opened his mouth to speak, but the door opened again, cutting him off. The next few visitors were people Carina hadn't met before. Nobility who weren't competing, there to wish her luck or praise her efforts. Some gave veiled insults or threats, saying there was no way she'd win against the others. Many tried to be her new best friend. Carina took note of each person, trying to remember their names and faces. The worst visit came when Lady Betania Liraste entered the room. Up close now, Carina recognized her features as the girl in blue she'd fought in the dark palace corridors the night before. She had the same sharp nose and arrogant expression as her mother.

"Good day, Lady Carina," Betania said, eyeing her carefully.

"Lady Betania. Please, sit."

"Thank you." Betania peered around the room. "So, this is how you conduct business, is it?"

"I see nothing wrong with my accommodations."

Betania scoffed, but sat primly on the sofa. "How are you feeling after that brutal race?"

"Fine."

"Well, don't go sharing all your darkest secrets with me. I was only concerned for your health. I hope you'll be healed in time for the duels?"

"The king's healers assured me I'll be fine."

Betania tilted her head, her eyes fixed on Carina's. Then she sneered. "I think I know your story. You were probably the best of the best wherever you came from, weren't you? The brightest talent, the loveliest face, the most praised. I imagine it must be hard to be so far from all that. So much here that is unfamiliar to you."

She's right, you know.

Carina forced her face into an impassive mask. Betania had no way of knowing what her words were doing. Carina wanted to say that she'd been a mere shadow of herself in her old home. That being here was finally helping her become the woman she wanted to be in so many ways.

You haven't really changed, child.

Silence did not come easy.

Then Betania caught sight of Merlin and her eyes lit up. "Oh, there he is! The loyal servant. I wondered if he'd be here."

Carina's hands formed fists. This game was infuriating. "He is my servant, why wouldn't he be here?"

Betania's smile spread, growing dangerously close to a leer. "Ah, but what kind of servant? That's what everyone is asking, you know."

Carina blinked.

Betania's gaze roved over Merlin, from his feet to his head and back more than once. "He is quite handsome, now that I see him up close. Shorter than average. Still, very striking. I really can't blame you."

Merlin managed to remain stoic, but Carina's face burned. "He is not that type of servant, and I'll thank you to drop the subject."

"Oh, defensive, are we?" Betania laughed, a chiming sound. "You know that's what they're all saying, don't you? That you sleep with a servant because you're not good enough for a knight. Not even good enough for a merchant. You're nothing but a tiny little bug in this tournament, *Lady* Carina, and believe me: you will be kicked aside like rats and feasted upon by the snakes of this kingdom."

She's right. You'll never succeed.

"Snakes." Carina's nails dug into her palms to keep her hands from shaking. "You mean like yourself?"

Betania only giggled, though her eyes stayed sharp. "I do love to maintain a reputation, but no. I wasn't referring to myself. Snakes are much better at hiding their true nature than I. Good day, Lady Carina."

Carina couldn't meet with anyone after Betania. She had sidestepped sycophants and faced her share of taunts, but now her heart was racing with rage and her mind was full of her father's voice once more. She paced the room, hands clenched in her skirts. After a full minute of this, Merlin stepped in front of her.

"Get out of my way, I have to move."

"Here," Merlin said, shoving a pillow into her hands. "Put your face in that and scream as loud as you can."

Carina didn't hesitate. The rage inside her escaped like a dam releasing, flooding her with frustration, the sound of her own muffled scream biting at her ears.

All the emotion she'd been taught to hold back, every retort she'd wanted to give her father, the questions she wished she could ask her old friends, the sadness she'd carried for so many years, and so much more, poured out of her in that scream. Betania's open threats and unapologetic anger had unlocked something within her. Her chest ached; her head pounded.

When the scream faded, she crumpled to the floor. Her breath had caught in her chest, and her eyes burned with unshed tears. She sensed Merlin kneel next to her, the warmth of his body close, but not touching.

"Carina?"

She sniffed, shaking her head. "I'm sorry."

"Nothing to be sorry for, my dear."

With a sob, she leaned into him and the tears began to fall. Anger—at herself and Betania and the world for being so cruel—had broken this dam, but behind the break was something deeper. Something she'd never been able to face:

Fear.

Fear that Betania was right. That Carina's father was right. That no matter how hard she worked, or how much she did, it would never be enough.

Merlin's arms, tentatively, wrapped around her. He stroked her hair from her face, and Carina found herself clutching the front of his tunic, his presence a comfort.

He pressed his cheek against her head. "I'm so sorry, Carina. She's a terrible person."

It wasn't only Betania. But Carina did not voice that.

Merlin smoothed her hair. "The last few days have been difficult, and you've handled everything with grace."

She blinked, finally opening her eyes, then slowly released the fabric of his shirt from her clutches, and sat back on her knees. Merlin offered her a handkerchief from his pocket, and she took it, drying her face.

"Feel any better?"

She nodded, not because it was the truth, but because at least she wasn't crying anymore.

Merlin watched her for a moment. "Is there anything you'd like to talk about? Anything you want to get out of your head?"

Carina gave a cynical laugh. "Sure, a lot of things."

"You know you can tell me," he said, "right?"

She met his eyes. "I know."

He seemed to wait a moment, maybe to see if she would voice her thoughts.

A knock sounded at the door then, breaking the moment. Merlin shook himself, then stood, offering her a hand.

Carina took it. "I feel like a terrible mess."

"Nonsense," Merlin scoffed. "Especially after all you've gone through, your emotions are running high, it makes sense to react this way. Now, do you feel better?"

She sniffed. "A little, yes."

"Good. Sometimes all one needs is a good cry." He squeezed her shoulder lightly, then went to the door. On the other side, Lyn stood waiting.

"I've sent the other visitors away," she said, "but the young man you've been sparring with just arrived so I thought you'd want to meet with him."

"You're correct," Merlin said. "Would you let him know we'll meet him out back in a few minutes?"

"Of course," Lyn said.

As she hurried off, Merlin turned back to Carina. "Let's get you sparring, you'll feel better burning off some of this energy you're holding."

Carina agreed. Her fingers curled into fists, the prospect of Excalibur in her hand bringing clarity to her mind.

19
AHNRI

Sweat poured from Ahnri's brow as he fought to keep up with Carina. The more he sparred with her, the more skilled she became. The races were still going on, only a few left before sundown, at which time the king's advisers would confer to award final points. Those moving on would be announced the following morning, and would immediately take their oral test. Those who passed *that* would be announced that same evening.

Then, Ahnri thought as he blocked a strike, there would be a day of rest and parties—the Midway Celebration—with a formal ball for all nobility that night. Medelians certainly liked their excuses to unwind. Then, the following day would be the final duels.

"Wait!" he called, backing up and blocking Carina's last attack. She pulled back, but did not lower her sword. He held up his hand and lowered his blade to his side. "I need a break, sorry."

She relaxed, and turned to where Merlin sat—drawing, as usual—and, after a moment, he brought them their water mugs. Ahnri took a few sips, pouring most of it over his face and head. Despite it being early winter, he couldn't seem to cool down. That's what living in a desert meant, though.

Carina sat on the ground, half-dead grass cracking beneath her. Ahnri was still fighting to catch his breath.

"Perhaps a break for food?" Merlin suggested.

Carina shook her head. "I'm starving, but full stomachs aren't good for sparring." She checked her blade for nicks and scratches while she spoke.

"One more go?" Ahnri said.

"Just one?" Carina grinned. "Are you getting tired, old man?"

"*Yira caneh dan su! Na!*" Ahnri said, Fugeran rolling off his tired tongue. "I'm your age, *yana*?"

Carina laughed. "I'm eighteen. How old are you?"

"Eighteen too," he said. Then he turned to Merlin. "How old are you?"

"Nineteen," Merlin answered.

"Really?" Ahnri frowned. "You seem older."

Carina laughed, and Merlin's lips thinned, holding back a smile. "I get that a lot, actually."

Ahnri smiled with them, unsure what the joke was. He cleared his throat. "Either of you excited for the Midway Ball?"

"Not particularly," Carina said. "I don't enjoy dancing much."

"Really?" Ahnri said. "You seem like you'd be a natural."

"Oh, I'm a fair dancer, but I don't—" Merlin cleared his throat and Carina stopped.

Ahnri glanced from one to the other. "Don't what?"

Carina shook her head. "Nothing. Personal preference, that kind of thing." She stood and turned to put her sword through a few practice moves.

That. That was a lie. A small one, but there it was. The first one he'd seen her tell, the first thing she was intentionally keeping from him. Ahnri tried to shrug it off, acting casual as though he hadn't noticed. "All right. Just trying to make conversation."

Carina swung her blade in a few arcs, dueling with an invisible opponent. "Less talk," she said with a grin. "More sparring."

Ahnri laughed and raised his blade. When had he last laughed? "Oh, I meant to ask, did you both hear what happened after the presentation of combatants last night? Apparently, someone attacked Sir Kemin, and he—"

"Stop, Ahnri," Carina cut him off, lowering her sword.

He frowned at her.

"I'm not stupid," she said.

Ahnri shook his head. "I didn't mean to imply you were."

"Your actions say otherwise."

"My lady?" Merlin said softly.

Carina paused then, taking a deep breath, and letting it out slowly. "I'm done trying to guard my words." Her shoulders squared, and her jaw set firm. "I know what you're trying to do. Yes, you're a spy, but I need someone to spar with, and you're incredible with a sword. So, you can either stop trying to wheedle information out of me and simply enjoy the chance to spar—which I doubt your master lets you do—or you can leave right now and not come back. I'll make do without."

Ahnri blinked, staring at her. There was something different here, now. The way she stood, something in her voice when she gave a command like that. In that moment, another side was revealed. A side with presence and power. If she spoke to the people this way, to the armies and townspeople, she could inspire them. The nobility would take time, but if they started now....

"Well?" Carina's voice broke his thoughts. "What's your decision?"

This was it. ChaNia was right, Carina was the best chance for a peaceful and prosperous Medelios. Ahnri bowed to her. "No more spying, my lady. No more questions, unless you give me permission to ask."

"Your word?"

"My word."

"Very well." She took a breath and her shoulders relaxed. "In that case, let's go again," Carina said, standing, "before we cool down too much."

"Right."

Merlin, who had watched the entire exchange, resumed his place against the wall, taking up his drawing pad. Carina already stood with her sword to her shoulder. Ahnri straightened to mirror her.

They sparred for another thirty minutes before agreeing to

stop. Ahnri was still a bit shaken from Carina's commanding moment, but he held on to the memory of it. He might never admit it in words but he truly looked forward to these spars. Carina was the best adversary he'd had in months, maybe years. He would rather lie to Matano than stop coming, and so he would.

20
CARINA

Two hours after her spar with Ahnri, Carina ducked through the fabric hanging beneath the tournament stands. Every seat above was filled. Carina cringed at the smell of so many bodies all around. All competitors were to wait there until the king's advisers announced those who would move on to the next stage of the tournament. Merlin stayed beside her, always close now. His presence was reassuring, comforting. As she stepped around her opponents, she received some stares of contempt, some nods of respect. She met both with squared shoulders.

"You're really very good at this, you know," Merlin said beside her.

Carina took a slow breath. All her life she'd hidden in the shadows. Now that she was so visible to so many, she felt uncomfortably exposed. There were, thankfully, large numbers of common folk in the stands cheering her name and waving small flags—a red background with a black raven above crossed swords, the Valio crest. How they'd gotten so many made in so little time, she had no idea. The attention made her want to curl away into a corner again. She took a deep breath. She wasn't that girl anymore. She could handle this.

The stands above her rumbled with movement and talk. "Merlin," she said. "What if I don't get through? Then what?"

"You will."

"But what if I don't?"

"Then I suppose someone like Betania will probably win and you'll have to challenge her or raise a rebellion. It's rare, but I've seen it happen."

She wanted to believe him. Believe that she would get through. That they would announce her name, and the nobility would see she was capable. She truly wanted this now. Now that she knew what it would mean for her, for the people of Medelios. She could fix things. She could help those who needed it most.

"Lady Carina," one of the king's advisers approached them. "I'm sorry, your servant will have to wait in the stands above. Only competitors down here."

"Right, of course. Thank you."

Merlin stood in front of her. "Look at me." She did. His face shone with pride. "You will be fine. I believe in you. I'll see you after." He took her hands and squeezed them tightly, then turned and disappeared into the crowd of families giving the same well wishes to their children. Within a few moments, only the competitors were left.

"I can hardly wait, can you?"

Carina turned to see Lady Rosaline behind her.

Rosaline threaded her arm through Carina's. "You'll definitely get through, you know. You did very well, and Nando Liraste was a mucking cheater. If I'd been against him, I would've strangled him for that stunt." She sighed. "I'm sorry you had to deal with that. The Lirastes have never been known for fairness."

"What was that, Lady Rosaline?"

They turned to see a group of Liraste family members surrounding them, Lady Betania at the front, watching them with a smirk on her lips.

Rosaline squared her shoulders. "Don't deny it, Betania. Every one of you has tried to murder off someone here. Maybe if you had the money, you could pay someone to do your dirty work for you."

Betania's face flushed with embarrassment.

"Even if you do get into the next round," Rosaline said, "there's no way you'll pass the oral tests."

Betania put a hand to her chest, a pained expression in her eyes as she tried to take control of the conversation. "I'm hurt, Rosaline. We have been studying for weeks."

"More like bribing," Rosaline said, raising a brow.

"Only the ones we can't persuade."

Rosaline rolled her eyes. "You're impossible."

"Impossible to beat, you mean," Betania snapped back

"Leave us alone."

"I only wanted to ask Lady Carina how her handsome

servant is doing," Betania winked, turning to Carina. "He's quite attentive, isn't he? You were holding hands earlier, weren't you? So sweet. I wonder what it would take to distract him away from you."

Carina's face went warm, her hands forming fists. "I've told you before, he's not—"

Rosaline cut her off. "It is none of your business what goes on between a woman and her servant, Betania. Whether they are that kind of close or not has no effect on Lady Carina's chance at the throne. You can take your curiosity somewhere else." Rosaline took Carina by the arm and led her away. "She's completely uncivilized, all of them are. The nerve, to confront you like that in public."

"Carina!"

She turned to see Sir Eron approaching.

"I've been searching all over for you." He paused, taking in her flushed cheeks and tense shoulders. "Is everything all right?"

"Yes, I'm fine." Carina said, trying to relax her muscles.

"Only Betania causing havoc, as usual," Rosaline said.

Eron frowned. "What was she saying?"

"Nothing," Carina said quickly. "It's nothing I can't handle."

Rosaline nodded her approval.

"Make way, competitors!"

A group of royal guards approached, surrounding a few of the king's advisers. Carina frowned. For the first time, she wondered why the king himself hadn't come to make these announcements.

As the group passed through the competitors, Carina recognized Sir Ilian, the wide-shouldered adviser who had interviewed her. He gave her a quick nod as he passed. Did that mean she'd made it? He and the others ascended the staircase to the stage-like landing. Dust trickled down from above as the crowd rose to their feet in excitement.

"Good people of Medelios!" Sir Ilian called. "It has been a difficult night of debate and consideration. Nevertheless, we feel the king and his council have made the best possible decisions. It is now time to announce the sixteen young competitors who will be moving forward to the next round of the King's Tournament."

Carina's palms began to sweat, her heart speeding up.

"In order by their houses, the advancing competitors are: Lady Alodie Baezona!"

The crowd cheered as Carina watched a girl with dark skin and a single streak of blue in her hair ascend the steps to the platform above them. Carina applauded along with Eron and Rosaline beside her.

Diman Baezona.

Eron Baezona.

Eron's face broke into a grin, and he hugged Carina in celebration. She let him, grateful when he let go to take the stairs and wave to the crowd.

"Lady Betania Liraste!"

Betania ascended the staircase, a smugness to her every step. Carina met Rosaline's gaze as they both raised brows in annoyance. Betania didn't glance at Carina as she passed, taking her place on the stand.

Wesley Liraste.

Simata Liraste.

Beatrice Matano.

Erica Matano.

Leo Matano.

Carina took a deep breath, counting up how many names had already been given. There were seven spots left.

Marius Matano.

Rosaline Matano.

Carina applauded along with the crowd as Rosaline took to the stairs. Carina's hands began to sweat.

Luka Teneo.

Syla Teneo.

And then, "Lady Carina Valio!"

She let out a sigh of relief. For a second, she forgot where she was and let the knowledge run through her: she'd done it. The first step.

She ascended the staircase slowly. At the top, Sir Ilian exchanged a nod with her. As she passed, he leaned forward and whispered, "Well done, my lady."

"Thank you, sir."

When she took her place, he continued reading:

Kemin Velando, the boy she'd met at the opening ceremonies, the one she'd saved from Betania and her cousins. He gave Carina a nod of respect as he passed her.

Last called was Luci Velando. When Luci had taken her place, Sir Ilian stepped forward. "People of Reinos, a cheer for the finest knights in all of Medelios!"

The crowd responded with gusto. Carina scanned the crowd, searching for one set of eyes.

There, halfway up and to her right, he stood still and calm. His hands applauded with the others, but his expression was serene, his gaze locked onto hers. Carina smiled back, a tentative pride beginning to blossom in her chest.

21
CARINA

"Lady Carina Valio."

Carina's eyes fluttered open. She'd been deep in thought, trying to remember the Medelian stories her mother had told and the history books she'd read. Trying to forget Eron's constant advances, Betania's arrogant air. She tried to focus on Merlin's encouragement, Rosaline's kindness, even Cait and Mar and their workers. The good things in her life right now.

The palace corridor where she sat waiting for her oral test was opulent beyond anything she'd ever seen. Not even the marble Reganian palace had gold-plated edges on the carpets or solid silver chandeliers and doorknobs. She wondered again how the king's conscience could stand it, knowing his people were starving and he had enough resources in his light fixtures alone to change it.

The adviser who spoke her name held open a heavy door, a stack of papers in hand. Carina stood, meeting his gaze. "Ah,

Lady Carina. Wonderful. In here, please."

She turned to Merlin, who stood up beside her.

"Good luck," he said.

"I haven't studied at all. What if I don't know the answers?"

He shrugged. "Make it up."

"Merlin!"

He grinned. "Don't worry, you'll be amazing. Just do your best."

Carina took a deep breath, then turned toward the adviser.

"Good luck, Carina," a voice drawled. Betania Liraste sat with those cousins who had advanced with her. Carina squared her shoulders, and passed them by.

"Who's her friend? A servant, or a lover?" A boy with them said.

Another girl scoffed. "If she needs a lover, I can think of far better prospects than that skinny thing."

"He's her *servant*," Betania crooned, watching Merlin. "I'd wager I could pay him better, though. Maybe we'll chat while she's testing."

The others laughed, but then Carina was at the door and entering a room she hadn't expected to see.

The council chamber was a wide space with a domed glass ceiling, the single room taking up a large section of the palace complex. There were three tiers of seats, with desks in rows. Eight each on the front two rows, with six on the back one, and a throne with a wider desk in the center of those six.

The king was here.

And all twenty-five advisers.

Had she known it would be *all* of them? She didn't think that had been mentioned. Her heart began to race like she had through that stupid course yesterday.

The adviser who led her in showed her to a podium on the floor, where every seat could have a good view of her. The walls around her were lined with gold pillars, framed mirrors, and brocades of deep red that she knew should've been comforting, but at the moment they only made her dizzy.

As the advisers settled, she tried to focus on Merlin's words: *You'll be amazing. Do your best.* She didn't like the way Betania had watched Merlin. It was a predatory gaze, one Carina recognized.

The door closed behind her and she was met by silence. A welcome reprieve from the nagging voices in the hall. Then, the adviser who had escorted her in spoke.

"Welcome, Lady Carina. I am Sir Celio Baezona. Allow me to introduce my associates:" he gestured to four others sitting on the front row, "Madame Rena Matano, Sir Ilian Teneo, Sir Leon Velando, and Madame Mara Liraste."

She was never going to remember all of them that quickly, so she didn't try.

"The five of us," Sir Celio went on, "are here to perform an interview with you, a test of sorts, before the king and his council. The questions may or may not be the same ones your fellow competitors have been asked, as we feel it's important to follow the flow of the conversation rather than an exact list. However, it will only be the five of us speaking to you, none of the other advisers, or his majesty, will be addressing you today.

Do you understand?"

She swallowed. Her hands clasping before her, hidden by the podium. "I do, Sir."

"Excellent. Let us begin."

He returned to his seat, shuffling a few papers as he did, and the man beside him spoke.

"Right," the man said, Velando, she thought. "To business. Lady Carina, please tell us what you know about the duties the Medelian monarch is expected to perform."

Carina answered as best she could. As soon as she was done, another question shot at her. History of Medelios. The pact of the Unbroken Lands. Trade, sanitation, contracts. Then on to her personal preferences, likes and dislikes; question after question, as though she were a target in an archery competition. She answered every one as concisely and honestly as possible. Slowly, to her own surprise, she began to relax.

The spectating advisers were a wonderful audience, nodding as she spoke and scribbling notes at times. Carina tried very hard not to look high enough to see the king—that would simply be too much pressure.

A woman with red braided hair said, "I wonder, Lady Carina, having lived most of your life in Regania, what you think of Medelios so far?"

"Oh, it's lovely," she said, accustomed now to answering quickly. "There are areas to improve, of course, but that's the case with any kingdom. And I've loved getting to know the people."

"Indeed," the woman said. "And what areas would you say

are in need of improvement?"

"Certain aspects of the economy would take priority, I think," Carina said, stepping out from behind the podium. "As I traveled through the Medelian countryside I came across far too many settlements that didn't have enough food or proper supplies. It is my opinion that a kingdom is only as strong as its weakest citizen. If our weakest citizens are starving, that's a potential problem for everyone. One that I think deserves immediate attention."

The reaction to this statement was by far the most discordant. The watching advisers murmured, leaning to address their neighbors in apparent confusion, or shock—she couldn't tell which.

Then Sir Celio said, "Certainly it's not as bad as you say. We haven't had any reports of such conditions."

"No, no," the other woman said. "She cannot be serious. This is some sort of ploy to gain our favor."

"That is a discussion for us to have in *private*, Madame Matano," Sir Ilian said.

"Now just a moment," the Velando adviser said, "I'd like to hear what exactly she's accusing us of. Are you saying, child, that we are neglecting our own?"

I don't believe you…

Carina shuddered. So many voices, and she wasn't sure whether it was her father's or if that was one of the advisers, on the edge of her hearing…

"Lady Carina?"

She took in a sharp breath. "Yes, sorry. I…I don't mean to

implicate anyone specifically, sir. I don't honestly know the reason why it's happening. But—"

"You see?" Sir Ilian said. "She admits she has no proof. It's false claims that should be ignored, that's all."

Lies...

The other advisers began to mutter again, and Carina clenched her fists, her blood beginning to flow faster and hotter. How dare they? They invited her in, asked her experience, and then invalidated it? Surely Merlin would agree this called for anger...but perhaps also control.

She took a breath, and waited for the voices to die down a little, her nerves shaking like an earthquake inside her. "Forgive me," she said, raising her voice, "have any of *you* been outside the capital in the past year?"

They all stared at her. Shock, curiosity, and even some raised brows met her gaze.

"If people were starving, we would know," Sir Ilian said, standing and leaning forward on his desk. "There are systems in place to keep such things from happening."

Carina squared her shoulders, steeling herself. "Again, sir, forgive me, but is it possible that those systems have been corrupted?"

Ilian paused, staring at her. "What exactly are you suggesting?"

"I am suggesting," she said, stepping forward, "that there are surely individuals and systems that should be checked by this council. I myself have seen members of the nobility abuse and mistreat the common folk. I refuse to stay silent about it."

"How dare you speak such things," Ilian said, his face red. "You come to our kingdom and accuse our nobility like this?"

Carina's voice rose. "You cannot tell me there haven't—"

"Ilian, there's no call for that," Sir Celio said, standing.

"How can she imply—"

"She must have some evidence—"

The room erupted into a clamor of voices. Advisers on the second row argued with those on the first; one on the third row was shaking a sheet of paper at someone on the second.

Carina put her hands to the sides of her head, trying to keep herself focused, grounded. Why was she here? Why had she thought this was a good idea?

A flash of memory: a sandaled foot stomping on her fingers; gritting her teeth to avoid crying out in pain. Things were always worse when she cried....

She shook her head, and found herself gripping the podium. She wasn't home at Valios Palace, she was in the palace of in Reinos, the capital of Medelios. She was competing to become heir to the Medelian throne. She was going to help the people of this kingdom. To raise them up. Give them a better life. Make sure they were fed and safe and...protected.

Protected.

The way she hadn't been.

She'd been traveling for so long, helping people where she could, she'd never once thought of herself as a protector. She didn't want to be a hero, or be given power or prestige, she only wanted to protect. To make sure no one ever had to go through what she had.

In order to do that, she had to win this tournament.

Bumps rose on her arms. From the corner of her eye, she glanced at her reflection in the mirrored walls, and for the first time, thought she could see what Merlin had when he made that sketch. A girl with steel in her, one who meant to help and protect. Not because she sought glory, but because she never again wanted to see anyone hurt the way she had.

Never.

She straightened, and stood as tall as her small frame would allow, her shoulders squared and head held high. And waited.

One by one, the advisers glanced her way, and one by one, they paused. They watched. It took some time, but Carina could be patient. She had to be.

When, finally, all eyes were on her, she took a breath.

"I mean no offense by my words," Carina said, her voice soft, yet sharp, carrying in the silent space. "I have spent an entire year traveling this kingdom. I have seen homes without doors or windows because the community lacked lumber or tools. I have seen children run barefoot, in tattered clothing, because there simply was no cloth available. I have seen nobility threaten to imprison someone for the simple mistake of spilling a bag of produce.

"I am not here to accuse anyone," she said. "Not yet. You asked what improvements I believe are needed." She paused, then gave a nod. "You have my answer."

Collectively, they seemed to squirm in their seats beneath her gaze. Sir Celio gestured once more to his fellow questioners. "Would anyone else like to pose a question?"

"I have one last," the grey-haired Velando man said, raising a finger. "If the rest of you don't mind?"

The others either waved for him to continue, or at least did not object.

"Lady Carina, you seem to have come from nowhere. Your story about Regania and your father fits with actual facts, nevertheless I can't help wondering what was it that made you leave your kingdom? Surely, despite your father's crimes, you had connections there, you had lands…"

His question trailed off, and Carina clasped her hands before her, gripping them so tightly it hurt. The truth about her past would come out eventually. She had to face it. Then something Merlin had said came to her mind:

We all have our trials and struggles, and I dare say you've had more than most. What matters is how we handle them.

Her past was part of who she was. If she couldn't speak of it, how true was she being to herself?

She sat up, preparing to face the painful memories, and told them everything. Certainly, she was taking more time than the other entrants, but as she spoke the advisers became more engrossed with her tale. Her mother's illness, her father's infidelity and abuse, his plot to overthrow the monarchs. Damari who betrayed her, Robyn who taught her, Lex who had believed in her, and finally, running away. She tried not to notice their stares, or the way some of them took notes, no doubt to review her story later, check it against more facts.

"When Alexander and his force were preparing to draw out my father's troops," she finally said, "I told them I needed to leave that place. There was nothing for me there, nothing I wanted anyway. I knew I wouldn't be able to heal in the place that had hurt me so brutally. So, I left. I traveled southern Regania for a year, then made my way into Medelios one year ago."

When she finished there was silence for a moment, until finally Sir Celio spoke, his voice rather more tender than it had been before. "Thank you, Lady Carina. This is more than sufficient for our needs. The advancing contestants will be announced this afternoon an hour before sundown, so you'll need to be at the tournament field then. Please, this way."

"Thank you, sir." She stood and curtsied to those still seated, taking a moment now to glance upward to the king. She couldn't quite make out his expression, but hoped it was a smile.

Sir Celio paused just before opening the door, and leaned toward her. "For what it's worth," he whispered, "thank you. Some of us have been trying to make this point for months, and I think you may have finally gotten through to the rest of them. I for one am grateful for your help."

She met his eyes, and part of her heart seemed to sigh in relief.

Out in the hall, Carina caught sight of Betania and her cousins hurrying to sit down, failing at their attempts to look natural. The expressions on their faces said plainly that they'd heard everything. Not that it mattered anymore, Carina had made that choice herself.

"Well," Betania said, her gaze sharp. "Bit of a heavy past you have, isn't it? I wonder what might happen if history were to repeat itself."

Carina's blood ran cold. The thought of being beaten, harassed, ignored, used. She wasn't that girl anymore. With ice in her voice, she said, "You wouldn't survive if you tried."

For once, Betania's haughty pride seemed to falter. And Carina had to admit, she got more than a little satisfaction from it.

"Carina?" Merlin's voice came from down the hall.

Carina left the Lirastes, following Merlin's call. He came straight to her and pulled her around the corner, out of sight of the others. "Well?"

"I think? I don't know, I—"

"Oh, stop that," he said, waving a hand. "Carina, you are one of the most intelligent people I've ever met—which in itself is saying something—but you have a terrible habit of understating your own abilities. Now tell me truly: how did it go?"

A small laugh escaped her, because she knew he was right. "Well, I told the truth. About everything they asked. And if they don't like it, I suppose we'll find out this evening."

Merlin beamed. "That was brave of you, and a wise choice."

Carina took a deep breath, feeling as though a weight had been lifted from her chest. Her smile came easier now that the test was over.

"Carina, I know it's only been a few days since the tournament started," Merlin said, "but you're doing remarkably well. I'm very proud of you."

Her heart swelled at his words, and as they made their way

out of the palace, a part of her realized this was the first time in her life anyone had ever said those words to her.

She hoped it would not be the last.

22
AHNRI

Ahnri's anxiety grew steadily while the combatants testing went on, and it made him sloppy. He wanted to know how Carina had done, wanted to watch or listen to her test if he could, but palace security was so tight he couldn't find a way in. He hoped that she had done well. And so, alley after alley, one eavesdropped conversation after another, he tried to gather what information he could until he found himself shambling into Cait's taproom as the morning rush was winding down, his nerves still on edge. He took a seat at the bar and waved for a drink.

He hadn't had enough alcohol since coming to Medelios. There hadn't been time to be properly drunk. It was a kind of art, after all. He downed a shot of something very strong, then asked for another. He didn't give time to let the first take effect before taking the second. He emptied his third in ten minutes just as someone sat beside him.

It was Merlin. He held a tray of food, and his own drink.

Ahnri set his glass down and raised his hand for another, then turned to Merlin. "Shouldn't you be with Carina?"

Merlin didn't speak, but picked up Ahnri's drink as it was set in front of him, downed it in a single gulp, then waved to the barmaid to bring another. Ahnri raised an eyebrow at him.

Merlin shook his head. "Some things need to be washed away with strong drink."

Ahnri ordered wine next, and raised his mug in a toast. Merlin toasted him and they both drank. They sat in silence for a few minutes, listening to the muted talk around them and the music from the other side of the room.

"Carina is getting ready for a lunch appointment," Merlin said, a hint of annoyance in his voice.

"With whom?"

Merlin glared at him, but then said, "Eron Baezona."

Ahnri stared into his mug.

"Why did you agree not to spy?" Merlin asked.

Ahnri paused before answering, mostly because he wasn't sure how to articulate his reasons. So, he simply said, "I don't know."

"Then I don't believe you."

"I can't change that."

"We know this," Merlin said. "I don't trust you, and you don't trust me. We are in mutual distrust."

Ahnri's fresh mug was placed before him. He ignored it, and stared at Merlin. "What will you do if I keep reporting to Matano?"

"Nothing. How will I know?"

"You could spy on me."

"No," Merlin laughed. "I'm not a spy. I couldn't sneak quietly through the night if my life depended on it. Carina might be able to, but she's far too recognizable at this point."

Ahnri tilted his mug, watching light reflect off the liquid inside. "There's something about her. I'm not sure if I'm imagining it or if it's a measurable trait, but I find her…intriguing."

"You sure you're not attracted to her?"

Ahnri snorted. "No. I promise you, she's *not* my type."

Merlin eyed him for a moment, and Ahnri tried his best to keep that box in the corner of his mind closed. Blue eyes and anklet coins; dark corners of the city, and views of the sunset….

"All right. listen," Merlin said, breaking Ahnri's reverie. "I'm choosing to believe—for now—that the agreement you made with Carina was honest and you plan to follow through. Tell Matano whatever you want about everything else, but nothing about Carina. Lie. If he asks, make something up."

Ahnri met his eyes, watching for signs of secrecy or untruth. But there was only a desire to protect the girl who may be this kingdom's best chance.

"I will." He still held a twinge of uncertainty about Merlin, but Carina he was sure of. And Ahnri could tell that in this, he and Merlin were the same.

"Thank you," Merlin said.

Ahnri took another drink, snatched a bread roll from Merlin's plate, and left the bar.

23
CARINA

When Eron had invited her to dine with his family, Carina wasn't sure what to expect. Given the attacks on her life already, she certainly didn't know whether she could trust him or his family. Aside from the visitors she'd met with and sparring with Ahnri, she'd mostly kept to herself. Now, walking through Nobility Circle in the middle of the day, it seemed that everywhere she turned someone noticed her. Groups stopped speaking when she came near, and watched her until she passed.

"Merlin," she whispered. "Are people angry with me?"

"I doubt it, more likely curious."

"I'm not sure how I feel about them staring."

"Pay them no mind, my lady. I'm only grateful they're not approaching you."

"Why?"

"Carina," he said. "You were nearly blown up, and survived a knife fight within hours of entering this city. Just because it's been a couple days doesn't mean it won't happen again."

"Right." She drew in a deep breath, welcoming the scent of rose oil she'd applied to her wrists and neck for comfort.

Soon they arrived at Baezona Hall. The front steps formed a semi-circle that led to a wide landing. A grand polished door, deep red with silver accents, stood twice the height of her bedroom door at the inn.

"Ready?" Merlin asked.

Despite an uneasy feeling in her stomach, she nodded.

A servant opened the door, standing aside to let them enter and take their cloaks. His posture was stiff, his eyes glazed, and Carina was reminded of Ahnri when he was in servant mode. The thought was a small comfort. She was, essentially, in a performance now, and needed to present the best image she could. Ahnri hid his emotions well when necessary, so could Carina.

The servant led them through wide halls decorated with portraits and intricate sculptures in clay and glass. Up a staircase and a corridor later they stopped at the entrance to a lounge where Sir Eron Baezona sat with his mother and father. They stood as Carina entered.

"Lady Carina." Eron's face lit up. "I'm so glad to see you again."

She let him take her hand and kiss it. "Thank you, it's nice to see you as well."

In her periphery, Merlin took a place to one side of the doorway, waiting to be called upon. There was a slight lift to one side of his mouth that Carina interpreted to mean, "*Good luck.*"

"Lady Carina." Barón Baezona gave her a pleasant smile. His wide shoulders were wide and his hair long, tied back at the nape of his neck. His hair color—a deep and intense blue—bespoke pure Calidian blood. "It's a pleasure to finally meet you."

"Thank you for inviting me," Carina said with a curtsey. "It's very kind of you."

"Not at all, young lady," Baronesa Baezona said. She appeared to be of mixed blood—like so many Medelians—with dark skin the same shade as Eron's, and similar black hair streaked with blue. Her eyes were shrewd, scanning Carina over carefully as she spoke. "We consider ourselves close friends to all nobility in the kingdom. Since you are now one of us, we feel it is our duty to get to know you."

Carina wasn't sure whether this was a compliment or not.

"Please, have a seat." Barón Baezona gestured to the sofas. "We've reserved the balcony dining room for our meal today so the extended family won't interrupt. It's near the kitchen and provides a lovely view of the back gardens. I hope you'll enjoy it."

"I'm sure I shall." Carina sat, running a hand along the upholstery fabric. The green velvet reminded her of Reganian forests.

Eron took a seat next to her, a little too close. She tried to politely scoot away while he addressed her. "Lady Carina, I would love to know more about you. Where did you live before you came to Medelios?"

Asking about her past already? She straightened her skirts as she formed her response. "Regania. I left there after some unfortunate events involving my father. The king was kind enough to let me retain my title."

Barón Baezona sat forward. "So, you were acquainted with King Alexander before you left?"

"I was, yes. He's a very wise king." She paused. "Are you close to King Jaltér?"

"Oh, not very," the baronesa said. "He's always been the private type, and even more so since his wife died."

"Yes, he's allowed most of the nobility to run amok, if you ask me," Barón Baezona said.

"I don't know if I agree, father," Eron said. "The relaxed structure since the queen died has been rather refreshing."

"According to whom?" the baronesa asked.

Eron stammered slightly. "The, the other combatants, my friends. People talk."

Barón Baezona scoffed. "They only enjoy not being punished for their inappropriate actions. Anyone without self-control is going to be sorry once a new king takes the crown." He gave a nod to his son.

"Father," Eron said. "It's a little early to be speaking like that, don't you think?"

"Nonsense," Barón Baezona said. "My son will make a great king."

Carina watched the exchange with curiosity. How often did they speak as a family for these opinions to be coming to light in front of her? She had nothing to add, and luckily a servant entered and announced their meal was ready. Carina stood and let Eron escort her to the dining room behind his parents.

"You look lovely, Carina," Eron said softly.

"Thank you, Sir Eron."

"Do you like my parents so far?"

"They're...very nice." Good. This was good. If she could keep all her answers short and vague, she wouldn't lead Eron on or give away any sensitive information.

The dining room was small, intimate. A rectangular table with five chairs filled the center space, and behind the head chair were wide windows opening to a balcony and, as promised, a view of the gardens. Barón Baezona paused at a small table to wash his hands in a bowl of water, and Carina did the same, followed by Eron and his mother. Merlin had already pulled out her chair when she went to her seat.

"Keep the conversation on them," Merlin whispered.

"How?"

"Talk about other nobles, the Hall, the silverware, anything but yourself."

She took a deep breath as he helped her sit. She squeezed his hand for a moment before letting go, and he gave a small nod of encouragement.

When the first course was brought out, Carina went weak at the smell. She'd always had a special place in her heart for delicious food, particularly the scents of it. When it was placed before her by a Somnurian servant girl, she leaned over and breathed in the fragrance of tomato, basil, and grains. As soon as Barón Baezona had begun to eat, she took a spoonful and hummed with delight.

"This is divine," she said before her second taste. "Your cook is very talented."

"Thank you," Barón Baezona said. "I'm sure you'll find the rest of the meal equally enjoyable."

Before they could throw another question at her, she spoke again. "You say you're familiar with all the nobility here?"

"Some more than others," Baronesa Baezona said. "But yes, we know them all by name."

"I've had such a difficult time remembering the major houses," she confessed. "How do you keep them straight?"

"Well, we interact with them often," Baronesa Baezona said with a chuckle. "You've hardly been here a few days, child. It's going to take some time."

"Of course," Carina said. "If you don't mind my asking, what are your thoughts about the Liraste family?"

Barón Baezona breathed a small laugh. "The Lirastes. Forgive me. They're a bit of a joke among the nobility."

"Eron said they've threatened to hurt you," Baronesa Baezona asked, leaning forward. "Is that true?"

Back on me again, Carina thought. "They have, though I doubt they mean anything by it. It's simply tournament competition getting to them."

Eron shook his head. "Even so, they shouldn't say such things. Why should they feel threatened by you?"

Carina blinked. She'd begun to think *all* the nobility were threatened by her—not that she'd done much to deserve it.

"My son speaks true," Barón Baezona said. "They have a history for threats, bribes, and assassinations. I know some of the nobility aren't fond of you, Lady Carina, and I would advise you to be careful. It would break my heart to see you hurt by one of them." He glanced at his son, then back to his bowl.

Eron shifted in his seat.

Carina tried to ignore whatever insinuations were in that exchange. "I'm always careful," she said. "My servant is very diligent in keeping me safe; I trust he will continue to do as he has done." She gestured to the door, where Merlin stood.

"Yes, your servant," Baronesa Baezona said, gazing up at Merlin. "I'm very curious. He's not Medelian, and he doesn't quite have the build of a Reganian nor the coloring of any nearby kingdoms. Where did you find him?"

Carina wiped her mouth to give herself a moment to think. To lie. "He's Ignatian. The snow kingdom in the north. His sister was my maidservant in Regania and when I began to travel, he accompanied me for safety."

Eron eyed Merlin more carefully now, and the barón and baronesa gave each other a glance that clearly said they thought she was lying. Carina's stomach twisted. They, too, thought she was sleeping with Merlin, like Betania said.

When the second course was brought out, Carina was distracted from her worry by the scents. Sweet honey-baked chicken over Somnurian rice, and fried banana fruit from Calidar.

"Where do you get such fine foods?" she asked.

"Everywhere," Barón Baezona said. "Medelios is a perfect

place to indulge in foreign foods. Every kingdom has a handle here, and we enjoy their imports. The more we buy, the more we sell to others, the more they bring, and we love every bit of it."

Yet the farming communities were suffering? Were the nobility trading needed local produce in favor of expensive foreign treats?

Eron spoke up. "I wonder, Lady Carina, I know we all hope to win heirship to the Medelian crown, but do you have plans if you don't? I, for example, will likely follow in my father's business of transporting goods to and from Calidar. What about you?"

How should she answer? Confident that she would win and needed no provisional plans? She didn't feel that. Or humble, hoping to remain in the city to serve the new monarch whoever it was?

A throat cleared in the doorway. Merlin.

Carina blinked. "Oh, I suppose I'd like to travel." She said the first honest thing that came to her. "Meeting new people and seeing new places would be quite as adventurous as running a kingdom, wouldn't you say?"

Baronesa Baezona's brow raised, a tight smile on her lips. "Indeed."

That brow bespoke a judgement Carina wished she were ignorant of. The baronesa seemed to hold disdain for a nomadic lifestyle. Which, Carina supposed, made sense. Still, she didn't have to be rude about it. They ate in silence, and Carina could almost feel the Baezona's planning their next question.

"Lady Carina," Baronesa Baezona said, concern in her voice. "I'm told you were attacked the day you arrived in the city, is that true?"

Carina swallowed. How would they know about that? "Not really, Baronesa. An explosive was thrown into the shop of Zanne the glassblower. We don't really know why or who was responsible."

"How terrifying," Barón Baezona said.

"My lady, you must be on your guard at all times," Eron said, suddenly eager. "I know you are capable, but evil lurks around every corner of this city. I would feel much better if you were in a safer place than a paltry inn."

Carina stared at him. "I'm not sure what you're suggesting, Sir Eron."

"Lady Carina," Eron leaned toward her, taking her hand. She twitched at his touch, but forced herself not to pull away. "You know, if anyone does anything to hurt you, or even if they don't, you're welcome to come to us. I know you don't have family here." He paused, his expression softening. "Let us be your family. We can offer you support, a home, servants, even financial support should you need it."

Carina blinked, shocked. Eron seemed kind—if not slightly naïve—but certainly his parents wouldn't allow this invitation to be made unless they were gaining something. But they appeared unsurprised.

She stammered. "I don't know what to say."

Baronesa Baezona took her husband's hand. "I suggested it before you came, and we all agree. You don't have to accept right now. At least say you'll think about it?"

Carina opened her mouth, but no words came to her. She wanted to decline immediately, but to do so without the appearance of consideration would be an insult to them.

"I'm flattered," she said. "I will keep the offer in mind."

"Wonderful," Baronesa Baezona said, beaming. "I do hope you'll accept; it would be lovely to have you here."

Somehow, Carina did not believe her.

Dessert was brought in then, a crumbling pastry covered in sunsetberries and lemon. Carina ate what she could. The food seemed less appetizing now somehow. She was about to excuse herself when yet another servant entered carrying a tray of glasses and a bottle of wine. The man carefully poured for them and placed one before each person.

"I believe a toast is in order," Barón Baezona said. "To two talented young people who have the potential to be royalty. Perhaps, even, together." He raised his glass to Carina and Eron.

Carina nearly dropped her wine. To her side, Eron was blinking fast, staring at his plate. She'd known he had intentions to court her, but this seemed to be too much even for him.

She lifted the cup as the other three drank heartily, pausing on instinct before letting it touch her lips. Merlin's words from earlier rang in her mind, "*...doesn't mean it won't happen again.*"

Beside her, Eron clutched at his collar, concern in his brow. Carina frowned, noticing the Baronesa doing the same. Eron dropped his wine glass. Dark golden liquid spilled over the table. She spun to face Merlin, who was already moving toward them.

He knelt over the baronesa. "Poison," he said. Hurriedly, he snatched a nearby porcelain jug for hand washing on a side table, and stuck his hand inside it.

One of the Baezona's servants appeared from the hallway and leaped at Merlin, knocking the jug out of his hands. They tumbled away from Baronesa Baezona, the water spilling over the carpet. Carina stood, her mind clearing, and drew a dagger from her boot. She had to help. She rounded the table. Before she reached them, a flash of *purple* light shone for a moment, and the servant went limp.

Merlin hurried to the Baezonas, muttering to Carina. "Stab him in the side, then give me your dagger and go back to your seat. They need to think you drank as well."

She didn't think. She followed his instructions. She stabbed the servant, a small twist in her stomach, then brought her dagger back to her seat as Merlin reached Eron and healed him. She then handed him the blade and laid down, pretending she was waking as the others were. Merlin held the dagger tightly, and offered a hand to help her stand.

Carina took in a slow breath.

At the head of the table, Barón Baezona gripped his chair and stood with a grunt. A moment later, he reached down and helped the Baronesa to her feet. Merlin helped Eron up as well, and for a moment Merlin's eyes widened, his jaw tense. She followed his gaze to the window where something shifted in the trees beyond.

Carina and the Baezonas took their seats. Spilled wine stained the tablecloth, but no one paid it any mind. Barón

Baezona finally noticed the blood on Merlin's clothing, and the dead servant on the floor. He pointed to Merlin. "You. Explain."

Merlin, who was still glancing at the window, shook his head. "It appears, sir, that the wine you were served was poisoned."

Barón Baezona gestured at the floor. "The poisoner?"

They all glanced at the body on the floor. The hard wood was darkened by water, and sprinkled with broken glass from the wash basin that had appeared to have fallen and shattered.

"Yes, sir," Merlin said. "He tried to stop me when I moved to help, so I stabbed him."

Carina noticed Eron's eyes widen at this.

"You did well," Barón Baezona said. "But how are we still alive?"

"It's lucky," Merlin said. "He was carrying the antidote in his pocket." He pulled a small bottle from his coat and held it up, clear liquid swirling inside. His vial of water, Carina knew. The Baezonas all appeared shocked, but Carina knew better. They'd likely been too far poisoned to realize he hadn't given them any kind of antidote.

Barón Baezona was beside himself. "Assassinations at every turn in the city and now even in our own house?"

Eron shook his head. "I for one am grateful we lived through it."

"Thanks to Lady Carina's servant," Baronesa Baezona said, seeming genuinely impressed.

Barón Baezona was staring at the body on the floor. "My

love, does this man seem familiar to you?"

The baronesa's eyes had gone wide. "Do you think?" she said.

Barón Baezona growled. Without another word he stood and stormed out of the dining room, followed closely by the baronesa.

Carina slumped in her chair and let out a sigh.

"I'm so sorry," Eron said.

She turned to him. "It's not your fault." She glanced at Merlin. "We're lucky."

Merlin opened his mouth as if to speak, then closed it, turning away in obvious frustration.

Eron shook his head. "I'm glad you're all right. I suppose my parents will be too busy with this to give you a proper farewell. Would you allow me to escort you out? Unless you'd like to stay here for the night?"

Determined, he was. "Thank you, but no," Carina said. "I'd rather be among my own things."

He led her back through the hallways to the main entrance, Merlin following behind. At the door, Eron took both of Carina's hands. "Lady Carina, because of such a terrible dinner, I feel a responsibility to keep you safe for the moment. Might I walk you back to your inn?"

She took a deep breath before answering. She had to stop this. "Sir Eron, I'm very grateful for your kindness, but I must decline. Perhaps when the tournament is over and things settle down, I might be able to consider walking out with a fine young man such as yourself."

His eyes lost some of their spark then, but he covered it up with a smile. "Even doling out rejection, lady, you are kind. I am disappointed, but you give me hope. For now, I will remain your loyal friend. And," he turned to Merlin, "I am confident this servant can keep you safe."

Merlin bowed and she watched Eron walk back into the Hall. It wasn't until the door shut that she turned to Merlin and yanked on his arm until they were out of earshot of the other buildings. "What was outside the window?"

He grimaced, then he found his voice.

"Ahnri. He saw me use magic."

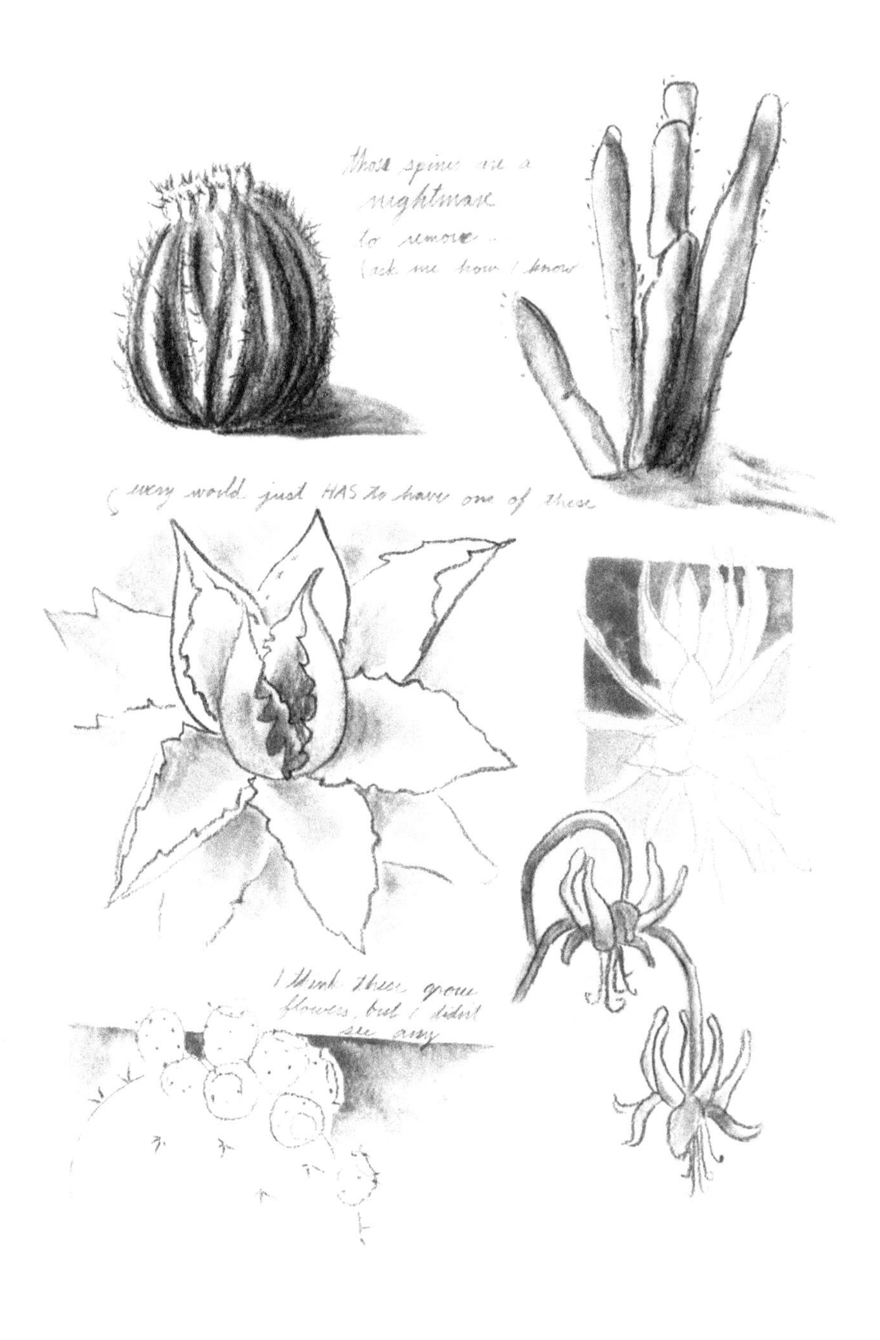
those spines are a
nightmare
to remove...
(ask me how I know
every world just HAS to have one of these
I think these grow
flowers but I didn't
see any

24
CARINA

Carina let the news sink into her mind, and her brow furrowed as they walked. "But...Ahnri? What was Ahnri doing at Baezona Hall?"

"Spying. Again." Merlin said. "Which was one step safer than the nomad."

"You truly killed him?"

Merlin nodded, shaking his hands out. "Death magic. From the shadows right to his chest. Very fast, very painless."

It had always unnerved her that death magic was drawn from shadows. It made simple darkness seem dangerous. That Merlin could end a life so quickly sent a chill down her spine. Yet, he had done it to protect her.

"Thing is," he said, "I noticed something through the window after I killed the assassin, then Ahnri was there after I healed the Baezonas. Looked at me like I'd betrayed him somehow."

Carina stared back toward Baezona Hall. Ahnri was probably long gone, and would likely be back at Matano Hall by now. "Ahnri? But he agreed *not* to pass information on us, didn't he?"

"Carina," Merlin said, drawing her aside into an alleyway. The space was thin and cramped, but he began to pace back and forth. "Twice I broke the law just now, and I used two different magics. If he saw me use both there's no telling what his reaction will be."

"Should we visit Matano Hall so you can talk to him?"

"What if he won't believe me? He'll bring it up when he comes to spar this afternoon either way. Might as well give him time to think on it." He sighed, running a hand through his hair, which fell back over his brow. "At least he doesn't know the full extent. He doesn't know about Excalibur. He probably thinks I'm a simple Vessel or that I'm wearing charms of some kind, but I can see how Death magic would frighten him. His biggest concern might be me helping you in the tournament, I—damn it, I should've been more careful."

"You did what you had to," she said.

"That's the truth behind all this," he said. He turned to face her. "I can't let anything happen to you. Eron might have put up a fight, but I get the feeling his parents would have thrown you at the assassin, and you didn't have your sword, and I—" He shook his head. "Life magic is all right, it lifts me up to use it, but I don't like using Death magic. It always leaves me feeling so *angry*."

And he did seem angry. His shoulders were tense, his face

flushed, and veins in his forearms stood out beneath his pale skin. Carina approached and laid a hand on his arm. As though she held a magic of her own, he relaxed under her touch.

"Thank you, Merlin. For doing what you did."

He sighed, placing his hand over hers. "Thank *you.*" He raised his head to meet her gaze. His eyes were intent on her, and she gasped at the emotion there. His gaze fell to her lips, then to the ground as he released her hand and turned away.

Something inside her fragmented, she couldn't be sure what. "Merlin?"

"Let's get you inside, darling," he said quickly, stepping past her. "It's too cold out here."

The sun neared the horizon, and Carina knew that in two hours they would learn which combatants were to move on to the final round of the tournament. She'd planned on working with Ahnri before the announcement anyway, but she found herself pacing the field behind Cait's Corner, swinging her sword to keep her hands from shaking, wondering if he would even come. When the gate creaked and he stepped through, she spun to meet him.

"Ahnri, listen—"

His sword was already out, and she caught his intentions a moment before he attacked. She blocked him, and used one of his own techniques to spin and thrust at his chest. He dodged and was back in an instant, his blade coming toward her shoulder.

Attack, parry, advance, retreat, dodge, spin. Carina fought harder than she ever had, as did Ahnri. Their spars of the past forgotten, each one brought out every tactic and secret strategy they knew to gain the upper hand.

Merlin stood off to one side, and—Carina knew—unable to help in any way unless he could get close enough to touch her. Magic didn't work from a distance.

Her heart raced; her grip tight on Excalibur. Merlin said the sword didn't grant her any magic or power, yet she couldn't help a sense of wonder—of certainty—when she held it.

If the destiny Merlin spoke of was considered magic, then Ahnri was right to suspect her—but there was no magic in this fight. Before even two minutes was up, Carina had disarmed him.

Her sword tip at his shoulder, their chests rose and fell with deep breaths. Carina lowered her sword and stared at Ahnri.

"Happy?" she said.

He gave a single nod.

Merlin knelt on the ground, running a hand over his face.

Carina let out a heavy breath, lowering her sword. "For the record, Merlin heals me when necessary, but I refuse to win this tournament by cheating during the events."

Merlin mumbled. "Took her a while to decide she wants to win at all."

"Well," Ahnri sighed, "if you fight anything like that in the matches, you stand a very good chance."

Merlin reached them and crossed his arms. "Satisfied?"

Ahnri raised a hand. "I want to say this: the fact that you have healing doesn't bother me."

Carina frowned.

"Everyone in the tournament has access to Cures," Ahnri continued, "whether through the king or their own private 'healer' who they pretend isn't using Life to fix them. It makes sense Carina would have access to healing. But Merlin, wielding two forms of magic is unheard of unless you carry a vessel." He paused. "Do you carry jewels or coins with the magic stored?"

Merlin looked to Carina. For a moment she hesitated, but something in her—something very similar to the feeling she'd had when she decided to trust Merlin—told her to trust Ahnri as well. "Tell him the truth."

"No," Merlin said to Ahnri. "I don't carry anything."

Ahnri's face paled. "Then how?"

"Merlin is not from here," Carina said, giving Merlin a sly smile. "He doesn't follow normal rules."

Merlin nodded to her, gratitude in his eyes.

Ahnri seemed to think about this for a moment. "And the sword?"

Carina's grip on Excalibur tightened. "What about the sword?"

"Is it magic too?"

"Yes," Merlin said, "though, it's not a vessel. I honestly doubt anyone *could* put magic into that thing if they tried, it's too full of itself."

Ahnri frowned, appearing confused.

Merlin sighed. "The sword can see when a person has the

right temperament, talents, and knowledge to make a kingdom thrive." He gestured to Carina.

As she watched, something seemed to click in Ahnri's mind, and his posture grew more relaxed. "I admit, Lady Carina, I have felt something different about you."

Merlin stepped forward. "How strongly do you believe that?"

Carina met Ahnri's eyes, and found genuine relief there.

"Of all the combatants, my lady," he said, "you would do the most good for this kingdom. You're telling me you knew that before you even entered?"

Merlin gave a nod. "Exactly that."

Ahnri turned to Carina. "That's a lot to live up to."

The fact that he simply accepted this information made her breathe a sigh of relief. At the same moment, doubts began to creep into her mind, like weeds she'd pulled a hundred times yet kept returning.

When Merlin spoke, there was a firmness to his words. "I've never once failed to put my charge on their throne. I'm not about to stop now."

"Well," Ahnri said. "If that's really a king-naming sword, I'd say it found the right person."

"King- and Queen-naming sword," Merlin said. "Of all the times I've guided rulers to their thrones, it's only once been a woman before now. Between the two of them, I'm not sure any man will ever live up to the example."

Carina watched Ahnri. He was someone else's servant. Yet, he'd given his word to her—and she believed him—that he would not spy on her. She took that to mean that even if he was helping someone else, he wouldn't be working directly *against* Carina. He seemed to believe the incredible facts about Merlin and Excalibur without question. But, why? Was he being honest?

As all these thoughts crowded her mind, one thing came through clearly: she couldn't keep being suspicious of everyone. Yes, Ahnri was her competitor's servant. But from what Carina had observed, Rosaline didn't have any closeness to him. And Carina trusted Rosaline too, as much as it was possible to trust her competition.

"Ahnri, can I ask you something?

"Of course."

"We've now explained to you that I was chosen by a 'magic' sword to win this tournament and become the next heir to the Medelian throne. You've just been told that Merlin is not from this world, and that he has access to multiple powers of nature, and you just…*believe* us?"

Ahnri shook his head. "When you say it all like that…"

"I want to be sure," she said, "that you understand what it is you're hearing. You say you believe that I am the best possible choice for the future of Medelios, yet, you're not even native to this land, are you?"

Ahnri ran a hand over his face. "No, I'm not. But I am always concerned with the stability of the Unbroken Lands. It's something my father drilled into me. I try to work with other spies and servants to help the best things happen."

"How do I know you're telling the truth?"

He paused, then simply said, “You don't.”

For some reason, that candid response made Carina's nerves settle. “Thank you.”

Then another question came to her. Why was this happening? She'd traveled on her own for two years, a small, single young woman, and never had she had as many attempts on her life as she had since arriving in Reinos. “Ahnri, are all the combatants getting death threats and assassination attempts, or only me?”

He cocked his head. “That's a good question. I haven't heard of any, but that doesn't mean they haven't happened. I see and hear a lot, but not everything.”

“The Liraste girls trying to get Kemin counts,” Merlin.

“Right,” Carina said. “That's the only one I'm aware of.”

“I can look into it,” Ahnri said.

Carina eyed him. “And you'll tell me what you learn?”

“I will.

“That would be wonderful, actually.”

“Ahnri,” Merlin said, “on your way out would you ask Cait to have a bath drawn for Carina? Tell her we sent you.”

“Sure. I'll need to be with the Matanos most of today. I'll find you tomorrow and let you know what I hear.”

“Thank you,” Carina said.

As Ahnri made his way to the inn's back door, Merlin turned to face her.

“Does it worry you at all that there have now been three attempts on your life?”

“Yes,” she said. “Though I would argue that my fight with

the Liraste girls was not specifically an assassination attempt."

"Did they or did they not try to kill you?"

"They certainly tried."

"Then it mucking counts."

"Merlin."

"And you just gave a *lot* of information to an individual we *know* has been ordered to spy on you."

Her eyes narrowed. "Yes, and he's said he wouldn't anymore."

"And now?" he snapped. "The only reason you have to make the call on whether to trust him is because he was *still* spying on you!"

"But he—"

"It is not my place to tell you what to do, Carina but I beg of you *be careful*." His voice was low, his fists tightly clenched. "We don't need him, or anyone else, we just—"

"Merlin, stop!"

He paused, finally meeting her eyes.

"Listen to yourself," she said, frustration brewing in her chest. "'Don't need him?' I would think we could use all the help we can get. Maybe he was watching, but he said he wouldn't spy anymore. And now he's agreed to help us—"

"Why are you so trusting of him all of a sudden? Only yesterday you told him to stop, and he promised he would, and now he's shown he hasn't."

She took a breath, closing her eyes for a moment. Merlin himself had taught her that getting angry at someone for trying to help her was futile. And she knew he was only trying to help.

But something had changed, and she found she did trust Ahnri. It was a feeling, more than anything, but she had to explain it somehow.

"Merlin, I can't keep distrusting everyone who might possibly be a threat to me. If I were still doing that, I would never have agreed to travel here with you in the first place."

That made him pause. The tension draining from his shoulders.

"I'm going to need more allies. I've been working on making friends with other combatants, but—spies, merchants, commoners—I'm going to need all of them." She shrugged. "I might as well start now."

Merlin crossed his arms. To Carina he seemed to be reconsidering, though he wasn't pleased about it. "All right," he finally said. "Those are good points."

"I'm incredibly grateful you're here to help me," she said. "But to say we don't need anyone else? Well, it feels like self-sabotage."

He ran a hand over his face as she spoke. "You're right…you're right, of course. I'm going to go talk to him. You need to clean up and get ready for the announcement tonight. But Carina," he paused, and his eyes softened then. "I might not always be close enough to save you. We've actually been very lucky that I have been so far. Please. Please take care who you choose to trust. You never know when another attempt on your life is coming, and at this point, we might as well assume another *is*."

Carina watched him go, then followed a moment later. She

understood his frustration. He was supposed to protect her…

And it was *her* job to protect this kingdom.

The best way to protect this kingdom from those who would harm it—and by extension its people—was to gain the throne and make change happen. In order to do that, Merlin was right: she had to also protect herself.

She would be careful, yes. But if helping this kingdom meant trusting Ahnri—and anyone else who was willing to help her—that was exactly what she would do.

25
CARINA

With the races over, the obstacle course had been removed and the holes filled in that morning while the tests were given. This was also where the final duels would take place, and that open patch of field was where the king's advisers now stood on a raised platform to announce the advancements to the final rounds.

Carina stood against the stands facing the advisers. Rosaline stood to her right, and Eron to her left. Merlin was in the stands somewhere, but she couldn't see him.

Beside her, Rosaline stood perfectly still, the epitome of calm. Confident as Carina had begun to feel, she couldn't help but fidget.

"Lady Rosaline," Carina said. "Do you ever worry?"

"No," Rosaline said. "Advance or not, worrying will do you no good."

She was right. Carina rolled her shoulders, lifting her chin to watch as the advisers began once again to name the advancing competitors. Those named took a place on the stage.

Alodie Baezona.

Diman Baezona.

Betania Liraste.

Marius Matano.

Rosaline Matano.

Syla Teneo.

Carina Valio.

Luci Velando.

Sir Ilian waited for the applause to fade before announcing that the following day would be a Midway celebration, including another morning parade, and a ball in the evening. The contestants would have that single day to rest before the final duels took place on the last day of the tournament, with yet another celebration after the winner was announced.

Carina smiled, waving as people in the stands cheered her name. It was a feeling she'd never known, being recognized and appreciated. Beside her, Rosaline gave a curious glance.

"What?" Carina asked.

"I'm impressed, that's all," Rosaline said. "Many didn't think you'd make it this far."

A small voice in the back of Carina's mind told her they might be right. Maybe she didn't deserve to be standing there. The image of her father's sword came to her mind, the one hidden under her bed at the inn. The one she'd tried to ignore, because Excalibur was the superior blade.

You're like that sword, the voice said. *Unfit...imperfect...*

She shoved the voice away.

Rosaline put a hand on Carina's shoulder. "But you've proven them wrong," she said, a gleam in her eye. "And now, of course, the real fun begins."

Carina frowned. "What do you mean?"

"Duels, Lady Carina," Rosaline said, her smile as sharp as a sword. "My favorite game."

26
CARINA

"Carina, look!" Merlin pointed to the sky.

On the canvas of deep blue sky, a white streak lit up, flying from north to south.

"I've seen those before. What is it?"

"It's a shooting star," he said. "Well, it's not actually a star, it's a meteor, which is a rock that fell through the planet's atmosphere and we're seeing it break into little bits as it does. But still. Pretty cool, eh?"

"Cool? Like, cold?"

"No, ah, it means…neat. Fun. Interesting."

"Oh." She nodded, turning to the sky. "Then yes, it's cool."

Merlin laughed.

They sat together on the front porch of the inn. Behind them, the bar was crowded with Carina's supporters. Mar had begun to worry they wouldn't have enough brew to last the winter if they kept up. Musicians played and people danced, and something stirred in Carina's chest. A sense of something foreign to her, something like…belonging. Like home, but more potent than Valios Palace had ever been. With each person who came to wish her luck in the tournament, her cheeks grew warmer, and the butterflies in her stomach flitted around as though they were celebrating too.

Golden light and music spilled through the windows behind them. There were even dancers and drinkers surrounding them on the porch and filling the street. Beside her, Merlin was fiddling with a bottle of sunsetberry wine. The wine was sweet tonight, fitting in with the atmosphere of celebration and excitement. From the corner of her eye, he pulled something from his coat, then the bottle glowed slightly white before fading back to normal.

"Merlin!"

"What?" He shoved his vial of water back into his coat.

"Did you put magic in there? With so many people around?"

"Do you think anyone noticed?"

She stared at him.

"Oh, come on. There's so much happening right now, I'm sure it's fine. If it concerns you, I won't do it again. Promise."

"You're the one who went mad when Ahnri caught you."

"That was different," he said. "I killed a man and healed three people in a matter of moments, and I *knew* he'd seen it all."

She shook her head. "I just don't want you to get carted off for illegal magic."

"A little flash like that, no one will think twice about." He set the bottle aside, and lowered his voice. "Aside from the, ah, recent attempts on your life," he said, "are you happy?" His eyes seemed hesitant, as though part of him knew her answer, and another part worried he was wrong.

"Of course, I'm happy," Carina said. "I didn't think I'd make it this far."

Merlin took her hand in his. "I knew you would."

She met his eyes. Surrounded by people as they were, she didn't expect anything more than to watch him for a moment. As she did, his grey gaze flitted from one part of her face to another. Her cheeks, eyes, mouth, as though he were memorizing each of her features. Her heart began to race, and the butterflies flitted in her stomach as she took the chance to do the same: his high cheekbones, deep-set eyes, thick brows, and black messy hair.

After a moment, Merlin's eyes grew sad. He briefly pressed his lips to the back of her hand, then let go.

Carina held her breath.

"Excuse me, my lady. I'll be right back." He stood and stepped into the inn, disappearing.

Her breath escaped her in a rush, her face growing warm. She stared at the hand he had kissed for a moment, trying to interpret her own emotions.

Then Cait came through the door. "What are you doing hiding against the wall, my lady? You're the guest of honor! People are waiting to see you!"

Before she could object, Carina was snatched and dragged

into the taproom. A whole group of people cheered as she entered, pressing forward to greet her.

One man introduced himself and offered her a dress for the Midway Ball. A young Somnurian woman promised her a custom necklace. Another man offered to care for her armor when the duels began.

Her head was spinning when a tall man, bald with a thick dark beard, pushed through the crowd to greet her.

"Good evening, Lady Carina," the man said, "Sylas Turner, I'm a woodworker by trade, and I have with me a gift I'd like to offer you." He pulled from his pocket a small, circular piece. Like a shallow bowl that fit in the palm of her hand, except it had a circle in the center and swirls carved out from there.

Carina frowned. "I'm flattered, Master Turner, but I'm afraid I've not seen anything like this before."

He chuckled, his amused eyes sparkling behind his spectacles. "Well, I was told you're a user of oils derived from plants, is that correct?"

"It is," she said, her curiosity piqued. She wasn't sure how that information got out, but it wasn't wrong.

"Well, this is what I call a diffuser, to be used with those oils. You see," he pointed to the circle in the center, "you simply pour a small amount here in the center, and swirl it around a bit. This spreads the oil out over a significant surface area, and the oil seeps into the wood, helping the scent to lift into the air."

Carina stared. She had always treasured her oils, and on her travels, she'd resorted to simply opening her vial and breathing the scent for a moment before stoppering it again, too afraid to lose what little she had left. But this? This would make a few drops last days.

"Sir, I can't thank you enough. This is such a kind gift."

"It's no trouble, my lady. We're all grateful you're here, and I'm happy to show it. Enjoy your evening."

Carina laughed. "Enjoy your evening as well, sir."

She waved to a few more people, excusing herself, and slipped back outside to her bench, to which Merlin had returned in the time she was gone.

"Where've you been?" he asked, as she sat next to him.

"Meeting people," she said. "You?"

"Enjoying the night. It's too stuffy in there."

They sat in silence for a moment, and Carina closed her eyes. The cold air bit at her skin, raising bumps, warmth beside her in the form of Merlin's body. She sighed, breathing in the smell of night and winter.

"Carina?" Merlin asked.

Exhaustion made her slow, and she only briefly noted the way his breath moved the stray hairs near her temple. "Hmm?"

"Would you like to dance?"

The thought was appealing, but her eyes were not staying open. "I'm actually feeling a bit tired. I think I'd like to go to bed now."

"Early to bed, early to rise," Merlin chanted. "It's a good habit to be in. Come on."

He offered his arm and Carina threaded hers through. She let him lead her to the inn's entrance, then paused. What was that smell?

"Wait," she said, turning back toward the street.

"What is it?" Merlin asked, following.

Shouts rose to the south of them, and Carina could smell something off. Something sharp. Smoke? But it wasn't the sweet smell of a cook fire, or the comfort of a hearth. This was the smell of something out of control.

"Something's burning," she said. "Something that shouldn't be."

27
AHNRI

Matano Hall buzzed with excitement. Of the five that had advanced to the test round, two had made it through to the final duels. Rosaline and Marius, the two cousins who, as Ahnri had heard it, had been sparring with each other since they were able to hold swords.

The entire extended family celebrated late into the night. Ahnri sat in his room staring out the window. The music and laughter from ground level had woken him every time he dozed off. He was supposed to spar with Carina in the morning before her duels began, but if he didn't get rest, he'd be useless. He was drained; unable to celebrate with the others, yet too restless to sleep.

He stared up at the sky, where stars dotted the blackness, a half-moon lighting the city. The glass of the window was chill against his cheek and soothed the slight ache in his head. He could probably go back to bed now, things seemed to be quieting down. He slumped in the corner where window met wall, letting himself relax for the first time all day.

The sound of running footsteps came to him. Probably another servant fetching something. Ahnri shifted in his corner seat. He needed to stoke the fire before he fell completely asleep, make sure his room stayed warm. A waft of hot air rolled over him then. Hmm…maybe he didn't need to stoke the fire. It certainly seemed warm enough. His skin not touching the window began to sweat. Sleep overcame him enough that his head nodded, before popping up again, and he took a deep breath on instinct.

Smoke.

He coughed. Shouts came from outside. Ahnri couldn't see his room. Only smoke. Fire? He crouched down to his knees, covering his face with an arm. A light shone through the crack beneath his door. He crawled to it and carefully felt for heat. It wasn't unbearable, but probably not the best escape route. He'd have to take the window—except…his game. Sticks. He'd hidden it in a loose brick of the fireplace in the parlor down the hall. He couldn't let it burn.

The box in his mind shuddered—the one where he kept the grief of Damond's death. He just had to get the game.

He turned to his bed and pulled off the quilt. Using that, he pressed the door latch, and swung it open. A blast of heat forced him to close his eyes. Darkness filled the hallway, small flames licking between the floorboards from the rooms below. The parlor was only ten paces away. He covered himself with the quilt, took a deep breath through his sleeve, and dove into the smoke.

Heat bit at his feet as he ran. Ignoring the pain, he burst into the parlor and his eyes found the fireplace. He ran to it and quickly pulled the pouch out, stuffing it into his pocket before turning to the nearest window. The heat here was unbearable; flames had come up the stairwell and poured over the wooden furniture.

A scream sounded behind him. Ahnri turned. At the far side of the room, Rosaline huddled in a corner. She also held a blanket, but hers was nearly burned away. Fire licked up her dress, burning her legs and arms, surrounding her with a reddish glow. She kept her face covered with her hands, but her cries of pain echoed through the room.

Ahnri ran to her and helped her stand. He tried to pat out the worst of the flames, but gave up—his own clothing was catching as it was—and pulled her to the window. The floor beneath them creaked in protest. He kicked the glass hard, shattering it, drawing the attention of onlookers in the street. A small windowsill was all Ahnri had to work with.

"Throw her!" A voice called. Ahnri could barely see through the smoke.

A group gathered together below, organizing into a tangle of arms. Ahnri held Rosaline around her waist. She was barely conscious. He took her face in his hands.

"Rosaline, listen to me. You have to jump, understand? If you don't, I have to throw you. Because this building is going to come down any minute."

She shook her head, her eyes glazed over.

The window sill creaked.

"All right, here we go." He picked her up. "Ready?" he shouted.

"Yes!" came from below.

As gently as he could, Ahnri threw Rosaline into the air. His fingers curled as she left his grip, and he watched her body fall. The group caught her, lowering her slowly to the ground.

The sill creaked again, and Ahnri turned to grip the frame above in time for the sill to crack and release from the building. His fingers shook, supporting his weight on only two inches of stone. He gritted his teeth and twisted his head to the group below.

Someone waved at him to move, maybe to jump, but there was no group to catch him. They were all surrounding Rosaline. Ahnri coughed, and moved his right hand a foot to the side, then followed with his left. When he got clear of the window, he anchored his feet against the wall, pulled himself higher, and reached for the roof's edge only a foot away. Both hands gripping, he strained his muscles again and pulled himself to the roof, rolling onto his side.

Against his back, the roof was warm. It wouldn't be long before the fire destroyed this too, and he wouldn't have anything to stand on. Ahnri forced himself to his feet and took in his surroundings.

Above, Kahn screeched his disapproval and swept down to the roof of the tavern next door. Ahnri went to the edge. He could barely see through the smoke, but he estimated a ten-foot jump. He might make it with a running start. More likely he'd hit the edge with his chest and knock the air out of himself. The building below him was crumbling, so he couldn't gradually go down the way he normally would.

Kahn flew off, staying above, watching. Ahnri took a few steps back and breathed deep, ran, and jumped.

As expected, he hit the edge with his chest, cracking ribs. The air in his lungs flew out in a huff. He managed to grip the thick railing as he gulped air, and again pulled himself up to roll onto his back.

Breathing hurt. As the adrenaline waned, the burns he'd suffered and the smoke he'd inhaled raged their pain against him. He writhed in agony.

But he was alive. Barely.

He could have died. He might still. He'd never been this close to dying in his life, even dueling crime lords and high-ranking officers in Fugera. Instead, it was saving a noblewoman he didn't care for in the slightest.

Forcing himself to his feet once more, he staggered to the other side of the tavern's roof. He looked down, wishing he didn't have to make the jumps in this condition, but there was nothing else to do. He steeled himself and jumped again, feeling every ache and burn on his body. He made it three jumps down before his strength gave out and he slid to the ground, landing in a pile of trash.

His brain was hardly functioning, his body doing everything on instinct. He forced himself to stand again and his left ankle gave out. Must've twisted it when he fell. He wasn't sure where he meant to go, but his mind cleared a little as he stumbled along. He'd nearly died. Could have died. *Should* have died. He had to find someone to clean and patch up his injuries, or he'd never be of use to—

An idea came to him as he limped down the street. He glanced back at Matano Hall where a crowd was still gathered, passing water from the nearby well and hardly containing the blaze. Could it be that easy? Could he fake his own death and be free from all obligation? It could work…if he got healed. He was hurt. Dying, he knew he was. He'd been burned, and he'd inhaled so much smoke. He wanted to fall down onto the street and never get up.

There was something at the back of his mind. Something he should remember. Something that could help. He shook his head, trying to figure out what it was. Then he sighted the sign above Cait's Corner. And it came to him.

Merlin.

Merlin could heal. He'd healed the Baezonas. Merlin was his only chance. The king would never allow his healers to fix a Fugeran servant boy.

Ahnri's body ached, his eyes blurring from the pain. He could hear people shouting, back toward the manor. Trying to focus, he crept around the side of Cait's to the gate that opened to the back field. Before he could get it open, his burned legs and twisted ankle gave out. He fell to the ground, cool cobblestones easing the fevered heat of his skin, and he slept. Perhaps he would die there. He'd consider it a mercy.

28
CARINA

Carina's eyes watered. Using the back of her hand, she swiped the tears away and blinked to focus on the onion in front of her.

Cait and her workers were not yet awake. The celebrations hadn't continued after the Matano Hall fire was doused, and instead the city fell into an uneasy calm. Though the sun would rise soon, no one seemed eager to get on with the Midway Celebration in light of the night's loss. It would happen, but it would be subdued.

Merlin entered the kitchen, carrying a small basket of carrots, potatoes, and other roots.

"How's Ahnri?" Carina asked.

Merlin sighed, setting down the basket. "Still sleeping." He began washing potatoes. "Shouldn't the Matanos' be searching for him by now?"

"Maybe they think he died in the fire."

"He'll probably be relieved if that's true. I get the feeling he didn't like them much."

Carina couldn't get the image out of her head, seeing Ahnri in the alley just outside Cait's. She and Merlin had followed the trail of smoke, then watched as Ahnri threw Rosaline from the second story. Merlin had gone to help, to see if he could heal the worst of Rosaline's injuries without being noticed, in case the king's healers were too late. But Carina had seen Ahnri climb up the face of the building and to the roof, where she'd lost track of him through the clouds of smoke. Minutes later, the roof fell in, the stones of the walls crumbled, and a water line was formed to try and put out the flames.

Merlin had pulled her away from the scene shortly after—there wasn't much more to be done—and they'd spotted Ahnri, burned and stumbling, turn into the alley beside Cait's. She was only glad they'd found him in time.

"What are you thinking about?" Merlin asked.

Carina shook her head. She'd paused in her onion chopping. "Last night."

"Hm. Someone is causing trouble."

"But who?"

"Who would want to kill off two top competitors in one shot?" he said. "Who paid that nomad to poison you and the Baezonas? Who threw the explosive into the glassblower's shop? Were those Liraste girls working on their own or were they paid or bribed or coerced? Could it all be the same person, or different? Do they see you *and* the Matanos as threats? There are four other families still competing, and they all have reason to come after you and Rosaline."

Carina sighed, scooping the chopped onions into a bowl and reaching for the carrots.

"Wash those first, please," Merlin said, cracking eggs into the bowl of onions.

She carried them to a sink nearby, already full of clean water. Once clean, she moved to the cutting board and began to chop, thinking all the while. "Betania, maybe? The Lirastes?"

"They do seem the obvious choice."

"They're the only family outwardly negative toward anyone. But they're that way with *everyone.* I mean, Betania and her cousins know it was me who stopped them the night of opening ceremonies. Betania tried to stab me then, who's to say she wouldn't start a fire?"

"And the fact you got away that first time certainly would have made her more vengeful. No one else has been aggressive toward you?"

"Not really." She thought through the names of everyone she'd met. "Eron wouldn't have done that, would he?"

"No," Merlin said without hesitation. "That boy hasn't got an ounce of cunning in his brain."

She held back a smile, focusing on the carrots in front of her. "You've never been fond of Sir Eron, though he's been more than eager to befriend me."

"And you rejected him, did you not?"

Her smile faded. "Oh gods, you're right. I can't imagine him doing it, but he does have a motive."

"A somewhat trivial motive, but a motive nonetheless." He

poured the egg and onion mixture into a pan over the fire. "Are you close to anyone else?"

"Merlin, you've been with me almost every minute since we met. If I was close to anyone, you'd know better than I."

He met her eyes. "You're probably right. What about that Velando boy, Kemin. You spoke to him at the party, right?"

"Yes." She remembered he was kind, and only wanted an excuse to get to the gardens for his own reasons. "But then I saved his life. He should owe me, not want to harm me."

"Just bringing up options. Anyone else?"

"There's no one else I've spoken to at length. Unless you count that glassblower."

"She was a close friend of Eron's, correct?"

She stared at him. "So, you *do* think Eron set the fire?"

He blinked, then shook his head. "No. No, we decided that already. There's not enough room in his head to plan it."

Carina laughed. "How would you know how smart he is?" she asked.

The tension in her melted away as Merlin's mouth twitched at the corners. "I may have listened in on his test yesterday. It happened right before yours, and you were busy trying to focus."

"Merlin!"

He grinned. "He's not very bright at all, that one. Charming, certainly. Handsome, I'll give him that. But his mind is empty as a poor man's pocket."

She rolled her eyes. "How am I going to speak to him now that you've said those horrible things?"

"It's not so bad," he said, turning to face her, meeting her eyes. "He can still offer to protect you from your faithful servant."

She laughed, a rush of heat flushing her face.

"Would you stir those eggs, please?" He pointed with a scrubbed potato toward the pan in the fire.

Carina turned to do as he asked. She hadn't cooked much even in the two years she'd been on her own. She'd mostly eaten food she stole that was already prepared, or paid for meals with labor. Merlin, however, told her cooking was a good skill to have, and decided this was the day to teach her.

"I think they're burning."

Merlin began to speak as Carina lifted the pan from the heat and immediately let go again. She'd forgotten to use gloves. Her hand was red where she'd gripped the handle. The pan crashed into the fire, eggs flying across the floor.

Heedless of the eggs he walked through, Merlin came to her. Carina's throat went dry as he took her hand in both of his, pouring his emergency water over her burn as the now-familiar white light began to glow. He was not cautious with his magic when no one else could see. Carina closed her eyes against it.

Her skin pricked, pulled tight, then relaxed. And then, as he had before, Merlin ran two fingers over the healed skin, and the contact sent bumps rising on Carina's arms. Instead of pulling away, he continued, running his fingers and then a thumb over the skin of Carina's palm.

"Does it hurt?"

Carina stared at their hands. Holding her breath, trying to

force her heart to slow slightly. She let it out, finally looking up at him. "Not anymore."

His hand tightened around hers. "Carina—"

The kitchen door opened, and Carina pulled away. She was shocked to realize how close they'd been standing. She gripped the fabric of her skirts as Ahnri entered.

His white-blond hair was a mess, singed in places. He rubbed his eyes with the heel of his hands and yawned. "Cait said you were in here. Can we talk?"

Carina glanced to Merlin, who cleared his throat.

"How are you feeling?" Merlin asked.

"I feel fine," Ahnri said. "Perfect. Which I assume I owe to you."

"You're welcome," Merlin said.

"I'm glad you're all right." Carina said. "Are you going to go back to the Matanos?"

Ahnri shook his head. "In Fugera, when a person saves another's life, their life is owed to the savior." He turned and met Merlin's gaze. "I would have died if you hadn't healed me. Therefore, my life is yours. Since you serve Lady Carina, I assumed I would become her servant as well."

Carina pursed her lips. "Doesn't that mean the Matanos should be—"

"Showering me with gold and jewels?" Ahnri shrugged. "Perhaps, but they don't follow Fugeran tradition. I do. I will go by to make sure no one is trying to find me, though. The Matano household should assume that I'm dead. As long as I keep my head down, I'm free to do as I please. And that means serving you in gratitude for saving my life."

Carina turned to Merlin. "Can he stay with you then? Sleep in your room?"

"Of course," Merlin said. "I'll talk to Cait and get it worked out."

Carina met Ahnri's gaze. "Thank you for this offer. I'm just glad you're all right."

"Ahnri," Merlin said, "did you get a chance yesterday to find any rumors of other assassination attempts?"

"A little," Ahnri said. "I did a little poking around and heard about an attempt on Luci Velando, and another on Syla Teneo. They're trying to keep both quiet, and as far as I can tell, no one even knows about the attempts on you."

Carina frowned. "I haven't exactly made them public, I suppose."

"Well," Merlin said, "Tonight is the Midway Ball. If you're Carina's servant now, we could use you there too."

"Yes," Ahnri said, "I can use the ball as a cover to find out more about possible attacks I might've missed."

Merlin clapped, grinning. "See, that's an excellent idea. This is why you're the spy."

"Thank you, Ahnri," Carina said. "You should rest until the ball."

"No," he said, "I need to move. I'll scout the city a little today and meet you before the ball. I'll let you know what I hear then."

"Perfect," Merlin said. "Take my cloak if you need."

Carina let out a deep breath, hoping they could learn

something today.

"Wait," Merlin said.

Ahnri paused at the kitchen door.

"You're going to have to let me cut your hair."

"What?" Ahnri said, his hand going to the singed long tail at the base of his neck.

"They'll be less likely to recognize you," Merlin said. "Don't worry, I promise I'm good with a pair of shears."

29
AHNRI

Fire.

He'd been in a fire. Flashes of memory came back to him as he made his way out of Cait's. There was still some soreness where he'd been burned and healed, but he had full range of movement. He also had a lot of information to catch up on. There might even be a chance he could fake his own death and escape Elya's service after all.

It was still early morning, the sun barely peeking over the horizon. He wore dark trousers, a white shirt, boots, and a dark cloak—all clothes of Merlin's. The Bones game sat in his pocket; he would not leave it anywhere else from now on.

His newly-cropped hair left his neck exposed, and it was unnerving. Ahnri already wished he had his long hair back. He stepped onto the cobbled street and began to walk north, pulling the hood forward to cover his face.

The streets were bare except for a few early-risers. Ahnri

ran through his options in his mind, then turned into an alleyway. He broke into a run, his hood falling back as he gained speed. The alley ended in a high stone wall, but Ahnri did not pause. Ten feet from slamming into stone, he angled his feet against the wall to his right and continued running. Two paces and he jumped from one wall to the other, hooking his fingertips on the top of the stone wall. His muscles burned, his body flowed; it was wonderful to move again.

He hadn't cared to try very hard while in the service of the Matanos, hadn't really scoured the city for information like this since arriving. But if it would help Carina, he would do it. From the wall's perch was a horizon of more alleys, wooden fences, brick walls, and buildings to scale.

Perfection.

Ahnri's face split into a wide grin, and he stood, balancing on the wall. Without a second thought he jumped to another wall and began to run along it. He turned right, then left, jumping from wall to wall until he reached Merchant Circle. From the alley there, he crossed the street and repeated the process once more. Sweat began to slide down his face and he wiped it from his eyes. Artisan Circle, then Farmer Circle, and finally Ahnri paused near the outer wall of the city.

The wall was only fifteen feet high, a simple thing to climb over except for the guards patrolling at the top. Ahnri walked along the inside, checking every so often for a clear shot. Before he found it, he'd arrived at East Gate. More people were moving in and out now, the sun fully up and beating on their faces and backs. Ahnri strode through, holding himself tall as a noble would. None of the guards questioned him.

As soon as he was out of earshot, he ducked off the road into a muddy ditch. His clothing wasn't fine, but it wasn't as rough as he needed it to be. He tore the shirt in a few places, and made a note to roll in the dirt before approaching anyone. The cloak would be his downfall. It was far too fine for a beggar, but maybe he could say some rich knight had thrown it out. It might be believable if it were dirty. Good thing he had mud available. He rolled in the mud, promising himself he'd replace Merlin's things, then angled himself toward the sun and waited.

A good disguise took patience, and as far as Ahnri knew, he had until sunset. Hopefully the Matanos already thought him dead, and Carina and Merlin wouldn't expect him back until they needed to leave for the ball.

He sat on the side of the road for over an hour, letting the mud dry, and pretending to beg from the farmers who passed. Some tossed a bit of food, most ignored him, and a few gave him a sympathetic smile and apologized for having nothing to spare. When the mud was dry, he stood and let it crack, falling off his clothing. He dusted some spots but left most of it. He could even feel some in his hair and on his face. That would help.

Imitating a limp, Ahnri hobbled down the road. Passing a few farmers, he finally approached one who hadn't seen him sitting at the roadside. The man worked across the field of grain, wielding a scythe as a younger man gathered and tied the stalks behind him. The farmer paused as Ahnri approached.

"Ho, friend," the farmer said.

"Beg pardon, sir," Ahnri said, shifting his accent a bit. "I've been traveling far, bound for the city. Ran out of food yesterday. Could you spare a bite of something? A small coin, perhaps?"

The farmer exchanged a glance with the young man, likely his son, then shook his head. "Wish I could, friend. At the moment we barely have enough to feed ourselves."

Ahnri let his face fall, nodding. "I understand, sir. Of course. Family first." He turned to leave. At this point he expected the man to call him back, offer something small in exchange for work, perhaps. But step by step, no call came. Ahnri shivered, even though sun beat down to warm his back. Maybe farmers weren't the best source of information. Still, he'd dirtied himself up for it, might as well give it one more shot.

He made his way toward another man, who was surrounded by ten or so workers. Some swung scythes, others tied bushels and loaded them into a wagon. This man might be better off than the last, perhaps he would have a gossiping tongue.

Ahnri paused when he came close. "Beg pardon, sir?"

The man in charge looked up from his work. "What do you want?"

Not friendly. "I've been traveling, bound for the city, and I ran out of food yesterday. Could you—"

"No," he said, walking toward Ahnri. He spoke next in a low voice. "And I'll advise you, *friend*, now is not the time for a spy to enter that city."

Ahnri gave his best confused face, but he couldn't help feeling impressed. "I don't know what you mean, sir."

The farmer nodded. "You're good, boy, I'll give you that. If you're really traveling in, be warned: the nobility are up in arms about a fire last night. If you're a spy, you'll have to pay me to find out anything else."

Ahnri's brow furrowed. He pulled a few coins from his pocket and let the fake accent fall. "If you're in the business of information, can you tell me who they suspect?"

"There've been a few names," he said, accepting the money. "All within the Matano family. Marius, Rosaline, Leo. Some suggest Barón Matano himself."

"Why would they risk sabotaging themselves, though? Surely there are other suspects?"

The farmer-who-was-obviously-not-a-farmer shrugged. "Could be. I also heard the foreign girl's name thrown out, the Jewel, but no others. Guards are searching the rubble for any clues. That's all I know."

That was enough. "Thank you, sir. I'll be off."

"Good day, friend," the man said with a hint of sarcasm.

"Good day," Ahnri said without turning back. He made his way back to the city. This time he slipped through with a full cart of a farmer bringing in his harvest. Inside the gate, he turned into the first alleyway he came to and wound through the city once more. He passed a tavern and swiped a cup, then made his way toward the palace gates across from South Arm. His muscles were nearing exhaustion by now; he *had* been extremely injured last night, after all. He took a shaded spot of wall about ten feet to one side of the gate, and crouched into the shadows, hood up. Waiting.

"The Matanos are staying in the palace," a passing woman said.

"That doesn't seem fair to the other houses, does it?"

"What else was the king supposed to do? Send them back to their manor? They can't very well stay at an inn."

"Lady Carina is, she's fine."

"Yes, well. We all know she's made of stronger cloth than most nobles."

Ahnri grinned at that.

He waited another hour there, but gathered nothing. Frustrated, he made his way back to Cait's. It was midday and he'd hardly learned anything new. Were people simply not gossiping, or had he lost his touch?

He shook off as much of the dried mud as he could before entering Cait's, went into Merlin's rooms to change, and then back out to the tavern to grab a drink and some food before he went out again.

"What'll it be?" the bartender asked, tossing their blue hair to one side.

"Strongest thing you've got," Ahnri said.

"That'll be our Jeweled Crusher," they said, reaching under the counter. They poured and spoke. "Just created today, my friend, in honor of Lady Carina, the Jewel of the People. This drink has three layers of alcohol, we've got sweet wine at the bottom, the middle layer is honey milk, and the rum on top," they paused after pouring this, then pulled out a match. "We light on fire."

Ahnri had to laugh. Of course, they'd be pleased Carina

had advanced. He stared at the small drink, a warm orange flame licking the edge.

They pushed it to him. "Blow, then drink all at once, honey."

Ahnri took a breath, blew out the flames, then tipped his head and threw back the drink. It was warm and sweet, but strong. As he swallowed it was like an iron fist to his gut. A wake-up call clearing his head.

He blinked a few times. "*Ya-NA*," he said, then let out his breath in a whistle.

"Told you," the bartender said. "Now wash it down with this, and you'll be fine." They passed him a mug of chilled wine.

Ahnri took a long gulp of the wine, letting it soothe his nerves. He sniffed, shaking his head, then had a thought. "So," he said. "That fire."

The bartender shook their head. "Something's happening in this city, for certain."

"Any rumors on who's behind it all?"

"I hear a lot, you know," they said. "So far this morning I've heard every single name of the final combatants suggested as a possible culprit."

Ahnri swore.

"I know," they said.

They went to help another customer as Ahnri shook his head and sipped the wine. He took a moment to scan the space and blinked at the man two seats down from him. Merlin's eyes were red and puffy, and a blue handkerchief sat crumpled before him. He absentmindedly spun a wooden spoon between his fingers.

Ahnri paused. There were dozens of people around, so he moved closer to Merlin before speaking.

"Is Carina all right?"

Merlin sniffed, wiping his nose with a sleeve. "She's fine, resting up for the ball tonight." His voice rasped like wood on stone.

Ahnri frowned. "Are *you* all right?"

Merlin's mouth twisted into a mocking smile. "Me? Why would you ask that?"

"Because I'm not usually great with emotions," Ahnri admitted. "I can remember facts all day but don't ask me to interpret why someone's crying."

"Fair."

"What's wrong?" Ahnri asked.

"Nothing."

"How are you and Carina?"

Merlin narrowed his eyes. "What do you mean?"

"I don't know, people talk. I thought maybe—"

"No," Merlin said, with finality. "Even if there were. Nothing could ever come of it."

Ahnri frowned. There was a tightness to Merlin's voice, a pain Ahnri might not have noticed if he hadn't gotten to know Merlin the last couple days.

Merlin turned to face Ahnri. "Can I ask you something?"

"Sure," Ahnri said.

"How do people move on from love?" Merlin asked. "I've seen people fall in and out of love so many times, it never seems to bother them."

"I've never really cared about anyone except myself, so—"

"Liar," Merlin shot.

Ahnri glared, the box in the corner of his mind threatening to open. "We are not talking about me. Listen, I see people go about with the ones they love and they're happy. When you're with Carina, you're happy. And so is she, even I can tell that."

Merlin sniffed, shaking his head. "I would only be a distraction to her."

"Or a comfort."

"Let's talk about something else, shall we?" Merlin said, taking a drink.

"You asked." Ahnri leaned on the counter, taking another drink of his wine.

"What about you? Where've you been?" Merlin asked.

Ahnri shrugged. "Around."

"I meant before Medelios. You're full-blood Fugeran, are you not? Yet you live here. What took you away from home?"

Ahnri stiffened, his brows coming together. He liked Merlin well enough, but anyone who knew Ahnri's whole story would be in danger. If Elya or any Fugeran spies ever found Kahn, they would also find Ahnri. He was risking his life staying in Medelios as it was.

And going back…well, he wasn't sure whether that was possible.

No matter how much he wanted it to be.

Ahnri turned his mug of wine, watching the red liquid ripple in the dim light. He shrugged one shoulder. "Nothing, really. I didn't have any family left, needed work."

Merlin stared at him for a moment. "You don't trust me enough to tell the truth?"

Ahnri sighed. "It's not that."

"Then what?" Merlin asked.

Ahnri scanned the room again. They weren't alone, though the bar had emptied quite a bit while they'd talked. The only remaining group sat around a table in the back corner playing cards. Merlin's brow was turned down, whether in worry or anger, Ahnri couldn't tell.

He sighed. "My loyalty to Fugera is true, but my loyalty to the current queen is not."

Merlin waited.

Ahnri continued. "Remember how I said that Fugeran tradition dictates that when one person saves another's life, the saved owes their service to the savior?"

"Yes."

"My parents died when I was three. My adopted father, Damond, was one of the queen's guards. Two months ago, he overheard some things he shouldn't have. He told them to me in confidence, worried he'd be killed for knowing it, and he was right. That same week, he was assigned to a different part of the palace, and he was killed by a group of 'intruders.' 'Murdered in combat,' the queen said."

"Two months?" Merlin stared. "Ahnri, I'm so sorry."

Ahnri shrugged, keeping that box locked tight. "I tried to run, but Elya's guards caught me. seven days in a cell and she offered me a sentence of royal service rather than death. *She* took it to mean she was saving my life, but—"

"A change of sentence is sparing you, not saving you," Merlin said, finishing the sentence.

Ahnri nodded solemnly.

"What was it Damond heard?"

Ahnri let out a breath, steeling himself. "Elya has a new adviser. She's put into her mind a very elaborate plan to take possession of the other Unbroken lands."

Merlin blinked. "All of them?"

"All of them."

"At once?"

"I'm not sure. All Damond told me was that the queen was gathering every Virus in the kingdom to create some kind of elite force. That's why I worried so much when I watched you kill that man at the Baezonas."

Merlin's face grew dark at this. "An army of Viruses would be devastating."

"They're pretty rare, though. When I left, she'd only managed to find three or four."

"Still," Merlin said. "Thank you for telling me this, Ahnri. As soon as Carina has some sway, you should have her inform the other monarchs of all this."

"Thank you," Ahnri said. "For believing me."

"You're welcome," Merlin said. "So, Elya wants you under her thumb to keep you from telling anyone about her plans."

"That's my understanding."

"Yet she trusted you enough to send you to spy on Medelios?"

Ahnri shrugged.

"That doesn't seem right."

"You have to understand," Ahnri said. "She trusts in the Fugeran tradition. She thinks I'm unwaveringly loyal to her, and so far, I haven't done anything to show her otherwise. I don't know how long she'll believe that."

"I see." Merlin ran a hand over his face. "Well. We'll have to do something about her before she realizes her mistake."

30
CARINA

Carina tried to rest before the ball but her nerves wouldn't let her. She ended up lying in bed with the diffuser the woodworker, Turner, had given her. Playing over the last few days in her mind.

Finally, as the sun began to set, a couple of Cait's girls came in to help her dress. They curled her hair and pinned back parts, letting the rest cascade over her shoulders. To her face they applied only trace amounts of rouge and kohl. The effort was minimal compared to what her father used to have done to her, and when she turned to the mirror, she gasped.

"My lady?" one of the girls said. "Is it not to your liking?"

"No," she said, "I mean yes, I—" She struggled to find the words. She had been either plain or paraded for so long, she'd never imagined that simpler makeup could make her feel more like *herself*. She let out a breath. "It's lovely, truly. Thank you."

Her dress was a new one Merlin had brought earlier, taking

advantage of the offer from the tailor she'd met at the party the night before. She was hesitant to put it on; it was far too lovely to actually wear. But when she finally did, something stirred in her chest.

Pretty dresses weren't a solution to every problem, but they certainly helped. The garment was both regal and comfortable. The fabric was deep scarlet, and soft against her skin, with flowers of a lighter red shade embroidered starting on the lower left of the skirt, and flowing up over her chest and right shoulder.

The dress fit perfectly, and made her feel taller. The short sleeves were cut and overlaid, allowing her arms full motion. She turned to admire it at every angle she could as Cait's girls gave her a few final touches. Elbow-length black gloves, and a simple silver comb above her right ear that they said was a gift from Mar. Last, she slipped on soft leather boots, a dagger hidden in each.

A knock came, and one of the girls went to open it. Carina turned to see Merlin standing in the doorway. His eyes widened, and his smile lit up. She realized in a moment that it had been some time since he'd worn that smile.

"Carina," he said. "You look radiant."

His voice held an emotion she couldn't interpret, and the way he stared at her sent a flutter through her stomach and chest, and a warmth to her cheeks. His focus was solely on her eyes, as though he truly *saw* her.

All she could think to say was, "Thank you."

The girls excused themselves, and Merlin stepped forward.

He wore a dark suit that matched her dress in its accents. Standing straight and proper as he was, he cut a striking figure.

"I have a gift for you," he said.

"Merlin, you didn't have to—"

"I know. I…here." He held out a small box.

She opened it to reveal a silver chain with a glass rose charm dangling from it. Nearly identical to the one she'd admired in Zanne's shop.

"Merlin," she breathed.

"I asked Zanne to recreate it for you, and she obliged. Hold your hair up?"

She did. The chain was cool against her skin. Merlin's fingers brushed her neck, sending bumps over her arms. The delicate glass rose rested in the hollow of her throat, like a shield against the rest of the world.

Merlin offered her his arm, which she took.

He led her out of the inn, cheers of support following them from the tavern. Carina noticed Ahnri perched on the back of the carriage as they climbed in.

"Merlin, have you spoken to Ahnri?"

"Briefly," he said. "He wasn't able to find much more than he told us this morning, I'm afraid. He's hoping to learn more at the ball."

"Right. Hopefully he does." On instinct, she clutched at her skirts, trying to calm her nerves.

Merlin took her hands in his. "Careful, love. Don't want to wrinkle your gown before we even get to the party."

The palace drive was lit by torches once more, and the

stone steps leading to the entrance were crowded with people. Merlin stepped out first, and helped Carina down. She was surprised again at how easy it was to move in her gown. Merlin waved the driver on and escorted Carina to the entrance.

"You know," he said, "Rumors say there are secret passageways in this palace."

She squared her shoulders and ignored stares from people around them.

"I'm not suggesting we break and enter or anything, but exploring might be fun sometime."

"Merlin."

"Just saying."

The main corridor led to a huge ballroom and even more faces that turned to her and began to whisper. She both wondered what they were saying and wished they would stop. Their expressions, both curious and critical, made her defensive, and without meaning to, she gripped Merlin's arm tighter.

He placed his hand on hers. "Look around."

"I am, they hate me."

"Not all of them," he said. "You're noticing the worst ones because they scare you. And rightly so. You are a threat to them. They will try to bring you down, as enemies always do. Sometimes they succeed, and your light fades, but not this time."

He squeezed her hand.

"Tonight, Carina? You shine."

He stepped aside, letting her arm slide from his as she entered through the archway into the palace's grand ballroom.

"Lady Carina Valio, of Regania."

The servant's voice rang through the hall. As she'd expected, nearly every head turned toward her. A warmth bloomed in her chest, a glow that Merlin's words had given her. She met the eyes of those who stared, which made them turn away in haste. Good. Let them be ashamed. Carina had no reason to be.

She descended the staircase to the ballroom floor and took in the space. A wide dance floor dominated the center, surrounded by circular tables with chairs. The sides of the room were lined with columns which held a second-floor balcony. Above that, the ceiling rose to a dome of stained-glass windows depicting the gods and their powers.

Much like the rest of the palace, it was certainly a sight to see.

"Ah, Lady Carina."

She turned to see Sir Ilian approach with a lovely woman on his arm, his thick frame parting the crowd easily as he moved.

"Lady Carina, my wife, Madame Rian. Rian, this is the young lady I told you of earlier."

Carina curtsied. "It's a pleasure to meet you, ma'am."

Madame Rian curtsied in return. "My husband tells me you had some concerns about our kingdom in your interview?"

Carina's brow arched in surprise. "Well, yes. I witnessed some things while traveling and speaking to citizens that led me to believe—"

"But she's seen the error of her ways, I'm sure," Sir Ilian cut her off. "The king cares a great deal for his people, and has always made sure that each citizen is cared for."

"On the contrary, sir, I see very little evidence of that. I am hoping to gain an audience with him tonight, which I hope will give me some insight."

Madame Rian smiled. "I have also heard rumors of the concerns you raised, Lady Carina. Despite my husband's doubt, I, for one, am glad you've brought them to the king. If people are suffering, I hope relief can be given."

Sir Ilian stiffened, but did not argue with his wife. "Well. We of course wish you luck, Lady Carina. Good evening."

Carina curtsied once more as Ilian swept away, pulling his wife behind him.

"I'm a little worried about him," Merlin muttered, coming up behind her.

Carina faced him. "Why?"

"I'm not sure. He seems to have a blind spot, but it appears his wife does not. It's just odd." He led her to a table on the edge of the dance floor, and helped her sit, then stood behind her.

"Should I be worried?" she asked softly.

"I wouldn't think so, but it never hurts to be careful."

A drink was brought by a palace servant, and Carina sipped carefully. She didn't want to lose her head tonight.

"Lady Carina." Betania Liraste came to their table and sat across from them. Her hair was pulled up in elaborate curls, the front fringe let down slightly to frame cunning eyes.

"Lady Betania," Carina said, frustration already building at the sight of the girl. "Good evening."

"A good evening indeed." She played with a purple stone

hung from a chain around her neck. "Care for a walk?"

Carina smiled sweetly. "Is that what you asked Sir Kemin at the presentation of combatants?" Betania's sneer faltered, and Carina rolled her eyes. "No, thank you. I have no need of a tour."

She scoffed. "You're such a bore." She stood and turned to go, then paused. She made her way around the table and stood on her toes to whisper in Merlin's ear. "And how are you, handsome?"

Merlin stared straight ahead, not reacting. Carina clenched her fists.

Betania clicked her tongue disapprovingly. "After my kiss I get nothing from you? Not even a name?"

Carina stood, nearly knocking over her chair. "Leave us."

Betania raised a brow, a laugh bubbling through her perfectly painted lips. "My my, you do have a short temper, don't you. Maybe those rumors are true, then? That *you* started the fire?"

"I did not."

"Defensive too, as usual. Hmm." Betania licked her lips. "Enjoy your evening."

As Betania left, Carina's eyes widened. She turned to Merlin. "You kissed her?"

"Are you all right?"

"Answer the question, Merlin."

He grimaced. "I didn't kiss her, she kissed me."

"*What*?"

A few people nearby turned at her outburst.

Merlin leaned closer to her. "During your test she tried to

flirt with me and drag me away. I wouldn't go. Then she…she grabbed my shirt and kissed me. In front of everyone there. That's when I left. Went around the corner to wait for you to finish."

She took a deep breath. Her hands shook. Why was this bothering her? "Why didn't you tell me?"

"I didn't think it was worth telling. I'm playing a lowly servant, there's very little I can do to keep a noblewoman off me without getting beheaded. Not that they're throwing themselves at me—that was a one-time thing."

"And tonight? Now? That wasn't throwing herself at you?"

"Carina."

She turned and sat, taking a gulp of wine.

"Carina," he knelt beside her chair. "Nothing happened. You know I care nothing for her. Please, don't turn this into more than it is."

Why did her chest tighten at that? She straightened her shoulders, clearing her throat. "You're right. It doesn't matter. It was just her trying to get to you, probably ask you to spy on me. You didn't return the kiss, I expect?"

He paused, and when he spoke there was a smile to his voice. "No, I most certainly did not."

She folded her hands in her lap, putting the matter aside. Betania was cruel, openly deceitful, and not worth Carina's time. So, why was her heart racing?

"Ah, there you are," a female voice said.

Merlin stood, taking his place behind her, and Carina turned to see Rosaline approach on the arm of Sir Eron. Eron beamed, crinkled lines appearing at the edges of his eyes. Carina stood and welcomed them both, motioning for them to sit.

Rosaline looked incredible. Not a single burn or scar on her flawless brown skin. A gold chain hung from her neck, its end hidden below her neckline. "Lady Rosaline, it's wonderful to see you feeling better. The king's Cures must be commended."

"Oh" Rosaline said, a blush darkening her cheeks. "I'm only grateful. The king allowed his Cures to use as much magic as necessary to heal me. The only remaining marks I have are…well, let's just say they're not proper to speak of in present company."

Carina pressed her lips together to hide her smile, and Eron gave an uncomfortable laugh.

"I was told your servant assisted me in the chaos," Rosaline added.

"Yes," Carina said. "He tried to help stabilize you before the king's cures arrived."

Eron eyed Merlin. "Your servant is far more gifted than I'd first imagined, Lady Carina."

"He has many talents, it's true."

Rosaline smiled. "Well again, I'm grateful. A servant for a servant, yes? Mine to spar with you, and yours helping me."

"He helped my family as well," Eron added.

"Did he?"

Carina's stomach began to twist at the direction this conversation was going. "Lady Rosaline, does anyone have any idea who might've caused the fire?"

"No," she said, her shoulders seeming to wilt. "And I'm

worried. I heard about the explosion that nearly got you, and then someone attacked Sir Kemin, now this? Who could be after so many of us?"

They exchanged frowns, and Carina worried when none of them had any suggestions.

"Enough talk of misery," Eron said, waving a hand. "Tonight is a celebration! We should be happy. Lady Rosaline, would you do me the honor of a dance?"

Rosaline nodded with that demure smile and stood, taking Eron's hand. They both bowed briefly to Carina before sweeping through the tables toward the dance floor.

"Carina," Merlin muttered behind her.

"What?"

"Come on." He offered her a hand, and she stood, winding their way through the crowds to a table in the far corner. There, King Jaltér sat speaking to someone.

"I think he's meeting with each of the remaining competitors," Merlin said. "I'll check." He stepped toward the table and spoke to the king's servants.

In a few moments the king's visitor was leaving, and Carina recognized Sir Marius, Rosaline's cousin.

He came close as he passed, stopped and leaned down to whisper in her ear, "Good evening, Lady Carina. Save me a dance?" Her face warmed as he pulled back and winked at her before moving on. After a moment, the king waved for her to join him.

She approached, curtseying before she sat.

"Yes, yes, proper etiquette and all, sit down," the king said, waving a hand.

Carina's eyes widened at this, but she did as told.

The king's face was drawn, as though something weighed him down. He didn't speak for a time, only ate his food and drank his wine, making sure Carina had some as well. Finally, he turned to her.

"I was quite impressed with your test yesterday," he said. "I admit some of the advisers did not want to put you through, but thankfully there was a majority in your favor and I was among them."

Carina blinked. Was he giving this kind of information to every combatant? "Thank you, your majesty."

"I'm told you have questions for me?"

"I do, sire."

He waved his fork. "Out with it, then."

She eyed him carefully. He was old, but he didn't seem frail. His eyes were sharp, but his hands shook as he ate. The first question was one she hadn't planned, but it fell from her lips with ease. "Why is magic illegal, sire?"

His grey brow raised, thoughtful. "That is a very good question," he said, "and one that is not often taught along with the law. Two centuries ago, a group of Viruses came together to fight against the throne here in Medelios. They killed many, particularly of the nobility. It was a struggle for our ungifted soldiers to defeat them, when they might die at a single touch. After much effort, we won. The queen, my great, great, great grandmother, created the law that all magic must be directed by royal rule, for the good and safety of everyone. Do you believe that to be a bad thing?"

Carina's chest tightened at the thought of so many deaths. "Not in theory, sir," she said. "But I do believe that the execution of this law has perhaps become more of a hindrance than a help."

He nodded slowly, poking a bit of potato with his fork. "Self-examination is always a good thing. You're probably right. Did you have any other questions? That can't have been the only one."

"You are quite perceptive, sir," she said. "I hesitate because my questions might be misinterpreted as offensive, though I do not mean them so."

"I was at your test, young lady," he said, a knowing smile on his lips. "I promise not to take them so."

She leaned forward, an odd eagerness filling her. "Why is there so much richness here in the palace, in the city, yet your people starve in the country?"

He met her gaze once more. "I am grateful you brought this up in your test, though my advisers are not. All day yesterday and today I've been ordering them to send missives out to the farthest settlements of Medelios simply to learn the truth. If things are as bad as you say, then we have a lot of work to do.

"You say my people are starving, that I could use my personal resources to help them, and you are certainly right. I could sell these things to other kingdoms, examine our trade and economy more closely, perhaps cut corners in places enough to allow the common folk to keep more of what they produce."

"Are there ways to find out where everything is going?"

"Certainly," he said. "At least there should be. Used to be I mean. The record keeping might need to be enforced again. And even then, it would take some work. But it is possible."

"Am I to understand then that you simply didn't know your people are suffering? That the lines of communication truly were broken?"

"That seems to be the case," he said. "My advisers I trust, but the nobility can be fickle. There was a time when altering reports was considered dishonorable, but in the time since my dear Eva died…" he paused, his breath catching.

On instinct, Carina put her hand on his.

He took hold, his grip trembling. "It's been difficult," he said, "to do everything required of me, when my heart aches with loss."

"I'm so sorry."

He squeezed her hand, and met her eyes. "Lady Carina, do you know who your enemies are?"

Her throat tightened. She did not, but she was too afraid to admit it.

"Keep close to those you trust," he whispered. Then raised his voice in farewell. "It was lovely to meet you, Lady Carina. I wish you the best of luck in the tournament. Good evening."

"Good evening," she said, standing. In an instant, Merlin was at her side, and escorted her away.

"Did you hear all of that?"

"I did," Merlin said. "At least he's not as incapable as we feared."

"No," she said. "Just heartbroken and lied to." A pang of sympathy struck her again, and she mourned for the old king. No one deserved to lose the one they loved.

31
AHNRI

Ahnri stood in a corridor off one side of the ballroom. He wore a fine dark suit, the same as every other palace servant. He'd taken a moment to rub ash through his short white hair to make it grey. He didn't like it, but it worked well enough.

He'd been moving around the room taking plates or drinks from the nobility in exchange for a snatch of conversation. All he'd managed to gain so far were rumors about Carina which he knew were untrue. She was not at fault for the Matano Hall fire, though many seemed to think so. He watched as Carina and Merlin left the king's table, wondering what information they might've gathered there.

"Evening."

Ahnri spun. ChaNia stood behind him, one thin eyebrow raised.

He shook his head. "Of course, you would recognize me."

"Anyone who actually knows you would recognize you."

She moved to stand beside him.

"How did you get there?" he asked.

"Secret passages, didn't I tell you?"

"That must make eavesdropping quite easy."

"Oh very. Have you gone by your old masters' yet?"

"No. I'm not sure I want to risk it."

"Don't bother. Matano is bragging more than ever and Rosaline is swimming in the glow of it while she manipulates my poor Baezona boy into thinking he has a chance with her."

"Does he not? She seems enthusiastic."

"Too much," ChaNia said. "Rosaline's better than that. She'd never be so crazy over someone she was truly interested in."

"So, it's an act."

ChaNia nodded.

"Why?"

"Who knows. Maybe if you were still in her good graces, you could find out."

Ahnri scoffed. "I was never in her good graces."

"Still," she said, putting a hand on his arm. "I hope you made the right move. Faking your death."

Ahnri stiffened. "Can I trust you to keep your silence on the subject?"

She pursed her lips, giving him a hard stare. "Listen, Ahnri. I consider you a friend. I would never turn you in for no reason, especially not now when Medelios needs every inside spy it can get. If my guess is right, your queen *will* come for you. She will want to be sure you're dead. And I will not be tortured for you.

If a knife finds its way to my throat and the only way out is admitting you're alive, I'm talking."

Ahnri met her gaze. "I appreciate your honesty."

"Always. Just make sure you don't tell me where you end up going after this."

Ahnri watched her go. He hadn't thought about ChaNia, but it seemed obvious now that she'd be one of the few who would recognize him. The other noble house servants had surely seen him in passing, but he was certain none of them would match him to the Matano servant who had died. Only ChaNia was that close to him, and that clever.

He made his way to a table filled with drink trays and took one up, readying to make the rounds once more. A glance at one of the high windows showed him Kahn's silhouette against the starry sky. ChaNia was right—the Fugeran queen would come looking. And when she did, Ahnri would need to make himself invisible.

A few paces away, Baronesa Teneo stood with a few of her nieces and nephews, her drink empty. Ahnri approached.

"—don't think we know, and I'm not about to announce it to them. That boy is trying to con my daughter into an agreement I specifically declined. I'll not have it."

Ahnri silently bowed and offered the tray.

Without breaking her sentence, she set her glass down and took a new one. "The whole lot of them are intolerable. They can't take care of themselves or their estate, and getting anything in writing is absolutely impossible."

Her words died off as Ahnri walked away slowly. She was

obviously speaking of the Baezonas. So, the secret deals hadn't played out, had they? Ahnri couldn't help wondering where Syla Teneo and Diman Baezona might be just then.

He continued around the tables that surrounded the dance floor. At a table in the corner, Barón Velando and Baronesa Liraste sat with their heads together, a few empty dishes in front of them. Without asking, Ahnri quietly began loading them onto his tray.

"—can't be allowed to advance again," Barón Velando said. "I know some are making attempts, but they are being rash. If they cause any more damage—"

"I know," Baronesa Liraste said, coolly. "I've already told Betania to stay away from her. Do you know who started the fire?"

"I think so, but they'd never admit it."

Now that was interesting…but he still hadn't gotten any names. Ahnri was tempted to turn around and hear the rest, but he was already walking back to the servant's station. And he doubted the conversation would continue long. He unloaded his tray full of dishes and wiped the tray off, ready to start again. A few more.

He took glasses from a group of young competitors who gave more of the same rumors he'd been hearing all night. If he wanted more on who was after Carina, he'd have to get to the heads of the houses. Who hadn't he seen yet? Barón Baezona, and Barón Matano. A moment later, he spotted both men only ten feet apart. He took a deep breath. Barón Baezona first.

Barón Baezona stood next to a group of men and ladies

whose drinks were empty. Ahnri picked up a bottle of wine instead, and approached, offering them refills. As he poured, he listened to Barón Baezona.

"—don't think it's right, personally. She's as valid a choice as anyone else."

"I agree," a tall woman said. Ahnri glanced at her, and recognized Barón Velando's sister, Lady Karya. "I think it's unseemly that she's been targeted the way she has."

Baezona, as always, kind and seemingly honest. At least his nephew was showing some initiative by sneaking around with a girl. Ahnri bowed himself away and turned to find Barón Matano. He also needed a refill on wine, so Ahnri approached.

"—certainly. But not fit to rule by any means," Barón Matano said.

Ahnri bowed low, shoulders slumped and his heart pounding in his ears. Without a glance, the Barón held out his glass. Ahnri poured, and listened.

"From what I've seen of her she's got the makings of a solid adviser and little else."

"Do you believe the rumors against her?"

"Rubbish. Whoever is trying to frame her shouldn't bother. She won't win regardless."

Ahnri slipped away and left the wine bottle on a table. He'd heard enough. It seemed that no one actually knew who was working against Carina, and that realization unsettled him. As he set down the wine bottle, he passed by Barón Baezona's group again, muttering softly. Curious, Ahnri slipped behind a pillar and strained to listen.

A younger woman was speaking, her voice weak. "Barón, I came to you because…I am worried."

"What is it, child?" Barón Baezona asked.

The girl stammered. "I'm not sure I should say here."

"Come now," Lady Karya said softly. "We will do what we can to help."

The young woman's voice trembled. "Assassins. Tonight. For Lady Carina. I can't even remember who said it, it startled me so much. I ran away as quickly as I could."

"Oh dear," Barón Baezona said. "She was targeted at our home yesterday as well, so I wouldn't doubt it. I believe we should agree to not speak of this. Without evidence and someone to accuse there is little we can do to help the poor girl."

Ahnri couldn't agree more. In a heartbeat he slipped silently away and out of the ballroom. He had to find Carina and Merlin.

The servants' corridors were dark, and he made his way in and out of the ballroom through them. His heart pounded in his ears. Carina had already suffered three assassination attempts; he wouldn't let them get to her again.

As he reentered a servants' passage, something slammed into the back of his head. He stumbled, pain shooting through him, but he didn't fall, and didn't check to see who had hit him.

He ran.

HOW does his arm bend like this?
I do not understand the ability to move like this!
I would legitimately break my neck

32
CARINA

Carina danced with a few young men, pretending to enjoy herself. All of them were kind, but after a while they began to blur in her mind and she was forced to admit the truth: there was only one person whose company she wanted.

"I need some air," she said, and dragged Merlin out of the ballroom.

Well-groomed gardens sprawled in a courtyard behind the building. A fountain carved from sandstone bubbled in the center. Thick-tiled paths wound through high hedges, walls of vines, and over small streams of water. Hearty winter flowers bloomed in rows along the path, citrus trees growing stout and wide so they had to duck around them. Carina breathed deeply of the fragrant air, letting tension release with each exhalation. Bumps rose on her arms, and she rubbed at them.

"Here," Merlin said. He shrugged out of his coat, and placed it over her shoulders.

"Thank you."

"Was there a reason you wanted to leave the dance?"

She sighed. "So many young men wish to spend time with me. I couldn't keep track of them all."

"Well, you never asked me to dance," Merlin said.

"That probably would have started even more rumors." She laughed, then sighed. "They've all been decent, I just can't bring myself to care about any of them."

Merlin gave a small nod. "Oh, there are many things the heart needs in life. Don't let yourself long for something when your better judgment has already decided against it."

His words made her pause, and in part of her mind she thought there *was* maybe something…but he was right. She wouldn't rush.

She pulled his coat tighter around her, pushing those thoughts away. They stopped on a bridge in the center of the gardens and Carina leaned against the stone rail, staring down into the still water of a pond. There were fish, gold and red, blue and purple, silver and black, flowing between each other. Then her vision shifted, and she noticed Merlin's reflection. He was watching her, something like contentment in his eyes. Then he turned to look out over the garden. A rush of gratitude came over her.

"Thank you, Merlin."

"For what?"

"Everything," she said. "You know you're the only person I really trust, don't you? I can't do this without you. It's a relief to know I have a friend. An adviser to help. When this is all over."

Genuine joy appeared on his face then. "You mean when you're queen."

"Yes, that," she said, letting out a laugh.

"Carina, you are an incredible young woman, and you will make a fantastic queen. I'm grateful to have known you."

"You sound like you're saying goodbye."

"Oh no, not yet. As long as I get the chance to do it, you'll know when I'm saying goodbye."

Her smile fell slightly. "What do you mean, as long as you get the chance?"

"Well, Excalibur will move on. Once you're established, it'll disappear and I'll have to go follow it."

Carina blinked. "Yes, but...you wouldn't just leave without saying goodbye. Would you?"

He gave a humorless laugh. "Well, it's not like I'm given much of a choice. Once it's gone, I follow. It *pulls* me away. I can stall sometimes but—"

"You said—" Her hands began to shake. "—you would stay as long as—"

"As long as I could. Until the sword moves on. I never know when that's going to be."

She took a step back. "You lied to me?"

"What? No, I—"

"Don't," she held up a hand to cut him off, anger boiling up in her chest. "You said you would stay as long as you could, but you conveniently left out the fact that you had no control over how long that would be. You should never have made that promise if you couldn't keep it."

"Carina—"

"Why wouldn't you tell me that?" she said, incredulous. "You knew I was afraid of you leaving, didn't you? Did you think I wouldn't notice when one day you aren't there?"

"You weren't even sure you believed who I was," he said, his voice growing fierce. "I couldn't tell you everything until you did."

"So, you were going to leave me behind and forget about me." It hurt to say it out loud. To admit that her fears would come true. "And why shouldn't you just leave, right? Leaving doesn't hurt you."

"Like hell it doesn't!" His words sliced through the air, and Carina flinched away. Merlin closed his eyes, taking a very forced deep breath. "You think this is easy for me? To pour all of my faith and belief into a person, become their closest friend only to be *forced* away from them?"

Forced...something clicked in her mind with that word. She'd misunderstood. This wasn't his fault, wasn't anything he had control over.

Merlin's voice was low and incensed. "That sword is the bane of my existence. You have no idea how much bitterness a person can harbor for a piece of metal."

Carina's anger suddenly seemed pathetic. How had she never put it together? He never touched the thing, never wanted to be anywhere near it.

"Why am I telling you this?" He spun away, fists pressing his temples. "Hundreds of years and I've never told anyone. No one would ever trust me if they knew how much I hated that—

that ice masquerading as flame."

She didn't understand his metaphor, but the vehemence in his voice made her shudder. She didn't stop him. The emotion in him now made him more human than she'd ever seen.

"You know why I'm rubbish at swordplay?" he continued, spinning to face her. "Because of Excalibur. I know the stupid thing won't harm me; I've tried. But I don't want anything to do with it beyond what I have to do. I take as much time as I can finding the thing because that's the only chance I get to be away from it."

He gripped the rail hard, his shoulders tense. Carina watched with wide eyes as he hung his head, his chest still heaving from the rant. Her heart pounded in her ribs and they stood silent for a time, the only sounds that of the water below, and distant noise from the party.

When Merlin finally spoke, his voice was rough, gravelly. "I'm sorry I didn't tell you. It wasn't on purpose." He turned to her, his expression pained. "It never occurred to me to specify that I had no control over when I go. That's what makes all this so frustrating, you see? I never chose to be this way. I was born like this. Call it fate or gods or the universe, but something connected me to that bloody sword without asking whether I wanted it."

Carina spoke, her voice timid and soft. "That sounds like a miserable existence."

He laughed, a cynical tone.

"Is there any way to break the connection?"

"Do you think I haven't tried?" he said, bitterness coloring every word. "Going my own way is physically impossible. I tried destroying the sword with hundreds of different magics and nothing worked so I stopped even attempting it. And killing myself? Well, you saw how well that works that day with the glassblower's fire. Futile effort, that one."

Carina's heart latched onto his words. "You've tried to kill yourself?"

He ran a hand over his face and sighed. "Yes, but—"

"When?"

"What?"

Carina stepped closer to him. "How?"

"No one wants to hear about that, I should never have said—"

"Merlin." She laid a hand on his arm. "Please."

He stared at her hand in confusion for a moment, then her face. Understanding dawned in his eyes. "You've…"

She nodded, swallowing hard.

"Oh, darling," he murmured, putting his arms around her shoulders.

Carina welcomed his embrace and held him as close as she could. She wrapped her arms around his waist and gripped his shirt to keep her hands from shaking, though that didn't stop the tears that rose unbidden to the surface. Closing her eyes, she pressed her cheek against his chest, savoring his warmth, his heartbeat, reminding herself that he was alive, and so was she. That they were trying to make the world a better place despite everything they'd been through.

"Do you want to talk about it?" he asked.

She sniffed, but didn't pull away. "It was four years ago, I think. Right after the autumn festival at the palace." Her hands gripped his vest, pulling him closer. "You?"

He nodded against her head. "Well, the first time, it was because I'd lost my…friend. My closest friend."

Carina heard what he didn't say. "Your wife."

His arms tightened around her. "Yes. She had been sick, and when I returned from helping someone, I found her dead. I stood in our cottage while it burned down around both of us. There were a few other times, it…I had a number of bad years." He ran a hand down her hair.

Before, remembering had been painful. But this, the sharing with someone who truly understood, felt different. Cathartic. She closed her eyes tight, holding onto him. "I jumped from my bedroom roof."

"How far?"

"Twenty-five feet."

He let out a shaking breath.

"They healed me. Some broken bones, a lot of bruises, and a fractured skull, but I lived."

They stood in silence for a moment. Carina couldn't bring herself to loosen her grip. As though if she did, some spell would break.

"Does it…" she hesitated, tears rising again. "Does it ever get easier?"

His hand rested on the back of her head, the comforting weight of it settling her into him. "It does."

She let out a breath. It didn't feel believable. "How?"

"Well, for me…it took seeing the true beauty of the world. Of lots of worlds, really. The purity of nature, the depth of humanity. Everything from a blooming rosebud to a monsoon storm; the strength of an athlete or the steel of one's character. Being able to sing, and dance, and see the incredible feats that life is capable of, I—" He paused, pulling back to look down at her, and he smiled.

Her breath caught in her throat at the sight. The brightness of it. The joy.

"With every person I meet," he said softly, "every individual I serve, I have to leave them eventually. I've come to accept that, in that sense at least, my life isn't in my own hands. But I know beyond any doubt that with every heartbreak, every loss, something new and miraculous and enchanting is waiting around the next corner." His knuckle traced along her jaw. "Carina. You shine with a light that this world needs. I'm glad you're alive, and I'm grateful to know you."

She couldn't speak. She pressed herself against him, her heart aching inside her as she buried her head against his chest, letting her tears fall onto his coat.

He responded by holding her more tightly. His hands on her back were warm, and her heart pounded a steady rhythm inside her. She'd never been able to speak of this with anyone before. And if she was being honest with herself, she doubted she'd be able to with anyone else.

Then, between two heartbeats, Merlin stepped away. The shock of cold winter air cut into her where his hands and body had been. The fracture that had appeared in her heart the day before seemed to widen.

A second later, a group of young nobles rounded the corner and passed over the bridge. She avoided their gazes, but they ignored Carina and Merlin, heading deeper into the gardens.

Merlin cleared his throat. "We should get you back to the inn. You've got a big day tomorrow."

Carina nodded, not trusting herself to speak.

33
AHNRI

Ahnri's head pounded with the ache from that hit. He ran through the palace halls, out a servant's entrance, and practically dove into the city. He tossed the servant coat as quickly as possible, letting the cold snap him into focus. It sent bumps rising on his skin and gave him even more of a reason to keep moving.

Someone knew. Someone was planning to kill Carina, and they knew Ahnri was working with her. He had to lose them, and warn Carina. He didn't pause. He ducked and jumped, and turned into the first alley he came to. A stack of boxes, a high wall, more running.

He chanced a single glance behind him as he leaped over another wall. He couldn't make out a face, but he could tell they wore all black.

Grime slipped under his hands as he jumped wall after wall. Running footfalls sounded behind him, not too close but still pursuing. He had to lose them, whoever they were. Right turn. Left turn. Up the side of a tavern and down a lodge. Through trash heaps and dog fields. Through every circle of the city. A guard shouted at them to stop. Neither did.

Soon it seemed all of Reinos was awake and watching the chase, as window after window lit up to see what was happening. Ahnri was past them before he was seen. He hoped his follower might be spotted. Whoever they were, people would ask questions. Ahnri ran, his lungs burning, legs pumping. He had to get a good lead and find a place to hide or he'd be too exhausted to keep this up.

Pushing himself faster, Ahnri gritted his teeth and sprinted harder. Behind him, his attacker grunted, and their run sped up as well. If they hadn't already threatened him, he might've been impressed.

They were maybe fifteen strides behind him, and he would have to be fast. He had come back around back toward the center of the city, and took a path leading between Nobility Circle and Merchants Circle. He hardly tracked what he was passing—a tavern, a chapel, a home, an inn. Then he spotted potential safety: a warehouse only thirty feet away stood wide open. Ahnri pushed himself toward it. If he could just—

His pursuer slammed into him. He fell to the ground and skidded across hard dirt, scraping his face. His vision blurred; they stood hovering over him. Something familiar rattled through his mind, before a heel slammed into his face, a gag was shoved into his mouth, and a sack thrown over his head.

34
CARINA

Carina and Merlin made their way through the ballroom without speaking to anyone and continued on until they reached the carriage yard. She followed his lead as they ducked between rows to find Cait's carriage. Making sure the driver was the same one they'd come with, they climbed inside. As the carriage began to move, Carina closed her eyes and took a few calming breaths.

She stared out the window at the dark buildings of Nobility Circle, then closed her eyes, rubbing at her forehead and temples.

"Are you all right?" Merlin asked.

"Just tired, I think," she said.

"There's room to lie down if you'd like?"

She considered this, but something caught her eye outside the window. "Could we visit that chapel?"

Without hesitation, Merlin stood and knocked on the

ceiling, signaling the driver to stop. Then he opened the door and offered his hand.

As Carina stepped out, she looked up at the beautiful building she'd first seen a few days before. This was what Rosaline had suggested she see.

The chapel's exterior walls were decorated with intricate carvings worn down by time and the elements. Approaching, she ran a hand over one, a vine wrapped around a hand that offered fruit. The stone was cool beneath her fingertips. Her heart skipped.

She crept to the front doors and pulled slowly.

The smell of incense—jasmine and fresh water weed—met her as she entered. High windows let in beams of soft moonlight, illuminating the dust in the air and benches on the floor, a single aisle breaking their lines down the center of the room, with an altar at the front.

"Why did you want to come here?" Merlin asked.

"I've never been very religious," she said. "But these spaces always seemed to bring me comfort."

"Is there something troubling you?"

There was, she just wasn't ready to admit it.

At the front of the room, beyond the altar, stood four statues. They were twice her height, portraying the gods. Amplia, Goddess of Life, stood to the far left in flowing robes. Her lips were turned up in a gentle smile, her hair and dress swirled around her full, round body as though she were underwater. Beside her was Sileo, God of Stability. His face was firm with a square jaw and wide shoulders. He stood like the mountains for which his power was attributed.

Next was Fina, Goddess of Death. Fina was small, thin, though stood as firm as Sileo. Her head was covered by a hood, eyes lowered to the floor. Was she sad? Her hands were held before her, together, palms up, as though offering something, but nothing was there. And last, farthest to the right, was Crescere. God of Growth. He was tall, willowy, and smirked with a mischievous air.

"Wow," Merlin said. "Those are impressive."

"Merlin," she whispered, "do you know how people become Vessels?"

"From what I've read, most are born to the powers. If they're not, then becoming a human vessel requires years of study, and then performing an act that mirrors the chosen power.

She let him continue speaking, his voice a comfort. The priests back in Regania had said that the four were partners, despite being so different. That they lived together in Vapris, and the very world and its foundations were created by their closeness and intimacy. Carina watched the statues again, thinking. If she had to follow one, which would she choose?

Merlin had stopped speaking. She turned, and found him watching her.

"Would you like me to wait outside?"

"Yes, please," she said. "A few minutes?"

"I'll be right through the doors," he said, placing a hand on her shoulder, and then it was gone. A moment later the door behind her closed softly.

Carina sat on a bench in the middle of the room. She had been traveling for two years, occasionally praying for relief and never truly finding it. When she left Regania she'd planned to find work and a place to settle down, begin a new, simpler life for herself. Nothing was ever right.

Then, in a moment of desperate panic, she pulled a sword from a stone. Whenever she held Excalibur, she felt strong. Not as though magic flowed from it, but some calm assurance that she could do what was required of her. Until she'd held it, she hadn't realized how uncomfortable her old blade had become.

Then there was Merlin. He could access the powers of the gods themselves, and yet the most powerful things she'd learned from him had nothing to do with magic.

A memory came to her then. One she hadn't realized she'd held onto. Herself, alone in her room, performing a practice dance with her sword before a flickering fire.

She'd done that too many times to count. But more than the setting, she recalled the emotions that had flowed through her in those moments. In that quiet space, where no one could see, she'd let herself believe she was strong. She'd let herself believe she was valuable, and bright, and worthy. Worthy of what? She'd never been able to define.

Now, she knew.

Carina had spent years of her life being told she wasn't good enough, to the point of literally having the lesson beat into her. Now, as she stood and held to the bench in front of her, meeting the eyes of gods, she knew.

She'd wanted to be worthy of love.

It was why she'd let herself be taken in by Damari so quickly, and why she'd pushed everyone away for two years after that. It was why she'd thought that helping others would fill that hole in her heart. And though the service had brough her joy, it hadn't healed her. Maybe she would never fully be rid of that pain, but if she'd learned anything about herself in the last week, it was that she deserved goodness. She deserved love, and life, and safety—as much as anyone she helped.

The statues facing her seemed more familiar now. As though they approved of her conclusion. She sighed, contentment filling her, and turned toward the exit.

A figure stood between her and the doors. Only a few paces away and dressed all in black, their face and head covered except for the eyes. They held a dagger loosely at their side, watching Carina.

She took a step back. "Who are you?"

"Your enemy."

Time seemed to slow as the figure's grip tightened on their short sword and they moved closer. The energy in the chapel shifted, and Carina let her instincts take over.

She leaned backward and to her right, the blade missing her chest by inches as the stranger attacked. Carina bent her knees to let one hand find the ground. Her left hand reached for one of her daggers, and with the other hand took the dark figure by their wrist and swept her leg out, bringing the figure to the floor with a grunt.

Carina bent their wrist backward, eliciting a cry from the figure and making the short sword drop. But the attackers other hand swung up and landed a sharp punch to her jaw, throwing her backward with incredible strength.

Carina landed on her back, her breath leaving her and her dagger flying from her grip. She tried to gulp in air as she struggled to draw her second dagger and stand, but the figure was faster, and swung an elbow at Carina's head.

It was as though a boulder had slammed into her skull. Carina fell onto the cool tiled floor, her palms sliding as she tried to stand.

"I wouldn't get up if I were you," the figure crooned.

"What are you—" Carina was cut off as the figure gripped her hair and pulled her head back so fast something cracked in Carina's neck. Then, before she could scream or struggle, a flask was shoved to her mouth, and sticky sweet liquid poured down her throat.

She tried to spit, to gag, to get away, but tiny amounts sank through to sit like a fire in her stomach. In mere moments, her entire body went limp. Exhaustion made her brain sluggish, though part of her mind screamed against the surrender.

"Finally," the figure said, and dropped her and the flask to the chapel floor.

Carina's head smacked against stone, pain shooting through her. Her body would not move, she couldn't even choose where to turn her vision. Yet she could feel everything.

Her hair was wrenched at again, her form dragged toward the front of the chapel.

Carina's heart pounded in her ears. Her mind scrambled for something she could do to alert Merlin. There was nothing.

She couldn't move, couldn't scream.

"You," the figure said, tossing Carina's body at the foot of the altar, "have gained a following to rival my own. And unfortunately for you, that can't be allowed."

The voice sounded feminine, but low, and through the chaos in her mind she couldn't place it.

"Normally I prefer not to get my hands dirty," they said. "Yet no one I paid could manage to kill you. So. Here we are."

The figure kicked Carina in the ribs and she wished she could curl in on herself. Memories flashed before her eyes. Her father's foot slamming into her stomach. His grip on her arms, throwing her at the wall. She pushed them aside, tried to remain in the present.

The figure in black stepped close to stare down at Carina, and she wished she could see *anything* that might identify them. Tears grew cold on her cheeks, her whole body frozen but her mind clear.

"The interesting thing about this poison," they said, "as I'm sure you've noticed, is that it paralyzes, but does not numb."

Terror filled her. Carina couldn't move, but her heart tightened, her breath quickened.

The figure raised their short sword. They reached out, lifting Carina's own arm, and slashed at the wrist.

Pain. Sharp and hot and stinging, it shot through her body and she wished she could pull away.

"It's not personal," the figure said. "You're simply the biggest threat right now."

The blade slashed again, and pain erupted at her side.

"I'll make it look like you put up a good fight."

Another slash, to her shoulder.

The figure stood, cocking their head to one side as they examined Carina. "One more." And they drove their sword through Carina's leg.

"That should do." They knelt beside Carina, eyes hard and dangerous. "Now, this paralytic is also a poison. It will keep you from moving for a good eight hours, and by then the toxins will have had time to close off your airways and blood flow. So. You stay here, bleed, and imagine all the ways I'll make a better ruler than you, and the pain will take you soon."

The hooded assassin stood and began to make their way toward the statues at the front of the chapel.

Carina still couldn't move. She wanted to close her eyes, pretend she was asleep, but couldn't even manage that. She would die staring at the ceiling of a chapel where she'd finally found peace.

The doors shook, as though someone was trying to enter.

"Carina?"

Merlin.

The figure swore.

Pounding on the doors. "Carina? What's going on?"

Darkness again, Carina's attacker was back, leaning over her.

"CARINA!" Merlin shouted.

A moment later, *CRASH!* A sound of broken wood clattering to the tiled floor.

Eyes narrowed, the dark figure swiped their blade across

Carina's throat, and ran.

Pain burned through her entire body. She could feel hot blood pouring over her skin. She couldn't see it, couldn't attempt to stop it. But she could feel every line as it slipped to the cool stone beneath her. She couldn't move, couldn't scream. Hot tears leaked from her eyes, her whole body ached. She stared into the rafters, wishing she could close her eyes and fall asleep before death took her.

Footsteps ran up the aisle. A moment later, Merlin knelt over her, his face twisted into a grimace of pain. His hand shook as he laid it over Carina's neck and closed his eyes. She could just made out a glowing white light, before darkness took her.

35
CARINA

Warm fingers brushed the skin along Carina's hairline. It tickled a little, but not unpleasantly. A hand rested against her face, then was gone. The mattress shifted beneath her. Part of her mind warned that she could be under attack. Her entire body seemed to be shuddering...humming. A single tone resonating through her very bones.

Then there was the actual sound. A different hum. A song. A voice.

Merlin?

Yes, it was him. This wasn't an attack. She was safe.

Merlin's hand held hers so tightly she wondered if he would ever let go. And then, it occurred to her that she didn't want him to. Her heart ached, and her skin grew warm.

His breath warmed her skin as his lips brushed the inside of her wrist. Her whole body roused at the touch, and her eyes fluttered open. His head was bowed, as if in prayer, and his cheeks were wet with tears.

"Merlin?"

His eyes shot open. "Oh, thank all the gods everywhere. How are you feeling?"

She took inventory of her body, wiggling her toes and flexing her muscles. She felt fine. Wonderful, in fact. Then her gaze truly fell on Merlin and she gasped. He looked terrible. His face was gaunt, the skin around his eyes dark and swollen, and his eyes themselves bloodshot. She spotted the bucket of water his other hand was dipped into.

"Merlin!" she cried, pulling her hand away from him. As soon as she did, the thrumming in her bones went away. "Have you been healing me all night?"

"The duels are today," he said. "*All* of them. You need to be at your best."

She got to her knees to face him. "Not at the expense of your health. Certainly, it didn't take all night to heal my wounds, why would you keep going once they'd finished?"

He waved a hand. "It's just a little sleep, I'll be all right." But his shoulders slumped, betraying the confidence in his voice, and his youthful frame suddenly weighed down by the years she couldn't see. "Never," he said. "Never have I failed to put my charge on their throne." He met her eyes. "And never before have I felt so close to seeing that failure."

"What do you mean?"

He stood and ran a hand over his face. "Assassins are always a threat. But I've never felt so…" his voice trailed off. "I can't fail *you*, Carina."

"Merlin?"

He turned to face her, and when she met his eyes—those stormy, troubled eyes—something snapped inside her. She reached out, took hold of his shirt. Pulling him close, she pressed her lips to his. Her arms wrapped around his neck, and his hands found her waist.

It was as though her entire body let out a sigh. She felt beautiful in his arms, as though she belonged there. As though she were enough, simply by being herself. And as he held her, the desire in her chest deepened. She pressed herself against him. She wanted him to hold her tighter, and tighter, and tighter, and never let her go.

Softly, his mouth parted hers, and she tasted sweet wine on his tongue. Their kiss became a fire, a slow burn, something that could last forever if given the right care. Merlin's hands pressed against her lower back, drawing her ever nearer, and she let out a soft hum of pleasure. She reveled in the heat, the contact; she'd never imagined kissing could feel like this.

But perhaps it was the person you kissed that mattered.

It was some time before they parted. When they did, Carina's heart was thundering in her chest. She clung to Merlin's shirt, staring at the collar—which was loose—and his chest beneath it, wishing with all her heart that they didn't ever have to leave this room.

And yet, that part of her mind she'd tried to block away came back as a slow trickle. Merlin could not stay. She'd known this from the very beginning. She would be robbed of passion as quickly as it had come.

Merlin cleared his throat. "Yes, I'd say you're definitely feeling better."

She let out a giggle, something, she realized, she hadn't done in a long time. Merlin beamed, and for a moment, she let herself believe they could have this.

Then her eye caught on the side table where the glass rose charm Merlin had given her lay.

The charm and chain were covered in blood.

Merlin followed her gaze. "Tell me what happened last night?"

She swallowed, letting the memories flood through her, holding on to him for strength. She told him the contentment she'd received during her time in the chapel, about the dark figure with eyes that bore into her, about the sticky medicinal liquid that made her unable to move but let her still feel everything. Talking through it was surprisingly easy. Like telling a dream, like it wasn't real.

He listened intently as she spoke, letting the story sink in. When she'd finished, he turned to sit beside her on the bed, crossing his arms. "We have very little to go on."

Carina thought for a moment. "Could we ask the king for help?"

Merlin raised a brow. "You'd feel comfortable doing that?"

"I'm not sure. Have you heard of a drink that can make someone unable to move?"

"No. Did it have a bite to it? Like alcohol?"

"No," she thought back. "It was sticky, and sweet. Like orange juice, but less tart."

"Well, we can start there," he said, standing. "Maybe I can find some healers and apothecaries and see if they know of such a thing."

"That's a start."

"Carina?" Merlin stood in front of her, catching her gaze. "Did she do anything to you besides what I healed?"

She shook her head. "Nothing. She only wanted to hurt me, then leave me to die."

Those words, more than any of the others she'd spoken, sent a chill down her spine.

Merlin ran a hand over his face again "She essentially did."

Carina ran her fingers over her throat, meeting only smooth skin. That sense of finality returned to her. "How did you know to come inside?"

"You'd been a while," he said. "I went to open the doors to check on you and found them locked. I knew immediately you wouldn't have done that, so I knocked, and you didn't answer. It only took me a few seconds to get water from the well, give myself some strength, and break in the doors."

She met his eyes. They pierced her soul, like a sword newly sharpened.

"I was nearly too late to save you, Carina," he said.

She took his hand. "You've never once failed to put your charge on their throne, right?"

He closed his eyes, a mix of exhaustion and gratitude in his expression.

"Thank you for being here for me."

"For as long as I can, darling." He stood, going to his door.

"Your first duel is in two hours. You probably still have time to spar with Ahnri, either way you should get ready."

She took a breath to try and focus her energy, then hopped to the floor and bent down to pull Excalibur from beneath her bed. Her hand didn't find the hilt right away, so she leaned her head down farther. And froze.

"Merlin."

"What?"

"Where is Excalibur?"

"*What?*"

Her chest seized. Her breath caught. Fear welled up in her throat.

"It's gone."

"WHAT?" Merlin said.

"It's gone," she said, louder. "It's not here." Anxiety clutched her heart as she forced herself to stand even as Merlin knelt to the floor.

Carina backed against the wall, forcing her lungs to open, to take in air. "Is…did it go?" she asked.

"What?" Merlin asked again.

"I mean," her voice trembled, "do you need to follow it?"

He paused, staring at her, his brows knit. He blinked twice, then said, "No. No, I don't feel the pull. I'm not done here yet. Which means the sword did not *leave*. Someone *took* it."

Carina slid to sit at the base of the wall, her knees pulled tight to her chest. One hand on her head, the other at her neck.

Merlin moved around the room with dizzying force. He checked floorboards, the walls, blankets in the corner, bricks of the fireplace, even inside the fireplace. As he stood, ash covering his hands, his shoulders were tense. Carina sank back into the wall, feeling suddenly weak.

Not good enough.

No. It couldn't be gone. The loss of it hit her like a boulder to her chest.

Never good enough.

Why? Why was her father's voice back? She was *winning*, doing well, and she'd been so confident last night, shouldn't it be going away? She put her hands to the sides of her head and started to mutter to herself in an effort to not hear her father.

"Carina?"

Carina, her father crooned.

"No, no, you can't be here," she said to him. "Go away, get out of my head."

"Carina? Can you hear me?"

I'm your father, child. I'll always be here.

"No, stop this," she screamed, tears cold on her cheeks. "I don't believe you!"

"Carina!"

She opened her eyes. Everything was blurry, but she could see the shape of Merlin right in front of her. He was speaking to her.

"Carina, focus on me," he said. "Breathe with me."

He's going to leave you.

Her panic froze. Merlin would leave. She'd known that all along. Known that he couldn't stay, even if he wanted to. For some reason, the truth of that, and the pain of that loss she'd come to expect, broke through everything. She blinked, feeling Merlin's hands on her shoulders, seeing his eyes staring right back at her.

Her father might remain in her mind, but he had left her *behind*, choosing his selfish plans over his own daughter. Merlin, however, though he would have to leave, would always be there for her.

"Merlin," she whispered, a plea.

He cradled her face in his hands. "Can you hear me?"

She nodded.

"Stay with me. Breathe."

She did. She kept her eyes on his. Cloudy, stormy, steely....

She breathed, and breathed, and breathed, until the air came easier and the pounding in her head eased. With surprisingly little effort, Merlin lifted her and put her back on the bed.

She closed her eyes, trying not to think too hard. "The sword is gone."

"Yes. The sword is gone."

"Why is the sword gone?"

Merlin shook his head. "Someone probably wanted to weaken you? Maybe they thought if you have to use an unfamiliar sword you'll be at a disadvantage?"

"Will I be?"

"No," he said. "No, Excalibur isn't granting you any power you don't already have. And really, no one can hurt it, so I shouldn't be worried, but this hasn't happened before."

That fact hit Carina in the chest. Merlin was how many

hundreds of years old, and he'd never had anyone try to steal Excalibur?

"The duels start in two hours." Merlin stood. "Ahnri should be able to find a sword you can use, or you can use your old one, I suppose."

He went through the door shared by their rooms. And a moment later, into the hallway, his steps quick.

Slowly, fear coiling in her stomach once more, Carina stood and knelt down to check under the bed again.

Her father's sword. She'd nearly forgotten she had it, and something about the sight of it sent an irrational anger boiling inside her.

Footsteps outside. She made her way to the door, peeking out to see Merlin speaking to Cait at the end of the hall.

"—haven't seen him."

Merlin's shoulders were tense. "Right. If you do, let me know." He looked back, worry plain in his eyes.

Carina's heart sank. Ahnri was gone as well.

Part Three

Resolve

36
CARINA

The tournament dueling field was made of loose churned dirt that sunk as Carina stepped onto it. Terrible for footing, especially since she'd been practicing on the hard-packed soil behind Cait's. Just another rock in her road, along with her father's sword that—after practicing with Excalibur all this time—was all wrong in her hand. She found she couldn't hold it for any longer than necessary. Part of her wondered if that was how Merlin viewed Excalibur.

She sat in a small wooden chair on one side of the rectangular field that had once been the obstacle course. Across the field was Luci Velando and her father, with a few servants surrounding them. Carina glanced at her sword, lying for the moment across her lap.

A moment later, Merlin knelt beside her. "How do you feel?"

"Nervous. Panicked. Afraid. Anxious. Petrified. Choose

one. Or all. Probably all."

He put a hand on her knee and squeezed gently. Her eyes closed, she relished the touch. Warmth spread through her, and recognized the power of Stability he gave. Her mind calmed, as though she'd been looking through fog, and now the sky was clear.

It wouldn't last, but it helped.

"Thank you," she said, noticing the section of dirt at her feet that had turned grey.

"You can do this," Merlin said."

"You're going to try to find Ahnri?"

"That's the plan," he said. "Will you be all right while I'm gone?"

She wouldn't say it out loud, the prospect of being parted from him—especially after the chapel—had her shaken. Yet, they had to help Ahnri. She gave a nod. "I'll go straight back to the inn after this."

"Good. Walk with a group if you can, stay around people."

A trumpet sounded from the far end of the field, announcing the arrival of the king's advisers.

"I'll be back as soon as I can," Merlin said. He took her chin between his fingers, meeting her gaze. "Focus. Put all thoughts outside your mind except survival and instinct. You have those in spades."

"But I don't have Excalibur."

"You don't need it. You already know it's named you heir. Have faith in that. All you need to remember is that she wants to hurt you, and you must not let her. Understand?"

"I understand."

Merlin stood and placed a quick kiss on her forehead. After a moment, he rounded the corner of the stands, out of sight.

Sir Ilian stepped onto a small temporary platform in the center of the field, waving to the people both across from and behind where Carina stood. When he spoke, his voice carried. "Good citizens of Medelios, today begins the third and final round of our tournament. Only seven duels stand between us and the winner. I dare say his majesty would be honored to have any of these young people take up his mantle, but only one can be victorious.

"Today's lineup is thus: one duel every half-hour until midday, two more this afternoon, and the final duel at one hour before sunset. First this morning, we see Lady Carina Valio against Lady Luci Velando. Second, Sir Diman Baezona against Lady Syla Teneo. Third, Lady Rosaline Matano against Sir Marius Matano. Fourth, Lady Betania Liraste against Lady Alodie Baezona. The next duels will be announced once we have winners from these four. For now, a round of applause for Lady Carina and Lady Luci!"

The crowd cheered, sending a thrill through Carina's body. She caught sight of Rosaline in the stands across from her, smiling demurely and applauding along with the crowd. Carina took strength from that. She could do this. She had to believe she could.

"The fight will end at first blood drawn," Ilian said. "If our combatants are ready?"

Luci stepped forward, and Carina mirrored her.

"Let the duel begin!"

The crowd exploded, making Carina's ears ring. She stood, taking up the sword she despised, and stepped forward. The loose dirt was awkward beneath her feet, but not as much as the blade in her hand. Luci strode to the center of the field with confidence, where workers were removing the stand. Once it was gone, Carina faced her opponent, and the crowd quieted. Luci raised her sword to her shoulder, and Carina did the same. They shifted to fighting stance.

Deep breaths, she told herself.

The first clash struck like lightning. Carina's sword was up before she thought of lifting it. Luci's eyes were wide, then narrowed. She came again. Carina blocked. Her fear and nerves still shook her. She twisted away, making sure Luci's next attack landed the flat of the blade on Carina's side. She cried out, wanting to grab at the aching skin through her armor, but Luci was coming again. Carina ducked out of the sword's path, backing away.

Her heart raced; her mind reeled. She shook her head. Luci came at her. Carina fell to the ground, dirt slipping beneath her feet. It flew in her face and she coughed, wiping it away. Then Luci's sword was swinging down. Everything went silent, and Carina's focus narrowed in on the blade. On instinct, she rolled to avoid it. Luci's sword stabbed into the dirt. She wouldn't be happy about that. Carina got to her feet and blinked, eying Luci as she stalked forward again.

Finally, Carina went on the offensive, testing Luci's strategies and limits for a moment, before backing off to let Luci attack again. Despite the ache in her side, Carina's mind was clearer now, and she could see Luci's weakness. She was flourishing, spinning away from blows unnecessarily. A plan developed in Carina's mind, but it would take time. Baiting Luci to let her think she was in control.

Carina attacked again, leaving an opening to her armored leg, which Luci took. The armor took most of the blow, but it still hurt. Another bruise. Carina stumbled backward, then gritted her teeth and swung again, leaving another opening. Luci's sword tip grazed Carina's hip, leaving a scratch in the armor there. Carina backed away more, watching Luci's face. The girl spun her sword, confidence pouring off her. Her every move spoke triumph.

One more, Carina thought.

She yelled, throwing herself at Luci. As she did, the flash of sunlight off her blade reminded her which sword she held.

Rage flooded her.

Stupid, idiotic child! her father had said. *Again!*

Luci easily blocked, making Carina spin away, dizzy and sick. As she had suspected though, Luci took the chance and slashed at her back.

Drills and tests, she remembered. *Swordplay, dancing, smiling through numbness. He'd put her through the muck of exhaustion physical and mental and then expected her to perform?*

The leather at her back was thin, and Carina had to twist with the blow to keep it from cutting her skin. She didn't stop the motion, and Luci's flourishing had turned her as well, exposing her back.

How dare you… Carina thought back at her father. *You were wrong…*

She planted her feet and waited for Luci to turn back. With a flick of her wrist, Carina slid the tip of her blade across the back of Luci's sword hand.

Blood began to drip freely before Luci's face registered her shock.

Carina stumbled to one side. She dropped her father's blade as though it burned her, and fell to her knees. Eyes closed, she buried her hands in the loose dirt while she caught her breath.

Her father. He'd made his choice. And it hadn't been her.

She glanced at the sword. It lay there in the dirt, nothing special about it except that it made her remember all the things she'd been trying to forget. Trying to move on from.

She forced herself to stand. The hits she'd taken made her feel like a creaking old wagon. Healers ran from the four corners of the field to see to them both.

Between the bustling healers, Carina caught Luci's gaze and gave a nod of respect. Luci's eyes narrowed before she too gave a nod of her own. Taking up her father's mucking blade, Carina made her way back to the inn, trying to calm her raging heart.

37
AHNRI

Ahnri could not remember his head ever hurting this much. He didn't bother opening his eyes for fear that light that might blind him. But his ears, ever aware of rumors and information, perked up before his mind registered it was hearing anything.

Two people were speaking nearby. A man and a woman. Whoever the woman was, she was angry, and if Ahnri had to guess, she was pacing the floor.

"It's not mucking possible," she said. "I slit her throat myself, she was practically dead already. I thought this sword might've been her vessel, but it doesn't have any power. There's nothing special about it except that I can't even nick the thing." She paused. "That servant of hers was there last night, I'm fairly certain. He got in as I left. I'd be willing to bet he's a Cure. Probably providing her with charged vessels for every event."

The man spoke, and Ahnri recognized his voice: Baron

Matano. "Does she know it was you? If she does, you can't expose her or she'll do the same to you."

"Who's to say she won't anyway?"

"She won't, for the same reasons. If she tells anyone you slit her throat, she'll have to tell them she was healed by illegal magic."

A grunt of frustration. "She shouldn't even know it was me. Besides, you saw her; there were no stitches, no scarring, not a mark. She's cheating."

A scoff. "Don't be so childish. You're a grown woman, Rosaline, and you're cheating far more than anyone else is."

Ahnri sucked in a breath. *Rosaline.*

"She's supposed to be 'perfect' isn't she? The *Jewel of the People*, they call her. What a load of muck."

"You're getting off track."

Rosaline grunted. "I'm going to have to fight this girl today, and if *she* has magic I may not be able to win."

"Why?" Matano said. "Is yours running out?"

Ahnri's eyes shot open. Rosaline was using magic?

"Yes. I used too much trying to follow that eavesdropping Fugeran spy of yours last night. The gem is almost completely drained."

"Will you be able to beat Marius and Betania?"

"Do you even need to ask?" Rosaline said. "They'll be going for a small cut. A mark that shows *precision in ability* and *respect for one's opponent.*"

"But you have no respect for them, I gather?"

"Correct." Rosaline's voice went low, and Ahnri strained to

hear it. "Particularly not Betania. She'll be lucky if she can walk off that field."

Matano sighed. "Your replacement gem should arrive at midday with the nomads—"

"They are never reliable, Father, you know that. They couldn't even poison that witch when she was with Eron. No. If I am to beat her, I either need to find her power and break it, or make certain I get a new gem in time. Preferably both."

"You don't even know if she's using magic to fight. Maybe she's only used it to heal herself, which the king is likely to forgive." He sighed. "I can send a runner to the nomad trails and see how close they are."

"Good," Rosaline said. "That's easier than spying on her. That stupid servant never leaves her side long enough for anything of worth to be done."

"Do you think her magic is related to that sword?"

Ahnri gritted his teeth, staying silent.

"I do. According to rumors she fights like a demon with it. Without it, she should be beatable."

"Luci didn't manage it."

Rosaline ignored that. "I've never heard of a sword that could hold much magic, especially one without a gem. We have to destroy it."

"You've tried, Rosa. Whatever it is, it can't be damaged."

"We haven't tried everything."

There was a *schik* of a blade being pulled from a sheath.

"Tell a runner to send for wood," Rosaline said. "I'm suddenly feeling quite cold."

38
CARINA

Carina couldn't stop checking over her shoulder as she made her way back to Cait's. Her mind kept fabricating horrible scenarios about Merlin and Ahnri. The next duel would begin soon. She knew she ought to watch, get a sense of her opponents' styles, but she couldn't focus.

She shoved her father's blade under the bed and paced her room. She'd already made sure the door between her room and Merlin's was unlocked from her side in case he returned soon, but checked it again. And again. She twisted her hands into knots, rubbing the skin raw between her fingers.

Was Ahnri safe? Was Merlin? Were they even still alive? Was Ahnri captured? She paused, her entire body freezing. What if they were tortured? Ahnri probably had training in such things, but he knew so much. And Merlin, he was strong in so many ways, but he couldn't die. Would they continue cutting him over and over again, letting him heal and be hurt until he cracked?

Flashes of her attack at the chapel filled her mind. The cuts, the tickle of hot blood trailing her skin, leaving her body cold at the foot of the altar….

She shook her head, rubbing at her temples. They would be fine. Of course, they would. They held secrets belonging not only to Carina, but themselves and each other as well. They would be fine. They had to be.

She sat on the trunk at the foot of her bed, letting her face fall into her hands.

"Gods and goddesses, what do I do?"

A knock sounded on her door. Carina stood, hurrying to open it.

Merlin stood in the hallway.

Carina threw her arms around his neck. For a moment he stood frozen, then his hands slid around her waist and pulled her close.

Carina held on, letting her heart slow. He was safe. He was here.

Once she'd assured her heart and mind that he was real, she loosened her grip enough to meet his eyes. "Ahnri?"

"Inside," he said, guiding her into her room. He shut the door behind them. "Well, I'm mostly sure I know where he is, but I don't know how to get him out."

"Where is he?"

"In the palace, as far as I can tell. I don't know where in there, just that he was taken in last night."

Carina frowned. "The king?"

"I don't think so, someone else is behind it." He narrowed his eyes. "You seem anxious, have you had any water since your duel?" he asked.

"No."

"Eaten anything?"

"No."

He sighed, letting his hands fall to intertwine with hers. His expression was dark.

Carina squeezed his hand. "Can you get Ahnri out?"

"Cait saw him talking to another servant the other day, a Somnurian girl in Baezona colors. I need to try to find her and see what she knows."

Carina took a deep breath, letting it out slowly. "I hope he's all right."

"Hey, look at me."

His eyes were so clouded it almost seemed like a real storm reflected in them. Carina couldn't have turned away if she wanted to.

"As long as he's still breathing, I can heal him."

"I know," she said. Then rose onto her toes and gave him a quick kiss.

His pale cheeks turned bright pink, and she had to admit she liked making him blush. He lifted a finger and traced her jaw, sending a shiver through her whole body.

"You know," he said, "I told Ahnri I couldn't let myself get too close to you because I'd be a distraction. He said it was possible I could be a comfort instead."

"He's very wise, you should listen to him."

Merlin's lips thinned in an effort to hold back a smile, then he leaned in to press his mouth to hers again. He was like a fire in midwinter: comforting and perilous and bright. Carina could only hold tightly to the fabric of his shirt as she lost herself in the warmth of his kiss.

How was it possible that only moments before, her mind had been a spinning mass of fear and worry? Now, in his arms, she had confidence that everything would work out.

His hands held her firmly against him, one at her hip and the other buried in her hair. Carina found it difficult to breathe, and for the first time in her life, that breathlessness was enticing.

Merlin pulled away, leaning his forehead against hers, and she closed her eyes. Part of her mind chided her for finding such joy when so much was going wrong. Ahnri was in trouble, she had more duels in a few hours, and they still didn't know where Excalibur was.

But she couldn't bring herself to be anything but grateful.

39
CARINA

Carina and Merlin made it back to the arena in time to hear the results of the second duel, watching for Ahnri's friend while the competition played out. Rosaline had won against her cousin, Marius, and Carina was happy for her. Rosaline accepted the win with poise, and Marius seemed frustrated by his loss.

They stayed to see the match between Diman Baezona and Syla Teneo—Syla won, and Carina was relieved by it—before waiting to watch Betania Liraste against Alodie Baezona. Carina didn't recognize Alodie, but from across the field she appeared competent, warming up with a sparring partner. She was taller than Carina, though shorter and thinner than Betania, who would certainly have the upper hand in strength in this fight.

Unfortunately, that meant Betania was warming up right in front of them.

When she noticed them, Betania approached. "Lady Carina."

Carina stood. "Lady Betania."

"I see you're still *with* your servant," she eyed Merlin, who stood beside Carina, eyeing him up and down. "You sure you don't want a real woman, friend?"

Carina's jaw clenched, anger roiling in her chest. She wanted to hurt Betania for continuing this. The drama, the childish attacks, the jealous jibes. Then Merlin's hand rested on the small of her back as he stood beside her.

"I promise, *lady*," Merlin said to Betania, his voice low, "were I spending my nights in any woman's bed it would most certainly not be yours."

Betania's eyes went wide, fury raging in her gaze. She raised her arm to hit Merlin. "How dare you speak to me—"

Carina caught Betania's wrist.

"Do not. Touch. Him."

Betania's fiery eyes lit upon Carina. "And what if I do?"

"I will break you."

For the first time, Betania flinched away. Pulling her wrist back, she swore, and turned to stalk back onto the field.

Carina's hands formed fists, wishing for something to hit. Merlin gently touched her arm, guiding her to sit. "She's only trying to provoke you."

"It's working," Carina said through her teeth.

She took deep breaths, calming herself. Betania's antagonizing had struck a chord. In such a short time, Carina had grown closer to Merlin than she ever had to anyone. He took care of her; he was her friend and her mentor—and more—all in one. His arm tightened comfortably around her waist as they turned their attention to the field.

The fight began as Betania swung her sword and Alodie blocked. Carina watched, wishing selfishly that Betania would be very *very* hurt by the end of the fight.

"Lady Carina?"

Merlin's body tensed as they both turned to see a girl with red hair and freckle stripes sitting behind them, wearing Baezona colors.

Merlin turned around fully, meeting her gaze. "You're Ahnri's friend?"

"Friend, associate, acquaintance. Call me ChaNia. You want to help me help him?"

The crowd rose to their feet, cheering louder with every block, every parry. Alodie was sweating, but far from giving up as she went in for another round of attacks.

"Yes" Merlin said. "Do you know where he is?"

"Mostly. I know the section of the palace he was brought to; I just need to narrow down the room."

In the space of a breath, Betania took full advantage of an opening. Alodie spun, nearly losing her balance, and Betania's sword slashed, cutting into Alodie's shoulder, just below the pauldron. She clutched at the bleeding cut and fell to her knees.

Merlin leaned closer. "I take it you already have a plan?"

Cures took to the field. Betania was breathing heavily, strands of red and black hair had come loose from her braid and were sticking to her skin.

"Meet me at the southwest corner of the arena in two hours," ChaNia said. "I'll get him out. I don't know who has him, but I'm worried he's going to be hurt."

The crowd burst into applause. In parts of the stands they stood, stomping their feet, while other sections only applauded, seeming uncertain.

"No one captures a spy and doesn't interrogate them." Merlin agreed to meet, then ChaNia stood and made her way through the crowd.

On the field, Betania straightened, finally turning to the crowd and waving to her supporters. Carina met her eye, and there was only hatred in Betania's gaze.

40
AHNRI

Ahnri sucked in a breath, pain coursing through his body. His head ached and his arms were rubbed raw from ropes tying him to a chair, and the pain. The pain of a red-hot iron being pressed against his skin.

Ahnri gritted his teeth to avoid screaming, as he'd been trained. If he screamed, he was likely to bite his own tongue off by accident or give away information. And he held a great deal of information he shouldn't reveal.

"You know," Rosaline crooned. "Everyone thought you died."

Ahnri glared at her, swallowing his retort and catching his breath while she wasn't burning him. *Do not speak*, he told himself. *Remain silent. Your life and your friends' lives depend on your silence.*

"A heroic death, really," she said, moving to circle him. "You saved my life, then lost your own. No one questioned your bravery or your end. It makes me sad to know you didn't truly die for me."

Ahnri wanted to spit at her. Instead, he took in his surroundings, now that he could see a bit more than before. The room they were in was dark, with a single window high in the ceiling. In that small frame, he thought he made out the shape of a bird, spreading its wings and leaping off into the midday sky.

Please let that be Kahn.

But there was a window. He wasn't in a dungeon, then. The room was warm with the glow of a fire, and richly decorated aside from the wooden chair in which he sat. Carpets lined the floor, and the walls were covered in paintings of landscapes Ahnri didn't recognize.

"Do you know why I brought you here, servant?"

Ahnri rolled his eyes. At least she didn't remember his name. He didn't answer.

"I brought you here because," her voice spoke right into his ear, her breath tickling his hair. "I saw you learn about the rumored attack on Lady Carina."

Was she trying to seduce him? Well. Good luck with that.

"You seemed fairly excited to learn about that. Are you working for her now? Were you going to warn her?"

Ahnri clenched his teeth.

"Still nothing?" Rosaline tsked. "Shame. Back to the heat, then."

The rod seared into Ahnri's flesh again. All thought left his mind as heat and agony rippled through his body. When the heat left his skin, it still burned, aching and itching beyond where the metal had touched.

He sucked in air and wondered if he could find a way to make himself faint. If he was unconscious, she wouldn't waste time torturing him, and he wouldn't have to deal with the pain. But he also wouldn't get any information that way. Maybe…

After a few breaths, he said, "What do you want?"

"Ah!" Rosaline said. "Are we finally making an impression?"

Ahnri gave her a flat stare.

She crossed her arms. "I want to know if you're working for Carina. Still sparring and training her? Do you know how she won her duel without her stupid unbreakable sword?"

Between gritted teeth, Ahnri said, "I will answer one question. In exchange for you to do the same." He twisted in his seat, trying to ease the pain of his burns. They would already be cauterized, so at least he wasn't losing blood. But the pain…

"You really have no room to be making demands," Rosaline said.

Pressure. Heat. Blinding pain. It was gone again in a moment, leaving behind that stretching, itching, burn. It seemed she was happy making small marks that would irritate him for days on end.

Rosaline set the poker back into the fireplace and removed the glove she wore. Going to a side table, she poured herself a drink and took a sip.

After a moment, she turned back to face Ahnri with a pout to her lips. "Out of curiosity, I will agree with your little compromise. What is your question?"

Ahnri's body was shaking now. He was about to go into shock. "Where…is…the sword?"

"Right here, of course." She motioned to a corner of the room where Excalibur leaned against the wall, snug in its sheath.

Ahnri closed his eyes. She would move it, now that he'd asked. Wherever he was, that sword wouldn't be here for long.

"Now my turn," Rosaline said. "Who are you working for?"

Ahnri lifted his chin. "Lady Carina Valio."

41
CARINA

One hour until Carina had to duel Syla Teneo. Until Merlin had to meet with ChaNia to get Ahnri out of trouble. After that, Rosaline and Betania would duel. And the winner of that match would, an hour before sunset, fight against either Syla or Carina.

She sat on her bed with a tray on her lap, pushing a berry around her plate with the tip of her finger. She was so close. So close to winning, to having the authority to make change, to help, to protect.

It felt wrong to sit in the silence of her room.

"Carina?" Merlin came through the door they shared and lowered himself onto the bed beside her. "Are you all right, love?"

She smiled at the concern in his voice. "Just nerves, I think."

"Understandable," he said, taking her hand. "Rosaline and

Eron have come to visit with you. Are you feeling up to it?"

Something twisted in the pit of her stomach. She knew Rosaline and Eron, there was no reason to be nervous. But again—she was unsettled. How could she have tea when so much was happening?

Rosaline and Eron were sitting close to each other on one of the sofas of Cait's sitting room. They both looked up when Carina entered, Eron's eyes lighting up at the sight of her. Rosaline curtseyed demurely.

"So good to see you, Lady Carina," Rosaline said sweetly.

"And you, Lady Rosaline," Carina said. "And Sir Eron."

She curtseyed to them both, then turned to sit opposite them. Cait's girls and Merlin brought in trays set with tea, and a plate of sunsetberry jam pastries drizzled with honey. Carina thanked the girl and waited for Merlin to pour her a cup of the warm tea.

He handed one to each of them, then leaned over to speak softly in Carina's ear. "ChaNia is outside, I'll be right back."

She tried to keep her face impassive. "Yes, please see to it."

His eyes were hard as steel, and he carefully squeezed her hand out of sight of the others, before he left the room, though he left the door wide open behind him.

Eron was already drinking his tea, but Rosaline stared at Carina. Blowing on her tea to help it cool, Carina took a sip. Rosaline's expression eased, and she took a drink as well.

Carina frowned. "How are you feeling about the tournament, Lady Rosaline?"

Rosaline's lips lifted in a sharp smile. "Quite confident.

And you?"

"Nervous, I admit," Carina said. Thoughts of Ahnri and Excalibur tumbled through her mind. "I am rather afraid of the prospect of possibly dueling you, Lady Rosaline."

"As you should be," Rosaline said, laughing softly.

Something in her laugh made Carina pause. She took another drink. The warmth ran through her body, refocusing her.

At that moment, Merlin reentered the room. He walked behind the sofa where Rosaline and Eron sat. When he was immediately behind them, he met Carina's eyes, and ran his thumb across his throat, then pointed to Rosaline.

Carina's blood ran cold.

Rosaline?

Rosaline?

It wasn't possible. Carina forced herself to smile. She'd had plenty of practice at that, thanks to her father. She could hide her shock. She had to.

She tried to focus, listening as Eron continued speaking, his eyes as bright as ever.

"Can you believe how far the two of you have come?" he said. "I don't mean you're unworthy of it, of course. You're both the finest women in Medelios. But that you were close friends from the first elimination."

She forced herself to remain calm. "Yes," she said, watching Rosaline. "You were very kind when Betania tried to embarrass me. I greatly appreciated it."

Rosaline appeared no different than before, but now,

Carina found smugness behind the demure expression. "Well, I couldn't have her poisoning your mind to think all Medelians are like her. Some are kinder, others far more cunning."

Carina froze. Fear gripped her and she couldn't speak. How had she missed this? How had she not seen it?

We must be ruthless…

Merlin cleared his throat.

Carina blinked. "Indeed, you've shown me well."

Eron laughed. "Ladies I hope you know how much I respect both of you," he said, setting down his tea and leaning forward. "Carina, there is a reason we came to you today. You see," he took Rosaline's free hand in his. "I have asked Rosaline to be my wife, and she has accepted."

Carina's composure cracked. Her jaw dropped, her mouth forming an "o" of shock. Fighting herself, she regained composure and pasted on a smile. Her hand holding the tea began to tremble, so she set it down, folding her hands in her lap. Eron turned to Rosaline, whose expression was one of calm contentment.

"Since we consider you a dear friend," Eron went on, "we wanted to tell you first. We plan to announce it tomorrow, regardless of the outcome of the tournament. Of course, I wish you both the best of luck. You're both so talented I don't think I'd be able to predict the outcome if I tried."

And yet, it seemed he was making his prediction by this gesture, wasn't he? His parents wanted the throne as much as anyone. They would've encouraged this.

And now, Carina knew the truth. Rosaline had tried to kill

her. Had very nearly succeeded, and now here she sat, leering like she'd already won. Rage boiled up in Carina's chest at the sight of this young woman, someone she had trusted from the beginning.

She took a breath and spoke the first thing that came to her. "How wonderful for you both. You're a very lucky pair to have found someone who cares so deeply for you."

At her own words, Carina's thoughts turned to Merlin.

Her mind was spinning.

Stronger, child. Faster!

She stood, and they followed. "I apologize. My time is quite limited today. I hope you'll forgive my abruptness, but I must be going."

"We should probably be going as well," Rosaline said. "We have an appointment with Eron's parents and, obviously, I have a duel in an hour and a half."

"Of course," Carina said. "I won't keep you any longer. Again, congratulations to you both." She curtseyed once more as they moved to leave, though Rosaline paused at the doorway.

"Go on, love, I'll just be a moment."

Eron made his way out, and Rosaline turned to eye Carina.

"We both know how this will end," Rosaline said softly.

What is the point of having a daughter so weak…

Carina gritted her teeth. "You're wrong."

The prim mask fell, and for the first time, Carina recognized the eyes that had stared down at her in the dark chapel.

"I'm not," Rosaline said. "You will throw the match, and I

will win. If you don't, there's no telling what will happen to dear Eron, not to mention that scum of a servant I have locked up."

Carina tried to keep her emotions from showing—the anger, the fear for the lives of her friends, the frustration—but certainly some of it leaked out in the tightness of her eyes and the tension in her jaw.

Rosaline's smile returned. "Good luck, Lady Carina."

42
AHNRI

Ahnri rested his chin on his chest, trying to breathe through the pain lacing his body. Rosaline had given up on torturing him and he'd tried to sleep while she'd been gone. He was mostly asleep now, but his ears made out a sound. A door opened in a nearby chamber. Ahnri held very still.

"You've cut it close," a man hissed. Barón Matano.

"It's your own fault for getting such a small one to begin with." That was Rosaline.

A door opened, flooding Ahnri with light. He held completely still.

"Still unconscious," Rosaline said, disappointed. She stepped away, leaving the door wide open.

"You really think you'll get anything out of him?" Barón Matano said. "I paid good money for him. He's the best spy we've ever had, I'm sure he knows how to hold up under pressure."

"Pressure, maybe," Rosaline said. "Not pain. Has it arrived?"

"I'm not sure I should tell you either way. Why not keep it for myself to use when you inevitably start a civil war in our kingdom because of your stupidity?"

"There will not be a civil war, father. You are overreacting."

"And you are too close to the situation to realize what you've—"

"*I* am going to be *queen*. And you will support me so that I can give you what you've been asking the king for for so long."

Silence. Ahnri carefully opened his eye a crack to see Rosaline standing before her father looking fierce.

Matano broke. "Fine. If you hadn't been so flamboyant, you'd have plenty left in the first one. I told you from the beginning to be careful with it."

"And I told you that I would use as much as I needed to win."

"You wasted it."

"What I did was necessary to keep my secrets safe, father."

"Secrets you've kept even from me."

"Yes."

Heavy footsteps retreated, and a door opened and closed. Ahnri peeked once more to see Rosaline standing before a mirror. Another door opened, and a voice spoke.

"You called for me, my lady?" A servant girl with a kerchief over her hair, her back to him.

"Yes, do you have a report on the attempts to damage that sword?"

Ahnri stiffened.

"Still nothing, my lady." Then, the distinct sound of metal grazing a sheath. The servant held Excalibur before her for Rosaline to examine.

"No amount of heat will soften it," the girl went on, "and nothing we've hit it with has had any affect at all. A blacksmith's anvil, horses, blocks of stone the size of me—nothing even leaves a scratch."

"Hmm. Where could Carina have found a sword like that?"

A knock sounded, and Ahnri heard the sword slide home, then soft muttering before the servant spoke again.

"The king wishes to see you, my lady."

"Of course. One moment. Take that blade, keep trying to break it. There has to be something."

"Yes, my lady."

Ahnri's door shut, and a lock clicked, sealing the darkness.

He vaguely made out them leaving, his thoughts focused on the sword. About getting it back to Carina. And Rosaline now had a new vessel from which to draw strength. Would Carina even stand a chance?

43
CARINA

Carina's cloak, though heavy and warm against the winter air, did nothing to ease her fear. She peeked to her side, catching a glance of Merlin as they walked to the tournament field. He was wary, searching, watching for potential threats. His eyes were still bloodshot, dark circles coloring the skin beneath.

It broke her heart to see him so tired, especially knowing it was because of her. On an impulse, she reached out and took his hand, squeezing lightly. "Thank you."

"For what?"

"Everything."

He smiled, though there was a sadness behind his eyes. Still, he held on, and gave her hand three quick squeezes in a row.

When they arrived at the dueling grounds, Carina removed her cloak and took her father's sword through a practice dance. She'd done this nearly every night for years, with this very blade.

It had become a ritual almost, and she remembered feeling calm, strong, and safe.

Why then, did this sword now bring back memories that hurt?

It's only a sword, she told herself. *So is Excalibur. They're just swords, and you know how to use a sword.*

The fact was, she had to think more intentionally when using this blade, and not only because Excalibur always felt more right. She couldn't focus on instinct alone because this sword unearthed memories of her father.

Merlin stood. Carina followed his gaze to see the Somnurian girl, ChaNia, waiting at the corner of the stands nearby.

"It's time," Merlin said.

To get Ahnri out. Rosaline would, they hoped, be here to watch Carina duel. Leaving her rooms in the palace unsupervised.

"Be careful."

"I will. Beat her," he said, pointing to Syla. He placed a quick kiss on the inside of her wrist before he disappeared behind the stands, following ChaNia.

When the stands began to fill, Carina set down the sword—hoping to forget she was using it--and donned her cloak again for warmth. She sat in her seat, watching from beneath her hood as people she didn't know bet on her life and fighting abilities.

Her back stiffened at the sight of Rosaline in the stands across from her. The girl smiled that same smile Carina had so often thought genuine. Carina raised her head and met the gaze, determined to be undaunted despite the anger and fear that warred inside her. At least Rosaline was here, and not in her rooms.

With the start time close, Carina took up her sword again and did away with the cloak, her bones humming in anticipation. Across the field, Lady Syla sparred with her mother, and Carina took a moment to observe. She had seen Syla's first duel, and so had a rough idea of what to expect from the girl. Only a few moments passed before a fanfare sounded and the advisers took to the field.

Sir Ilian was there, speaking to the other advisers around him. He caught Carina's eyes from across the field, and his shoulders grew tense.

Certainly, he wasn't still concerned about her?

Illian spoke with another adviser, who made their way to the center of the field and began to introduce Carina and Syla, while Sir Ilian spoke with Syla and her mother. Syla's eyes narrowed as he finished. The announcer completed his intro.

Syla strode forward. Carina took a deep breath, and stepped onto the field.

Syla's dark eyes were intense as she approached Carina. Her hair was black and streaked with gold, cut short, framing a lovely face of perfect copper skin and sharp features. Carina stopped near the center of the field and raised her sword hilt to her shoulder. Syla did the same, and they both readied themselves.

Syla struck first. Determination flashed in her eyes before

she moved and Carina was lucky enough to catch it. She raised her blade in time to block, and Syla gave a grunt as she shoved Carina's sword away. The blade nearly knocked from her grip.

Not good enough! her father shouted.

Carina shook herself. They separated and began to circle, Carina's heart beating faster every moment. Then, Syla came at her with a series of forms Carina didn't recognize. It was all she could do to ward them off, narrowly avoiding strikes to her abdomen, legs, and throat.

Faster, you stupid—

Carina…breathe…

Her breath burned in her lungs. How long had they been fighting? Syla's strikes began to slacken, and Carina put all the energy she could into a swing toward Syla's feet. The girl stumbled and fell to the ground, but her sword was quickly up to block Carina's next attack. Syla leaned back on one hand and with a grunt, shoved Carina's sword away. Carina backed off, careful not to lose her footing the same way. Before she'd set her feet, Syla was up again.

Syla did not pause. Carina retreated with each attack, trying to find a weakness, some opening she could exploit. There was none. Syla was relentless. Carina knew, if she stepped outside the huge field, she would forfeit the duel. Without losing eye contact with Syla, Carina tried to guess how close the edge was, based on her position on the field. If she was right, it was coming up fast. She had to circle somehow, get on the other side of Syla if she stood any chance at all.

Stay with me…

Carina gritted her teeth, readying herself to move. As Syla drove her blade in a thrust to Carina's stomach, Carina turned sideways and dropped the tip of her sword, deflecting Syla's. Syla's momentum threw her forward and Carina spun, ending up behind her opponent.

Carina had a split-second to set her feet before Syla whirled and kept advancing. The girl was strong, fast, and showed no mercy. Carina dodged a strike and knew she had to end this fight quickly, on her terms, or she would be overpowered.

Carina retreated with each attack to the center of the field—she wanted this to be as visible as possible so no one could claim she cheated. She tried to fight back, but Syla gave no openings. Then Syla let down a strike from above with so much force Carina fell to the ground.

She still had her sword, the mucking sword that kept distracting her, but somehow the memories were held at bay for the moment. She raised it, but Syla did not hesitate, thrusting her blade toward Carina's chest. Carina let out a cry of frustration. Angling her sword sideways, she caused Syla's blade to slide down and past Carina, striking the dirt above her shoulder. She rolled, and as Syla's blade raised for another blow, Carina flicked the tip of her sword at the inside of Syla's forearm.

Syla dropped her sword and staggered back as a line of blood trickled down her hand to drip in the dirt. Carina shuffled away, out of striking range, just in case. Healers ran toward them, but Carina knew it wasn't a bad wound. She wouldn't even have a scar.

Carina met the girl's eyes, full of frustration and confusion. The healers were done wrapping her arm, and were trying to ask questions. Syla shoved them away and stepped to Carina.

"You could have killed me," she hissed.

"As could you have," Carina replied.

A cold laugh. "I tried," Syla said. She paused. "My uncle says you're bad for Medelios. Says you don't trust the king and can't be trusted yourself."

Carina nearly rolled her eyes, but refrained. "I didn't trust the king at first. Your uncle took that to mean I meant ill for the kingdom, but that couldn't be further from the truth. I only want to help."

Syla searched Carina's face for a moment, then gave a short bow. "You're a good fighter. Strategic and smart. I wish you luck."

As she walked away, Carina's eyes flicked over the crowd, unconsciously searching for Merlin. Instead, her gaze settled on a different face. Rosaline stared, expression set, void of emotion, before turning and hurrying out of the stands.

44
AHNRI

Pain lanced through Ahnri's side, fully waking him. He wasn't being prodded right now, but the pain. The pain was still there.

He pushed the thoughts aside and looked up to the high window in the wall before him. Bright sunlight. Was it still the same day? He had no idea how long he'd been asleep. Or unconscious. Same thing.

He was on the floor now—no chair—and crumpled in a heap. Though he was alone. He searched as much of the room as he could see from his vantage point with his hands tied behind him and his ankles bound. His injuries kept him from moving much. Certain the sword was not in this room, he focused on his breathing and tried to awaken his senses now, before someone came to check on him.

He took a number of deep breaths, suffering as the burned skin on his chest and torso stretched. The air helped clear his mind. His hands were tied behind him, but they, at least, were free of injury.

He tugged at his bindings for the millionth time, and still had no success. He sighed, letting his head fall to the floor—carpeted, but damp with his own sweat. Sweat made him think of the Fugeran sun, and Remi's eyes, so like the sky...then of Queen Elya. And that made him think of Damond.

Ahnri usually tried to ignore the fact that the boy he loved was the child of the woman who had murdered his father. Remi was kind, compassionate, if occasionally a little full of himself. But it was always to hide his own insecurities. Elya wanted Remi to be perfect in the same way she'd wanted Damond dead.

The boxes in his mind—Remi, Damond, Isille, the tower city, all of them—cracked with the realization that he might never get a chance to fix any of it. Elya deserved to pay for what she'd done to Damond, and Remi deserved to know the truth about why Ahnri had been gone for so long. Why he'd had to leave the city without so much as saying goodbye.

Just like Damond had been there one morning, and gone the next.

Damond had taught Ahnri many things. The most important of which was to know where your loyalties lie, and stand by them. Ahnri could still remember sitting by the fire as a young boy, hearing stories of Damond's experiences and wishing he could be as brave one day.

So much for that. What good was bravery when Ahnri couldn't even free himself? But loyalty? Ahnri was now loyal to Merlin, and therefore Carina. If he did somehow get out of this,

Merlin could heal him again, making Ahnri even more indebted. He didn't mind. Merlin was good, and smart, and honest. Ahnri would serve him in any way he could.

A grinding sound came from somewhere nearby, followed by a muffled curse. Ahnri blinked. It wasn't from the main room, but sounded as if it came from a wall. Through the pain, he forced himself to sit up.

Part of the wall slid away and someone crawled through. When the girl turned, he recognized ChaNia, her red hair covered with a kerchief.

"Ahnri?"

"Here," he said. It came out more like a croak.

"You need a drink," ChaNia said, approaching him. She unsheathed a dagger and cut his bonds. "Hurry, we don't have long."

Ahnri forced himself up, and lost his balance. Instead, he crawled, following her to the opening in the wall. She shoved him inside, and slid it closed behind them.

The tunnel was cramped, and Ahnri had to pull himself forward on his elbows rather than crawl on hands and knees. He shuffled as fast as he could go with his injuries, ChaNia following behind him. He'd gone twenty feet when his head collided with the wall in front of him.

"ChaNia?"

"Left. There should be another in ten feet or so, go right."

Ahnri crawled, and ChaNia gave him further directions. The tunnel sloped downward in some places, leveled out in others. Ahnri's breath was coming hard now, his arms and injuries aching from movement and pressure. The burns on his body screamed their misery, and Ahnri wanted nothing more than to stop moving, pass out, maybe sleep. But the thrill of being freed ran in his blood, and he channeled that energy to keep him moving. Through the pain, he pressed on, focused on finding each new turn or bend that ChaNia described.

It took an eternity, but he reached a dead end at which ChaNia told him to knock firmly four times, pause, then knock three times. He did. A moment later the wall opened to afternoon sunlight and fresh air, and Ahnri breathed deeply of it. He tumbled from the tunnel onto hard-packed dirt, and rolled once before settling on his back. The ground upset his burns, and a figure stood over him.

"Oh, Ahnri," Merlin said. "Come on, let's get you out of here."

45
CARINA

Carina's head ached. For a moment she wished Merlin were around only to ease the pain behind her eyes. Part of her chided herself for it. Excalibur would leave, and then Merlin, and she'd be left to deal with headaches on her own. Perhaps it was good she started now.

The stands were nearly full when she took her seat. She'd decided to keep her father's sword with her rather than leave it at the inn. Every time she glanced at it, she tried to remember the peace it had once brought her. It was a struggle. The voices and memories in her mind mixed with the chatter surrounding her.

"My money's on Lady Rosaline."

"I've got no money, but I hope it's her too."

Foolish child…

"If Lady Betania takes the throne, I'm moving to Somnuria."

"Why Somnuria? I think I'd prefer Regania. Nice and isolated."

...breathe.

It seemed a great many people were pulling for Rosaline to win. Which made sense when Carina thought about it. To them, Betania was cruel, where Rosaline was a kind-hearted soul. Carina herself had been drawn in as much as anyone. These people didn't know what Rosaline had done, or might do. To them, the Matanos were a noble house that paid their workers—not enough, Carina thought—had no debts, and appeared to be upright.

One of the royal advisers began to introduce the fight. Betania warmed up on their side of the field, looking around in confusion as Rosaline wasn't anywhere. The moment the adviser said Rosaline's name however, she came around the corner of the opposite stands, drawing a sword from its sheath. She walked as though she were about to practice, not fight to blood.

Carina's hands curled into fists, her nails pressing into her palms. The two girls met in the center of the field. They raised hilts to shoulders and took up fighting stances. Carina held her breath.

At the first clash of steel, Carina knew how this fight would end. Betania didn't stand a chance.

Carina tried not to think about the possibility of herself against Rosaline.

The duel did not last long. At twenty seconds, Rosaline's blade cut into the back of Betania's legs, severing the muscles and causing her to crash to the dirt.

As healers ran to stabilize Betania, Rosaline's gaze fell directly on Carina. An expression that said plainly, *you are next.*

Carina's fists tightened, and she wished Merlin was still with her.

Rosaline walked off the field the way she had come. She did not pause to wave at her supporters, nor check on Betania's status. As she turned the corner, she casually sheathed her sword.

Carina turned her attention to Betania. Tears left lines through the dust on her face, and she screamed as the healers put her on a stretcher and lifted her off the ground. The healers released four legs from the sides of the stretcher and set it down as a table, beginning to work immediately rather than remove her from the field as they normally would.

Snow began to fall. Thin flakes that melted as soon as they touched anything. A bucket of water was hastily brought out, splashing over the edges until the man carrying it set it beside the stretcher. Then, one of the healers put a hand in the water and one on Betania's right leg, and a soft white glow began to flow from his hand. More water buckets were brought. Betania's injury would require a great deal of Life magic to heal. More, perhaps, than the king was willing to ration.

Strings of curses came from Betania, likely directed at Rosaline and the pain. Carina couldn't help a pang of fear in her chest. Despite everything, her hand went to the hilt of her old sword, and managed to find comfort in the firm grip.

46
AHNRI

"Up. Up now." ChaNia whispered as she closed the door they'd come through. She tucked her head under one of Ahnri's arms, and Merlin did the same on the other side. Together they dragged him out of the alley in which they'd arrived.

Ahnri may have closed his eyes a few times—the fainting he'd wanted to fake threatening him for real now—but he never fell, thanks to his friends. Through a soft snowfall that melted before it stuck to anything, he trudged, leaning against them. A few minutes later, they ducked into a deserted building.

Sunlight filtered in through shattered windows and onto the dirty floor, showing only a few rough-made furnishings. Without a word, Merlin took Ahnri under his arms and helped him to a clean cot that had been set up near a fireplace.

ChaNia tossed a water skin to him, and he drank gratefully as Merlin scanned him for healing, a small bucket of water at his side. ChaNia stoked a nearly-dead fire, and Ahnri scooted toward it. He watched her slip chunks of meat onto a stick and hold it over the coals. Juices sizzled as they dripped onto the flames, and his mouth watered.

"Are you going to tell me how I just escaped the palace?" he asked.

Merlin looked up from examining Ahnri's side. "Ask her, I only met you at the tunnel."

ChaNia pulled the meat off the heat and tested it, squeezing a chunk between her thumb and forefinger, before putting it back. "I hadn't seen you and was getting worried. He knew where you were but couldn't get you out. I told you there were hidden passageways in the palace. It's only lucky that Rosaline had you in one of the connected rooms"

Ahnri rubbed at his arms to warm them. "You have my thanks. Both of you."

Merlin gave a quick smile, and went back to cleaning and healing Ahnri's many wounds.

They sat in silence for some time, waiting for the food to cook while Merlin began to explain that there were some burns he wouldn't be able to heal completely because they'd already closed over too much. But the very fresh ones, he could. Ahnri clenched his teeth together every time. He'd been unconscious the last time Merlin healed him, and he was grateful for that now. Each small burn he'd been given by Rosaline was like a hot needle was sewing up his skin as they closed.

It was half an hour before Merlin was done. ChaNia took the meat off the fire, and handed the entire stick to Ahnri. He took it gratefully and began to eat.

Merlin stood. "I need to get going. Rest, Ahnri. As much as you can, all right?"

"Right. Rest." Ahnri began to close his eyes, then remembered Rosaline's conversations. "Merlin, wait."

Merlin turned back.

"Rosaline has a vessel."

Merlin frowned. "A real one?"

"I'm afraid so. She said it had run out, but her father gave her a new one. Maybe an hour ago?"

Merlin ran a hand over his face. "All right. At least now we know what Carina's up against. Thank you, Ahnri, that information cost you more than it should have."

"And she has the sword."

Merlin swore.

"Does Carina need it?"

"Not particularly," Merlin said. "But I'd like to get it back."

"Sword?" ChaNia said. "The one she's trying to damage?"

"Yes," Ahnri said.

"She's not gonna be able to," Merlin said.

"Maybe not," ChaNia said, "but she's trying everything. I think I can get it out, but I might not make it in time for their duel."

"When is that?" Ahnri asked.

Merlin met his eyes, worry clear in them. "Just over an hour."

"Right. I'll be there," Ahnri said. "Good luck."

Merlin ducked out.

"Will you be all right alone?" ChaNia asked. "I need to get

back before they realize I'm gone."

Ahnri nodded, swallowing another bite of meat.

"Good. You sleep. I'll be back in time to get you to the final match."

As she left, Ahnri collapsed back onto the cot. He had no idea where they'd left him. As his eyes closed, he thought it didn't matter where he was, so long as he could sleep for a little while.

47
CARINA

The stands were a jumble of movement as the sun neared the horizon. Being the final match, everyone in the city wanted a view. Carina went toward her place on the north side of the field, and her heart swelled with relief when Merlin rounded the corner.

But he held no sword.

She shook herself. It didn't matter. This one was just a blade, and she'd won two matches with it already.

Merlin wrapped his arms around her, and she held on, letting herself relax against him. The crack inside her shuddered.

She stepped back to look him over. "Are you all right?"

"Of course," he said, his hands falling to rest at her waist. "And so is Ahnri. But the sword is still…ChaNia says Rosaline has it and she's trying to damage it."

Carina swallowed. So. She would have to do this with her

father's blade after all. The prospect made her shudder. But she was nonetheless determined.

That blade had come to represent something in Carina's mind, and she struggled to put it into words. But she would use it, and she would do good with it.

Merlin tipped her chin up to meet his eyes. "Remember what I told you when we first met?"

"Merlin." She couldn't help a small laugh. "You said a lot of things when we first met. You'll have to remind me which one you mean."

He grinned. "All Excalibur did was identify you, and really it only does that for me. No one else here even knows what it is, and yet a huge number of them believe in *you*."

Her gaze unfocused for a moment, then refocused on the stands around them. A huge portion of the crowd were raising flags with her colors, calling her name and wishing her luck. More people than she'd have imagined possible.

Her father's blade. Propped against the rickety wooden chair.

Channel the pain.

Beat Rosaline.

Protect.

"You can do this, Carina."

With a few deep breaths, Carina took up her old sword and began to warm up her body. Her practice dance was one of slow control this time. Her eyes closed, wind and light snow brushed strands of hair out of her braid and over her face and neck.

The stomping of feet over the stands echoed in her ears,

and small bits of conversation drifted in and out of her hearing range. A strong scent of fire smoke and mud came to her, making her nose crinkle. She let her mind clear as voices and bodies, wind and scents, moved around her. As she ended the dance, she remembered something Rosaline had said.

She opened her eyes. "Merlin?"

"Yes?"

"Rosaline might have Eron."

"Okay," he said, "I'll find him. You focus on the fight."

He slipped away, disappearing into the crowds that gathered to watch. Carina sat, trying to force her mind to clear.

Her father's voice was still there, in her mind, except now he was shouting through a wall, or a window. Like she knew he was speaking, but couldn't make out the words.

The old sword lay across her lap.

A moment later, Merlin had returned. "Neither Rosaline nor Eron is here yet. Ahnri and ChaNia are going to watch for him."

"Thank you," she said, letting out a deep breath. Merlin knelt beside her.

"Nervous?"

"Yes."

"Me too."

She couldn't look at him. Instead, she stared at the sword. Her hand rested on the handle. Everything about this weapon was familiar to her, almost too familiar.

Merlin placed his hand on hers. "Promise me something?" he asked.

"What?"

"Make her hurt."

This made her turn to meet his gaze. He was completely serious.

"She has hurt you, Carina. She has hurt Ahnri. I know you prefer to mark lightly to win, but Rosaline will not give you the same courtesy. She tried to kill you once; she will try again, and she has magic on her side to do it."

Carina swallowed a lump rising in her throat. "I don't want to kill," she whispered. "I've never had to go that far, I don't want to now."

Merlin took her hand in his. "Then don't. You and I both know you hold fire inside you. If ever there were a time to let it out, it would be now."

Her jaw tensed at his words. She thought of everything Rosaline had done, how many times she'd tried to hurt her and the people she cared for, and a burning began in the pit of her stomach.

Merlin squeezed her hand three times. "Do not underestimate her."

"Welcome, citizens of Reinos!" an adviser called from the center of the field. The crowd erupted with applause and cheers, chanting Carina's or Rosaline's name. "Welcome to the final match of the King's Tournament!"

More cheers, and Carina stood, weighing her father's sword in her hand.

"I present to you, Lady Rosaline Matano," cheers from the south side of the stands. "And Lady Carina Valio!" The roar behind Carina shocked her out of her focus. She turned around.

Her side of the stands were completely filled, everyone standing because there seemed to be no room available to sit. Were so many people with her?

In that moment, it seemed to finally sink in. She'd done this. She'd made it to the final match, in the King's Tournament. Not only that, but she'd managed to gain more support than she'd imagined possible. The realization brought a warmth to her chest that she clung to.

"Combatants, please take the field!"

Carina turned away from the crowd to face the field. Empty, save for a royal servant, and the girl Carina had to make sure could never hurt her or Medelios again.

Rosaline's mask was gone. Her face no longer held any hint of the friendship she once pretended. No doubt she expected Carina to be taken aback by this, but Carina only returned the stare. A glint of white sparkled at Rosaline's neck, and Carina breathed deep. That had to be the vessel. How to get to it, she didn't know. She would have to get extremely close, regardless. A plan began to form in Carina's mind.

"Will you yield?" Rosaline asked.

"No," Carina said.

"Shame," Rosaline said. "I actually rather liked Eron." She motioned to a corner of the stands behind her. Carina's gaze was drawn to where a servant stood, holding Eron by an arm.

To anyone in the crowd it would appear that the man was simply escorting him, but Carina could see the fear on Eron's face, the firm yet unnatural set of his shoulders that said he was trying to appear confident. She hoped Ahnri would be nearby.

Carina and Rosaline took up their positions. Carina did not raise her sword to her shoulder, and neither did Rosaline. This was not a fight of respected enemies; this was a fight to win. The crowds quieted. Or perhaps that was only in Carina's mind.

Time seemed to slow for a moment. The stone at Rosaline's neck gave off a subtle glow. Enough to grant Rosaline strength, not enough to draw any attention unless you knew it was there.

Carina readied her blade. For the first time since she'd pulled Excalibur, her hand tightened willingly around *this* sword.

Channel the pain.

Win.

Protect.

You can do this.

Rosaline's sword came in a blur. Carina dodged the blow. There was no time to attempt a counter attack as Rosaline struck again. She moved fluidly, yet unexpectedly. Carina recognized the style; it was the speed and strength that shook her. Rosaline seemed to flash from one place to another and hit with the power of ten. It shouldn't have been possible.

But it was, only with magic.

Carina ducked, dodged, and parried where she could. Rosaline was ruthless. Her sword flashed like lightning through the air. Carina had to remove the vessel.

Weak—

Stay with me…

She let Rosaline come at her. Being a small and quick target, she was able to block or avoid every attack, some only by a finger's breadth. But any attack Carina attempted, Rosaline parried and turned into another barrage.

Minutes passed until Carina realized she was nearing the edge of the field. Like Syla, Rosaline seemed to be trying to drive Carina out to force a forfeit. She held her sword over her head. It was all she could do to stop Rosaline's attacks from landing. Carina's arms ached from the effort. Rosaline's eyes were narrowed in anger and frustration.

Rosaline's blows suddenly increased in strength, and the vessel at her neck shone brighter. Carina fell to the ground, holding up her borrowed sword with both hands. Rosaline swung again, and again, and again, still fast and strong, but her form was sloppy, desperate. Carina caught a flash of light.

The vessel.

Summoning every bit of vigor she had left, she dove for Rosaline's feet. They both fell to the ground, and Carina lunged for Rosaline's neck. Nails left scratches on Rosaline's skin, but Carina gripped the stone. She tore it off, and threw it outside the bounds of the field.

"NO!" Rosaline let out a cry even as she seemed to wilt.

Carina didn't trust herself to speak as she stood, taking up her blade. They began to circle each other.

"I'll still kill you," Rosaline growled. "And this time, you won't have anyone to save you."

At her words, Carina sought out Merlin at the side of the

field. But he wasn't alone. Someone held his arms, and by the way he stood, Carina guessed there was a knife at his back.

Merlin met her gaze and nodded for her to continue.

Breathe...

Rage poured through her at the sight, but she understood. He would be all right. She'd seen him survive a lot; he would be all right. So, she played the part, spinning toward Rosaline, letting her fury take the reins.

"You will *not* harm him."

"If you so much as cut me they have orders to kill. Your servant will be dead. You'll have a crown, and you'll have no one left."

Carina charged forward, thrusting her sword at Rosaline's chest. The girl dodged, knocking Carina's blade aside, the intensity of her attacks lessened now without the vessel powering her. Carina spun and slashed again, quicker. Rosaline barely caught it on her own blade.

They were an even match now. The two fought with skill, speed, and agility borne of years of training.

"You'll never win," Rosaline said, her voice nearly a growl.

"

Carina watched not only Rosaline, but the sides of the field too, waiting for some kind of sign that it was safe to act. To hurt Rosaline for hurting her.

A blow landed on Carina's armored shoulder, and she staggered back.

Idiotic, wicked girl!

"Shut *up*!" she shouted, tears beginning to burn behind her eyes.

She'd lost focus. Back into the fight, she scrutinized Rosaline. The girl was growing tired, but would not relent. Their swords flashed, meeting and dancing away, wrath in every movement. Carina watched, waiting for the opening she knew would come, and finally, she saw it. Rosaline's sword swung a hand's breadth too far, her body turning just so—

You'll never be—

"I already *am.*"

Carina slashed at Rosaline's leg. The blade cut through the straps of her armor, into flesh.

A cry of pain, and Rosaline fell.

Silence. Carina backed away, her pulse pounding in her ears. She held to her blade.

I knew you could.

The crowd around her exploded in sound. Healers ran toward Rosaline. Carina's vision blurred as the tears behind her eyes finally fell, drawing lines through the dust on her cheeks.

In a corner of the field, Eron stood with Ahnri and ChaNia. At their feet, Rosaline's servant lay in the dirt with his arms tied behind his back. Carina let out a breath of relief, then turned to Merlin.

He stood, holding a dagger over the man who had been holding him. There was blood on his shirt, and he appeared shaken. But he met her gaze, and gestured to the stands.

As the cheers and applause quieted, every eye in the arena went to her. Though she was exhausted, drained, and really only wanted to sleep and cry and spend time with only one person, she took a breath, and made her way to the center of the field.

She tightened her grip on her sword. *Her* sword. It may have been given to her by her father, but she'd claimed it as her own. She would use what he'd given her for good, both for herself and those around her. Peace. Her racing heart slowed; her hands steadied. Then, she began to speak.

"Friends," she began, projecting her voice as best she could. "I know I was not born or raised in Medelios, as so many of you. But I grew up hearing my mother tell stories of this great kingdom. She spoke of its trade, its prosperity, its people. Its brightness and love of life.

"In recent years, it seems that brightness has grown for some, and dimmed for others. It has become unbalanced, and unfair. I'm not here to accuse anyone of causing it, because certainly, it does not fall onto one person to break a kingdom. What I can do, is try to lead us toward healing what has been hurt.

"Medelios has great potential. The people here—all of you—are strong, determined, and ready to do what is required to thrive. Right now, I worry for the safety and security of this kingdom. There are those who would take advantage of that. Ununified, we are vulnerable and exposed. But if we work together, we can make Medelios not only as prosperous as it once was, but stronger. Greater. A beacon of power in the Unbroken Lands which no one would dare try to attack or overthrow."

She met the eyes of those in the crowd. The energy was there, warm in her chest. She could feel it, and hoped they could as well. Finally, she said, "I have tried to follow the guidance of my heart as well as the laws of the land to the best of my ability. I am not perfect. And I admit I cannot accomplish this dream alone. I will need the help of every Medelian in this kingdom to do it. If you will support me as your future queen," she knelt, the cold dirt crunching under her knee, "you have my solemn vow that I will protect you. I will serve you, and this kingdom, for the rest of my days."

For a moment, nothing happened. Carina's cheeks flushed with embarrassment and she bowed her head, staring at the ground. Then—right in front of her—a young boy, perhaps twelve, sunk to one knee.

That boy was a rock dropped into the still pond of the crowd. Behind him, others knelt. Before Carina's heart could comprehend what was happening, every person in the stands had fallen to one knee, heads lowered toward her.

Her eyes filled with tears, and she let them fall. Pride for this kingdom and its people rose to overflowing within her. A knot loosened in her chest. If she could win over this group of Medelians, perhaps others would follow.

From one side of the arena, someone called out, "His Majesty King Jaltér Salina!"

All heads, including Carina's, turned to see the king himself take the field. A soft smile touched his lips, and his tired old eyes glittered. As he reached Carina, he extended a hand to help her stand. Then he held her by the shoulders and said softly, "What you have done, I've only seen one other person do in my lifetime. You inspire greatness, Lady Carina Valio, and I am proud to name you my heir."

He turned to the crowd, raising his voice beyond what she would've expected he could. "Change is never easy. But it would be impossible without all of you. You have seen history made this day, and judged this young woman as worthy to be your future queen. Take your experience and tell your friends, tell your families. Tell every Medelian you can reach, and invite all to come to Reinos in two days' time to celebrate Lady Carina's coronation as Crown Princess of Medelios!"

The crowd erupted. Applause and cheers and stomps drowned out every other sound, and Carina couldn't help the smile that spread across her face as Jaltér led her from the field.

She glanced behind to make sure Merlin was following—he nodded to her, and she knew he would stay close.

They passed Rosaline, whose leg was now wrapped in a thick bandage, healers still working on her. Tears streaked her face even as she glared at Carina.

Silently promising herself she'd deal with the Matanos later, Carina asked, "Where are we going?"

"To the palace, of course," the king said. "We'll have a celebration tonight and get you situated and comfortable in your new rooms. Tomorrow we'll need to find you reliable handmaidens, and advisers, and begin your training in the policies and practices of running the kingdom. Not that you'll need much training, of course," he said. "You're already very well-educated, and I daresay you learn quickly. It won't be long before you're filling your own responsibilities."

Carina wanted to sing in victory and sigh in resignation at

the same time. This would not be easy, but she'd already known that. She would listen to everything King Jaltér taught her, taking it all in, in an effort to make things better.

To protect Medelios.

48
AHNRI

Ahnri couldn't wipe the grin from his face. Taking Rosaline's servant by surprise had been easy with ChaNia's help. Then, Eron had the sense to land a perfect punch on the enemy's temple, which knocked him down. They'd tied them up, and that had been the end of that. Ahnri was glad of it.

Most of the citizens began their celebration on the palace lawn, but Ahnri and Merlin were allowed in—Carina's orders—and they made their way to the ballroom. Food and drink were being provided, and musicians started to play.

They found an empty table and sat in silence, watching the bustling crowd. Ahnri noted Diman Baezona and Syla Teneo sneaking off into the servant's halls.

"Well," Merlin said, "now what?"

"Actually," Ahnri said. "I wanted to speak to you about that."

"Oh?"

"I'm indebted to you for saving me many times over," Ahnri said, reverently. "I owe you my life. If you ask it of me, I would follow you wherever you go, but I have a feeling there are some places I won't be able to follow."

Merlin gave a humorless laugh. "You would be correct. What is the proper custom for when a savior wishes to release the saved from all obligations?"

Ahnri leaned back in thought. "You could order me to go about my life as though you had never saved it. You could possibly order me to serve others as payment for my life, or something similar, but that's up to you."

Merlin's brow furrowed in thought. "In that case, Ahnri, I have only one request. Now that Carina has succeeded in winning the heirship, I don't know how long I'll be staying. While the people love her, and the king as well, I would prefer to leave her with at least one person she and I both know she can trust without fear."

"You want me to stay here as her servant?"

"Servant, spy, or something else." Merlin said. "I'm sure she can assign some job to you if you'd like."

Ahnri considered this. He'd planned to disconnect himself from Queen Elya but no attempts had ever worked. He didn't know whether the queen had been told of the fire, or Ahnri's apparent death. But after all this, months away from home, there was a part of him that wanted nothing more than to go back.

"Fugera is in danger," he said. "Maybe I could ask for Carina's help in stopping Queen Elya."

"I'd be willing to wager she'd help without question."

"Probably, but it's risky." Then, unbidden, his mind opened that box in the corner where he kept all his memories of Remi locked away. The prince who had been a friend to Ahnri for years, and then they'd grown to be more. And everything had been perfect, until everything fell apart.

The other box, the one that held his pain at Damon's death, seemed to shake, begging to be opened. But Ahnri instead grasped onto anger. His jaw tightened at the thought of hurting Elya the way she had hurt him. But if he went back to Isille, he knew those boxes would *all* open. They would *all* need to be faced.

"There you are!"

Ahnri and Merlin both turned to see Carina approaching. She'd cleaned up, and now wore a lovely red and gold gown, and a gold circlet resting on her brow.

She paused. "Did I interrupt something?"

"No, no." Ahnri stood. "Merlin was just giving me some very good advice."

Merlin stood as well, and Carina eyed him warily. "How are you feeling?" she asked.

"I've been better, but I'll live. As usual."

"Good. Ahnri?"

"Yes, your highness?"

Her cheeks darkened slightly. "You don't have to address me as such yet, please."

Ahnri grinned. "If you say so."

"I spoke with the king about you, and he—we—want to

hire you. We'd like you to help us organize a new Medelian intelligence organization, of which, if you'd like, you will be the head."

Ahnri's eyes widened. *Head* of a royal spy setup? He would be set for life. And if Elon ever did come for him, he would have an army of mercenaries and assassins to protect him. Not to mention, if he wanted to go back to Fugera, he would have the kingdom of Medelios behind him. It was the kind of opportunity he'd never thought to dream of. It was perfect.

"Yes," he said, grinning wide. "Yes, I would be honored."

"Fantastic!" Carina said. "I'll need you to start thinking about who you'd like to work with, and how to handle recruitment and training. We need to be certain of proficiency and skill, as well as Medelian loyalty—though I'd prefer to do that through encouragement rather than threats."

"I understand. I'll begin tonight."

Carina smiled, relieved. "Thank you, Ahnri. I look forward to working with you on this. It should be—"

"Ahnri!"

The three friends turned toward the call as ChaNia came near, carrying a sword. Ahnri immediately recognized Excalibur in its sheath.

"I don't know how it's still in one piece," ChaNia said. "Rosaline ordered everything done to it to try and break it. Nothing worked."

"Yeah, that tracks," Merlin said.

Carina took the blade, thanking ChaNia. Though she seemed troubled as she held it. As ChaNia left them, Carina turned to Merlin. "Now, about you."

"Yes, your highness?" Merlin said.

She rolled her eyes. "Will you stop? I'm not a princess yet."

"You've always been a princess, darling," he said.

The two exchanged a long and silent glance, and Ahnri cleared his throat. "I'll leave the two of you alone, shall I?"

Carina blinked. "Sorry, ah. Ahnri, would you mind taking Excalibur to my new rooms? The king said they're in the southwest wing, a few doors down from his."

"Of course," Ahnri said, taking the blade.

"Thank you. Merlin, will you come with me, please?"

Merlin bid farewell to Ahnri, and followed.

As evening turned to dusk, and dusk to darkness, Ahnri circled the ballroom five or six times, watching the people. Just watching. He'd be seeing more of them in the future, but that didn't change how interesting it could be to simply observe.

Carina made rounds as well, Merlin by her side the whole time, until they retired to her rooms some hours after sunset. The party continued without them, by order of the king. Ahnri thought it was likely to go all night.

Most of the nobility seemed rather shocked at Carina's win at first, but played it off as though they'd known all along she would win. And as word got around that Rosaline had cheated by using a charged vessel in her fights—and that the king would put her on trial the following day—the mood shifted to one of genuine astonishment. Lady Carina had won the tournament under her own power, defeating even an over-powered opponent?

Yes, she'd won their respect now.

Ahnri made his way to the gardens, where the cool night air made bumps rise on his skin. A screech from above made him turn skyward, and Kahn glided down to settle on a tree branch nearby.

"What do you think?" he asked, stroking the hawk's feathers. "Care to make a new home here?"

Kahn clicked his beak, settling onto the branch and closing his eyes. Ahnri knew the feeling. Now that they had a firm purpose, he felt more content than he had in a long time.

49
CARINA

"Staring at it won't change anything," Merlin said.

Carina stood before the fireplace, holding Excalibur before her. The pristine metal gleamed yellow and red and orange in the light of flames. Part of her ached to throw it into the fire, even though she knew nothing would happen to it if she did. She would only burn herself getting it out.

The suite of rooms she'd been given as the heir were spacious and grand. Now, with the party settling down, Carina stood facing the fireplace in her private sitting room. It was warm, everything soft—the carpets, the furnishings, the drapes, even the candlelight. It was a good room in which to feel pain. She already felt it: a widening chasm inside her growing ever deeper with each breath.

She and Merlin had spent the evening celebrating. Carina accepted congratulations from person after person, with him always a step behind her. She had tried to force herself to ignore the inevitable. To enjoy the sweet victory.

The distraction only lasted so long.

"How can you stand it?" she asked, sliding the blade back into its sheath.

He shifted on the sofa behind her. "It's always easier when I meet the next one. Gives me a sense of purpose, I guess. Something to do to keep my mind off what I've lost."

"You think it'll be the same for me."

"I can hope."

"That I'll throw myself into the work of a kingdom and simply forget you."

He didn't answer.

"It won't work."

"You are very young yet," Merlin said, softly. "And young love can be a fickle thing. I've lived a long time my dear, and I've seen people fall in love many, many times. Who knows but there is a man far younger than I who will charm your heart, and before you know it you'll go willingly into his arms."

She placed the sword on the mantle and turned to face him. "I'll always love you, Merlin."

He stepped toward her and took her hands in his. "I wouldn't want it any other way."

Carina leaned up and pressed her lips to his. The sensation was better than she remembered. His arms wound around her waist. The sweetness of his kiss overwhelmed her, passion and desire rising like a flame in her heart and body. Carina held on to him tighter than she ever had, afraid he might disappear from her arms at any moment. When they parted, Carina's eyes burned with tears as she leaned her forehead against his chest.

A lump formed in her throat. "How long do you have?"

"I don't know." His hands were warm against her back. "I never know. Sometimes it leaves right after a day like today, and sometimes not until months after. Once I was there for three years before the sword disappeared."

She blinked, wiping tears from her cheeks. "I want more than three years."

"I know."

"I want a proper goodbye—no, I don't want a goodbye at all."

"I know, love."

They stood like that for some time, wrapped in each other's embrace. Carina didn't want to ever let go. Her mind raced and her eyes sought out the sword once more. There had to be a way, didn't there?

Merlin pulled away and took her chin in his fingers, tilting her gaze up to meet his. For a moment, he stared into her eyes, his mouth opening and closing, as if deciding what to say.

"I could stay," he said. "Spend my time with you, help you learn, advise you, and I would be more than happy to give whatever you wish of me. Or…"

The fissure in her heart widened at his pause.

"I could leave," he said.

"Leave?"

He dropped her hands, taking a step backward. His eyes were darker than she'd ever seen them, like clouds signaling a thunderstorm on the horizon. "I could leave now. Take the sword with me, even. You'll never have to worry about how long we might've had, never wonder what might've been had I stayed, and never lose the chance to say goodbye."

Goodbye.

Carina wanted to punch him for thinking to leave her right now, and yet…here was a man she trusted with her life, a man she knew loved her as much as she loved him, offering to walk out of her life to save her pain. It would still hurt, but this way she would be prepared. It would be on her terms, not fate's. Merlin didn't offer this because he didn't love her; he offered it because he did.

She touched the charm at her neck, the glass rose he had given her. The one thing she would have to remember him by. But she wanted more. She squared her shoulders and met his gaze.

"One night?"

Merlin's frame shuddered, as though his resolve was wavering.

Carina stepped toward him. "Will you stay with me, Merlin, for one night, and then..." she swallowed, "then you can take the sword and go."

The corner of his mouth twitched, and he nodded in understanding. "As your highness commands."

Carina rolled her eyes. "Please, don't—"

His mouth was against hers, eager and fierce, and for a moment she couldn't breathe. Merlin surrounded her; his hands framing her face, then in her hair, then at her back, untying the laces of her dress. Carina held onto his shoulders as he lifted her by her waist, carrying her into the bedchamber beyond.

The bed was draped with curtains, making their time together sacred in Carina's mind. She committed as much as she could to memory: the feel of Merlin's lips on her body; his hair tickling her face, his hands bringing her pleasure; the specific bright smile he wore all that night, the distinct depth of his gaze. And all through the night, they spoke in whispers. He told her more stories, she shared all her secrets, and for a while it seemed that together they could fly to the stars and back. She spent much of her time staring at him, touching his face, trying to memorize every feature, every stray strand of hair, and the specific, familiar, grey of his eyes that shifted with his mood.

It was an entire night of saying goodbye, without ever speaking the words.

She tried not to fall asleep. She didn't want to lose a single moment with him. But between the stress of a day of duels and a night mingling with so many people, she couldn't stay awake all night.

When a beam of sunlight shone through the bed hangings, warming her skin, she woke. Blearily, she reached out to the other half of the bed, and looked around. But Merlin was gone.

She'd known he would be, but that didn't make it easier. The crack that had begun to form in her days ago had widened, and she knew it would take a hundred decent men to fill the space left by this one.

Rising from bed, she wrapped a dressing gown around her and went into the sitting room, to the mantle. Excalibur was gone, a note left in its place.

You can do this. I believe in you.
I love you, Carina. I always will.
-Merlin

For a moment, the old panic began to tighten inside her. Her hands shook slightly, and she closed her eyes, forcing herself to breathe. Then a voice came to her. Not her father's, but Merlin's.

"*Stay with me, Carina*," it said.

Her breathing eased. She stood in her room, holding that note, until servants came to help her dress for the day. She had responsibilities now. She would be expected to be present for her trainings and fill the role of a princess. To make a difference in the lives of her people. She could do that. She was ready.

When she was dressed, she found a small box in her wardrobe and placed Merlin's note inside. There it would stay as she followed the palace servants out to begin her new life.

Ahnri will return in

CLEVER

Book Three of

THE UNBROKEN TALES

ACKNOWLEDGEMENTS

I've discovered the frustrating thing about writing acknowledgements, for me at least. And that is that I have to write them months before the book comes out. As a result, I'm terrified I'll fail to thank someone who helped between the time I write this and the time it's published. But if that does happen, please know I'll add you in future printings/editions.

This book has been through twelve drafts over the last nine years. Probably more, because I tend to mush my drafts together. A lot has changed from those early pages, but it's all led to this final version in your hands. It feels like it took on a life of its own in the last couple of years, and I am incredibly proud of what this story has grown to be.

First and foremost, I need to thank my husband, Brandon Cole, for his constant support. He is the one who lifts me up when I stumble, who holds my hand when I'm afraid. He brings me tacos when I'm stressed, and doesn't get upset when I spend too much at Swig (I'm doing better these days). Thank you, my love. I couldn't do this without you.

To my kids, who are so patient when Mom has her work time. They love me so much, and I love them, and I hope they see me telling my stories and understand that it makes me a better person, and therefore a better mom.

I need to give a huge thank you to everyone who has read this book from its very beginning to now—sometimes multiple drafts and sometimes small sections—to give thoughts, feedback, and insight. Apologies in advance if I forget someone: Brett Werst, Gina Denny, Rachel O'Laughlin, Francesca Zappia, Megan Jauregui Eccles, Emery Jonas, Rosalyn Eves, Heather Romito, Stacey Leybas, Jaylee Kennedy, Shauntel Simper, Ruth Olson, Katy White, Robert West, and Richard Fife.

To Shauna and John Granger, thank you for reading through my fight scenes way back in 2014 and telling me what to fix. The tips and guidance you gave has made every fight scene I've written since feel real and genuine.

An enormous thank you goes to my copyeditor on this book, Amelia Martin; I'm sorry I used "but" so many times. I can't promise I cut all the ones you wanted me to. I *did* however cut some other ones, so hopefully they balance out. (Let the record show I cut one from this paragraph.)

Shout out to the teen early readers! Will H. and Karen A., your reactions and notes give me LIFE. I hope you'll read the next one early too. I would love to have you. (Also, any teens interested in reading an early draft and giving feedback on the next book, email me at the address on my website's contact page. :)

Gratitude forever must go to the always-amazing Kirk DouPonce for this stunning cover art. You know the artist is talented when you can't stop staring at the piece. It's been my desktop for months and I just can't get over how gorgeous it is. Thank you, Kirk.

The maps were done by Dewi Hargreaves who also did the maps for TARGET. I'm amazed at how different the styles look, even though they're made by the same person. Dewi, you do fantastic work! Thank you.

The interior art of Merlin's sketchbook pages was done by the incredible Danielle Prosperie. We met thorough the Sanderson fandom, where she often does beautiful fan art for the Cosmere and other properties (seriously, check her out, she's @felcandy.art on Instagram). Danielle, I swear I looked at dozens of artists' portfolios before finding your sketch work, and I could not be happier with every piece in this book. I think Merlin would be as in love with your work as I am.

A very special thank you must go to my Patreon supporters! You may be few, but you are wonderful: Peter Harris (tuckerized as Sylas Turner), Suzanne Musin (tuckerized as Zanne the glassworker), Jennifer Johnson, Brett Werst, and Shauntel Simper.

Thanks also to the friends whose names I borrowed to tuck you in as well, though you may never even know: Cait (Cait's Corner) Petersen, and Marieke (Mari) Nijkamp.

My ARC readers have been incredible! To all of you who read and left reviews, thank you for taking the time and a chance on my books. I will forever be grateful:

Chloe (Allysen) Hey, Hilary Amick, Catherine Angland, Sophia Bidny, Sarah Blair, Siena Buchanan, Zaya Clinger, Em

Clover, Lynette Cole, Michelle Cowart, Gloria Cox, Michael Cox, Sarah Cudlipp, Danielle Dispenza, Caleb Duvall, Sara Dye, David Fallon, Angjelina Glasnović, Ashley Goodwin, Kel Hale, Eve Hammond, Peter Harris, Jodie Heiselt, Emily Henman, Erika Kuta Marler, Emme Landers, Daniel Latimer, Jeanette Lestina, Brianna McNabb, Liia Alice Menke, Adina Morgan, Kaelyn Morton, Ashley Nasburg, Carter Powers, Andrew Pratt, Jayda Ray, Brooke Shanklin, Annalee Shumway (Hi Mom!), Lauren Skidmore, Karissa Tedrow, Emily (EB) Thompson, Lena V., and Stephanie Whitfield.

Lastly, to the incredible individuals who gave this book sensitivity reads, for cultural, personal, and mental health purposes: Eileen Doherty Souza, Shauntel Simper, Ruth Olson, and Veronica Pomboh. I couldn't have gotten all these details right without your help. Thank you for sharing your experiences with me, for being vulnerable, and for being honest. I hope we've made a book that will touch the hearts and minds of many.

I always cry when I write thank-yous, and this time has been no exception. My heart is full when I think about how blessed I am to be able to tell stories. And while self-publishing is not easy, it has been so incredibly rewarding. I thank my God for putting me on this path, and for guiding me every step of the way. I'm proud of my work, and I hope you enjoy reading it.

Follow Darci for Updates

DISCORD: Join the DarciVerse Discord channel to talk with other readers, ask the author questions, and get early access to advance copies, swag, and more.
Go to Linktree.com/DarciColeAuthor and click "Join the DarciVerse Discord"

SOCIAL MEDIA: @darcicoleauthor on Facebook, Twitter, Instagram, and TikTok.

NEWSLETTER: Receive emails updating you on Darci's writing progress and process and be the first to know about awesome deals.
Visit www.DarciCole.com to sign up.

PATREON: For as little as $2/month you can receive early looks at new books and projects as well as deleted scenes and bonus content for The Unbroken Tales.
Go to Patreon.com/DarciColeAuthor

About the Author

Darci Cole is an author, narrator, and podcaster in the fantasy genre. She and her husband run Colevanders: a wand shop catering to lovers of magic and cosplay. She loves Harry Potter, oracle cards, pretty dice, and Supernatural. While she spends most of her time wrangling children, she also enjoys beta reading for her friends and acclaimed authors. Darci currently lives in Arizona with her husband and four children.

CPSIA information can be obtained
at www.ICGtesting.com
Printed in the USA
LVHW100253121022
730516LV00006B/227